YEAR OF THE
DRAGON
LORD

Be blessed & Keep an eye
on the Moon!
Milly O'Neal
2016-02-26

Callista—
You are a precious jewel! Daddy is so
proud of you & in love with you, it's almost
blinding at times. And I'm proud of you
& love you, too.
　　　　　　　　Huge blessings
　　　　　　　　　　Milly Also

Please enjoy.
all. O.

MILES O'NEAL

YEAR OF THE
DRAGON
LORD

nine realms
press

First Edition, 2015
Printed in the USA.
ISBN: 978-0-9971129-0-0
Publisher: Nine Realms Press, Round Rock, TX

Illustrations: Alli Gray
Cover and interior design: Allison Metcalfe Design
Editing: Inksnatcher and Sharon O'Neal
Library of Congress Control Number 2015920272
05 09 12 19 20 55 57

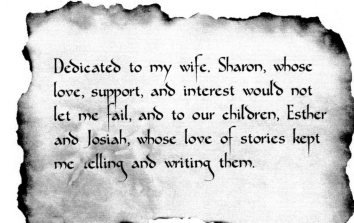

Dedicated to my wife, Sharon, whose love, support, and interest would not let me fail, and to our children, Esther and Josiah, whose love of stories kept me telling and writing them.

TABLE OF CONTENTS

Prologue	Am I Cursed?	1
Chapter 1	Comings & Goings	11
Chapter 2	The Absolute Best	21
Chapter 3	Druids & Kings	27
Chapter 4	Offense Taken	37
Chapter 5	On the Hunt	43
Chapter 6	Family Affairs	47
Chapter 7	In a Pig's Eye	59
Chapter 8	A Royal Audience & a Beating	71
Chapter 9	King's Justice	81
Chapter 10	Quests Unveiled	89
Chapter 11	A Welsh Surprise	99
Chapter 12	The Dragon Lore Master	107
Chapter 13	Seeking Santana	115
Chapter 14	The Voices	121
Chapter 15	Revelation & Truce	127
Chapter 16	When Dragons Laugh	135
Chapter 17	Awake in a New World	145
Chapter 18	Insult on Top of Injury	153
Chapter 19	Fever Dreams	163
Chapter 20	Unbalancing Debts	173
Chapter 21	Dragon Madness	179
Chapter 22	Two More Return	187
Chapter 23	Justice for James	195
Chapter 24	Ancient Blessings & Curses	205

Chapter 25   Glasgow Calling 213
Chapter 26   An Unexpected Visitor 217
Chapter 27   History Lessons 227
Chapter 28   Fair Trades 237
Chapter 29   Visions 247
Chapter 30   Illumination in the Fog 257
Chapter 31   Merlin, Elijah, & Dunvegan 267
Chapter 32   A Strange Name 279
Chapter 33   The Decrees 287
Chapter 34   A Brief Respite 299
Chapter 35   Argyll Pounces 309
Chapter 36   Bittersweet Victory 313

Pronunciation Guide 322
Glossary 323
Afterword—And Forward 325
Acknowledgements 327
About the Author 329
Community, News, and More 333

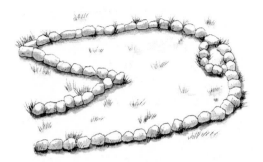

AM I CURSED?

Gerald didn't always know where he was, but he was never lost. You have to care where you are to be lost. Gerald mainly cared where he wasn't, so as long as he wasn't back in Kenwield, he was content. One spring morning, long after the last snow had disappeared from the most remote valleys, he followed a game trail to the edge of the forest. There in a stony glade covered in tender, new grass sat a girl about his age. She gazed dreamily at the trees.

Gerald froze too late; he had already caught her attention.

"Ho!" she called. "Who are you?"

Gerald walked tentatively into the clearing. "I'm Gerald. Who are you?"

"I'm Sally. I've never seen you before." She took in his ragged clothes, stained green and brown by weeks of sleeping in pine and fir branches. "Are you a forest sprite?"

"Of course not. I'm a boy. Are you a forest sprite?"

She giggled. "No, I'm a girl. I guess we're just folk. What are you doing?"

"Walking. Walking forever, I guess."

Sally gazed at him solemnly. "I'd get tired."

He grinned, an engaging smile missing two teeth. "I do."

"Well, sit down and talk!"

He sat. "Actually, I'm hungry. I've not found any berries today."

"I have some bread. It's the rest day, so I don't have to do anything. Here." She offered him half and was astonished at how quickly it disappeared into a mouth no bigger than hers. "I guess you were hungry!"

"Starved. Better now." He pulled out a skin and drank some water. "Thanks. Thirsty?"

Sally shook her head. "No, thanks. I have some, but I want to eat first." She started on the remaining bread.

After she ate, they talked about her village, Kiergenwald, and the village Gerald grew up in, Kenwield. Then she asked about his parents. "I don't have any," he said matter of factly.

"That's silly. Everyone has parents!"

Gerald shrugged. "Not me. Mine disappeared." He lowered his voice and looked around. "I think a dragon got them."

Sally's eyes widened. "Oh, no! I'm so sorry!"

Gerald froze. "You believe me?"

Sally's eyes slitted. "Shouldn't I?"

"Yes!" he almost shouted. "Only nobody does. My uncle tried to tell me they just went somewhere and they'd be back, but I think it's because he didn't want to have to take care of me. But I couldn't do everything on the farm; I'm only eight. The ox ignored me and the donkey kept trying to bite me. The chief wanted my family's home, so I called him out in the middle of the market and offered to sell it. He gave me some gold. Not much, but if I hadn't taken it, I think he would kill me."

"What? Kill an eight-year-old?"

"Yeah. Kenwield's not a real nice place."

The bread finished, Sally drank from her water skin, then stood up. "Let's play house."

"How do you do that? I don't see a house here."

"Oh, we just pretend. There's a place I always play house in."

"All right. I like to pretend. What do we do?"

"What grownups do. Hunt, cook, eat . . . well, we just did that. . . ."

Gerald stood up, staring thoughtfully around. "We should build a house here."

"From what?"

"Stones. Like this." Gerald ran around picking up rocks, then set them side by side in a neat row. "We don't have to build it high, but we can lay it out. This is the front wall of the main hall."

They worked until late afternoon laying out a home worthy of a village chief. Afterward they sat down, exhausted. "Now what?" Gerald pondered.

"I guess we sleep together. It's what grownups do."

Bundling up their cloaks over a few soft branches, they soon fell asleep with Gerald's arms around Sally and her head on his shoulder, the way they had seen their parents lie.

Her parents found them at dusk. Wallace raised the torch high and Samantha gasped. "Who is that boy? Why are they sleeping together?"

Wallace laid his hand soothingly on his wife's arm. "They're only children; it's innocent enough. Another few years, aye, it'd be to worry. But not now. And somehow I like the look of him, vagabond though he may be. See how he protects her in sleep? And he has the look of a king."

Samantha snorted, but quietly. "A prince, perhaps, but one in need of a bath and new clothes!"

"We've been that ourselves, love. Why don't you wake them up? I'm just glad there be no bears or wolves about."

Later that evening, having made a hut for Gerald from poles and skins, Samantha and Wallace talked quietly around the fire. "That's quite a story he told, Wallace. What do you think?"

Wallace stared into the fire. He and Samantha came from long lines of seers, and he often saw best looking into the flames. "From what I've heard of Kenwield, I don't doubt it. Dragons? I'm not so sure, though you know the rumors of one or two nearby. But the rest I can believe. And the boy seems both regal and honest."

"And you trust him with our daughter."

"Don't you?"

She laughed. "You know good and well I trust almost no one."

"Your parents trusted me, and so did you. Sally trusts him, and she's a lot like you." He looked through the fire into a time or place Samantha could not see.

After a few minutes she asked, "What do you see, Wallace?"

"This boy. We are all bound up . . . in a good way. Don't fear. I see nothing clearly, but everything I can see includes Gerald. He will make a good brother and son." He smiled. "We could do far worse than this lad Gerald. In fact, I feel it would be a mistake not to take him in."

"All right, my love. I've no idea why, but I'm inclined to trust him, too. Now, let us be off to sleep together." She mimicked her daughter's voice. "It's what grownups do."

Wallace grinned and squeezed his wife. "Aye, lass, it is."

Shortly after breakfast the next morning, Wallace emerged from the house dressed to ride to battle. Gerald immediately asked, "Where are you going? Is Kiergenwald at war?"

Wallace smiled and shook his head, his long, red hair flying freely. "Nae, lad. But we go to patrol the borders. There are savages about."

"And worse," said Samantha solemnly as she walked up leading a horse.

"But we'll nae talk o' that," Wallace said. "Gerald, take good care of these two lasses for me while I'm away."

"As long as need be, sir."

"Good manners, lad, but I'm nae sir. Just call me Wallace. Everyone calls me that but family. They call me Dad, or husband, or cousin or such."

"Wallace it is." But Gerald looked a bit uncomfortable.

Samantha put her arm around Wallace's waist as he pulled on deerskin riding gloves, faded with age but still strong and supple. "Gerald, did Kenwield have a lot of English blood?"

"I think so. Why?"

"The English use titles more than most Scots. Other than kings and dragon lords and such, there are no titles here. We're all just folk."

Out of the corner of his eye, Gerald saw Sally grin. She added, "No sprites, just folk."

Wallace laughed, then glanced up. "Ho! Donny and Sims!" Two more riders dressed for battle rode up. "Well, we're off then."

Samantha grabbed him and kissed him fiercely before he could mount his horse. "Be careful, dear heart."

He laughed and was on the horse so quickly Gerald had no idea how he'd done it. "It's the wild men 'as need to be careful. We'll be back in a fortnight." He spun his horse around, whirled his hand over his head, and the trio galloped off north.

Those he left behind stared at the riders' backs and the dust veiling their dwindling forms. A thought struck Gerald. "Is he your warlord?"

Samantha's eyes were glued to her husband. "We have no warlords. He is our battle chief."

Eventually she turned and faced the children. "Gerald, I should wait and let Wallace tell you, but I think you should know. If you like, our home is your home. We will adopt you and be your family, and you will be a son to us. If Wallace could have waited a day to ride, we'd have offered this formally and had the ceremony tonight if you wished."

Gerald's eyes grew distant. After a long silence he spoke. "I miss my parents. I want a family more than almost anything. But what if I lost you, too?" His voice rose in pitch. "And what if I'm cursed?"

Sally laughed. "You aren't cursed!"

Samantha dropped to her knees to be eye level with Gerald. She put her hands on his shoulders. "Why do you think you're cursed, Gerald?"

Gerald turned his head to look past her. "Everything I try goes wrong. The cows I worked hardest on died, or ran away, or got stolen. . . ."

"Gerald, please look at me."

"You don't understand! Jamie and I went climbing. He fell down the mountain and died. Glen and I were helping haul hay, and the wagon fell and his legs were crushed. But the worst . . . after Mom told me about dragons . . ." He shivered, paused, and went on, ". . . I kept asking her what their names were like. She said it wasn't safe to say their names. Finally she told me one. She said everyone thought he was dead, so his name should be safe. The next day . . . the next day she and Dad went out to look for some missing cows. They never came back, and we never found them. We did find Dad's sword. It was kind of melted."

Finally, he looked into Samantha's eyes. They were sad, gentle, and loving. Like his mother's eyes. And they were full of tears. He fell into her arms and cried for the first time since his parents had disappeared six months back. Samantha cried with him. Sally looked away, tears rolling down her face. She couldn't imagine losing her parents.

Samantha let him pull away, but not too far. Her gentle hands on his cheeks directed his face toward hers. "Gerald, please. Look at me. You are not cursed. Things happen to all of us. I'm sorry about your parents and friends, but if you were cursed, those things should have happened to you. Charmed is more like it, to walk away unhurt from all those things. As far as your parents go, I don't know, but it's not your fault. No one can predict dragons."

"Do you think it was a dragon?"

"I don't know, but it could have been." She looked apologetically at Sally. "They've been seen in the area."

"What?" cried Sally. "Nobody told me!"

"The less said about them the better," Samantha replied. "And as Gerald knows, no names. Even dead dragons might turn out to be live dragons after all."

"But nobody believed me!"

"Your father and I did," Samantha said quietly.

"Wait!" demanded Gerald. "Did you really see . . . a . . . a dragon?"

"Yes!" she stated defiantly.

"I always wanted to see one. Only now I just want to kill them. What did it look like?" Gerald was torn between vengeance and curiosity.

"Gorgeous . . . magnificent . . . terrifying . . . huge . . . and green. It was so long it went on forever, with gigantic wings, a barbed tail, and claws that could easily kill an ox." She shuddered. "Smoke from his snout. He started to look my direction, but I fell on my face in the dirt and hid." She turned red.

"I'm glad you didn't look. I hear their eyes can freeze you like a statue."

"Enough!"

Both children jumped at Samantha's tone.

"The less said about them, the better."

They nodded.

"Gerald, don't say the name. . . ."

Gerald shook his head violently.

"What did it sound like? The name?"

He thought a minute, eyes unfocused. "Like a waterfall, something roaring. No, like a roaring fire. That's it."

Samantha started. "She spoke his name in his own language! I'll ask no more."

During lunch, Gerald suddenly spoke up. "Do you want my gold?"

Samantha almost dropped her grouse breast. "Your gold? Whatever for?"

Gerald blushed and looked at his plate. "I know it's not much, but it's all I have to offer."

"For what? A dowry for Sally?"

Sally nearly choked. "Mother!"

Gerald looked horrified. "No! I mean, she's lovely but . . ." He turned even redder. ". . . We're only eight!"

"Then for what should I be taking your gold, if not yet my daughter's hand?"

"Mother! What do you mean, 'yet'?"

Samantha smiled, but the seer in her noted what was and wasn't said, and wondered.

Gerald finally got past the choking sensation enough to speak. "In Kenwield we don't just barge into a family. We pay our way."

Sally was shocked speechless.

Samantha was neither. "You may need that money someday. We don't. But even if we did, we do not buy families here. Families are for love and duty—not one or the other, but always for both. We like you and trust you, and we don't want to see you alone. Besides, you'll earn your keep, the same as we all do, however long you decide to stay. If you do." She raised an eyebrow.

Gerald stood up awkwardly but bowed fairly gracefully. "I am deeply honored by your offer, and gratefully accept."

Samantha smiled. "The formal offer can't be made until Wallace is home, but I promise it will be, and in fact it might as well have been. Your gracious reply is well spoken and duly accepted." She bowed her head briefly. She glanced at Sally, who did the same.

"You all seem so regal," Gerald said wistfully.

"We're descended from lesser kings of both the Irish and the Scots. And Wallace said you have a kingly look."

Gerald reddened yet again. "I'm no king, nor even prince, that I know of."

"Time will be the tell. But for now, since you are through eating, go help with the herds." She pointed west. "Occam is over yonder hill with the kine. He is our herdsman."

After Gerald was out of hearing range, Samantha looked at her daughter with a soft smile. "He'll do."

"Mother!"

"Don't you agree?"

Sally's face softened; she looked dreamy. "Of course . . ." Her expression hardened again. "But please don't say that around him!"

CHAPTER ONE

COMINGS & GOINGS

Gerald worked hard that fortnight, to prove as much to himself as to anyone else that he was not cursed, and perhaps even blessed. Indeed, it seemed that all he turned his hand to worked out well. He found a new calf Occam couldn't find, saved a neighbor's goats from a wolf, and brought in several wild cattle. Gerald could almost believe Wallace would be proud of him.

Wallace and his party never returned.

Two days after the last day they should have returned, Wallace's first cousin, Cle, returned from patrol. Within hours of hearing of the missing party, Cle led three of the village's best scouts toward Wallace's last stop.

One man returned the next day, his horse spent from a long, hard run. "Wallace and the others never got to that post. The other three rode back down the line to find them. We thought someone should warn you."

Samantha thanked him and went back to watching for her beloved's return, sure in her heart he was dead.

Nine days later an exhausted search party came in by the route Wallace had left. Cle climbed slowly down and embraced Samantha.

"Wallace and the others never got to the third post. Somewhere between Chloe and Serr, they just disappeared. No sign of them at all. Dermid holds Chloe. He said Wallace and the others spent the night there and left at the crack of dawn." Cle looked around, eyes settling on the newcomer. "You'll be Gerald?"

Gerald nodded, his heart pounding.

"Wallace told Dermid and the rest about you. Said you're a good lad, will be a good man, and he knew you'd take care of his family. You'll do that?"

Stunned, Gerald nodded again. Words refused to come.

"Samantha, I'm sorry. We were attacked twice; we can't search without a larger party. The savage bands are bigger and better organized than we thought. But I don't think it was them."

"I know, Cle. You'd have found their bodies, desecrated."

He nodded, pain evident in his eyes. They hugged again and Cle turned to go.

"Cle! You're limping."

Gerald finally spoke. "And what happened to your back?"

Cle froze. "You can't see my back."

"It's the way you walk. My father walked like that."

Cle turned around. "We nearly lost the second time we were attacked. But we killed a few and the rest fled. We got hurt, though. I'm going to let Myrna look at my back." It was said that Myrna, Cle's wife, could nearly cure the dead.

Samantha nodded. She called the children, went inside, and began a long, low wail that seemed to last for days.

As soon as the formal mourning period was over, Samantha burned the clothes she'd worn on her wedding day and those in which she'd heard of Wallace's death. "Thus I choose to walk away from the pain. Never from the memory, or the good times, or the good things he left us. And now, after death, new life. As head of this household, Gerald of Kenwield, I extend to you the arm of family, our name, our love, our bond, our duty, our heritage, and ask from you the same, if you so wish." She held out her right arm.

Recovering quickly, Gerald reached out and they grasped each other's forearms. He sought desperately for the sort of things to say. "I so wish, and accept, and offer you all that I am, as your son, as man of the house unless and until you take another husband, and as a brother to your daughter, so long as we shall live."

Samantha brought out wine and a curious goblet of something that wasn't quite marble. They all drank. Gerald officially had a family again, though in practice he'd been family since the day they'd met.

With Cle's and Occam's help they turned Gerald's hut into a real room, part of the house. When it was finished, Sally smiled.

"Now it feels more like family with you living in the house!"

The next four years passed normally enough. Gerald helped with the home and farm, made friends, and generally enjoyed being part of a family again, something he had given up on when he left Kenwield.

Samantha never allowed Gerald to use his gold for any of their needs. On his twelfth birthday she told him, "We can always trade cows and their meat, milk, or hides. You have doubled the herd size and befriended everyone in the region so that we get favorable trades. You claimed and marked more pasture and more crop land. We're fine. Save your gold. You'll need it one day."

She spoke with Cle, a trader at heart, who taught Gerald

how to buy, sell, and trade, Over the years he gained more gold, silver, other metals, and a few small gems. Cle called Gerald the brightest pupil he'd ever had.

At thirteen Gerald was ready to start formal training in the arts of battle. Since he could go any time that year, he chose to wait until his friends also came of age. The time arrived and five young men prepared to depart after harvest.

The day before Gerald was to leave, Cle and Samantha presented him with all he needed for the trip—clothing, bedding, and food. Then Sally told him to close his eyes. He did so a bit nervously, noticing what he thought were smirks on his mother's and her cousin's faces. When told to look again, Sally was kneeling before him, holding a sword in a sky blue scabbard of overlaid scales.

Eyes wide, Gerald took the sword, then helped Sally stand. He pulled the sword from the scabbard. Had he not grown quickly for his age, it would have been too big. As it was, he knew it would be some time before he could wield it as well as he could his own, smaller sword. Yet it felt wonderful in his hand. He waved the sword carefully, then peered closely at it.

"It's beautiful! And it's covered in runes. What do they say? What sword is this?"

Sally spoke. "It was my father's. He called it Draebard, Dragon Singer. With it he could summon dragons, either to do his bidding or to their death. The runes represent the names of dragons. On one side, the side with the fang, are the names of those he killed. On the other, the side with the eye, are the names of those with whom he spoke. There are more of the latter than one might expect, but more of the dead than I could have guessed." She looked at Cle, who took over.

"Do nae wield this until you know how. My father had a dragon sword as well; it went to our eldest brother, Samwise. At sixteen, celebrating a victory over a horde of savages, he had too much to drink. He drew the sword and called the name of a dragon he had learned from a scroll at yon castle. The next day, riding out with his company to hunt cattle thieves, the dragon he'd named descended and demanded to know who had called his name. The captain drew his sword; he and his horse were burnt to a crisp for his insolence.

"Samwise, shaking but determined, rode his horse forward and drew the sword. 'Here is your bane, wyrm!' he cried. For a moment, the dragon stared back. Just as everyone began to breathe again, the dragon pounced. With Samwise in one foreclaw and the horse in the other, he flew away. My brother and the sword were both lost to us."

Gerald swallowed and sheathed the sword. "I promise, Cle. I will not even draw the sword until I know what to do with it, and never will I wield it without the knowledge and practice to win."

"Good lad!" Cle slapped Gerald on the arm. "Put it away, and wear your battle sword for now."

"I think I will rename it, though. Not Dragon Singer, but Dragon's Death. Draenacht."

Samantha placed a gentle hand on his shoulder. "Do nothing rashly, Gerald. I know you have lost your mother and two fathers to the fell wyrms, but I ask you to not even so much as change the sword's name until you have learned all you can at Cair Parn."

"Yes, Mother." He smiled. "I can seldom refuse you." He paused. "But I am no dragon lord. How can I carry this sword?"

Sally spoke first. "But you will be a dragon lord, even if untried. We all saw it the day we met you, whether we understand or no. We knew you were different and kingly, but we never expected such an august personage to wander in out of the woods to sleep with an innocent young lass." The twinkle in her eye belied the mocking tone of her words.

"I am but glad Samantha had no sword in her hand when she found us; she might have felt I besmirched your honor."

Samantha laughed. "You have no idea. But Wallace saw, and when he pointed it out, so did I." She sighed. "We lost a good man in Wallace, and the region lost the best sight of any in a hundred years. But Sally shows promise to outdo her father."

"Hardly fair," the girl noted, "when he's not here to defend himself. . . ." The joke died on her lips and Cle changed the subject.

"Supper is in an hour. Dress up, lad, you're one of the guests of honor. The village has never before had five new recruits to send at once. It's grown quite a bit since my day. I went with only one other, and Wallace was alone from Kiergenwald in his class."

The feast and dancing went late as they were wont. Gerald would have preferred to turn in early to be rested for the morrow's ride, but as a guest of honor he really had no choice. He managed to appear to drink more wine than he really did; this left him the least muddled when they headed out at dawn the following morn. Thus he set the tone for his tenure at Cair Parn, never overindulging, ever vigilant. But he kept his motivation to himself; few of his classmates or instructors soon guessed how much his hatred of dragons drove him.

Gerald, Eoin, Justin, James, and Sholto set out for Cair Parn with food for three days, a meager selection of clothes for all seasons, and whatever weapons they chose to carry for the journey. Each took a few personal items as well, but none of them owned much.

A miniature Draebard ear ring dangled from Gerald's right ear, a present from Sally. Eoin and James wore identical silver bands with gold inlay about their upper left arms, twin gifts from their identical twin mothers. Justin carried in a leather pouch a few things he didn't really discuss. Sholto wore, as he had since first appearing in Kiergenwald with his mother, four lead crosses—one on a chain about his neck, one from each ear, and one attached to the top of his right boot.

They rode fairly quietly through the morning except for

Eoin and James, who sang in their beautiful, tenor voices. After lunch, Justin finally called to Sholto, riding alone in front of the others.

"Sholto! You've lived nearby for over a year, but we hardly ever see you or hear a word. Want to tell us your story?"

Sholto shrugged. After a moment he dropped back to ride beside the others. "If you'll tell me yours." As always, he was soft spoken.

"Of course!" Justin looked at the others, who nodded. "Do you want us to go first?"

"Nae, I'm fine." His eyes went distant for a few breaths. The clop of his sturdy pony's feet on stone was the only sound nearby; the others' mounts picked their way through grass and sand.

"I come from Carlisle, on the border. Do ye know where that is?"

Eoin spoke up. "We lived there a while with an aunt and uncle when me mum was sick. Thought she was going to die. I was about six."

The rest knew only vaguely, as in "southeast a ways" or "well past Glasgow" (which they knew only by name and reputation).

"Da was a lead miner. He worked for his uncle, a harsh man but he paid fairly. Da found his own little lead vein on our land where Ma kept the sheep. He was digging a shaft one evening, about fifteen feet down, when the wall collapsed. Rocks crushed his head."

Sholto was quiet a moment; the others joined him in it.

"Ma sold the land to Da's uncle. She bought a wagon and we became travelers. We joined a group of traders, a dozen wagons going between mining villages, farm villages, craft villages, and Glasgow and Edinburgh. The second time we came ta Kiergenwald, in the fall two years ago, Roy MacGregor's wife had just died o' snakebite. He dinna want ta work or eat. Ma got him ta eat, then traded some food for some of his wife's clothes. She cleaned his house for him in return for our staying there a week. What a mess that was!

"When we came through the next spring, we stayed there again. Before we left, he asked Ma ta marry him. She said she needed ta think on it, as she dinna know as she could take a chance on losing someone again. When we left, she told me all this. I pointed out she was stuck with the possibility of losing me. That night I asked if she loved him.

"She took a long time answering. 'I barely loved your father when we married, but I grew to love him dearly. I think I can love any good man. Not every woman can, but that's just how I am. What do you think? Is Roy a good man?'

"I told her I thought he was. She laughed and agreed. We left the traders the next morning, went back ta Kiergenwald, and they were married a week later. Roy and Ma said they took the first year to get ta know each other better, but now they're starting ta talk more with people."

"What about you?" Eoin pointed out. "We hardly know you."

Sholto shrugged again. He did that a lot. "Everyone says I just don't talk much."

James smirked. "There's a simple explanation for that. You don't! In fact, Norbert told everyone at first that you were mute."

Sholto gave a rare smile. "Well, if Norbert said it, everyone knew it was true." They all laughed. Gerald's cousin, Norbert, wasn't known for being very bright, or for needing much in the way of facts to form an opinion.

Sholto looked at Gerald. "Ma said you were a trader, too?"

Gerald looked uncomfortable. "Not really. I like to bargain, and I'm pretty good at it."

Sholto shrugged. "What else do you think a trader is?"

The others urged Gerald to go next. Between Sholto's

questions and his friends' additions, Gerald's story went on for a while. It was getting dark as he finished. They found an open spot in a thicket for a camp. They wove grass to cover the openings and slept hidden away, having no idea who was about. Each took turns on watch; three boys slept while two watched. Thankfully, it was a quiet, uneventful night.

CHAPTER TWO

THE ABSOLUTE BEST

The next morning, Eoin told his story. He didn't recall too much from before his mother's sickness, other than playing with his sister and friends, learning to plant crops (which he loathed), and never having enough meat.

"Which reminds me," he said. "What about meat for the trip? We don't have much."

"We will," Gerald said, refusing to add more. A few minutes later he waved at the others to halt and left their trail to follow a game trail. Before long he came galloping back on his pony, yelling, "Ride! Ride like the wind!" Hearing the angry squeals that followed Gerald, his friends obeyed.

About a mile up the trail their horses and ponies jumped a steep, if narrow, ravine. Gerald had them hold up. A few seconds later a furious sow bolted up behind them. She saw the ravine too late. Trying to stop, she succeeded only in slowing enough to hit farther down the wall than she would have otherwise. She lay at the bottom with what appeared to be a broken neck and a thoroughly crushed snout.

Gerald looked over and shook his head. "Not worth trying to get her out of that." He hoisted a squealing sack over his shoulder. "Roast piglets!" His smile quickly faded. "Too bad their mother had to die, too. I prefer to kill one or the other, not both."

Eoin laughed. "She would have preferred to kill you!" They made a fire and cooked the piglets right there. They ate half of the pork, then wrapped the rest in leaves and cloth for later. Eoin finished his tale.

"A healer in Carlisle saved Mother. We moved back here, grew potatoes, barley, and wheat, and raised sheep and goats, same as most everyone else. Father taught me a bit about fighting, and I got my first sword." He pulled a small sword from its sheath and held it up in the sunlight a moment before replacing it. "Nothing that great. I've tried Father's claymore. It's too big for me but this is too small."

Sholto reached behind his head and pulled a long sword from a sheath behind his back. "It's not a claymore; I don't want something that big yet. But I traded for the longest sword I could wield. I wear it like a claymore and practice with it. That way when I get the real thing I won't have to learn anything new but the weight and length."

The other boys all whistled approval.

After a moment Justin spoke up. "As you know, my father and grandfather are smiths. I grew up playing around iron, steel, and fire, and I remember trying to use a hammer before I can remember anything else. I'm terrible with a hammer at an anvil, but I can use a war hammer better than anyone my age within three day's ride.

"I can't sing like James and Eoin. I can't trade like Gerald or you. But I can run like the wind for hours and hours and hours."

His friends chimed in with stories of Justin winning races, winning games of Shinny, and of his long legs occasionally tangling and tripping him at embarrassing moments.

"But the absolute best . . ." Eoin started.

"Oh, no!" Justin said, leaning well off his horse and punching at Eoin.

Eoin laughed and moved his horse a little farther away. Justin almost fell, but his much-discussed long legs saved him.

"The best of all was when a trading caravan came near Kiergenwald just before you moved here, Sholto."

Justin hung his head and hid his face in his hood.

Eoin seemed not to notice. "This was a large caravan. It normally wouldn't have stopped at such a small village, but there was a heavy storm coming. Gerald's Aunt Freda met them as she was hurrying home from who knows where. She led them to her farm at the edge of the village. The storm lasted two days. Trying to woo the caravan's leader, Freda threw a feast for them. The next morning they set up shop to trade, out of gratitude. We saw things we had never seen..."

James took over. "And the chief among those things was Justin, smitten with love. But Justin's first love was no mere lass his age. No, he had to fall in love with a woman the likes of whom we'd never seen. A vision of beauty who left us all breathless. She had hair almost as red as Justin's face."

"A woman," added Eoin, "over twice his age!"

Gerald felt for Justin, but it was too late to stop the story. And it wasn't as if Justin hadn't told tales on his friends.

James continued. "Justin decided to dance for her. He's a fair dancer, but he tried too hard. As he twirled and leaped, his legs wrapped round each other like lovers, and as he landed, spinning, he fell."

"But," Eoin almost yelled, "he didn't just fall. He fell onto her display of jewelry, knocking it down, and then he fell right . . . into . . . her lap!" Eoin and James had to stop; they were nearly falling off their horses laughing.

Sholto was laughing, too, but managed to gasp, "And then?"

Justin pulled his hood back, his face still red. "She said . . . she said . . . 'It's not a very effective surprise attack, but I was certainly surprised.'"

At this point the others all howled. Once they calmed down

Justin continued. "As I got up to run away, she clasped my hand and held me fast. 'You have a good heart. I've no wish to embarrass you. If we meet again, it will be as the first time. Pretend you do not know me and I will pretend to not know you. Is that agreeable?'

"What could I say? I agreed. I helped pick up her wares; she put her boards back up, and I left with my tail between my legs. Later Norbert brought me a small package. He looked at me strangely and left. In it was a simple ring of silver wire with a note. 'Whether we meet again or not, though I feel sure we shall, let us be friends.'"

He turned redder but would say no more. The others had never heard of the ring before. They agreed later they had never seen him wear it and suspected it was in his pouch.

James started his story over supper (leftover piglets and bread). "My mom and Eoin's mom are twins."

"I wondered," said Sholto.

"Why didn't you ask?"

After the inevitable shrug, Sholto thought about it. To everyone's surprise, he answered. "Growing up on the border, we tended to mind our own business. Then as traders, we always collected information, but we seldom asked unless we had something to trade. I forget up here that it's all right to ask."

Justin laughed. "I hear in parts of the highlands, even if you do ask, you'll seldom hear more of an answer than, 'aye' or 'nae.'"

Gerald looked solemn, or perhaps stern. Sometimes his friends weren't sure. "What is it?" James asked.

"Just thinking about trading information. I hear with dragons everything is a trade or a debt. I want to trade to get them all in my debt. Then I'll be safe until I can kill them."

Nobody answered. These moods were rare, but when Gerald was in them nobody encouraged them.

They decided to let James finish his story the next day. This night passed as uneventfully as the one before.

After breakfast they took turns washing in a stream before mounting up for the day's ride. At Gerald's suggestion, no more than two bathed at a time while the others stood guard. Gerald watched his fellow guards with fierce joy, having no doubts they would make the village proud during their time at Cair Parn.

He thought of Cle, Wallace, and others. Ignoring Norbert, Kiergenwald had a reputation for warriors and dragon lords far above its meager size and wealth. He grinned happily. If he and his friends could end the scourge of dragons, the village would go down in history.

Once they were on the move, James resumed his story. "One of the healers told me that a lot of twins don't live, or maybe only one lives. They're usually so small at birth they have a hard time surviving. And they're rare enough to begin with.

"Our moms were not very sickly for being twins. In fact they were the healthiest twins anyone had heard of. Eoin and I were born a few weeks apart and grew up like brothers. It was tough when they moved away. I used to have nightmares that my mom would get sick, too, and they'd both die. Even a year after they came back and Aunt Enya was fine, I'd still wake up sweating and thinking they'd both died in the night.

"Then one day Eoin and I were in a big field hunting rabbits. We heard something crying just inside the woods, so we went to look. We found some newborn kits, acting hungry. We put them in our empty game bag and started back for the village.

"Half way across the field, the biggest wildcat I'd seen, almost as long as my arm, leapt straight up at me from the grass. I dropped the bag and fumbled for my knife. Eoin leaped in front of me, dirk in hand, ready to fight, but the cat was shredding the bag, letting the kits out. We just watched, and soon she had them free. She snarled at us, batted them until they started back to the wood, and followed them, turning frequently to watch us.

"I don't know why, but watching that cat gave me the trust that our moms would always be there for us."

He looked apologetically at Gerald. "I'm sorry for all the times we talked about moms being forever after that. I never thought about yours. . . ."

Gerald shrugged. "At least I got another. And once the dragons are gone, that will be one less reason for moms or dads to go."

They all nodded, but Sholto realized something. "Without the dragons, would we have to fight the English again?"

"Might be. But at least they can't swoop down out of the sky, catch us unawares to wreak their mayhem, and fly away."

"True enough."

A few minutes later Sholto stopped suddenly atop a hill. As the others came up beside him, they saw a lone druid standing in the path a dozen yards ahead. His robe was white, as were his hair and beard.

"Hail, Sholto! Your time has come!"

CHAPTER THREE

DRUIDS & KINGS

"How many weapons is he wearing?" Eoin demanded. He could see a curved sword, at least two knives, a spear, an axe, a small trident, and a staff.

Sholto replied quietly. "More than you see. Maybe twice that many." After a deep breath he hailed the druid. "Well met, Struan!"

He spoke again to his traveling companions. "You see the others by the trees to the left and right? His horse will be with one of theirs in the woods. I'll be back soon."

Sholto dismounted and walked to the waiting druid, who had not moved since calling out. They spoke for several minutes. The druid nodded and gazed a moment at the lads atop the hill, then turned and walked down the path. His companions moved out of the shadows to meet him.

Sholto returned to his friends and climbed onto his horse. "This is it, then. I ride with them."

Everyone tried to talk at once. Justin won out.

"What do you mean, you ride with them? You are to appear before the king before this day is over!"

Sholto sat quietly for a few seconds before answering.

"About a year ago, Struan came to our house to stay for a few days. Many priests, both druid and Christian, do so. Father MacPherson arrived that night. They spent two or three days talking and arguing—about life, death, God, and everything. The third evening, Struan had a dream. He said a shining man with wings, a terrifying man of fire, appeared and told him to take me as apprentice one day. Struan could not say when, only that the winged man promised to tell him at the right time.

"Father MacPherson was adamant it was no good. But the next night he had a dream. He said the same man—an angel—visited him and told me I should go with Struan. He was stunned, but he had been visited before, and was certain it was no evil.

"And now Struan is here and I go. To what? I have no idea. But if Struan and Father MacPherson agree, it will not be boring. Please give my apologies to King Donald. Fair travels!"

He clasped each of their arms in turn, then rode off to meet the druids, now also mounted. They rode into the forest a bit away from the main trail and faded into the shadows as if they had never been.

The four remaining trainees rode on, alternately silent and locked in heated discussion about what had happened, what it meant for Sholto, and how the king would react.

Gerald worried the least about the king. "From what Cle and Samantha have told me, King Donald has close ties to the druids and to the church, something few have managed to do."

James nodded. "Then again, the druids and Augustinians get along better in our region than in others, or so I hear. My cousin says that in Wales there are no more druids at all."

"No druids?"

"Aye. And no druids in Ireland since St. Patrick. Few in England since Merlin. Only here in Scotland . . ."

Justin jumped in. "There are fewer druids than there were, though, even here. I've heard the druids say so, and Father

MacPherson."

"I guess the father's happy about that?" Gerald wondered.

"Not precisely. He loathes their religion, but says they're good men and know many things others have forgotten. Mum says that's why he's here in the wilds of Scotland, that he got in trouble for not being tough enough on the druids across the water."

Eoin snorted. "Then they never heard him argue with them. I've heard the likes of what Sholto spoke of. When they get wound up ye can hear 'em a mile away!"

"I know. But the church on the continent seems to be quick to brand a man a heretic and kill him. The church here still teaches love, for the most part."

They argued and discussed things as they rode. They were surprised to come suddenly upon the castle. It was just after noon, and they hadn't expected to reach Cair Parn before dusk. A sentry on the wall above the gate raised a hand in salute. They saluted back and urged their horses on more quickly, thinking of their new lives inside the castle.

As they approached the gate, two warriors dressed for battle rode out on war horses. The warriors stopped at a line of knee-high, alternating, black-and-white stone blocks and waited for them, relaxed but alert.

"See that line of stones?" Gerald asked.

"Hard to miss," Justin replied.

"Those the arrow stones?" Eoin asked.

"Yes," replied Gerald. "Cousin Cle says they stop visitors there because the king's archers can easily hit a man's head at that distance if he turns out to be an enemy. And they can have the portcullises ready to drop by the time even the fastest horse can get to the gate."

A moment later they were at the arrow stones.

Gerald spoke for them all. "Greetings, warriors! We are here from Kiergenwald to learn the arts of battle and serve King Donald."

The older of the two, who appeared to be about thirty, studied each of the boys in turn. "We expected five. You are four. Where is the fifth?"

"Sholto was met by the druids. They had a claim on him." Gerald shifted uneasily, not sure how this would be received. "Sholto sends his apologies, but apparently he had no real choice."

"There is always a choice. But if druids are involved, perchance the king will not object. Wait here." He spun his horse and rode quickly back to the gate.

The younger horseman spat to one side. "Druids. Things always seem a bit weird when they're involved."

Eoin spoke up. "Father MacPherson agreed with the druid."

The man's head came up. "Did he now? Christian and druid agreed?"

"Aye. Both had dreams of this."

"That's right strange. I've not heard of such."

"Nor had we," admitted Gerald, "but they do get along well where we live."

"Aye, here, too. But they're still a bit strange."

The older warrior returned. "The king is not surprised by this. Follow me."

He turned and rode again to the castle. The new arrivals followed him, trailed by the younger warrior. Once in the courtyard they dismounted. "My name is Folkvar. This is Tunstall." He indicated the younger man. "Unload your mounts and stack your gear in yon corner. The grooms will see to your horses."

As soon as the horses were free the grooms took them away. Folkvar bade the recruits retain their weapons. They followed him through half the castle. As he approached a great set of doors, he spoke. "Folkvar and Tunstall with Kiergenwald's young warriors." The doors swung open. A moment later, the four brash young men found themselves suddenly nervous before the king.

Donald sat on a throne covered in deep purple. He wore purple and red, with a light gold crown upon his head. The boys fell to their knees and gave their names.

"Welcome to Cair Parn! Though Kiergenwald is small and quiet, the village is well known and honored here in the heart of my realm. This is my captain, Murdoch." He nodded to the warrior in green and black standing to his right. "He is my right-hand man, the captain of the army, and one of my most trusted advisers and friends."

The king glanced at the man standing on his left. "This is Dragon Lore Master Cuthbert, of similar qualifications, save that he concentrates on dragons rather than warfare." They all took in the ancient, regal figure dressed somewhat like a druid, other than the deep red hue of his robe. Despite his obvious age and white hair, he gave them a boyish grin.

The captain spoke. "If you are prepared to swear fealty to the king, present your weapons."

Three swords appeared. Eoin held out an axe, fearing his sword too small.

The king smiled. "I swore allegiance to my grandfather with an axe."

Eoin felt a little better.

The captain spoke again. "Repeat after me: I . . . " (he waited as each said his name) "do solemnly promise . . . to serve King Donald faithfully . . . to render him honor . . . to defend and protect the king and the realm . . . and its people . . . against all enemies . . . be they human, dragon, or beast."

The king smiled kindly. He looked each of them in the eye before speaking again. "I accept your oath. In return for your fealty, and your spending two years learning the arts of warfare and at least two years afterward in the army, I will provide you a home here, shelter elsewhere, food, clothes, weaponry, a horse, and whatever else you need during that time. I will be fair, balancing justice and mercy, both to you and through you. Do you so agree?"

As he looked each of them in the eye, they replied. "Aye, my lord!"

When done, the captain spoke. "Arise, young warriors!"

They rose, sheathing their swords while Eoin sheathed his axe.

"Folkvar, take them to put their gear away, then show them the dining hall. You know where they are quartered?"

"Of course, captain. Follow me!" He spun and left quickly.

Only James seemed to have been ready, but the others quickly caught up.

"Lesson number one!" Folkvar called over his shoulder. "Always be ready. You must obey any order given by your superiors." He glanced back. "For now, that's every man at arms, including young warriors ahead of you. Beware the rest of the castle; the cooks and pages love giving orders to see if you will follow them. Do not berate them or argue; simply smile and go on your way."

He stopped at a crossing hallway as two maids went by carrying loads of linen. "Save in battle, yield to others in the castle, and often without. Even our grown warriors do this. It is not demeaning, but a sign that we, too, are servants, not lords. I know that the English do otherwise, but that is their misfortune.

"All know that the English teach classes or companies of men. We teach each warrior as his own man. While there will be times when a large group is with a teacher, most teaching time will be in small groups or paired with someone who will teach you the skills they know best.

"Since we do not march to war as the so-called Great Armies do, we will spend no time on marching. We will spend a great deal of time on practical battle skills. By the time you are deemed warriors, you will be as skilled in the use of the sword, axe, knife, spear, and bow as men several years older in armies elsewhere, such as England. Even Edinburgh and Glasgow teach this way. It is one of many reasons the Scots are known as the most dangerous fighters in the isles."

They had reached a barracks.

"You may claim any empty bed. Note the number. You do know your numbers?"

They all nodded.

"Good. Report your bed number to the barracks page. That way we can rouse you in the dark for guard duty." He waited as they piled their belongings on four bare beds grouped near the far end of the barracks. "Come on, it's time to eat!"

Once in the mess, Folkvar escorted them to a table where several folk their age were eating and addressed them. "These are the recruits just in from Kiergenwald. Go over the basics with them, get to know each other, take an extra hour, then report for sword drill." He left to get his food and sit with the warriors.

One of the lads finished a bite and pointed to one of two windows to the kitchen area. "That's where we get our food. They'll hand it out."

At the window they were each handed a large, rough, wooden bowl of stew with a large piece of bread on top. Returning to the table, they found a small pile of spoons.

"These are the clean ones, then?" Eoin asked.

The oldest looking of the group nodded. "Help yourself."

As they sat, Gerald sniffed the stew. "Well, it's not boar. Something new!"

"It's decent. Venison and bear. Drinn," he pointed with his chin to his neighbor on the right, "and I killed them two days ago. We chased a stag through the woods, and it ran into the bear. The bear knocked it down and hurt it too badly to run.

We killed the bear, then the stag. Took all four of us to dress them and haul them out. I'm Dree, by the way."

The recruits introduced themselves, then met Drinn, Peter from Erie, and Thomas the Usually Quiet, who just smiled when introduced.

Dree continued. "We're called young warriors until our two years are up. We're not warriors until then, no matter how many men, beasts, or dragons we kill, although the king and his men may call us warriors or anything else they please.

"There are four more of us who are out riding with warriors to protect a caravan to Inverness; there have been reports of shipwrecked pirates turned land raiders. There are several more your age ahead of you but behind us. They're out on patrol with warriors, improving their tracking skills.

"Folkvar explained the basic teaching method, right?"

James, having the least food in his mouth, answered. "Very basic, yeah."

"Good. Most instruction is in small groups or one on one. Some of it will be with warriors, some with us. The warriors teach the things they know best. We also teach either what we've mastered or what we most need to master. No fear; we'll be sure to have a warrior watching to help out. But Cuthbert . . . you've met him? Right. Cuthbert maintains that the best way to learn something is to teach it. Seems to work. Of course, having a warrior who knows it nearby helps, too. Otherwise Drinn here might teach you to thrust when you should parry, and you'll end up spitting each other. Not that we'd want you for dinner."

Drinn spoke up. "At least I know to use the sharp end of the spear!"

Justin laughed. "That sounds like a tale worth hearing!"

Dree waved it aside. "Time enough for tales in the barracks. I assume you can all ride well and handle some sort of weapon?"

Gerald was annoyed. "Aye. Can anyone survive otherwise?"

"Perhaps not in Kiergen. . . ."

"Kiergenwald."

"Yes, there. But we have had people show up who could barely hold a sword, and one who had never held an axe."

Eoin interrupted. "I bet they were from cities. I met several such in Glasgow and Edinburgh. Seemed strange to me, but some of them—not all—are raised soft."

Thomas broke in. "That was it. I recall one lad. The first time he drew his sword it flew out of his hand and across the room. The captain had to duck, and the pommel still grazed his head."

Dree pointed to the warriors getting up. "We have an hour. Let's use it wisely. If you're through eating, we'll tour the castle while we talk."

Gerald asked, "What about our dishes?"

"They'll get picked up."

"Lead on, then."

Dree gave Gerald a cool look. As they stood, Gerald was amazed to see that Dree was very nearly the shortest of the group. His natural authority had made him seem larger. "Sorry. I just meant that we're ready to go."

"Then let's go." Dree spun on his heel and headed for the door.

CHAPTER FOUR

OFFENSE TAKEN

Everyone chimed in as they toured the castle, but Dree and Drinn provided most of the immediately useful information. Peter spoke up when horses were mentioned. The others laughed.

Drinn noted, "Peter should have been born a nobleman, a horse breeder. He doesn't talk much, but when horses come up, there's no stopping him!"

Peter laughed with the rest. "I suppose he's right. Back home, I did breed horses, but we only had a few of our own. I brought mine, Padraigh. He's the equal of any I've seen here, save the king's and Murdoch's, and perhaps one other.

"If you want to keep your horse and it's battle trained, you may. Otherwise they'll be sent back to your homes, and you'll have one of the king's horses while in his service. Stay long enough serving him and the horse is yours, even when you leave.

"We don't have a lot of extra time, but I spend mine down at the stables. Back home I'm known as the best breeder and vet in several days' ride, but here I've met my match."

"Imagine that," said James. "How old are you?"

Peter grinned. "Same as you, I reckon. Thirteen or nearly

so? I thought so. But I've already helped my uncle breed two stallions that sold for record prices in our part of Ireland. He said I could have my pick of his horses, and I picked Padraigh. They're going to breed him here, too. . . ."

Laughing, Dree held up a hand to interrupt. "See? But you need to know about places horses aren't allowed.

"This is the stair to the keep. Up we go. On watch, there's one warrior or young warrior on each of the four outer walls and one on the roof of the keep. The keep watchman is an extra pair of eyes for anything the wall watch calls out. We refer to these watches as 'the wall' and 'the keep.'"

They came out into an open room with small windows. "This is the battle floor. If an enemy were to overrun the castle, those needing protection would be above, and the guard would make a stand here." He pointed to large chests around the room. "Each of these has extra weapons in it, and room for a man to hide if he chooses. But that's for surprising the enemy. Woe to the guards who let anyone past this floor!"

"Has an enemy ever gotten up here?" Justin asked.

"No enemy has yet breached the castle walls, but we plan for the worst. Back to the watch; once a wall calls out something interesting and the keep calls or signs that he sees it, the wall goes back to watching everything in his direction while the keep tracks whatever interested the wall.

"He's also higher, so he can see farther. The keep also watches for dragons.

"There's a runner posted by every wall, and on the roof at the base of the keep, to carry messages to the captain of the guard.

"If too many things are happening, the captain of the watch sends more men to the keep. If we need more men on the walls, we're preparing for battle."

They came into a well-kept, ornately decorated room with a highly polished table and massive wooden chairs. "This is the keep's dining room. King Donald, Captain Murdoch,

Cuthbert, people like that use it. Quite a bit of business seems to happen here. As you can see out the window, we're already above the outer walls, so you can see a good ways off.

"The upper stair is behind this hanging of William Wallace. All the stairs are like this, narrow with lots of corners to make fighting your way up as difficult as possible. This next room up is where Cuthbert spends a lot of his time.

"Oh, hello." Dree got quiet as he realized Cuthbert was engrossed, his noble nose inches from a large book on the table, taking notes on loose paper next to it. They went on, the stair this time hidden behind a heavy wall hanging in the back of a closet. The hanging was painted to look like the wall.

"This is the final stair to the roof. 'Hoy the keep! Dree and company bringing recruits learning the castle.'" He turned to the new arrivals. "Always announce yourself to those on watch, here or elsewhere."

As they blinked their way into the early afternoon sun, they saw a watchman facing them. A familiar voice rebuffed them.

"About time ye got here. What took so long?"

"Cle!" Gerald ran across the roof to embrace his cousin. His friends followed him and clasped arms with Cle. Gerald noticed Dree giving him a dour look; perhaps he didn't think warriors and young warriors should behave this way. Nobody else seemed to care.

"Cle, what are you doing here? Are you here for long?"

"No, Gerald. Only yesterday and today, here on business. I leave at daybreak tomorrow. But a couple of the men came down sick, so I told Murdoch I could take a watch.

"You're in good hands with Dree and Drinn and their lot. I've seen no better group of young warriors since my time here. See that you live up to their mark." He smiled at Gerald and his friends. "Not that I've any doubt of it. Enough talk. I'm on watch."

They all stood at the wall a moment, looking into the distance. Justin imagined an invading army, James an assassin darting from cover to cover. Eoin and Gerald said nothing of what they imagined, but both thought the keep a perfect place to watch for dragons.

"We'd best go," Dree commanded. "We've still an hour of sword drill and we're nearly late. That would not do."

They arrived in the courtyard just as Folkvar did. He directed them to sets of targes (round shields) and wooden swords. "Be careful! These can still break bones," he noted. Then he paired them up—Gerald with Dree, Drinn with Eoin, Justin with Peter, and James with Thomas.

He watched approvingly as they tested the swords. "It appears you all know how to hold your targes as well. Good. You notice the spikes are not mounted; we'll add those once you've proven your skills at defense.

"All right. I want the new recruits to attack first. The rest of you defend only for now. I want to see what they're capable of."

Folkvar let them go two rounds of a minute, then had the recruits rotate among the older boys. He repeated this until each had gone up against all the rest. After each round he made suggestions.

"Take a brief rest." Folkvar looked at the older boys. "Well, what do you think?"

"They're not bad at all!" Thomas said.

"Better than I was when I arrived," admitted Drinn.

"They'll do," Peter said with a grin.

Dree looked thoughtful. "Definitely some good material. But Long Shanks here," Dree gestured at Gerald, "needs help with his footwork."

Folkvar arched an eyebrow as Gerald bristled. "It looked good to me, but you're the one fighting him. Spread out toward the corners. That's it. If your opponent isn't going to be able to block, pull your swing! If you are too hurt to continue, fall to one knee or drop your sword. Go!"

Within seconds, Gerald had used his long legs and arms,

and his "inferior footwork," to move Dree against the wall and disarm him. Dree looked daggers at Gerald but said nothing. Thomas disarmed Justin with a tricky twist of his sword. The other two pairs went a full two minutes before Folkvar called time. They battled the same people thrice more. Twice Dree managed to best Gerald; the final match was a draw. The others fared more or less the same.

"Gerald," Folkvar said as he reached out. "Let me see your sword hand."

Gerald grudgingly held it out. It was swollen; he wouldn't be able to bend his fingers in the morning. "How did you fight with this?"

"It happened at the end, sir. Just as you called time."

"Did it now?" Folkvar looked long and hard at Dree.

"I couldn't help it, Folkvar. I'd already started my swing when you called."

"Hmmm. I thought I heard a hit after that. Your reflexes are usually better than that, Dree. Be more careful."

"Yes, Folkvar. Sorry, Gerald."

Gerald heard no apology, only hollow words. He'd offended Dree earlier, and now he'd beaten him, even if he'd lost twice. He could imagine Dree saying, "This will not do."

Gerald foresaw long days ahead. If Dree called him Long Shanks again he wouldn't take it. What self-respecting Scot would?

CHAPTER FIVE

ON THE HUNT

The first week at the castle was a bit rough for Gerald. As the tallest boy in the new class, he was targeted for everything from jokes to fights to extra duty. His natural affability, along with the wisdom to know when to fight, when to back down, and when to simply defer, stood him in good stead. No one called him Long Shanks. By the end of the month he was simply another excellent student—top in his group at many things—harassed only by a trio of older boys. Chief among these, of course, was Dree.

At the end of the first month, the classes were divided into teams of four and sent out for a weekend to hunt for meat and to kill any predators they found. Gerald was the youngest on his team, led by his nemesis, Dree. By now, the short, second-year fighter with a pock-marked face seemingly loathed everything about Gerald, from his height to his accent to his easy way with words to his smooth skin. It looked to be a long year.

In the woods, Dree begrudgingly deferred to Gerald's craft, though that woodsmanship galled him as well. He might be forgiven this as Gerald seemed new to the woods and Dree had hunted them dozens of times. Yet Gerald was as at home as if he'd been born there.

In reality, he had been born there. This same wood extended to Kenwield, but Gerald refused to even think of that village if he could help it, and never brought it up without real need.

The second day of the hunt, Dree chastised his force. "We haven't killed so much as a sparrow or a mouse. We have no meat to take back, the wolves we saw have all gotten away, and despite the tracks, we have yet to see a bear."

Drinn interrupted. "I think my horse stepped on a centipede."

"We are not going back empty-handed! Spread out and blow your horn when you kill something!" He whirled and rode off toward the nearest edge of the woods.

A half hour later Dree had stopped on a game trail again to listen. He heard grunting in nearby brush. His horse jumped and whinnied as a boar broke from cover. It raced straight for him. As it ran past, he struck with his spear, but the boar lurched sideways and caught his horse's leg. The horse screamed and fell, throwing Dree into a tangle of thick, thorny vines. The boar skidded to a stop, tossing brush in every direction. Time slowed. Even thirty yards away, Dree thought he saw individual bits of dirt on the boar's tusks. Its beady eyes glared with fury. Dree saw death in those eyes, heard it in the rising thunder of hooves on hard ground.

As the boar gathered speed, Dree heard a second sort of thunder. The boar had covered about half the distance to Dree when a horse came flying out of the woods. As the rider passed the boar, it squealed and went down, sliding in its death throes almost to Dree. Impossibly, a sword had been run all the way through its neck.

Seconds later Gerald rode back, hopped off his horse, and helped Dree up. "Are you all right?"

"Yeah." He stretched. Sore, but alive and unbroken. "Um, thanks."

Gerald bowed. "You were right."

"About what?"

"We are not going back empty handed!" He laughed and clapped Dree on the back. Dree winced. "Oh. I'm sorry!"

Dree looked at Gerald's honest face and decided it had truly been an accident. He grinned. "No, we aren't. Blow your horn; we'll let someone else cut this thing up."

While they waited, Dree discovered that his horse had two broken legs. Sadly, he slit the horse's throat and caressed its head while it bled to death. "I hate killing a horse. But what else can you do?"

"Nothing," replied Gerald as he worked his sword out of the hog's neck and cleaned it.

"I meant to ask, why the sword instead of your spear?"

"No room. I was coming between the trees at a gallop."

Staring at Gerald's horse, Dree asked, "Where is your spear?"

"That's the other reason." Gerald laughed. "I ran it through a boar without realizing he was on the edge of the cliff by the riverbank. He's probably a mile downstream."

"Why didn't you follow him 'til he went to ground?"

"I heard your horse shriek and saw you through the trees. I was less than fifty yards away. You seemed to be falling so I came with all speed."

Dree stared at Gerald. "It's a good thing you did! Ah, here are Drinn and Justin. Did you get anything?"

Drinn grimaced as Justin answered. "No. We split up. We each heard something and stalked it in the brush, only to find out we were tracking each other."

Dree and Gerald roared with laughter, Gerald almost falling over.

Dree continued. "Too bad, but all is not lost. We need you two to dress this boar and make a sled for it while we go find the one Gerald sent down the river and do the same for it."

An hour later they were busy butchering the second hog. Gerald's spear had broken somewhere in the river. They arrived at the castle as dusk settled, covered in minor glory and hog blood. Dree rode behind Drinn.

On the way back Justin managed to get a moment alone with Gerald. "What's with Dree?"

"I guess things are all right now."

"Just like that?"

"Well, I saved his life rather than chase my boar downstream. Maybe that helped a wee bit."

"I suppose it might!"

As the story got around (and Dree made sure it did), Gerald found that everyone now accepted and even respected him. By the time he went home for planting season, he'd been given his own team for hunting—unusual for a newcomer.

Gerald arrived alone in Kiergenwald shortly after sunset the first day of the first week of spring. His friends were several hours behind, having stayed to visit with Sholto after encountering him along the way. No one spoke to him. Gerald supposed they didn't recognize him; it was night and he'd grown and bulked up over the late fall and winter. He took care of his horse, loosed it in the pasture, and nearly ran to the house. Inside he found Sally, sitting and staring into a fire.

"I'm home."

Sally gasped, jumped up with a knife in her hand, then dropped it and ran to him. She hugged him fiercely.

After a moment he realized she was crying. "Sally, what's wrong?"

It was almost a minute before she could answer. "Mother. She's dead. A dragon took her." The tears started again.

As it sank in, Gerald began to weep, too.

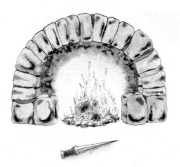

CHAPTER SIX

FAMILY AFFAIRS

Gerald realized he was squeezing Sally too tightly. It had to hurt, but she was holding him for all she was worth. He felt a hand on his shoulder. He managed to speak between sobs. "Cle?"

"Aye. Gerald, I'm so sorry."

"Why was Sally alone?"

"She insisted, Gerald. It's been near a week."

Gerald realized Cle called him by name rather than "lad."

"A week? Why wasn't I sent for?" He managed to sit down on a cushion, cradling Sally in his lap. She was barely sobbing now.

"Samantha made us promise not to."

"She what?"

"Before she went to the dragon."

"Before she went to the dragon." Gerald could feel rage eating the pain. He knew it was a bad idea, but it felt good. His voice rose. "What dragon, and why would she go to it, and why would you let her?"

"Eat and I'll tell you all." He set a tray down next to Gerald and Sally.

"How can I eat?"

Cle used a tone Gerald had previously only heard at the castle. "Eat! Sally needs to eat, too, and she won't eat if you don't!"

Gerald picked up two pieces of meat, handing one to Sally. She just held it as he ate, so he tore off a piece and put it between her lips. She gave in and started chewing. He rubbed her cheek with the back of his fingers.

Cle looked at them a moment before starting. Though only fourteen, they looked at least sixteen, and might have been married.

"Someone called a dragon. Or at least said its name aloud."

"Who?"

"We don't know. A dragon showed up demanding to know who had called its name. They always know where and when they are called, and they never lie about that. No one in the village spoke up. When no one confessed, he ate the mayor's son, Smeert. He said he'd be back for a person a day until someone confessed or the village was gone.

The second day we'd all talked and thought, and were no closer to knowing. The dragon showed up, got no satisfaction, and roasted the first person he got close to, my great aunt Mathilde. Uncle Padraig flew at the monster in a fit of fury. It killed him and flew off.

"The next morning, Samantha called Sally and me together. 'If anything happens to me before my son gets home, promise me you'll not send for him, but let him finish his term. It's only a few days, and I see it as crucial.' We asked what could happen and told her not to be morose, but it seemed important to her, so in the end we agreed."

Sally nodded miserably and sobbed a little.

Cle continued. "That afternoon when the dragon showed up, your mother was waiting for it. She ran out of the woods wearing red dragon scale mail, which is why no one intervened. Few had heard of a woman dragon lord, a dragon lady as some called it, but here was one before us. She wore a red scabbard and wielded a sword that fair sang as she waved it.

"'Be gone, Drachmaeius! Your bane is before you. We know not who said your name before, but I, Samantha, say it now, and warn you to leave or perish.' She stopped mere feet from the dragon, half the height of its snout, the sword blazing like a fire before her, a fierce love driving her, as if the village itself had taken on life to guard its children.

"Time froze. I don't believe a one of us breathed for a minute. The dragon looked ready to fly. Then it laughed, the most terrible sound I've heard in all my life. Your mother stood firm in its face, sword pointed straight at it. Finally it said, 'The sword Draeblood I recognize, Samantha, daughter of Kiera daughter of Kindra, and the mail, but not your authority to wield and wear them. Yet for your love of kith and kin, and your boldness, I will accept you in lieu of my lawful prey.'

"He roared fire like we have never seen, but it did not harm her, despite her so called lack of authority to wear the mail. Then he snatched her up and flew away. She dropped the sword, and somehow the scabbard. But she is lost to us.

"I had not been there the days before when the dragon showed up, but I was waiting that day. But the fiend landed far from me, close to Samantha. I could not have got there, even had I started running the instant he showed, but I wish to God I had tried." He looked stricken.

Gerald shook his head. "But the mail! He cannot hurt her while she wears the mail!"

"He can hold her hostage till she dies of starvation or thirst. He can drop her from a great height."

"Has none gone to look for her?"

"Where, Gerald, where? No dragon has nested within a month's ride of Kiergenwald for a century. And we don't even know the direction; dragons seldom fly off straight toward home. They are quite secretive. I'm sorry. She was like a beloved sister to me."

Gerald heard the pain in Cle's voice, and knew how deep the truth was. He sobbed. "There must be something."

Cle's hand found his shoulder again. "If there was, we'd have done it."

Sally spoke up. "We held the ceremonial funeral three days later. We had the pyre with her favorite clothes on top. Just as it reached its hottest, the widow Karyn screamed, 'I can't take it,' and leapt atop the pyre. She was dead almost instantly, nothing we could do. Most people thought she couldn't take Mother's death, but she and Mother didn't get along at all. She was too practical for suicide. Cle and I think she had named the dragon and went crazy because Mother and the rest died for her foolishness."

They sat silently a moment. Sally finally remembered to eat again. Gerald started to, but something stopped him.

"Wait. The dragon's name. Cle, you said the dragon's name!"

Cle sighed again. "Aye, lad. When your mother named Drachmaeius in our hearing and he accepted her as substitute prey, he freed all who heard her of the curse of using his name when speaking of the matter. But we can't just yell his name out or curse it. That'd still bring him. And you can't use it since you weren't there. And don't get any ideas of running off to fight him yet!"

Gerald shook his head, which almost made him lose his meager supper. "No, I'll wait 'til I can use Draebard aright. Where are the sword and scabbard?"

"I'll get them." Sally jumped up, ran into another room, and came back a moment later. "Cle and his men recovered them, and we hid them well. Some people. . . ." She rolled her eyes disgustedly.

Gerald examined them and sadly handed them back to Sally. She lay them beside her on the floor.

"Let's keep them hidden. Just show me where they go."

Sally reddened a bit. "We hide them inside my mattress. There's a slit in the side by the wall."

"Isn't that uncomfortable?"

"No. I don't sleep that far over."

Cle sighed. "We have a problem to discuss."

Sally sat back down by Gerald. "Will you hold me?"

For a brief second Gerald felt uncomfortable. Then he saw tears on Sally's cheek, and realized he was close to tears again as well. He put his arm around her and held her close. "The property?"

Cle gazed at the fire. "Aye, that, too. But the problem right now is that the law doesn't know if she's alive or dead."

Gerald gasped; Sally cried a little harder.

"Since she was still alive the last time we saw her, she's just considered missing until a month passes with no sign of her, or she's found. You recall that's what happened with your father."

The teens nodded.

"The pyre was a ritual acknowledgment, but you two have to decide if you want to have her declared legally dead or wait out the month."

The room could have been a tomb. Gerald felt cold and stiff like a corpse. From Sally's expression and rigidity he knew she felt the same, or perhaps worse.

"It doesn't matter," Sally finally spoke, almost gasping for breath. "I won't think of her as dead until I know. But I don't really expect to find her alive. A man or woman might keep her alive out of cruelty, but a dragon's revenge is much swifter."

Gerald closed his eyes; he could see Samantha as plain as day, but she seemed a statue. His eyes flew open in a mild panic.

He realized something. "I thought you could say the dragon's name?"

"I can, but I don't want you to get used to hearing it and say it without thinking."

"Don't worry. I won't say it without thinking. But I'll think about it until the day I can say it and teach him what swift revenge is."

Cle shook his head. "Be careful, Gerald."

Even lecturing, Cle still called him Gerald. It felt good. It would have felt even better hearing Samantha say it.

"Living for revenge, even against a dragon who deserves it, will eat you alive."

Gerald smiled grimly. "We'll see who eats who."

"Gerald!" Sally jumped out of his arm. "You can't eat dragon!"

Gerald laughed. "Maybe not, but Draebard can. And will."

"Oh." She settled back down near him, but not as near. She looked at Cle and nodded. "If Gerald can stand it, I think we should petition to have Mother declared . . . dead." Her voice didn't quite break.

The men were proud of her.

Gerald nodded. "She's right, it doesn't matter. I will live as if she were here, but I hardly hope to see her again."

Cle looked long at each of the youth, seeing the maturity, knowing they were right, weighing his next words. "Then on to tomorrow's problems."

"The property," Gerald guessed.

"The property is one," agreed Cle. "It would entail to you or Sally if either of you were fifteen. Since neither of you is of age to inherit, it goes to the closest relative of your mother—to a brother or sister, a father or mother, an uncle or aunt, a cousin, a nephew or niece, in that order. The more steps removed, the larger the portion retained by the village."

Gerald jumped up. "No!"

"Yes, I fear it is so. Sally's drunken whore of an aunt by marriage, Freda."

More than once, Gerald had seen Freda try to seduce Cle right in front of his wife. He was always amazed no one had killed Freda. The thirty-year-old woman had even eyed him lustily the day he'd ridden off to the castle. He avoided her as much as possible.

"There's only one way, Gerald." Cle gazed steadily at Gerald but said nothing else.

Gerald looked at Sally; Sally looked at her hands in her lap. It took a minute but eventually it dawned on him what Cle was suggesting. He reddened and thought frantically.

"Can't we just call the dragon and say Freda did it?"

His feeble joke didn't help. "There's no other way, is there?"

Cle shook his head. Sally looked up, her face almost expressionless. "Is the idea that bad?"

Gerald reddened more. "Of course not! You're wonderful! It's just that . . . that. . . ." Reasons they couldn't do this lined up in his head like English soldiers. They were just fourteen. She was practically his sister. He had to return to the castle. They had never kissed. Could you marry someone you hadn't kissed?

Sally dropped her eyes to her hands again. "I know."

They sat quietly a long time, occasionally hearing the crackling and popping of the logs in the fire. Eventually Gerald found words. They slipped through his lips unexpectedly. "Sally, will you marry me when, well, after we are of age? It might have to wait a bit if I'm off at the castle."

Sally looked from Gerald to Cle and answered formally. "If my cousin permits it."

Cle laid his knife on the floor close to his right hand, then laid his open hands palms up on his knees. "What gifts do you give Sally and her guardian as your promise?"

Gerald thought for a moment. While he had occasionally dreamed of a day like this, he had assumed it was far off. "Wait," he said and ran outside. A moment later he returned.

"I promise my life as yours, Sally, with Cle and God as my witnesses. Sally, I have no ring; I offer you my most treasured worldly possession, this sword and scabbard."

Sally gasped and Cle grunted in awe as Gerald, now on his knees, picked up the sheathed Draebard and laid it in Sally's hands. "I, Gerald, will be your husband in due time. This is my promise."

Sally stared at Gerald a moment before responding. Her voice finally showed up. "I, Sally, promise to be your wife. All that I have will be yours as well." She wanted to say more but could think of nothing. Cle's smile suggested it was enough.

Gerald spoke again. "And Cle, I give you this gold nugget as a promise of more, that you shall have half of the gold I now own, and if I have more on my wedding day, half of all the increase 'til then." Gerald handed Cle a nugget the size of the older man's thumb.

"Gerald, that is well given, but it is too much!"

Sally snorted. "So I'm not worth it? What did you give for Myrna?" A hint of a smile accompanied the challenge.

Gerald spoke, cutting across Cle's retort. "No, Cle, it is too little. I have no doubt that I owe my life to this family, and certainly I owe them my happiness, and my chances—at arms and now at family."

Sally blushed, causing Gerald to blush and Cle to laugh.

Gerald continued. "If Wallace or Samantha were here, I would offer it to them. And as it is a good faith offer," his voice rang with authority, "it cannot be denied without utter dishonor."

Cle raised his hands as if to ward off attack. "Very well! Half your gold. Sally's worth far more than that."

She smirked.

Cle became formal again. "Clasp hands, you two." Gerald took Sally's left hand in his right. Cle unwound a swath of MacLeod tartan from his arm, wrapped it around their clasped hands, and blessed them.

"Now, to fulfill the vow, and may I never hear these words

come out of my mouth again, you must kiss your sister."

Gerald blanched.

"Yes, full on the mouth, Gerald. Go on, now. I must witness. Tartan and a kiss are how our families cap the hand fasting."

It felt an eternity before Gerald found the courage to move. It took another eternity to get his hand to her cheek, his face near hers. She held her breath; he found himself sweating. Finally, their lips met. It felt like . . . it felt like . . .

"Just a quick kiss to seal the vow!" Cle chortled as they hurriedly pulled apart, their faces hotter than the fire.

The hand-fasted couple found they couldn't look at each other but each was secretly glad their hands were still tied together. "Now the law has to recognize you as legal heir, Gerald, so that's settled. And . . . when do you two plan to get married?"

"What? Legal age? I'm barely fourteen!"

"No, Gerald, but once betrothed, you are treated as if you were of legal age for all intents and purposes, except that you can't actually get married yet. And Sally's past twelve."

"I . . . I don't know?" He looked helplessly at Sally.

"After you're sixteen? Finished with military training and two years of service?"

"Oh, that's right. That's what we agreed to. I . . . I've always loved you, Sally, since that first day in the clearing. When you went to sleep on my shoulder, I wanted us to really be a family. I have ever since. . . ."

"I know. But I don't even want to think about really being married just yet. Can we decide when we're sixteen?"

"Let's do that. When I'm home for planting."

They realized they were still holding hands and let go, slipping out of the tartan, which Gerald folded and handed to Sally. Cle rejoined their hands. "Might as well get used to it. Just don't go past the hand for now, Gerald." He tapped the knife and grinned ferally.

Gerald grinned back. "She has a sword, and you think I'm worried about that little toy?" He got up to search for more to eat.

A moment later the sound of a horn outside the house made him jump.

"It's just Cle," Sally laughed. "He has to make the announcement, brag that he's marrying his cousin off, and make sure everyone knows that neither the property nor I am available."

"You?"

"Of course, you big ox. If you hadn't offered, I'd be fair game, and anyone might have tried to marry me, gaining a wife and the property. That's why I was sitting with a knife when you arrived. I was afraid of who might come for me."

"Why didn't Cle just say that instead of threatening me with Freda?"

"It's how we do things. He has to make sure you will do the right thing for the right reason." She smiled. "Even if he already knows. Like I said, it's what we do."

"Well, I'm stuck now, and so are you." He glanced nervously at the door. "I guess we have to go out now? I hear lots of voices."

"Yes, I think it's time." She gripped his hand tightly.

The crowd roared as they stepped outside, but the jubilant yelling quickly faded, shouted down by an angry male voice.

"He can't marry his sister! That's unnatural. We'll be cursed!"

Sally glanced at Gerald and growled. "It's Norbert, Freda's son."

"I should have known."

Cle's voice shouted down Norbert. "You oaf! He's adopted from another clan. No blood relation at all!"

"It doesn't matter! The law is clear. A man cannot marry his sister and a woman cannot marry her brother. No exceptions!"

"The law also makes it clear that adoption is legally as binding as blood, but in no way entails extra burdens."

"There's no burden, there is simply no betrothal. And so, I wish to propose!"

"Then I claim blood vote."

The crowd fell totally silent as Cle's words rang out. Blood vote was a fight to the death, with the point of law decided in the victor's favor. It had not been invoked in the region for at least fifty years.

Norbert licked his lips. "I . . . um . . . I . . ."

"Do you yield, or do we vote?"

Norbert drew his knife and threw it to the ground. "I yield!" He spun on his heel and stomped off, muttering furiously. The crowd cheered Cle and jeered the retreating Norbert.

Cle picked up the knife and examined it critically. Shrugging, he cleaned it and stuck it in his belt.

"Cle had best watch his back," said Gerald.

Sally laughed. "Norbert is terrified of real warriors. He only had one year of battle training."

"What? Only one year?"

"He was sent home as 'unruly, untrainable, and a menace to the safety and lives of all around him'. Father couldn't recall ever hearing of that happening. Except for Norbert. He's a big slug." Her voice had dropped to a whisper.

Gerald's neck prickled. He guessed out loud as he turned around. "Ho, Freda!"

"Hello, my handsome young nephew. And Sally." Her hungry eyes never left Gerald's face. "Congratulations. I hope you're very happy with your child bride."

As Sally's hand gripped his tighter, Gerald spoke up quickly. "Thank you, I'm sure we will be. Good evening, aunt. I'm sure you must be tired. We children won't expect you to keep up with us." He turned, hauling Sally with him, but not so quickly he missed the rage crossing Freda's face in the firelight.

As they stepped into the crowd for hugs and back slapping, he stopped. "I've really loved living in the house, but for your honor, I suppose I can't do that now."

Sally smiled, her tired, red eyes nevertheless glowing greenly. "Cle took care of that. He and Myrna are moving in until you leave for training. They'll sleep in our parents' bedroom. We hung a full door on my room, which I tie shut at night from inside for a little more protection if I'm alone."

"Tied shut? What if there's a fire?"

"I have my knife."

"So you do. And a sword. Although I may need that back some day."

"Done. And there are two swords, one for each of us."

"Wait. Girls don't get trained at the castle. Where do you learn to use a sword? And fight dragons?"

"I have no idea."

"We'd best find out!"

And thus a brother and sister were engaged to be married and none could speak against it.

CHAPTER SEVEN

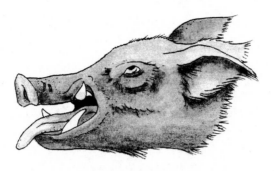

IN A PIG'S EYE

The castle, and especially the barracks, felt somewhat empty. Dree and the rest of his year's trainees were off on their quests, a standard part of second-year training. No one would tell Gerald and his friends anything else. Even as each of their older friends returned, they learned nothing.

Captain Murdoch addressed the issue. "A quest is a very personal thing. As such, we want you to come up with the idea on your own when it's time. So stop asking and stop trying to listen in on conversations." He looked pointedly at Justin.

Eoin spoke. "But a quest by all accounts involves danger. What if knowledge of another's quest might save a life?"

"A worthy quest is certainly not without peril. But King Donald would never approve a quest with little chance of success. And you may pick everyone's brains after you declare, before you leave." He bid them good day and left them to their lessons.

Over the next six weeks their friends returned, one at a time. They would see the king, then return to their lessons and to helping teach the younger warriors. It was all very secretive and unsatisfactory, but there was little choice. No one wanted to anger the captain.

The summer passed fairly uneventfully. The young warriors practiced with weapons and targes from two to four hours a day, while their arms and legs grew stronger than ever. Eoin and James proved the best at axe, hammer, and knives. Gerald alone was tall enough to use a claymore, though it was still a bit unwieldy for him. Justin was the only one of the four with much skill at archery. He could easily hit a gourd the size of a man's head out past the standing stones, both from the wall and from the keep.

Though all were good at tracking, they got much better, learning also how to foil trackers even as they tracked someone. Gerald and Eoin proved the best at this.

The captain had observed that the four looked born to the saddle, but they still learned a great deal about horsemanship, especially with respect to battle. They spent several days riding various horses until each found the one best suited to him (or vice versa, as Peter was fond of saying).

All grew their hair out, as befit men and warriors. While they thought little of it, an outsider would no longer have seen children but young men—strong, courageous, and deadly to their enemies. They began helping train new arrivals.

Peter quietly became a warrior. Gerald was the first to notice that though Peter wore his new belt proudly, he also wove a green cord with a few small, green stone shamrocks through it. Gerald smiled to himself, understanding well the need to feel connected to home.

When the weather cooled all young warriors were sent home, along with half the warriors, to look after the harvest. As it had taken Gerald a couple of days to adjust to the bed and life at the castle each time he arrived there, he now found it took even longer to readjust to his bed and life at Kiergenwald. Things felt strange for a few days until something (he couldn't have said what) shifted and he again felt at home. His fourth night back he fell asleep as soon as his head hit the pillow, and he awoke refreshed before sunrise.

The harvest was slightly better than average that year. There were the inevitable nasty comments by Freda and Norbert, mock challenges by friends, and advice from other teenagers. But the biggest problems Sally and Gerald faced came from dealing with each other. They were not quite out of their awkward years and had seen each other as brother and sister for so long that they weren't sure how to act.

They also found that people treated them differently. This ranged from respect to mild advances by slightly older members of the opposite sex (never mind Norbert and Freda, who were so blatant the clan's elders finally threatened to disown them) to snide comments by those jealous of their new status as effective adults. At least two of their friends tried to hand-fast someone, but their parents weren't having it.

Gerald tried to explain to his friends that it wasn't the jolly ride they thought. After a day of bargaining with traders for his grain and goats, he told Justin, "They think I must be covering for a sick parent or that we're desperate somehow, so they won't deal fairly. And some of them get angry when they find out I know what I'm doing and what things are worth."

"Yeah," Justin agreed, "but still. You get to do it, and you came out well in the end."

"True. But it's not like we're getting rich."

Justin laughed. "Remember how we were dreaming only last winter about being adults?"

Chagrined, Gerald admitted he did. Realizing how his friends saw him somehow made him appreciate it all a bit more, and he smiled more and worked even harder. And when he played, he still played for all he was worth. In many ways it was the best of both worlds.

The second week of harvest, Gerald and Eoin were loading sacks of barley onto a cart when they heard a woman's scream. Running through the stalks, they almost fell across a bloody Freda laying in the dirt. Rushing up the row straight at them was the ugliest sow Gerald had seen, with eyes like hot coals, and foaming at the mouth.

Gerald found himself running at the beast, screaming, sword drawn. As they closed Gerald leapt up onto the row to his left, crouched, and as the pig raced by, swung his sword to hack its legs off. The madly squealing pig nosed into the dirt. Gerald ran up behind it and severed its spine with a furious stroke to the neck. He spun around, looking for more hogs. None came. He finally realized the squealing he still heard came from two nearby sources—Freda and baby pigs.

From the shape and angle of Freda's legs, both were clearly broken, accounting for her pain. She had several squirming baby pigs wrapped in a barley sack, explaining the sow's rage. Others began to show up. Cynthia, an elder and healer, supervised as two of the men ran back for branches to make a sled. Freda screamed and passed out when Cynthia straightened her legs, setting the bones enough to move her.

Norbert, who always assumed the worst, was working another field and heard the story in its entirety before he got back to his mother's home. He found her drugged and asleep, her legs tied up in splints. After a moment he left and went to find Gerald. He found him back at work, unloading barley for the threshers.

"Gerald! I come to thank you. Everyone said Mum would be dead if t'weren't for you."

"That may well be."

"You're all right, Gerald. Thanks for saving Mum." He held out his arm. Wonderingly, Gerald clasped it.

"You're welcome."

Norbert grinned and walked off. Gerald shrugged, looked at his workmates, and resumed unloading barley.

Over the next few days, the healers settled into a routine of watches for Freda. On the fourth day she was lucid enough to ask for Gerald.

"Must I?" he complained.

Cle and Sally laughed, but Sally turned serious. "You saved her life; she has every right to see you. Be gracious, Gerald. Besides, it's not like she can chase you down to ravish you!"

She walked with Gerald to Freda's house. Once inside, Sally hung back. Annoyed to find himself alone, Gerald moved to Freda's bedside. "I'm here, aunt."

Freda opened her eyes and took Gerald's hand. She struggled to speak. "Thank you . . . Gerald. When I was lying in the dirt in pain . . . I wanted to die. I tried to scream for you to kill me, or let the sow do it, but all I could do was cry. But now I'm glad I'm going to live . . . even if I don't know if I will walk again."

"Of course you will, Aunt Freda."

"Of course you will," chimed in Sally, wearing the same, slightly amazed look as Gerald.

"We'll see. But be that as it may . . . I had four piglets. I want each of you to take one. . . . It's not much thanks, but . . ."

"You don't need to do that," Gerald said softly.

"Maybe not, but I'm doing it."

Norbert cleared his throat just behind them, making them jump. He held two piglets, one in each of his huge hands.

Freda fell back asleep and Jason, the healer on duty, waved them out.

Once outside, Norbert spoke, "One of the piglets died. But she wants you two to have the larger ones, so we kept the runt."

"Let me trade with you," Sally said.

"No! She said you were to have the best, and you shall."

Gerald smiled as they accepted the piglets. "So be it. We thank you, Norbert. I have to go now to get ready to return to Cair Parn. Be seeing you." He and Sally left Freda's home.

Sally laughed. "Bacon and ham for us!"

"Eventually," agreed Gerald, "but you will have to build strong pens for them. They're harder to keep in than cattle."

"I know. We had pigs before."

"Why don't you now?"

"They started dying with some form of madness. We had to kill and burn them all."

"I've heard that dragons like pig. Too bad the dragon didn't eat them. Maybe it would have died."

"And maybe it would have gone mad. That's all we need, a dragon going crazy, foaming at the mouth."

"I think they're all crazy. Wait. What do you mean, foaming at the mouth?"

"When the pigs went mad, they drooled constantly. It looked like bubbles all round their mouths. . . . What's wrong?"

Gerald almost dropped his piglet. "Where do we put these for now?"

"There's the goat pen. It's empty and will hold them for a day or two. Now, what's wrong?"

But Gerald seemed bent on putting the piglets down as quickly as possible. Once they put the piglets in the pen right behind the house, Gerald furiously wiped his hands on a rag hanging nearby and insisted Sally do the same. Only then would he relax even a little.

"Sally, I'd forgotten. I don't know how, because I've dreamed about it almost every night. But the sow that tried to kill Freda. . . . It's eyes were blazing red, and there was saliva all around its mouth, like a foaming river. . . ."

Sally gasped. "Gerald, you must be mistaken! Someone would have noticed!"

He shook his head. "When I cut her legs off, she nosed into

the dirt going really fast. Her snout was just a ball of mud after that."

"Oh, I hope Freda doesn't go mad."

Gerald smiled. "Especially since she's just stopped acting mad."

His smile disappeared. "What about the meat?"

"The hog? We ate some of it yesterday. Most of the village has by now. But it was all cooked. I've never heard of anyone getting the madness that way, so long as the meat was cooked. And everyone knows you have to cook pig meat or you can die, anyway."

"I hope you're right, but it's too late to do anything now. Only . . . what about Freda?"

"You'd better go tell the healers. Don't look at me that way! You saw the sow; you need to talk with them. Wait, why are you going that way?"

"To tell Jason. He's with Freda."

"We'd best tell Cynthia. She's the eldest healer."

Cynthia was at home asleep, having spent the previous night watching over Freda. Druze, her granddaughter, agreed to wake her when Gerald assured her it was urgent. Cynthia, ever conscious of custom, waited while Druze brought wine and bread. She blessed it and offered it to her guests. Once they had taken their portions, she leaned back to relax. "Now, my young hero, what brings you to waken an old woman from her slumber?"

"Old woman?" snorted Sally. "You run most of us off our feet!"

The healer shrugged. "I cannot help it if some of the young let themselves get old before their time."

The gleam in Cynthia's eye told Sally she would play this game all day. "I will rest my young old bones for yours since they cannot sleep at the moment, while Gerald tells you his news."

"Very well. But it is chilly in here. Druze, please bring both of us old women some blankets."

The girl hurried off to find light coverings.

"Now, Gerald, what tidings?"

"Sally and I believe the sow that attacked my aunt may have been mad. Its eyes were blazing red, and its mouth foamed like a spring where the women have washed clothes with too much soap."

Cynthia's eyes were wide. "You did not know of such madness?"

Gerald hung his head. There was no reason to feel ashamed, but he did. "No, Mother. I have heard of mad animals, but never the symptoms. When I chopped her front legs off, she fell into the dirt snout first. By the time anyone else got a good look at her, any foam was wiped off and her snout was covered with mud. Her eyes were lifeless. I'm so sorry. . . ."

"Do not blame yourself for what you do not know, son. Just continue to learn so that what you do not know grows ever smaller. I must go to the other healers. Thank you for telling me." She leaped up from the rug on the floor like a woman less than half her age. "Feel free to stay and eat and drink if you like." Then she was gone.

Gerald stared after her. "I forget what a whirlwind she is. Her face says she's sixty, but she thinks and moves like she's twenty."

Sally punched his arm. "Well, don't go getting too excited, Gerald. It's me you're engaged to, not her!"

"Thank God! She'd outlive me and probably outdo me my whole life!"

"And you think I won't?"

"Well, it's not so bad with you not having a fifty-year head start."

Druze stuck her head in from the other room. "I heard that!"

Gerald reddened. "I'm sorry!"

"Don't be." She grinned. "I feel the same way. She knows, and loves it."

At the harvest feast a week later, nobody commented on the lack of hog meat.

Gerald and his friends had to leave for the castle the morning after the feast. As Gerald was checking that his pack was secure on his horse, Sally ran up.

"No need to run; I won't leave without saying goodbye."

"Gerald." Sally spoke between gasps; she had run hard. "Freda started sweating during the night. She's burning up, but she gets chills, too. She aches. She isn't hungry, and Freda is always hungry."

"Nobody gets the sweating sickness this time of year."

"No."

"Does that mean . . . the madness?"

"It might. The healers aren't taking any chances. Nobody can get close to her or the three still attending her. They say it could be the sweating sickness."

"But nobody thinks so."

"Not really, no."

Gerald hung his head. "So she's going to die."

"We don't know. But if it's the madness . . . or the sickness . . . probably."

A tear wandered down Gerald's face.

"Gerald, are you crying for Freda?"

"I guess so. And Norbert. And Jason."

"Yeah. I never thought anyone but Norbert would love Freda, but I think Jason was thinking of marrying her."

"Are you serious?"

"Yes."

"Then she's definitely mad."

"What?"

"Well, she must have gone mad. Where else could he have caught it?"

They both laughed, but not for long. It was so unfair that after years of making the village miserable, Freda seemed on the verge of turning her life around and was probably, almost certainly, going to die. And not a nice death, by any account.

"Sally, I have to go. I'm to meet the others at the Fallen Stones at noon. I should have left by now."

She grabbed his arm. "Be careful, Gerald."

"Of course, Sally." He wondered if she would let him kiss her goodbye.

"Good. Otherwise I'll end up married to Norbert."

He rolled his eyes, shrugged her hand off his arm, and made to climb onto the horse. She grabbed him, turned him around, and kissed him much harder than any fourteen-year-old in the region had ever been kissed. Then they were apart, wide eyed and a bit out of breath.

"And I'd much rather have you than Norbert." She reddened to match her hair.

Completely out of sorts, Gerald bowed, scrambled onto his horse, waved, and rode off. As Sally waved one last time, Cle stepped from behind a rock.

"Oh! I thought you would have been here, Cle."

"I was, but just as I started to announce myself, you grabbed Gerald and attacked him. I didn't think it was the best time to interrupt, so I disappeared for a moment."

"I'd have seen you!"

Cle smiled broadly and shook his head. "I walked up behind Gerald. You should have seen me, but your eyes were boring into him. I doubt you'd have seen a dragon consuming

Gerald's horse with a wall of flame!"

Sally reddened still more as her cousin hugged her and they walked back toward the house.

Freda was declared mad a week later and had to be restrained. The next morning they found her dead, a knife through her heart and a torn piece of tartan around her right hand. Later they found Jason, his body smashed at the bottom of a nearby ravine, the matching strip of tartan around his left hand. No one admitted to handfasting the two, but all were glad for them. They hoped they were together in the afterlife. Norbert was livid that his mother had been killed, yet grateful she'd not had to live through the most brutal stages of madness. A few days later he formally gave his family's holdings to Sally and rode off into the woods. No story ever returned of his fate.

CHAPTER EIGHT

A ROYAL AUDIENCE
& A BEATING

When Gerald and his friends from Kiergenwald returned to the castle, they were met at the gates by Dree and Drinn standing guard. Drinn spoke first. "Salute your betters!"

Taking in the guards' new belts signifying their warriorhood, the arrivals clasped forearms with their friends and congratulated them.

"I suppose this means you've moved out of the barracks, then?" Justin asked.

"No." Drinn glanced at Dree and raised an eyebrow.

Dree spoke, but like Drinn his eyes were ever past his friends, watching the approach. "We had the option of moving to the warrior barracks or staying this year. We wanted to stay with Peter and Thomas. The captain liked the idea; he says maybe we can whip you into shape faster if we stay close."

The younger crowd groaned. Eoin spoke up. "What happened when you became warriors? We've not heard, but we noted there was never a ceremony this past year, only a dribble of new warriors."

"We were taken before the king. We swore fealty as warriors and he renewed his vows. He gave us the new sword belts and we returned the old ones. That was it. Nothing fancy, no meal, no gold or jewels, no fair maidens, no land." He sighed as if deeply disappointed.

"Still," Drinn grinned, "we could hardly refuse the honor."

"True. We were outnumbered. All the king's advisers were there with their swords drawn. Though they were saluting us, they could as easily have had our heads."

Gerald laughed. "And here I thought you two the mightiest warriors in Scotland!"

"Of course, but it's terribly rude to fight the king and his advisers in the throne room. No self-respecting man or dragon would have anything to do with us ever again!"

Drinn glanced toward the castle. "You've missed lunch, but if you hurry with your horses and gear, there should still be some scraps available."

They hurried. There were.

"Here you are. We should have known. Why would we look all over the grounds this magnificent day? Any fool should have guessed you'd be sitting morosely, staring into a fire."

James's voice called Gerald back to the present, but he didn't look up as his friends entered. "It's nice outside, is it?"

Justin struck an astonished pose. "Do you mean to say you haven't set foot outside today?"

"No. Yes. I mean, I've been in here all day, thinking."

James snorted. "Brooding, more like it. Is it Freda again? None of us could stand her, including you, so why are you so miserable?"

Gerald stared deeply into the flames. He was only now understanding what he felt and couldn't yet really explain it. A touch on his shoulder startled him.

"Ho ho!", chortled Dree. "Got you for once! Well, pull

yourself together. You're wanted."

"Wanted? By who?"

"By whom? By the king himself."

"What?" The fire forgotten, Gerald sat up straight. "Why would the king want me?"

"How do I know? Why would anyone want you, you great lout?" Dree grabbed Gerald and, despite being a foot shorter, easily hauled him up out of his chair. "The captain said to find you and take you to the king. Now let's go!"

Pausing only to grab his sword belt, Gerald hurried after Dree. The other boys followed, but not too closely. Eoin muttered. "Is he blasted or blessed? And are we as well?"

Justin laughed quietly. "We're safe enough as he only asked for poor Gerald. But I wonder why?"

"Just so it's not more bad news from home," Eoin grunted. "I don't think Gerald needs any more bad news."

The others nodded. James replied, "I don't think it can be. The captain would have told him, or if it were something about the village, we'd all be called."

Coming around a corner, they nearly collided with Dree and Gerald.

Dree was speaking quickly and softly. "I'll announce you to the guard. You have to go in alone because he only called for you."

Gerald nodded, saving speech for the king; he felt like he only had a few words in him at the moment.

Dree's voice rang out loud and clear. "Gerald of Kiergenwald, at His Majesty's request."

The guards never moved, but the door opened. With only a slight push from Dree, Gerald entered the king's audience chamber.

"Why am I so nervous?" Gerald asked himself. "He's only a petty king, not a high king." He looked up at the man on the throne thirty feet away. "Because a king's still a king, and not to be trifled with," he answered himself.

"Come!" the king called.

Gerald walked quickly forward (too quickly, he thought), and dropped to his knees as the trainees had been taught, otherwise at attention. "Your Majesty!"

"Rise, Gerald of Kiergenwald."

Startled, Gerald managed to comply.

The king looked at him for a few seconds in silence. "How many hogs have you killed?" His voice was gruff yet cultured, commanding but kind.

"Hogs, Your Majesty?" Gerald thought desperately. "Three."

"Only three? I'd have thought at least a dozen by now."

Gerald had no idea how to reply, so he stalled. "Why is that, Your Majesty?"

"Who is your father?"

"My father is dead."

"You come from Kiergenwald?"

"Yes, Your Majesty."

"But you are from Kenwield, I think?"

Dumbfounded, Gerald merely nodded.

The ghost of a smile played across the king's lips. "Did your father kill a lot of hogs?"

"I don't recall, Your Majesty. I was eight when he was . . . when he and my mother vanished."

The king's smile faded, but his face softened a bit more. "I thought so. Taken by Argyll, I suspect."

"Argyll?"

"Argyll," the king agreed. "A dragon who fled the Western Isles and settled in the northwest highlands, but sometimes followed the savages south, seeking strife and war. He loved to fly over battles, roasting everyone alive, then return to feed."

"What a brute!"

"Yes, quite a brute. Your father and others hoped to destroy Argyll, but they all simply disappeared, in some cases with their wives."

"Did you know my father?" Gerald gasped, "Your Majesty?"

The king smiled. "That was nearly your second omission! But yes, I knew your father. He was a great warrior, was Angus, but he kept a quiet life in Kenwield. He lived up to his name. He killed several dragons and more wild hogs than anyone cared to count. Do you recall eating a lot of pork as a child?"

Lost in the turn of conversation, Gerald was quiet for a moment. "Yes. I recollect ham and bacon almost every day, as far back as I can think. Sometimes sausage."

The king nodded. "I should think so. He kept our larder well stocked, as well as your village's. That's why he had so much land and a bit of gold from trading the meat and skins."

"Gold?" Gerald looked confused.

"Yes, gold." The king's smile vanished. "You didn't get the gold?"

"No, Your Majesty. My uncle and the village chief hated me, and after my parents were dead I sold the chief all the family property for a small bag of gold."

"What else did you take with you? His sword? Armor? Horse?"

"He was on his horse when he disappeared. I don't recall any armor or a special sword."

"What?" The king leaped up in anger. It was all Gerald could do not to turn and run. A hand on his shoulder nearly made him faint. "Steady, lad," a quiet voice behind him whispered in his ear. He'd not heard anyone enter.

"Your Majesty. . . ."

"Hush, young warrior! Let me think. . . . Your father was a humble man, but a dragon lord, and I'll wager would have been among the best had he lived. He came late to the knowledge, but took to it like a beaver to a dam. He practiced his killing thrusts and strokes on hogs, because they are the closest thing to a dragon in feel there is. Aye, I heard about how you saved Dree. That's what first brought you to my attention. Then you saved your aunt. . . ."

"But she died!" The hand tightened gently on his shoulder. By now he knew the captain stood behind him.

"Through no fault of yours. But back to your lands and other things. Murdoch!"

"Aye, Your Majesty!"

Gerald felt the captain draw to attention.

"Take the lad back to Kenwield. This is the third and worst tale I've heard of Ogilvy. He hasn't paid taxes on these lands he's acquired, nor has he reported the armor or sword. Twice this week I've heard rumors of beatings and worse. Take a squad, bring him in, and appoint Roger as chief. And hug Ailsa for me."

"Aye, Your Majesty, but I'll make sure all know it's in the king's name." He nodded and touched his head.

Gerald did the same, and they turned to leave.

"Oh, and Gerald," the king called.

Gerald spun sharply, "Yes, Your Majesty?"

"I never congratulated you on your engagement. A bit surprising for one so young."

Gerald blushed, nodded thanks, and spun around to leave, ignoring Murdoch's smirk.

As the doors closed behind them, Gerald turned to Murdoch. "Hug Ailsa?" Gerald recalled her as a beautiful woman who looked younger than her middle-aged husband, Roger.

"Aye, Ailsa. She was the king's first love. Her father was the laird of the northern highlands. But she loved Roger, and the king's—well, he was only a prince then—his mother loathed all McElroys, so Ailsa McElroy was out of the question as a wife. But they remained friends, though by all counts Roger is very jealous."

This frank talk appalled Gerald, who'd grown up believing kings were people best seen and honored from a distance. He said as much to Captain Murdoch after making sure nobody was close enough to hear.

"Aye, as a rule, that's not bad policy. But Donald is as good as they come, though he can't hold his ale as he should."

Gerald missed a step, causing Murdoch to laugh.

"We rode together against dragons. He was my prince then. Six dragons we killed, seeking the one who ate your parents. Five denied knowing anything and Argyll refused to talk, but all had killed too many people and tried to kill us, so we killed them. We thought surely Argyll had done it, but we never found any evidence among his plunder. So we don't actually know." He shook his head sadly. "We may never know."

Gerald said nothing, thinking of how much had been taken from him by dragons and selfish people.

"We ride at daybreak three days hence. Be ready."

"Yes, sir! Sir, why am I to go?"

"You are going to get your heritage back for what was paid for it, plus interest."

"Interest?"

"Oh, yes, we must be fair." Murdoch smiled grimly. "You'll see." With a clap on the shoulder, the captain turned and headed to his quarters.

Gerald suddenly found himself surrounded by Dree and his friends from home. Once he managed to hush their questions, he told them what had occurred in the king's audience chamber. Their reaction was all he could have hoped for. Justin summed it up.

"It's not fair! His father's a dragon lord. His second mother is a dragon lord. . . ."

"Don't you mean dragon lady?" Dree interjected.

"Lady dragon lord. Whatever! He has one dragon sword,

his fiancée has another, now he's inherited a third, and armor, and land, and gold, plus half the land Norbert left his fiancée. Next he'll be in the king's guard by his fourteenth birthday!"

"Oh, did I leave that part out?"

The others stared at Gerald, astonished. "You oafs, I'm joking!"

They dunked his head in a nearby horse trough.

After supper the next evening, Gerald sought out Dree. "I need some help."

Dree nodded, and Gerald explained. Dree tried to argue, but he could see how much it meant to Gerald. Dree also remembered his first year and how nervous he'd been. "All right. I'll do it. The main warrior's practice room in five minutes."

"Warrior's? I'm not allowed there!"

"You are with me. Meet me at the gate, but don't go in 'til I get there. You'll be fine."

Despite curious looks and the odd glare or two, they made it to the practice room without anyone challenging Gerald's right to be there. Once inside, Gerald moved to the middle of the room and stood at attention with his back to the door. After maybe thirty seconds of silence, he heard Dree draw his sword. He flinched and grimaced. He heard the sword go back in the sheath. Then out it came, and the flat caught him across the back. He gasped and cursed himself for the weakness.

Fifteen minutes and many bruises later, as he took a blow behind his knees without moving, he heard a furious roar.

"Dree! Cease that at once!" Despite his aches, Gerald spun around so quickly the captain would have been proud. But it was the captain glaring at them as Dree nervously sheathed his sword, and he looked anything but proud.

"Sir, I can explain!" Dree blurted.

"I'm sure you can," the captain agreed coldly, "but I'll let young Gerald explain. Well? Why was he beating you with his sword?"

Glancing quickly at Dree, Gerald took a deep breath. "I asked him to."

The captain just stared. "You what?"

"I asked him to."

"To what? Beat you like a dead cow?"

"I guess it does look crazy, sir, but yes. You see, when you came up behind me yesterday in front of the king and touched me, I flinched. I never want to do that again, sir. Whether in front of King Donald or Ogilvy, or facing a dragon or an army. Whatever happens, I don't want to be caught off guard, and I don't want to show weakness or dishonor the king. Or you. Or my comrades. Or Scotland . . . or myself, sir."

Murdoch glanced back and forth between the two young men, as if trying to decide. Finally he shrugged. "I'll leave you to it, then."

Gerald sighed. "Perhaps we should find somewhere more private."

"Why?" Dree asked.

"Good point, lad," Murdoch said. "Anyone might walk in and think what I thought."

"What did you think, sir?" Dree asked.

The captain squirmed just a bit. "I thought you might still have a grudge, Dree."

"What? He saved my life!"

"I know, and you have my apologies, Dree."

Dree nodded.

The captain continued, "I'll post a guard."

"Sir, I'd rather nobody else knew."

Murdoch smiled at Gerald. "I meant to post myself as guard, if you must know." The boys were awestruck.

Finally, Dree spoke. "There's no point, sir. He hasn't flinched for several minutes, and he took some pretty good licks, as well as a long series of drawing my sword but not touching him. I don't think more would help, and I'm afraid he's bleeding a bit already."

"I'll say he is. Come with me, Gerald. Dree, you're dismissed." He hesitated. "Good work, Dree."

Dree nodded and hurried out. Following him, Murdoch shook his head as they walked down the hallway toward Murdoch's room.

"Where are we going?"

"I'm going to put something on your wounds, lad. If ye take those to the healer, there'll be talk."

"You don't believe us?"

"Aye, I believe. But not everyone will, and not everyone would understand. Best keep it quiet. Interesting technique, but if it works, good for you."

Once in Murdoch's room, the captain had Gerald remove his shirt and leggings. His eyes widened at the extent of Gerald's wounds. "I hope it was worth it."

"It was. If it works."

"Dree thinks it did. But the pain isn't over yet. . . ." As he daubed salve, it stung a great deal where Gerald's skin was broken. Gerald managed not to flinch or call out, to Murdoch's delighted surprise. "I'd say it worked."

Gerald smiled, then winced inwardly as salve hit another spot without skin. But neither Murdoch nor the mirror saw any change in Gerald's expression.

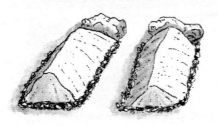

CHAPTER NINE

KING'S JUSTICE

Two mornings later at sunrise, a dozen men and four young warriors rode out for Kenwield. Half the warriors rode in front, including Captain Murdoch. The young men rode in the middle, with the rest of the warriors behind as rear guard.

"Rear guard for what?" Gerald wondered aloud.

Dree, now official leader of the young warriors, replied. "Savages. Beasts. Highwaymen. Dragons. Anything but hogs; then they'll call you."

Gerald smiled. "They'd best. I've a long way to go to catch up with Father." The smile faded. "But highwaymen? Against the king's warriors?"

"Aye!" one of the nearby warriors, Donald of Lochlorien, replied. "Some of them are crazier than savages. If they even think they see a weakness they'll attack. As none of you are full grown yet, they'd no realize you are already deadly foes. By the time they knew better, one or two of you might have fallen to an arrow. But with us riding rearguard, they'll try naught."

Gerald could see his point. All the warriors on this trip were big men, well-muscled, with a deadly look.

"What of the Britons and their knights?"

Donald waved a hand in dismissal. "Paugh. Since the dragons came, we doona fight each other. Our southern neighbors have become just that, if only by uneasy truce. Dragons seldom notice small battles, but real war brings them faster than vultures or eagles. Besides, they canna more afford to lose warriors than we; they were hurt far worse in the early dragon attacks."

James spoke up. "We always heard they were still our enemies. Why is that?"

"Oh, there's no love lost, that's true. But mostly I think what ye hear of such is from the older folk who heard it from their grandparents and so on."

"That's true," said Dree. "My grandparents spoke of it, though they admitted they'd never seen an Englishman in person save traders and sailors, and them not too hard to get on with."

At this point Folkvar, whose mother was of the Vikings, broke in with a long tale of a knight and a trader under a spell, and the conversation wandered into epic tales (mostly lies), as is wont to do among bored fighting men. And so that evening they came near Kenwield. They camped at Inverhost, an outpost hidden from Kenwield by several tall hills, ready for supper and a fire.

"We'll enter at daybreak," Murdoch ordered. He looked at Gerald. "You'll ride by me." He waved behind him toward Kenwield. "Reports are that Ogilvy is still a sluggard, sleeping till mid-morning. We'll greet him and invite him to an early breakfast."

The men roared their approval.

The party rode into Kenwield with the rising sun glinting redly off their spear tips and targes, Captain Murdoch and Gerald of Kenwield in the van. But when they called for

Ogilvy, they found he was gone. Gerald's uncle, Errol, who had profited much from allying with Ogilvy, had somehow heard of the king's mission. He and Ogilvy had fled an hour earlier.

Half the warriors and two of the young warriors stayed behind to inventory Ogilvy's and Errol's lands and leavings. Their abandoned wives were none too happy but cooperated. Murdoch's men assured them they would not lose what had rightly been their families' lands and properties.

Murdoch and his force caught Ogilvy and Errol around noon, their horses too laden with gold and other treasure to keep up any sort of fast pace. They chose to give no quarter.

Dree shook his head and said, "They died the death of utter fools."

No one disagreed. Gerald looked on their hacked and bloody bodies with only minor pity; he knew these men to be thieves and murderers.

"Why," intoned Dree, "did the village suffer them to rule?"

Gerald glanced at Murdoch before answering. "King Donald appointed Ogilvy, whom all thought a good man. Ogilvy appointed Errol. Once they were in power they became greedy and ruthless. If we spoke against them, it went badly. Several people died or disappeared. At first I wondered if they had killed my parents, but they were cowards at heart."

Murdoch nodded as four men started digging shallow graves and the rest looked through the loot. Dree and Gerald were tasked with stripping the bodies of all but their kilts and vests. The bodies were laid in the graves with crude, wooden plates made on the spot, each plate holding a little earth and salt. Murdoch would not bury even such men as these without proper rites. Rocks were laid over the graves.

Captain Murdoch pondered aloud whether markers were needed.

Gerald laughed hollowly. "The only reason anyone would care would be to see if they'd been buried with stolen valuables. I've never met anyone more despised than these two. They were kind enough by accounts to their women folk until they married; then even their wives learned to hate them."

Murdoch shook his head as they mounted up to return to Kenwield. They ate bread en route, and went slowly to save the horses. "Well, Gerald, that's a bit more interest paid than I expected, but they insisted."

"They were always greedy."

They rode on in silence a few minutes.

"Folkvar, tell them of Viking funerals," Murdoch suggested.

Folkvar smiled. "The Vikings have funeral pyres for their warriors, either on a ship or on a mock ship on land. If the man is a chief, one of his thrall girls will join him in the afterlife." Before anyone could ask, he added, "There is always a volunteer. Mother tried to explain it once, but I don't think she quite believed it, herself.

"All Viking men are warriors, including the traders, priests, and artisans. Many of the women are warriors as well; few of my mother's people are not warriors. She told me of a man named Asgrim in their village who was small, with useless, twisted legs. He rode about on a little cart. When their village was attacked, Asgrim first heard the raiders and led the attack, rolling down the hill, swinging his sword, singing a battle chant. After the fight, all the raiders were dead. They found Asgrim underneath the giant raider chief. Asgrim's sword had run through the raider's belly but the raider broke Asgrim's neck when he fell. Asgrim had never been to sea, but they made his pyre on the raider's ship, a funeral fit for a chief, save that he had no thrall."

Gerald looked at Dree, who seemed to have no questions. When no one else spoke, Gerald finally asked, "What's a thrall?"

"A thrall," Folkvar replied, "is a serf, a slave. With a great chief or warrior, a thrall woman might volunteer to join a man in the afterlife."

"She would kill herself?"

"No, she would drink things that made her very happy, almost delirious, and help her see into the next life. Then she would be sent to join him."

"Oh. And she would volunteer?"

"Yes. A wife could do this if she wished instead. But Asgrim had neither thrall nor wife."

The party was silent for a while; Gerald was glad for the quiet as he pondered what it would be like to join Sally this way if she died first, or vice versa. He kept his peace but decided he didn't care for the idea. Had he asked, he'd have found that Folkvar felt the same way. But Gerald had yet to learn that politely minding your own business was not always best.

They arrived two hours after the most glorious sunset Gerald could recall, with the northern lights following suit in a spectacular array of greens and purples after nightfall. Murdoch and his party took turns standing guard, not because it was needful, but because the king's men always stood guard. Gerald and James were glad when their watch was over at midnight. They awoke to the smell of ham. "Just my luck," Gerald said. "Someone else got the hog this time."

"Don't worry," chortled James. "I'm sure there are plenty more where that one came from."

"There always are."

Roger and Ailsa were made chief and chieftess at high noon. Justice was meted out to the few people who had cooperated overly much with Ogilvy, primarily in the form of repaying with interest what had been taken from others. Two men were tried for brutality and murder. The brute was beaten and stripped of most of his property to repay his victims. The murderer was executed and his head posted on a stake at the main village gate. That was Folkvar's idea, but everyone approved, even the man's family.

The accounting and redistribution of stolen property and goods took that afternoon and the better part of the next day. When all was said and done, Gerald had his parents' lands back and Ogilvy's wife had a bag of gold. Unbeknownst to anyone, it was larger than the one Ogilvy had given Gerald. He felt sorry for the woman; Ogilvy had treated her horribly.

Gerald's family's land was near the center of the village. He gave the land to the village for a commons or whatever else they wished to use it for.

Ogilvy's and Errol's wives offered Gerald a tenth of their own lands by way of apology, but he declined. "You have done me no wrong, and have likewise suffered. I do not hold you to account for the crimes of your husbands."

They thanked him lavishly, kissing him and kneeling before him while he blushed and his friends roared with approval and laughter. The women insisted he take gifts for his betrothed, including gold and copper jewelry, two silver and gold chalices, and a matching flagon. Of the latter items Ogilvy's wife said, "I've no idea from whence these came. But when things simply appeared as these did, I assume they were ill gained. Please take them. If you do not want them, do with them as you wish."

Gerald stammered his thanks to the women.

Dree later remarked, "For a fourteen-year-old, you're getting quite the hoard. Your part of Wallace's and Norbert's lands, the other parts by marriage, uncountable dragon swords, and all this loot. You're halfway to being a dragon yourself!"

"But why didn't you take the lands, Gerald?" Folkvar wanted to know.

"I don't claim this village; I will not let it have a claim on me." He stared around at the villagers. "I bear them no ill will, but I have no real friends here and no good memories after my parents' deaths."

Eoin jumped in. "Not even the kisses?"

"Don't be jealous."

"It's a shame your father's sword and mail were gone," Folkvar added.

"The mail would be nice, but if I got any more dragon

swords, I wouldn't know what to do with them!"

"My birthday is coming up."

Everyone laughed.

The celebration lasted until nearly daybreak the next day. Murdoch let his party sleep 'til noon. He left two of his men to better prepare the village defense against savages. The rest rode back toward Cair Parn after Gerald made arrangements for Sally's gifts and his new wealth to be sent to Kiergenwald.

Shortly after starting home, Gerald rode up beside Murdoch and asked quietly, "Did you remember to hug Ailsa?"

Murdocuh grinned. "Of course! After explaining and with warriors nearby! But Roger seems no longer jealous. He laughed and said to hug the king back for himself and Ailsa. Then Ailsa added that I should kiss the king for Roger."

"All of Cair Parn will want to see that!"

"Even I won't see that. Now get back by Dree before he wanders up to hear what we're discussing and I put you both to work in the stables for a month shoveling muck!"

The remaining two months of the year passed with few noteworthy events. Winter arrived with cold and snow as expected, but there were plenty of skins and furs available. The winter promised to be neither colder nor wetter than usual.

Some druids came to the castle a week before the winter solstice. A dozen or so warriors, young warriors, and castle staff rode with them to Ballymeanoch—near Kilmartin—to celebrate Yule. They never discussed their celebration with anyone else.

Father MacPherson and two acolytes showed up to hear confession and hold Christmas mass. About half the castle attended. Gerald was surprised at how beautiful the songs sounded. Even his voice blended well. He missed Drinn and Thomas, who were off with the druids.

"The singing is always like that," said Murdoch the next morning after breakfast. "Even my cousin sounds good Christmas Eve, and normally he sounds like a hare having its throat slit."

Gerald wondered who the cousin was but asked nothing.

The day Thomas returned, he received his warrior's belt. Later he told those from Kiergenwald, "I saw your friend Sholto, but only from a distance. He seemed to be off roaming in his mind. He looked well enough and the priests said he's fine, he was just seeking answers."

"What answers?"

Thomas shrugged. "They said that was his business."

Thomas and his classmates remained in the young warriors' barracks for the time being.

Drills and preparation for spring continued. The second year trainees began to swap and hone ideas for their spring quests. Everyone but Gerald got excited about these discussions. As he had yet to learn any dragon lore or fighting skills, his quest would not involve dragons. All he really wanted out of life right now was to fight and kill every dragon on the planet. Sighing, he tried to think of something worth doing.

Two nights before he had to declare his quest, Gerald woke sweaty and excited from a strange dream. Awake but still seeing the dream clearly, he knew he had his quest. He'd have to confide in the king's seer and get his backing, but then he'd be set.

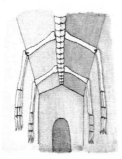

CHAPTER TEN

QUESTS UNVEILED

As custom demanded, all second year young warriors assembled at dawn the morning after the spring equinox before Murdoch and the king. Each young man stood a foot from the edge of a crag near the castle, his back to the drop. Tradition said that more than one young warrior had been pushed off the cliff for failure to have a bold enough quest. Gerald wasn't sure he believed it, but wasn't sure he didn't, either. It was too late to second guess his choice, but that didn't stop him from looking at it from every possible angle and rethinking how to present his case.

As each young warrior in turn announced his intentions, the rest of the troop cheered.

It was Gerald's turn. He took a deep breath and tried to speak clearly and strongly. The cliff at his back kept him solemn.

"Two nights ago, I dreamed true. I knew it to be so as I have dreamed true before. Still, I appealed to Torquil and he meditated and agrees the dream is true."

As Gerald paused, the king glanced at his seer. Torquil nodded, but his eyes never left Gerald.

"A great sword was lost to my family, Draehamar. The dragon who ate my parents also ate my Uncle Samwise and took the sword. He has hidden it a week's ride from here, not wishing to keep it with his hoard or even near him. He scored a cleft in a great tree with a claw, put the sword inside, scorched the tree to shrivel it, and buried it—sword end down—at the edge of the forest. I mean to get the sword."

Admiration shone on the captain's face, but the king immediately saw a flaw in the plan.

"How do you propose to get at this sword, buried as it is and inside the trunk of a great tree?"

Gerald ignored the murmuring of his comrades in arms. "I plan to take something the dragon values greatly to that spot and call his name."

The silence was deafening. Under the gazes of his masters, the cliff began to seem inviting.

"There is an egg long lost to the dragons. I did not know until yesterday that Torquil knew of this and has long sought for it in dreams and study."

Again Torquil nodded.

"I saw in my dream the cave where this egg lays hidden. It is an egg of the dragon who now fashions himself Lord of the Western Isles, an egg that never hatched but was hidden by great warriors. The dragons revere even their dead offspring, and especially of that wyrm. I will find the egg, call the dragon as I did in my dream, and trade the egg for the sword. I will also promise not to use the sword against it in trade for its promise not to harm me or seek me for the sword's sake."

The king's guard stood silently behind the king. Their faces registered everything from awe to astonishment to unbelieving smirks. After a moment the captain spoke.

"I notice these conditions are rather specific. Why is that?"

"I don't want to rule out using another sword on that vile murderer once I am a dragon lord."

"And how," the king wondered aloud, "did you name the dragon to Torquil so he could deem if the dream were true?"

"I spelled it. Backwards. There are tales that writing the

name can bring the beast the same as speaking its name, and none of the wise claim certainty it is not so."

The king looked back and forth between his advisers a moment before speaking. "It is a good quest. Let it be so!"

The king's guard beat their swords on their targes, a sign they deemed this the worthiest quest possible. A couple of his comrades started to cheer, but a stern look from Murdoch quelled them. The remaining young warriors announced their quests, all worthy, but none so ambitious—or as likely to kill them—as Gerald's.

After the king rode off, Murdoch dismissed the class for the day's hunt, but only after reminding them that their announcements, having been sanctioned by the king, constituted binding vows. Any who failed to try their hardest to accomplish their quest would be banished from the kingdom. While most of the others looked solemn, Gerald grinned like a thief. His life revolved around his plans to eliminate dragons. Backing down was not an option.

That evening at the castle, Dree was aghast. "That's insane! You know nothing of dragon lore yet!"

Justin started to reply angrily on Gerald's behalf, but Gerald waved him silent.

"Angus, my father, was a dragon lord. There were dragon lords on Aileen's, my mother's, side as well. Wallace, my adoptive father, was a dragon lord and Samantha, my second mother, wore dragon mail and a sword and taught me much about dragons and their habits.

"I have spent several years learning from my cousin Cle, a dragon lord of some renown. I have spoken to every bard, healer, and seer who has come anywhere near my home. I have spent hours polishing mail and sharpening steel for the lore masters, seer, and dragon lords at Cair Parn. While I am far from a dragon lord, or even a dragon lore master, I am neither ignorant nor a fool."

"I never said you were either, but I crave pardon for my words; I had no idea. And I crave pardon from your valiant friends." He bowed to show he was not jesting. "Truly your lineage and village are very blessed. I was raised not to look down on things for being small or out of the way, but this exceeds all I've ever heard. I pray we may one day fight dragons side by side!"

"For my part, Dree, I pray we do so as well. I could ask for no better men at my back than those I have found here, whether of age or not." He smiled at Dree, but also at James, Justin, and Eoin, his fast friends from home.

Eoin spoke up. "Now that we have declared, Dree, we may hear of quests past. What was yours?"

Dree smiled wryly. "At the time it was rather grand, but compared to Gerald's..."

Gerald waved that away. "Samantha always said comparing ourselves to others leads to lessening one or the other in our minds. Every quest I heard this morning is as worthy as mine. Some were just not as ambitious . . . or insane."

"Still," James laughed, "I wish I'd known of yours earlier. I might have striven higher!"

It was Justin's turn to laugh. "Let that be a lesson to all of us! Strive higher than we can reach from the beginning!"

Eoin would not be deterred. "But what was yours, Dree?"

"I claim elder rights. Speak of yours first, all of you."

"That's cruel. Do you realize how hard it's been waiting all year to find out what your quests were? It's practically all we talked of for a month!"

"Of course I know. We had to wait to hear about those from the year before us. Now, elders right! Out with it, varlet!"

Undaunted, Eoin shrugged. "There is a druid priest far south of here on the eastern coast near Dover. He claims to have relics of Merlin's. My family has always had seer-warriors in it, ever since Merlin granted the gift to one of my ancestors, William of Danbury."

Drinn jumped in. "William of Danbury! He came to conquer Scotland!"

"No, that was his descendant, centuries later. True, the one you speak of was appointed by the king of England to help subdue the Scots, but he and his troops arrived at the border just as the first dragons arrived in the isles. While some of his contemporaries chose to wage battle and thus doom their own men as well as their enemies, Danbury arrived at Stirling Bridge under a flag of truce. He spoke with Wallace and Moray, and made alliance to fight the dragons. At great loss they prevailed and their example spurred others to do the same. King Edward, facing rebellion by his knights, agreed to meet with Robert the Bruce, and they signed the Treaty of Carlisle on Hadrian's Wall, acknowledging Scottish independence and bringing the uneasy peace we have held the past four hundred years."

"But what of your quest?" demanded Dree.

Eoin smiled. "I plan to meet with this druid and see if these relics indeed be Merlin's. If so, I will support him in his bid to build a shrine and establish a safe haven. If not, I will inform him of the truth."

"And if he doesn't believe you?" asked Dree.

"Or simply doesn't like it?" added Drinn.

"Then what happens happens." Eoin shrugged. He looked at Justin, who then spoke up.

"I heard of a girl my age who was captured by a slaver. She was sold to a hermit who lives in the wild hills of the north. It is said he keeps bears for pets, though I think such would little like the rocky wastelands thereabouts. I aim to free the girl and take her home, with bear rugs, if the rumors are true."

"What of the hermit?"

"Slavery is outlawed. If he chooses to fight, we fight."

Dree nodded in admiration. "And you?" he looked at James.

James looked at the floor.

"Go on, James," said Justin. "Your quest is my favorite."

"Mine, too," chimed in both Eoin and Gerald.

James looked up uncomfortably. "I know there is honor in it, but I still feel like a thief."

Dree and Drinn stared at James until he finally continued.

"When I was young, my village was well off. We were a village of traders, and my family did well. But a party of savages raided us after the harvest feast three years ago. They killed most of the men, raped the women, and took everything that looked shiny or valuable, and some of the women and children. I have good reason to believe I know where they are. I have leave to take five warriors, scout the village, and steal enough to prove my case. If I can present that to the king, and some from my village can identify it, the king will send a party to deal with the raiders and restore the wealth of my village."

This was unheard of; a quest was always undertaken alone. No king in memory had allowed such a thing, much less blessed it. Thomas the Usually Silent finally spoke.

"And you have men willing to go, letting a lad lead them?"

James smiled grimly. "Aye! I could have a dozen. Over half of the men from that village who yet live are here in the king's army. They have long wished to know where these raiders live."

"And how do you know?"

"A seer told me."

"Who?"

"I'm not at liberty to say."

Dree looked at Gerald, who smiled and shook his head. "No, not me. I think one dream is more than enough for me this year!"

"Very well," said Dree. "And now for mine. Perhaps you have heard of the Great White Stag?"

"Of course!"

"Yes!"

"Who hasn't?"

"But," objected James, "he's here, isn't he? I mean, on the king's lands?"

"Of course. But he wasn't always."

James rolled his eyes. Dree looked into the distance, eyes shining.

"I sought him for nearly a month. I tracked down every reported sighting that had any merit, but found not the slightest trace of unusual spoor. About the time I decided he didn't exist, I found him near the English border. I skirted south and stalked him north another fortnight, well into Scotland. I finally cornered him on a rainy night at the end of a ravine.

"I built a wall of branches and vines between the trees and the low cliffs, trapping him. There was plenty of grass and water in his end of the ravine. He wouldn't be happy but neither would he go hungry or thirsty.

"I built a signal fire. Two nights later my horse, Dunstay, woke me up. He is of the royal fighting stock, keen of sense and trained to wake his master in case of danger. A trio of brigands was sneaking up on my camp with knives in their hands and murder in their eyes. I left the fire low and climbed a tree. When they attacked my bedroll, I leapt down and clove the skull of the first with my sword. I took the next one's head off before they recovered. Alas, the third was a brute of a man and knew well how to fight. I hurt him a bit but he hurt me more, and I thought I was doomed until Dunstay attacked him from behind. He bore him to the ground and trampled him.

"We moved camp, I burned their bodies, and the next day my signal fire brought a king's patrol. Over the next week, the stag got used to us enough that when we roped him, we were able to lead him back to Cair Parn, though that took another fortnight, and he charged us more than once.

"The beast was two feet taller than me, plus those glorious antlers. The king released him onto his preserves, and neither the white stag nor his offspring may be hunted, by royal decree. None have seen him since, but there are several fawns this year clearly of his lineage."

He bowed as the younger men clapped.

Drinn and Thomas excused themselves as they had next watch on two of the castle walls. The rest went to bed and slept. For Gerald, though, sleep came late as he went over in his head all he could remember of the dream. He thought about how much he still did not know, and wondered just how big a dragon might be. His dreams that night were full of white dragons the size of small mountains, with antlers like giant oaks.

The next morning Gerald wolfed down his breakfast.

James objected. "Slow down! You're the one who taught me to take my time and savor the bacon, yet you just ate a half pound in the time I ate one slice!"

Gerald swallowed, drained his coffee, and laughed. "Sorry, I have something to do before muster. See you then!" He moved as quickly as he could without getting called out by a superior. Even so he received a few quizzical looks and a couple of glares.

As he expected, the Hall of Warriors was deserted. He'd come to gawk here when he first arrived, and later to study the statues and ponder their history. This time he had eyes only for the ceiling.

Where most halls would have a giant timber at the peak of the roof, this hall was topped with a series of large, ivory colored rings, smaller rings at the ends and huge rings in the middle set face to face—the backbone of a vanquished dragon. Where other great ceilings might have descending timbers, the bones of four huge legs seemed to hold up the two sides of the roof, ending in magnificent feet—four cubits across and six long—with wicked claws. Most of the tail and much of the neck were elsewhere, along with the skull and wings. Still, Gerald got a feel for the sheer size of this dragon, one he'd been assured was only slightly above average. It must have been the size of a standard trader's ship. He shivered.

"It's a sight to ponder, lad."

Gerald jumped, spun around, and came to attention. "Your Majesty!"

The king waved that away. He came to stand by Gerald, placed a hand on his shoulder, and stared at the ceiling. "I've never slain a dragon. My grandfather slew this one, Fraener, also named Graekel. No other dragon has been known to claim two names. Rumor has it Fraener was crazy, even by dragon standards." He smiled. "Whatever those may be."

"It was huge."

"He. He was huge to us, but not really huge as dragons go. Yes, note that the feet reach the ground! He was near as big as this hall, and more than thrice the length you see here." He turned a penetrating eye on Gerald. "You've taken on a lot. Having second thoughts?"

Gerald drew up even straighter, hoping the king's hand would drop from his shoulder, afraid it would do just that. It was nerve-wracking and thrilling having the king's attention this way. "No, Your Majesty. I'd sooner die than not face these monsters down."

The king's hand dropped to his side. He turned to face Gerald. "Monsters? Is that all they are?"

"What else?" Gerald was confused. The king didn't seem to be playing games.

"Of old, not all dragons quarreled with men. Many would speak with those they deemed worthy, or those they respected or feared. Quite a few seemed content to live at peace with us, but too many people hated and feared them. The peaceful dragons were slain, left for parts unknown, or learned to hate us." He stared Gerald in the eyes. "Because we deemed all dragons monsters."

"I have heard of dragon lords who talked with dragons. But that is all in the distant past. . . ."

The king shook his head, a gesture so common Gerald was amazed to see it in his king. "My grandfather spoke of his father as having spoken with dragons as equals. I have spoken with dragons I would not, and will not, kill. Cuthbert has spoken with nearly every dragon in the isles, and more beyond."

"You speak of your ancestors as dragon lords. What of your father? What of you?"

"I was but seventeen when my father and grandfather died. A cave they were sheltering in during a severe storm collapsed. I was crowned three days later. As you will learn in your dragon lore class soon, the one time a king may not lead in battle is against a dragon, unless he is already a dragon lord or if there is no choice. We have lost kings to dragons, and the people grew tired of it."

"But Murdoch said the two of you had killed six dragons."

"I helped but only killed one. Murdoch slew the rest."

He smiled a sad smile. "I have little doubt you will be the youngest dragon lord in Scotland, probably younger than I was when crowned." His smile brightened. "But do not feel bad for me, Gerald. While most men wish to be dragon lords, few become so and even fewer become kings. I am privileged to be the latter. I refuse to live with regrets, especially given this realm I am blessed to lead."

The king glanced at the window. "You are nearly late for class." He clapped Gerald on the back to send him on his way. Gerald was late to class, but to everyone's amazement, Murdoch seemed not to notice. Gerald suspected he knew where he'd been. The captain and the king both seemed to know everything that went on in the castle. He reckoned that was a good thing, and was again grateful for them both.

CHAPTER ELEVEN

A WELSH SURPRISE

The second year students hoped to hear Drinn's and Thomas's stories the next evening after sword practice, but James and Justin had watch. The weekend was set aside for hunting. Gerald was told to hunt something besides hogs for once. He brought back a crane, a dozen rabbits, and a hedgehog. He commandeered a page to help carry these to the kitchen.

"It doesn't count as a hog, you know," Gerald said laughingly to Myles, the butcher who met him at the kitchen courtyard gate.

"A hedgehog? What for?" demanded Myles.

"I shot a rabbit with my sling. It tumbled into a bush. Ready for snakes, I had my knife out. Something bit me, and I killed it before I realized it was only a hedgehog. I never waste what I kill. The dogs will eat it."

The butcher smiled. "I have a better idea. I'll take it." He carried off all but the crane; he'd be back for that soon. Gerald laughed and sauntered off to the barracks, wondering what wild dish Myles would come up with.

James looked up from sharpening his knife. "Drinn, he's here. Out with it!"

Drinn grinned. "Sit down, Gerald. Your friends are dying to hear my tale."

"So are we all, Drinn," Gerald said as he bowed in mock honor. "Will you grace us with it?"

"The bards tell of a fruit tree in Greece long ago, blessed by Aphrodite and Hermes. It makes the skin fair, gives the hair sheen, and cures many diseases. It was said to have made it to western Europe, but none knew its name. I sought this fruit. I sailed with a Spanish merchant, and spent two months sampling every fruit I came across.

"I fought no glorious battles, only skirmishes with highwaymen and drunkards. I did manage to cut off the hand of a slaver who thought I would fetch a pretty price.

"Alas, I found no fruits worth fighting for, but I brought back samples of those I believed unknown here. Two the king's sister Kirstin delighted in, and so I was pardoned for failing in my quest. Later it was found that the pomegranate was good for the skin, and had healing qualities as well."

"What does it heal?" asked Justin.

Drinn grimaced. "I have no idea. I only know that Kirstin was sick and then she was better. Since none would discuss it, I thought perhaps a womanly problem, but one of her maids assured me it was otherwise."

Thomas grinned. "He'll be engaged to that maid before long."

Drinn grinned. "I just might. And now, Thomas, your turn."

Thomas stood and began pacing, as was his wont when he had to talk. "Mine was somewhat like Justin's. Oh, not at all like it in how it came about, but . . . well, decide for yourself.

"The gamekeepers felt there were not as many hogs about as should be. Being a practical man with little imagination . . ."

Dree's left eyebrow went up. "Little?"

"Fine. Very little."

"That much?"

Thomas cuffed Dree as he walked past. "Barely, but yes. I chose to track down the hogs and bring any poachers to justice. Little did I know!

"Starting in the area the wardens thought problematic, I wandered pig trails for days. I tracked every bit of game I could find. I began noticing things: broken branches higher than the game accounted for; here and there the spoor of a horse. Eventually I found clear tracks and trailed them to the English border. A few miles across the border, north of Carlisle, I found a village of the savages. They had pens full of hogs, and one pen was clearly full of the king's pork."

"How could you tell?" wondered Eoin.

"The royal hogs have tails dyed black."

"What? Who would do that?"

"We did. And you will, next year." Thomas grinned at their shocked looks. "But fear not, laddies. There are tricks, and you'll learn them same as we did. And you'll learn to hate that end of a pig."

Everyone laughed.

"I already did," said Drinn, "unless it's cooked!"

"Anyway, each night I lured a hog to the gate with a fresh ear of corn. Then I walked it back into Scotland proper, and ran it into a ravine two hours from their village. I took a different route each night. I used a stout, long branch to roll a large stone across the little entrance. By the fifth night I was having to distract guards. The eighth night I scattered their horses. After that it was too dangerous. So I spent the next two days scouting 'til I found a king's company camped in the woods. I alerted them and then rode back to the village and stormed through it calling them every foul name I could think of, screaming all the way and hacking at the poles holding their roofs.

"Since they'd been watching the livestock, I caught them off guard. But they soon came hard after me. I led them straight to the king's men. That took care of that, although I almost lost my head to a sentry I suspect was sleeping until we nearly rode him down. Fortunately he missed me, but got the fiend close by."

Everyone laughed appreciatively.

Suddenly James spoke up. "Thomas had best be careful or he'll lose his title. That was hardly his usual unusually quiet."

They all laughed again.

"The English think we are crazy, sending 'young lads' as they like to call us, on such quests," Eoin said.

"Ah," laughed Drinn, "but all know the Scots have the best warriors. And who has more dragon lords? Scotland!"

"And Ireland," noted Gerald.

"Britain has a few," replied a sobered Drinn, "but the Welsh have none at all."

"What? No dragon lords?"

"No. Nor dragons."

"No druids, but also no dragons. Maybe that's a fair trade."

"A bit hard on the druids, don't you think?"

"True enough. But how can that be?" Gerald wondered. "The Irish have plenty of dragons and to spare!"

"None know," Drinn replied.

"The Welsh are brave enough." All eyes swept to Dree as he spoke. He nodded. "My Uncle Threbus chased the dragon Glorious across the water."

"Glorious?" interrupted Gerald to general laughter.

"Glorious," agreed Dree. "An odd name for an odd dragon. Uncle Threbus chased it into Ireland, where he killed it with the help of a woman named Irene. She hated dragons as much as our Gerald; a baby dragon had badly cut her hands when she was young. She could never after use a sword.

So she played hound, lure, and trickster for anyone who would wield a sword for her, and had helped kill more dragons than had most Irish dragon lords. Or most Scots, for that matter."

Dree ignored the inevitable protests and muttering.

"Afterward they talked long of dragons, and she told my uncle of Wales. He determined to go and see for himself.

"Irene told him that the Welsh would have no dragon lords on their soil, so he hid his scale mail and went as a soldier of fortune. He sailed from Wexford in Ireland to Aberystwyth in Wales. The first night he visited a tavern. He got properly drunk and started a good natured argument with a Welshman about why they had no dragons. They were happily flinging insults at each other when my drunken uncle, never as witty as he thought he was, ran out of things to call the Welshman, and said something on the order of, 'perhaps you give them your daughters to bed'. The Welshman, enraged, drew his sword and ran my dear uncle through."

The younger lads' eyes went appropriately wide.

"Quickly coming to his senses, the Welshman called for the city's elders and explained what had happened. Within two days, he set sail with my uncle's body, two elders, a seer, and his daughter. They braved the winter storms to sail up the coast to the Mackinnon lands in the north. They brought his body to my Aunt Toll and asked for a hearing.

"My people made them wait three days while news rode out and people came in. The whole clan wanted to know why a Welshman was bringing one of our own back dead, and why he demanded a hearing.

"He got his hearing. He testified, the elders testified, the seer testified, and his daughter testified. He begged forgiveness. The rest of the Welsh begged for leniency. He offered to pay any reasonable blood price as proof of his sincerity. Clan Mackinnon forgave him, blessed him, asked half of the blood price for his widow, and sent them on their way."

A chorus of incredulous shouts halted the story as Dree knew it would. Waving them quiet, he finished. "Only the week before, while Aberystwyth slept, a pirate ship had entered the harbor and taken a dozen captives. The next morning the city awoke to find some of their leaders and prominent citizens tied and held at sword point in the square.

"The pirate chief told the people they had two choices. They could watch their friends die and then all fight for their lives, or they could provide the pirates with gold, food, and twenty of their comely daughters as wenches. The mayor spat in the pirate chief's face and got his throat slit for it. The furious locals attacked and the pirates fought. They killed half their captives, but had to fight their way free without killing the others. The Welsh fought to keep them from their ship, but eventually they attained it. When they were out of arrow's reach they turned the ship to fire their cannons at the town.

"It was then a Welshman sprang from hiding on the ship, kicked a lantern down into the hold, and leaped overboard before the pirates could react. A small explosion rocked the boat and flames sprang up. The Welshman had got to the ship well ahead of the pirates and emptied several of their powder kegs, then spread oil and pitch around. The pirates were burnt alive, drowned, or killed by the citizens if they made shore. The Welshman who scuttled the ship was half drowned and frozen, but survived.

"They later discovered that the pirates had managed to get away with two of the Welsh lasses, including the niece of the man who killed my uncle. Both were found dead in the sea with their throats slit by the pirates—no doubt for revenge. That was why the Welshman flew into a rage at my uncle's poor joke."

Nobody spoke for a while. Drinn cleared his throat. "At any rate, nobody knows why the dragons avoid Wales."

"Perhaps," observed Gerald, "they're afraid of angering the Welsh."

Drinn laughed. "But the Welsh aren't taking any chances. As Dree's tale shows, they can be brave enough. But they figure that dragon lords might attract dragons. The only dragon lord they'll allow is one who speaks with dragons and only kills when he has to. Or so they say; when was the last time we had one of those?"

Most were sure of the answer—quite a few years. Gerald knew better but kept that to himself. He laughed. "Well, I'll be happy to speak with the dragons. As I kill them."

The next morning there was a ruckus at the captain's table—a shout of surprise, then a great deal of laughing. Everyone attempted to see, but only the table closest, the oldest warriors in training, might know what was going on.

That afternoon, the younger trainees heard the news while grooming their mounts. Dree grinned from ear to ear as he explained.

"We found your hedgehog, Gerald!"

"I didn't realize I'd lost one. In fact, I never had one!"

"Ah, my friend, but you did. A very dead one, the same one you need have killed in honor after it first drew blood from your finger."

"I gave that to one of the butchers to give to the dogs."

Dree grinned even more gleefully. "Best not say that near the captain! I believe your butcher is best friend to the captain's cousin, the cook for the captain's table. He brought a special dish for the captain in honor of his birthday. He put down the platter, whisked away the cover, said 'Wal LA' or some such French thing, and there . . . there . . . there was the hedgehog in all its spiny glory, a tiny apple in its mouth!" Everyone burst out laughing.

"The captain recovered quickly and praised the hedgehog. He went on and on until the cook relaxed. Then the captain grabbed the hedgehog, and quick as you please had his arm round the cook's neck, brushing his greasy hair with the hedgehog!"

The older teens laughed, but the younger ones looked

stricken. They weren't sure who should be more offended, the captain or the cook, though their sympathies lay fully with Murdoch.

"You ninnies!" chortled Thomas. "The cook is the captain's cousin! They grew up playing jokes on each other. The cook is nearly his cousin's equal at wrestling, and many is the time one of them has taken the other by surprise to throw him in the river and both went swimming."

Gerald felt stupid. It had never occurred to him that his captain had a family. Or a birthday. He'd seen Murdoch almost like a dragon, existing just as he was for centuries. He wondered what the captain's mother and father had been like. Startled, he wondered if the captain was married. He was sure he had no sons, but perhaps a daughter. . . .

What a girl the captain's daughter would be! Gerald was sure she would be a warrior as well as a lady. Probably quite pretty, too. Like Sally. Sally? Gerald reddened, but thankfully nobody noticed. He was engaged. He didn't need to be thinking about other women, even imaginary ones. He suspected that Sally, like her mother, was perfectly capable of being a warrior.

That got him thinking about why the dragon had not recognized Samantha's authority to wield the sword. He'd have to ask someone about that.

CHAPTER TWELVE

THE DRAGON LORE MASTER

His next rest day, Gerald sought out the dragon lore master, Cuthbert. He eventually found him in the castle keep, staring out the window with a pile of scrolls and a few books at his feet.

"Master Cuthbert?"

The man hardly moved. "Ah, young Gerald. But I suppose you hate that."

"Hate what, sir?"

"Being called young anything."

"Not at all, sir. I am yet young."

Cuthbert looked at him keenly. "Well said, Gerald. I'd wondered when you would seek me out. That's quite a quest you've set yourself, especially for a first year."

"I know, sir, but that isn't why I've come. At least, not the only reason. Not today."

"Really." The old man's gaze grew more intense beneath his bushy, white eyebrows. Gerald had seldom been very close to this master, and only now realized how terribly old he seemed. His hair had long ago turned from grey to white. Yet for all the lines in his face and the shagginess of his brows and beard, the man radiated a kind of strength to match his well-known wisdom. Gerald was tempted to bow.

"Then if not that, or not only that, why are you here, loather of dragons?"

"Dragons took my parents, both my natural parents and my adopted parents. I suspect the same one. But the strangest thing was that when he took my mother, she was wearing dragon scale mail and carrying a sword—both of which he claimed to recognize. Yet he said he didn't recognize her authority to wear or wield them. I want to know why."

The old man was silent for a moment. "And you saw and heard this yourself?"

Gerald reddened, as much in anger as embarrassment. "I've never seen a dragon. They took my family but I've never even seen one. My sister, my cousins, the whole village saw it. He carried her away months ago, and she hasn't been heard of since."

"What of the dragon?"

"He hasn't been there, either. He only came because someone called his name."

"What?"

"Yes, some fool called his name. We think we know who, because she leaped on Mother's ceremonial funeral pyre and died. She had no other reason to do that."

Cuthbert looked out the window for a moment. "I believe you are right in that."

Gerald just stared. How could this lore master possibly know that?

Cuthbert smiled sadly. "I know what you're thinking. We'll come back to that. So you don't know what became of your mother, and the mail and sword are lost as well."

"Not the sword. Or the scabbard."

"And how did this come to be?"

"Mother had the sword drawn when the dragon grabbed her. He snatched her up so suddenly she had no chance to use it. It fell. Somehow she got the belt and scabbard off as well, and dropped them just as he took flight with her. They are well guarded back home."

Cuthbert ran his right hand through his long, tangled beard. "I had no idea. One less sword lost. That is good! But your mother gone. . . ." He stared sadly into the distance.

"But you want to understand." Cuthbert's voice slowed; his tone became both thoughtful and definite.

"A dragon sword starts out like any other sword. Well, like any other good sword. A poor sword will nearly always fail against a dragon; dragons are too strong, even apart from their magic. But a good sword, wielded by a strong heart, may cleave a dragon. Once bathed in a dragon's blood the sword becomes a dragon sword, with a certain, inherent ability to hurt dragons."

"These things I know," Gerald said with somewhat veiled irritation.

Cuthbert smiled gently. "Always best to start with the foundation. Now, once a man—or woman, as rare as that may be—has slain a dragon, any dragon sword is more lethal against dragons in his or her hand. But the sword itself cannot, or perhaps will not, fight dragons. So no matter the heart of the bearer, if he or she is not a dragon slayer, the sword is just a sword for him until it has tasted dragon blood. A dragon sword in the hands of a dragon slayer is very effective. In the hands of a dragon lord—whether man or woman—it is almost always lethal."

"Why did you say, 'dragon slayer?'"

"To have killed a dragon is one thing. To have killed many, or to have spoken with dragons as their equals, that is a much bigger thing, and only then do we call a person a dragon lord. But a sword becomes a dragon sword as soon as one vanquishes a dragon with it . . . or simply cuts it and then bargains with it. Drachmaeius . . ."

Gerald gasped.

". . . recognized the sword Draeblood, and likely the mail. No doubt he knew the dragon from whose scales it was made. I wonder how your mother obtained it. . . ."

"Nobody is sure. No one had seen it before."

"Curious. But to go on, dragon mail is only fully effective against dragons when worn by the person who killed the dragon, or by their descendants. A sword, however, must be won anew with blood by each owner.

"Now, why did you gasp?"

"I don't recall. Perhaps because you spoke Drachm... the dragon's name. Or the fact you know so much of what happened. How do you know? How can you say his name?" Gerald realized he had been scanning the sky since the name was spoken.

Cuthbert laughed. "Two reasons, lad. One you can use yourself, though I wouldn't if I were you. Drachmaeius is a wily old thing, and more aware than most dragons. Which is saying quite a lot.

"Each and every stone in this keep, and many scattered throughout Cair Parn, have bits of dragon bone in holes bored into them and sealed up, as well as some ground up in the mortar. While bits of bone are not as effective as entire bones, much less skeletons, they are effective enough, especially in the quantity we have here. I could curse every living dragon, and those about to be born, and not a one of them would bother to come seeking me. They know the protection of this castle, and that I seldom set foot outside its walls. Even then I go protected in various ways."

At first Gerald thought Cuthbert looked smug. Then he realized the man was simply supremely confident. Given that he had lived so long, Gerald assumed he had good reason.

"What of the courtyard?"

"It matters not if there is a roof if enough bone is around you. Any relic of a dragon around you is protection—its scales, its skin, or its bones. We use scales for mail, bone for homes and skin for . . ." The old man paused, his eyes twinkling. ". . . I think we'll save that for class next year. If I don't hold something back, you'll have no reason to pay attention!"

Gerald laughed. "And how do you know so much?"

The lore master waved a hand in deprecation. "It's my job to know. I am the lore master. I am a dragon lord who has spoken to many dragons, and killed only when absolutely necessary. When you meet Santana, the dragon of your quest, the first words out of your mouth should be, 'The Great Dragon Lord Cuthbert of the Lothians sends his greetings.' I assure you that he will then hear you out."

Gerald stared suspiciously. "Why?"

Cuthbert looked taken aback. "Why? Because I am the chief of the lore masters. I have spoken with more dragons than anyone living. Have you heard the king speak of his most precious treasure, the one he guards safely in the keep, where none may steal it?"

Gerald nodded.

Cuthbert sighed. "I am that treasure. Other kings have sought to kidnap me and to buy me. Dragons sought to kill me, 'til they learned they could trust me with their secrets—and that though I am loath to kill dragons, I am deadly when it comes to self-defense."

"But if you stay here, how do you speak with them and learn news such as that of my mother?"

Cuthbert leaned back in his chair and closed his eyes. His long, white hair fell around his face like a landslide. "There are ways I will not speak of with you yet, if ever. But one way is through the birds. You know the huge black birds, the Great Crows of Glasgow?"

"Of course, sir."

"The dragons call the crows their Voices. Long ago, they were bred and trained to speak with men and dragons. I have heard that dragons did this; I have also heard that Merlin's ancestors—the faeries and druids—did this. I suspect each played a part. The Voices act as messengers. Alas, there is much I do not hear, but I hear much. . . ."

He gazed longingly out the window. "Soon, I will know all I wish..."

"How is that, master?"

The old man shook himself. "You will know soon enough. Meanwhile, do not overrate what using my name will do for you with Santana. Use it to gain his attention, and so that he knows I know of your quest. After that, avoid his eyes and keep your wits about you."

"Sir, why do some of the dragons have Scottish names and some not? Santana is from nowhere in the isles, I'll wager."

"And you'd win that wager, young Gerald." Cuthbert briefly bowed his head. "Dragons live long. Not forever as some think, but close enough that it matters not to mortals. They go where they will, for reasons men cannot ken, so a dragon named across the sea may suddenly decide to take up residence in Scotland or vice versa. They take their names at hatching and never change them. A very great dragon from the Far East, Li Ping, lives in the heart of Britain. Andrew, from near London, lives very near Rome. Tomorrow either of them could be half a continent away."

A thought struck Gerald. "Do you . . . do you know the dragon who killed my birth parents?"

The ancient head shook vigorously in denial. *How very like a dragon he is,* thought Gerald. *Or how like I think a dragon must be. Wise and old and young and powerful and full of life.*

Cuthbert explained. "I do not know a thing until I truly know it. So I do not know that your parents were killed by dragons." He held up his hands to ward off Gerald's protests. "I strongly suspect it, even believe it. But I do not, as of yet, know it."

Gerald dropped the subject. He smiled. "You also mentioned meeting with Santana. What else should I know?"

Cuthbert eyed him curiously. Gerald realized he'd gone back and forth between being at ease and being nervous through the interview. "I don't think, Gerald, that I shall tell you much else right now. I have a strong feeling you will have no problem dealing with Santana, which I would never have said before meeting you. Santana is a most reasonable dragon, but dragons hate dragon swords for obvious reasons. And they have learned to be suspicious of humans, in your case with good reason."

Gerald flushed.

"Good. Gerald, you cannot yet understand, but do not hate all dragons. Dragons, like humans, come in good and bad. Few dragons hate all humans, and fewer still are truly evil. If you must hate, save your hatred for those who deserve it. Hate will eat you alive, but over years rather than quickly as a dragon would eat you. It is better not to hate at all."

"You don't know what it's like," Gerald began.

Cuthbert cut him off. "You have no idea what I know and don't know, or what it's like to be me. Do not waste your breath with such drivel."

Gerald flushed again and bowed. "Yes, sir. Is there anything else I should know about dragons now?"

"If you must fight a dragon, the most vulnerable spots are the eyes, the nostrils, the mouth, behind the knees, and what in a human would be the armpit. In that order. Oh, and of course any spots where scales are missing.

"And now, you'd best go. I have much to think on and you are about to miss lunch."

Gerald went, getting to the dining hall just in time to be served. He thought long and hard about the great lore master and all he'd learned, and marveled at how much he still didn't know.

CHAPTER THIRTEEN

SEEKING SANTANA

At last Gerald understood why everyone kept after him to not hate dragons. Flying! Dragonback was much faster and more fun than horseback, and the worst dragon was far more formidable than the best stallion. Of course, you had to keep them under control or they'd flame you, but that was doable.

He spied two young ladies below. He swooped lower, warning Santana not to hurt the girls. Sure enough, he'd recognized them: Sally and the captain's daughter, Jillian. They'd become thick as thieves on meeting and tended to ignore him. But they wouldn't ignore it when he flew by on an upside-down dragon! Santana refused the command and started trying to turn his head to roast Gerald with his breath. Gerald hauled on the reins when they suddenly snapped! Santana's head swung round, the great eyes full of vicious joy. . . .

Gerald woke in a sweat. He hated dragons more than ever, and these dreams about Sally and a daughter the captain probably didn't have were getting absurd. He stared out the window at the full moon. It looked ice cold against the thick band of stars. He'd have to ask Cuthbert about riding dragons, but he had a feeling that was silly. After a half hour, he fell back asleep. He missed seeing his first dragon by about two minutes as it flitted across the moon on its mysterious dragon business.

The dragon's passage was not unnoticed on the castle walls. Justin signaled by barking twice. Across the castle, Eoin glanced up, as did the guards on the other walls, before returning their vigilance to the ground below. Only the guard atop the keep watched the dragon out of sight. Inside the keep, Cuthbert's brows knitted in his sleep. He soon relaxed and snored more deeply.

A week later, on the first day of April, the young warriors set out on their quests. There was no fanfare, but the king and his warriors all turned out to honor them and see them off. The king addressed them as a group. "You arrived here on the cusp of manhood. You have ridden that cusp for months. Now you go forth to prove yourself—to yourself first, to us second, and to everyone else last." He smiled. "There is nothing else we can do. You are each prepared. I believe you are all perfectly capable of achieving your goal, of finding glory, of winning renown, of vanquishing your foes, of liberation, of finishing whatever tasks you have set yourselves. Go forth knowing we await your return with faith and pride, that God goes with you, that your cause is just."

Arrayed in vee formation about the king, the other warriors clashed swords or spears on targes as they roared their approval. Those on quest rode their mounts proudly, if perhaps nervously, single file through the castle gates. As Eoin, the last rider, passed the gate, the portcullis was dropped with a resounding clang, proclaiming to all that there was no turning back. Gerald, in the van, raised his quest banner and with a scream of battle lust that would have frozen many foes in their tracks, galloped off northeast. The others followed suit toward all points of the compass.

The king and Murdoch watched the dust settle as the last horse and rider disappeared into the distance along the river.

Murdoch spoke first. "How many do you really think will make it?"

The king frowned a moment, something others rarely saw. "I want to say all of them. I know that seldom happens, but this is the strongest class in over a decade. Yet Torquil is uneasy, and Cuthbert will say nothing save that he expects to see Gerald return safely but changed."

"Changed? How?"

The king smiled tiredly. "He will not say. But I know his expressions, and he's feeling a bit smug. I suspect Gerald is about to find that he really knows next to nothing about the great wyrms that have defined so much of his life."

"That man almost scares me."

"Cuthbert?"

"Yes. He knows more about dragons . . . and about what goes on with dragons . . . than any man ought to know."

The king laughed and clapped the captain's back. "He does indeed, Murdoch. He does indeed. If Merlin were here today and could commune with dragons, I think he'd look like Cuthbert."

"Commune with dragons. . . . I have heard that dragons could once talk mind to mind. I wish Cuthbert could commune with them thus. That would answer so many questions."

"Aye, but it might answer questions for them as well, so I'm just as glad he cannot."

Murdoch nodded; it was a good point. "You think Gerald is ready for this, then?"

"I asked Cuthbert the same question. He said that Gerald needs to learn and he's likely ready enough, but if not he never will be. He also said that Santana is an excellent teacher."

"Santana is the dragon with the sword?"

"Yes."

Murdoch thought for a moment. "Torquil will not say who he thinks may not return?"

"Only that he sees a head on a pike, a quest banner over a body. He says the head is one of ours, yet wears a face he cannot see. It is a boy crying for someone lost."

Murdoch grimaced. "I like that not, but there is naught we can do save wait and do our jobs. And mine is to put Dree's patrol to work on the southern border with Tunstall's men, to learn better the art of tracking."

"I understand Drinn is already quite the tracker."

"Aye. He can teach Tunstall a thing or two, but he has things still to learn as well. For sure he has a natural ability. When they return from this fortnight's outing, Gillian wants to take him for a month to play cat and mouse. He claims, if you can believe it, that before Drinn is of age the lad may surpass him."

"I can believe almost anything, but that would be a sight to see."

"Aye. And I hope we do!" Murdoch saluted the king and left to give final orders to Tunstall and Dree.

Gerald was soon skirting the fringes of the wood. As a child he'd both longed to meet and feared to encounter Ghillie Dhu, spirits of the forest. By the time he'd started training at Cair Parn, he considered the Dhu a fairy tale. But now, looking across the moors as a late afternoon mist arrived, and with the forest urging him to both stay and go, he wasn't so sure. He was alone in a land haunted by everyone who'd ever disappeared, whether to dragons, his fellow man, or something else. All he was sure of was his horse, his weapons, and his skills—and the latter were impressing him less by the minute.

He thought back over all he'd learned: tactics, skill at arms, the little he'd learned about dragons. He thought of Torquil, of Cuthbert, of visions, of dragons. He wished for a Great Crow to come, but then he remembered the crows could as easily tell the dragons of him as him of the dragons. He reminded himself of the king's speech, that he was a man engaged to be married, that he dreamed true, and of his farewell kiss from Sally. The last memory carried him well into the moors and the mists.

Despite the fog, it was easy to follow the trail he'd chosen amongst the rocks and tough grass. He frequently let his horse graze a moment and drink; he had but a few more miles to go today. He planned to camp at a deserted outpost in the hills for a couple of days. Torquil had advised him to spend some of his time on the quest thinking about dragons and praying. Cuthbert agreed. Gerald's trust in these men was great, so he would do as they suggested.

He came upon the wall, mostly in good repair, soon after dusk. He scouted the ruins; they were empty save for a few rabbits, two of which he managed to kill. Dogs or wolves had been there in the not too distant past. Gerald moved his horse into an interior storage room with no windows and a sturdy door. He set up camp in the guard room outside it, a room with a barred door and slit windows. He expected no trouble but prepared for it as would any prudent man on the edges of the wild.

He slept well that night but dreamed constantly. Amid dreams of Sally and his parents (all four of them discussing a proper punishment for his foaming at the mouth like a mad pig), a festival at Kiergenwald, and racks and racks of ham at Cair Parn, he also dreamt of dragons. He was negotiating with Santana to dig up the sword in the tree when a rush of wind nearly knocked him over. Drachmaeius had arrived to claim the egg, followed shortly by the Lord of the Western Isles and the ghost of Glorious, both also claiming the egg. Santana offered to dig up the sword and use it to divide the egg into three parts, one for each of the other dragons. Drachmaeius suggested using the sword rather to divide Gerald between them, but Glorious objected that he couldn't eat, and Santana pointed out that Gerald was barely a morsel for any of them, craving Glorious' ghost's pardon.

A nearby howling and his horse's answering snort awoke Gerald. Shivering (from the cold, he told himself, not the dream), he wrapped his furs more tightly about him and went back to sleep. If he dreamed again he couldn't remember it when he wakened shortly after sunrise.

At least, he thought with a wry smile, Jillian hadn't shown up. As Cle had often told him, "Small victories provide strength while waiting for chances at the bigger ones."

Gerald hunted throughout the day, focusing on his prey to the exclusion of all else. Later he wondered if that was how dragons felt. Perhaps he would ask if the right chance arose. But from what Cle and Samantha had taught him, Gerald knew that all one does with dragons hinges on debt. Every bit of knowledge gained put you in the dragon's debt, or removed it from yours. Gerald reckoned he wouldn't be asking trivial questions of Santana.

That evening as Gerald cooked a cony stew, a racket arose outside his guardhouse. Hand on sword, he moved to a window to look out. A flock of black birds, the largest crows he'd ever seen, stood or walked everywhere he could see in the yard, on the ground, on fences, on nearby roofs. Gerald wasn't sure what to make of it until one of the crows called him by name. Then he felt really off balance.

"Gerald of Kiergenwald, come forth. I have a message for you from the great Santana."

Hesitating only a moment, wondering whether the crows were alone or a dragon hid nearby, Gerald took a firm grip on his sword, unbarred the door, and walked warily into the twilight.

CHAPTER FOURTEEN

THE VOICES

As Gerald stepped into view, the crows' noise intensified for a few seconds, then quickly tapered off. As silence settled over the outpost, one of the larger crows hopped up to Gerald. Its head was at least three inches above Gerald's knee.

"I am Gerald of Kiergenwald. Who calls me?"

"For now, the Voice of Santana speaks with you."

Gerald pondered this but made no reply. The crow's voice was harsh and cold. Gerald was surprised it was understandable, coming from a beak.

The Voice continued. "My name is my own, but when I speak for a dragon, I speak with his or her name."

"Well met, Voice of Santana. What does the great dragon wish to say to me?"

"Santana has heard that a great warrior seeks him. Usually this means a dragon lord. But all Santana has seen is a boy, untried save with beasts and his classmates. Santana wishes to know why you seek him. Do you seek death?"

Gerald laughed, both at the question and at the realization he was free to speak the dragon's name; what else was he after but to see this dragon face to face? "I may seek death, but not my own. No, I come to bargain with the great Santana. He has something I desire, and I have something he desires. But before I say more, I send Santana greetings from the great dragon lord and lore master, Cuthbert of the Lothians."

Santana's Voice immediately hopped back and began cawing with several nearby crows. Five of them soon flew away in different directions.

"Santana had no idea his visitor was so highly favored as to come with Lord Cuthbert's blessing. I have sent someone to tell him."

"Several someones, it would seem."

The crow regarded him for a few seconds before responding. "Why is your hand on your sword?"

Gerald dropped his hand and bowed. "I beg your pardon. When I heard the noise of your arrival, I did not know what to expect. I did not know who you were or what dragon you might herald. A wise warrior is always prepared."

"Are you a wise warrior, after all?"

"I hope to be both some day. And since you are one of the Great Crows who mediates between men and dragons when necessary, I will trust you."

Again the crow hesitated. "We always send several crows. They fly at random at first, so that none knows their path. Also, this way if one or more is attacked or finds a storm, the message still gets through."

It dawned on Gerald that dealing with these crows must be like dealing with dragons. He had withdrawn a threat (however unintended) and offered honor to the crows, so the Voice in turn had paid the debt with information. He realized he would need to check with Cuthbert before sharing with others anything he learned from the crows lest he find himself in their debt. While obviously not as dangerous as dragons, he wouldn't want to have them as enemies if he could help it.

Then he wondered whether the debts were really between men and dragons, since the Voices represented them. He definitely needed to know this.

"Will Santana see me?"

"That depends. What do you wish to trade? And if I may be so bold, that does not look like much of a dragon sword."

Gerald placed his hand on the sword hilt. "If I may?"

The crow nodded, an odd gesture for a bird.

Gerald drew the sword. "As I trust the Voice of Santana can tell, this is no dragon sword. It is for brigands, highwaymen, the king's enemies, and meat for my belly." He sheathed the weapon. "While I have a dragon sword, it is not here. I am no dragon lord, and come in peace."

"Very well. But you still have not answered my question. What do you wish to trade?"

Gerald almost said he would only tell Santana, but something stopped him. He could see Cuthbert clearly, imagine his voice, what he might say if he were here. "Treat the Voice with respect, the same as you would treat the dragon. When he says he speaks for the dragon, he also hears for the dragon. For all intents and purposes, while you talk, he is the dragon, save that he cannot burn you up. But ware the beak and claws! Not just his, but the whole flock's."

Gerald glanced around; there were a lot of beaks and claws, all large, and all very pointy.

"I would trade an egg of the Lord of the Western Isles for the sword Draehamar." The crows began to speak amongst themselves, but Gerald overrode them. "And my promise never to use the sword against Santana for his promise not to seek to harm me over the matter, or during anything pertaining to the trade, or my journey home afterward."

The crow began to walk around Gerald, staring at him as he did so. "You are young; Santana does not believe you have had your full training, yet you have been with Cuthbert so you know something of dragons. Never have we heard of one who is not yet a warrior attempting something so bold. You know, I assume, that a bargain made with a dragon is binding on both parties, that neither party is capable of breaking trust?"

"I do. But that sounds as if Santana doesn't trust me. I have not impugned his honor; I will not have mine impugned, either."

"There is yet no basis for trust beyond the magic from the time of creation that binds men and dragons in their bargains. But no disrespect was intended."

Gerald bowed his head. "Then pray continue."

"You do not have the egg with you."

"And Santana does not have the sword with him unless he has dug it up very recently. If the bargain is accepted I will lead Santana to it."

"And you plan to return straight home with the sword?"

"That is my plan. That will change only if some great need arises. What does it matter?"

"I do not know whether it does. And what will you do with the sword?"

"I have no plans, save to recover the sword. It is of value to my family. You know it is of no use but in the hands of a proven dragon lord, and such will have his or her own sword."

"And what of the egg?"

"I do not know how old it is. It is intact, and contains the dead infant, well preserved."

"And how do you know this?"

"I, Gerald, am descended from both dragon lords and seers. I have seen it in a true dream. Torquil of Cair Parn has seen it in a dream as well, and Lord Cuthbert agrees that we have dreamed true."

"Gerald, in most things, I know how to speak for Santana, having been one of his Voices for nearly two decades. In this case I will speak with him directly and bring you his answer. How did you plan to find him?"

"Voice, I have seen his country, but not his lair, in my dreams. I would ride there and meet him wherever he wishes."

"Very good. Will you ride tomorrow?"

"I had planned to wait another day, but can leave tomorrow."

"Good. If you leave at daybreak and ride at the same pace you used coming here, either I will meet you on the way tomorrow and tell you to turn back, or Santana will meet you in the hills in three days."

"How do you know what pace I used coming?"

"Santana sees a great deal of what goes on hereabouts, both through his own eyes and those of his Voices. Three days?"

"Very well."

"Good day, Gerald of Kiergenwald, and safe journey."

"Good day, Voice of Santana, and safe flying with a good nest at the end." He bowed.

The Voice of Santana stared at Gerald for a moment, that inscrutable bird stare, and then took flight. The rest of the crows took to the air a bare instant later. In seconds Gerald was again alone in the deserted outpost save for his horse, who began snorting as soon as quiet had descended in the birds' wake.

Gerald's sigh of relief was interrupted by the smell of smoke. His stew was burning.

He managed to sleep well that night, but his last thought before he fell asleep, and his first on waking, was that there was no turning back now. This both comforted him and made him nervous as he prepared to get up and really begin his adventure. More than anything he wished he were home in Kiergenwald, before Samantha disappeared, having a meal with her, Sally, and Cle. Then he snorted in disgust. "I'm fifteen. I'm on my quest. I'm a young warrior! I shouldn't be wanting my mummy." Smiling at his folly, he turned out his horse to graze and began packing his bedroll.

Three days and he'd face his first dragon. Unless Santana refused. But Gerald would not be refused. One way or another, they would meet soon.

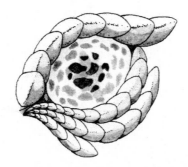

CHAPTER FIFTEEN

REVELATION & TRUCE

Gerald spent the next three days riding uneventfully across the Scottish moors. He'd always heard them referred to as bleak, but Gerald was as comfortable in the open with no change in scenery as he was anywhere else. The main exception was when he looked for a spot each night to camp. While the moors were full of hills and high ground was more defensible, he really wanted spots that were at least somewhat guarded. He knew that late in the afternoon he'd start looking for a cave or similar shelter. The first night, right before sunset, he found a cave just large enough to stand and swing a sword in. It showed no sign of ever having been used by more than small animals.

The second night he camped in a ravine under overhanging rocks. The low cliffs were crumbling; anyone or anything attempting to climb down would give themselves away—even if they didn't slip and fall. That night he ate little, having seen no game the past two days.

The third afternoon he found neither cave nor sheltered ravine. The weather was mild with little wind, so he chose to camp at dusk on the highest nearby hill. He built a fire down between the hills to avoid advertising his presence and roasted mutton from a scrawny sheep he'd killed midday. He had seen a boar that morning, but it sensed him (or something) and ran. He'd twice had chances to kill wild birds, but wasn't sure how the crows would feel about that. He laughed quietly. "If hogs were Voices I'd be afraid to kill any pig. Then I'd be in real trouble!"

As he laid out his bedroll, he silently cursed Santana for not showing up. Perhaps he had misunderstood and the dragon would appear after three days, rather than on the third day.

With his horse tethered a few cubits away to alert him to anything sneaking up, Gerald crawled into his blankets. Adjusting his pack under his head, he relaxed and looked at the stars. A fast moving cloud obliterated them for a few seconds. His horse whinnied. A few breaths later the hills around him lit up and echoed a deafening roar.

Jumping to his feet, sword already in hand, Gerald realized that his hill was surrounded by a ring of fire. A great, dark shape flickered in and out of view amidst the flames. He raised his sword in a trembling hand above his head and shouted.

Or tried to. He only managed to croak. He swallowed, set his mind, and tried again. This time he managed a shout. "Santana! Here I am, Gerald of Kiergenwald!" He dropped his sword into a standard salute in front of him, a position which still allowed him to immediately wield it if need be. Considering the size and speed of the dragon and the sheer volume of flame, Gerald wasn't sure it would matter, but he was not going to back down. Tremble, yes. Back down, no.

The fire ceased almost instantly. Everything went black while his eyes tried to adjust to the sudden darkness. Gerald resisted the urge to do a sudden 360 scan to see if Santana was sneaking up on him. But what need had the dragon for that? He could cook Gerald to a crisp from twice his length's distance. Gerald stood his ground.

Three lights appeared on the hilltop directly in front of him—two enormous eyes and a small tongue of fire as the dragon spoke.

"We are here."

"We?" asked Gerald, desperately wishing he could see better. He could see the eyes just fine, though; they were large and slanted, green with slightly brighter green irises like polished emerald shields reflecting noonday sun. They spun slowly with a liquid effect, as if they were green, molten lava, constantly in motion. They both drew Gerald in and made him queasy. He tore his own eyes away just as the dragon responded.

"I, Santana, and my Voices. Never in my life has a dragon lord, much less a mere warrior—never mind an untried youth—sought me out. Men have fled from me or tried to fight when I appeared. Some have offered rash bargains to save their hides after having angered me, but none has been so rash as you, Gerald."

Gerald had wondered exactly how to speak to Santana, and whether he would be able to show enough respect to not offend the dragon. Having now seen the beast—or at least its eyes and mouth—and some of its capability, respect was no longer an issue.

"I . . . I greet you in the name of the great dragon lord, Cuthbert."

The huge, yellow and green eyes blinked. "Cuthbert has sent word of you through my Voice. This is one of the reasons I am here."

"Great Santana. . . ."

"You make free use of my name, young one. Why is that? I heard you do this even when you spoke with my Voice."

Gerald bristled; even without experience with dragons, it was clear the dragon spoke this with some derision.

"You named me first, Santana. And as I planned to speak with you no matter what, why should I not use your name?"

The flames lengthened slightly; Gerald hoped that wasn't a bad sign. He had no way of knowing Santana had just chuckled, delighted at Gerald's blend of honesty, innocence, and purpose.

"Cuthbert told me you were brash and unlearned in dragon lore. We dragons have strong feelings about the use of our names."

"Then perhaps you should not be so free with the names of others. Respect calls out respect."

Again the flame lengthened for an instant. "Perhaps so, young warrior. Perhaps so. Now this egg. Describe it to me."

Gerald closed his eyes to think solely on the egg. They popped open on their own due to Santana's proximity. He firmly shut them again, determined to follow through. He pictured the egg. "It's about three cubits long, in shape somewhere between a ball and a chicken's egg."

He opened his eyes and asked, "Do you know what a chicken egg looks like?"

"Yes. Tiny."

Gerald mostly stifled a laugh and closed his eyes. "It's sort of blueish, mottled with light brown and green." He hesitated. "Kind of like looking at a spring sky through a budding tree."

"Very well so far. What else? Look closely!"

Gerald tensed, then relaxed as much as he could. In his mind he moved closer to the egg, reliving the dream. "It has some sort of veins in it. They're reddish-gold, and they look like the blood vessels under my skin. Faint but definite. . . ."

"And how do you know what is inside?"

"In my dream I opened the egg as if it were a chest, looked, then closed the shell; it sealed as if it had never opened. The baby was a dull, light brown. Not at all like you."

His eyes having adjusted, and with the help of the full moon and stars, he saw that Santana's hide and scales were a silvery color. In the reflected light Gerald saw hints of every color he knew. It looked as if a rainbow had mated with the night sky and their offspring had come to life before him.

"Did it have horns? Ridges on its back?"

"No. Just a face—eyes, ears, snout. Lots of tiny, sharp teeth.

I could sort of see its spine through its hide. It was curled up in a ball like it was sleeping, but the eyes were lifeless."

"Tell me, young warrior, of the eyes." Gerald noted that the dragon wasn't being so free with his name. He wondered at this; it seemed like a good thing.

"They were dark brown. Almost black, yet they looked as if they had once held red, green, blue, every color there is."

The flame disappeared for three breaths, but the eyes bored into him. Gerald remembered not to stare at them. The flame reappeared, longer again.

"You may look safely into Santana's eyes for now, Gerald. When I agreed to treat with you, you became safe from my eyes until we resolve to either strike the bargain or not."

Could dragons read minds?

"Thank you, Santana; that is a great honor. But I prefer not to develop the habit of looking into the eyes of dragons. Otherwise Gerald might not last as long as he otherwise would." Gerald had guessed (correctly) that it was perfectly fine to occasionally use Santana's name so long as he used his own just as often.

The great eyes blinked. Once. Twice. Three times. "No man has looked into the eyes of the Lord of the Western Isles and lived, save three dragon lords, and these will not discuss the color of those eyes. You have seen what few have seen, Gerald, the color of those eyes, even if only in faded glory. It is not for me to reward or punish that, but I offer you this freely, without debt. Sharing that knowledge could win you great wealth, great respect, great honor, great fame. But it could also win you the enmity of the most fearsome dragon within a week's flight. Think on these things."

Gerald bowed. "I shall, Santana. And yet I feel indebted. How can I repay you?"

"You can be honest with me. I have heard that Gerald of Kiergenwald wants only to kill dragons. Yet he comes to me ostensibly to bargain fairly. He promises not to use the dragon sword he calls Draehamar, which we call Murder Most Foul, against me. Yet I have also heard that he especially hates me." Santana's great tail lashed like a cat's. It was disconcerting. But there was a lot of that this evening. "I would know the why of all of these."

Gerald's heart seemed to stop. He knew he quit breathing for a moment. How much should he say? How much was fair in terms of what Santana had told him? Then he realized it didn't matter. The truth would at least repay the debt, and if he overpaid, Santana would be in his debt. He licked his lips, said a quick prayer, and replied, feeling at last the old, familiar anger.

"You took my parents. You took my uncle, and perhaps my second father!"

"I took your uncle, yes . . . albeit an uncle you never knew. An uncle who called my name, then attacked me."

Gerald waited, but so did Santana. Gerald finally spoke. "What of the others?"

"What of the others? I can tell you who took them, in trade for the egg."

"But it was not you?"

"No. It was not me."

"Thank you, but I prefer to press my initial offer."

"Very well." Gerald could now see that Santana was draped across the hill. As far as he could tell the dragon might be totally relaxed, if a dragon relaxed. He was realizing by the minute just how little he knew about them. What folly to be here!

Stifling such thoughts before he could panic, Gerald hurried on. "I have wanted only to kill dragons, yes. But many whose voices I respect have told me this is folly. I am not completely convinced, but I can put that aside until later. Since you tell me you did not kill the others, I suppose I must accept that."

He wasn't sure just what Santana did; he guessed it was

a growl. The ground rumbled and the dragon's eyes began to pulsate, the green light brightening and fading every few heartbeats. Gerald swallowed and continued.

"I have a dragon sword at home, Draebard. I left it there and brought only this sword, untried save for meat to eat and brief battle with a handful of thieves and murderers. I come to bargain, not fight. That is all I know to say on this."

"And would you use another sword against me if the opportunity arose?"

"Let us say if need arose, just as I am sure Santana would roast Gerald if the need arose."

The flame lengthened, but Santana made sure to keep it away from Gerald and his horse. "Yes, he would. But having spoken with Gerald, Santana hopes the need does not arise. So far you have spoken well, if you have not told all you might..."

Gerald hadn't planned on interrupting, but it popped out without his thinking. "Nor have you."

Santana smiled, a magnificent and terrible sight. "You have the makings of a very great dragon lord if you can get over your hatred. Perhaps even if you cannot, but then there will be war between us and you like few have seen. I would rather count you as a friend, Gerald, but will count you as a meal if that is not an option."

"It is too early to speak of such things, Santana, but for now I am content not to do battle with you."

The eyes pulsed again. "Such wisdom. Come, I agree. You go to the cave wherein lies the egg. I will go to the sword the night before you arrive there, free it, and carry it to this cave when you call me. We will trade there. It's not," he continued, as Gerald opened his mouth to speak, "that I mistrust you. We have, after all, a binding agreement. But if, for example, we were beset between the sword and egg by a horde of hateful dragon lords, you might be killed while I defended myself. I want the egg, and I trust you with the sword far more than most, despite your abiding hatred for my kin and myself."

Gerald started to argue, then stopped. It was true. Or was it? He wasn't quite sure. He'd have to sort it out later. "Why did you not then wish to go to the egg first? Oh. Never mind. That would be harder to carry and protect."

"Very good."

"My horse is tired. Can we wait until morning to leave?"

Santana arose. "As you say. I will see you at daybreak." He spread his mighty wings, shook himself, and took to the air. Gerald watched the great shadow cross the stars and moon, heading north. He noted the graceful beauty of the wings— neither bird wings nor bat wings, but with elements of both. He was amazed to find himself thinking so poetically about a dragon, something—someone—he'd sworn to kill only a week ago. He had a lot to think about.

But that could wait. He needed his sleep. It dawned on him his mount had made little noise or fuss during his discourse with Santana. It took him a moment to find the great steed— lying on his side with a stunned expression on his face. Gerald hadn't realized horses could faint.

He patted the horse awake and made sure he had water and grass in reach. Then he lay down and quickly fell sleep. Sally stayed with him that night in his dreams, alternately urging him to kill the dragon or to handfast it. Gerald woke with a slight headache, a dry throat, and two very large and very green eyes a few yards from his face.

He managed not to yell.

Or to faint.

Barely.

CHAPTER SIXTEEN

WHEN DRAGONS LAUGH

I'm impressed," said Santana. "You hardly flinched."

Gerald was more honest than he meant to be. "I'm not sure I could have moved."

Santana snorted, causing Gerald's horse to try to bolt.

"I dream sometimes of waking up to green eyes, but not yours, dragon. I hope that doesn't break your heart."

Santana's eyes spun deliriously. "My mate will be very glad to hear that. She can be quite jealous."

As Gerald stood up he realized that he was not as tall as Santana's head. While Santana had been speaking, Gerald noticed the dragon's largest teeth were longer than his forearm, the smallest almost the length of his hand. He had never seen a live dragon; the scale intimidated him anew. He'd have to get over that. "How?" he asked himself, and laughed.

"What's so funny, young warrior?"

A dozen clever retorts danced a jog through Gerald's mind, but he wasn't really as rash as Santana seemed to think. "Dealing with dragons, or at least with a dragon, as you are the first I have met, isn't quite like I expected." Noting the dragon's expression, he went on. "All right, not much at all like I expected. Not that I had too many expectations."

"We are even. You are very unlike what I expected as well. And so far neither of us is in a hurry to kill the other, so perhaps this will work out well for everyone."

Having finished striking his meager camp while they spoke, Gerald mounted his horse and stroked its head to calm it. "You asked why I wanted the sword, and what my plans were. Why do you want the egg? What are your plans for it?"

"Ho ho ho!" Gerald was glad Santana had moved a little farther away as a thin flame shot out of his mouth as he laughed.

"That is an affair of dragons seldom mentioned to men, and then only to a great dragon lord. Perhaps one day you will know, but not today, Gerald."

Gerald stared at Santana. The light was changing for no apparent reason, and he saw images flicker and fade, dragons appear and disappear. Whole seasons flashed before his eyes; dragons came and went, fought and treated. Vaguely Gerald noted that Santana never seemed to age or change.

Santana stared at him intently, waiting for him to speak. "What is it you see, Gerald of Kiergenwald? Where are you walking beyond the veils of here and now?"

Caught up in the scene fading into the distance, Gerald replied without thought. "Just as dragon bones protect us, possession of another dragon's offspring offers great protection—for you as well as for us. For some reason I cannot fathom, this is even truer if the offspring is dead; it is absolute protection. The Lord of the Western Isles would grant you anything to get this back, and whether you traded the egg away or not, you would be safe from him and any with whom he is allied, including dragon lords."

Gerald felt betrayed. Why had no one told him of this? For an instant he thought of reneging and keeping the egg, but he had given his word and it was an irrevocable bargain. Santana backed away and hissed, then rumbled somewhere deep inside. The ground vibrated, bringing Gerald quickly back to the moment. His hand went to his sword as he scanned for the threat.

"Warrior! You cannot know this. You must not speak of this to anyone. If not for our bargain I would have pounced as you spoke." The dragon's head was constantly in motion now, the great neck weaving, the head rotating, as Santana considered Gerald from many directions.

Catching the change in address, Gerald sat up straighter, wondering even as he did whether he was becoming arrogant. This dragon was yet again destroying his world, making it anew, causing Gerald to look deeper into his own identity as well as into the nature of everything around him.

"Is the Lord of the Western Isles very like you, Santana? In my seeing he seemed to be. Had I made the bargain with him, it would be no bad thing for men or dragons, but from all I have heard, there are dragons I should never have made such a bargain with. Is that so?"

"These things are so. The Lord of the Western Isles and I have much in common, having the same mother and father, although he is a thousand years older than I. Listen. If it is acceptable, when we are alone save for my Voices from whom I keep no secrets, you and I will speak as equals. You are not yet a dragon lord, but I will treat you as one, for in my mind you are.

"There is no record in the memory of any dragon alive of one your age being a dragon lord. A few your age have killed young dragons, or become an equal to a dragon youngling, but that is all."

Gerald felt like his head was spinning. "Yes, that is acceptable. But I thought a dragon lord had to . . . well, kill dragons."

"A dragon lord is not lord over dragons, though many foolish humans believe this. He is a man the dragons treat with respect, as an equal in some way. But to be named dragon lord by dragons requires that the man has been seen as equal by at least three dragons, whether by word and deed, or by vanquishing them. Not even a decree by the Lord of the Western Isles can make one a dragon lord. I know that people see this differently, but dragons remember when the laws that hold all things together were laid down. We recognize those and we reserve the right to ignore man's folly."

Gerald bowed. To his astonishment and amusement, Santana bowed his head to Gerald. "Don't look so surprised, youngling." Santana smiled. "When a dragon says equal, he means equal. To think otherwise is an insult."

"I meant no insult."

"I know, and none was taken. But while I will trust Cuthbert for most of your education, I will train you in some things."

Gerald laughed. "You have already taught me far more than Cuthbert!"

"You have not yet been his pupil. Tell me after he is done with you if you still feel this way.

"Now, we have been moving slowly so we can talk, but let us eat some distance. Let your horse go as fast as he can until he tires. I will meet you there, wherever there is." As he spoke the last word, Santana leapt into the sky, the beat of his great wings nearly knocking Gerald off his horse. The young warrior screamed his battle cry and his horse leapt forward like the wind. No horse, much less a horse with a rider, could win a race with a dragon, but they could certainly try.

King Donald's horses were some of the best in Scotland. If a man served in the king's army for two years beyond his training, he won the right to take one of the retired horses as his own. While these horses were no longer young, they were still at least the equal of many in the land. But if a man served four years, he could keep the warhorse he rode those years. Gerald planned on doing just that.

Fionnlagh was, indeed, an excellent steed. He slowed a bit after a half hour but still kept up a good pace 'til lunch. Gerald killed a small pig. He cooked and ate what he could and left the rest for scavengers; he had no time to cook or cure the leftover meat. He rode slower that afternoon, but by day's end was into a region of tall hills and crags he'd never seen or heard of. He hadn't expected to ride off the map in his head for another day.

He started to make camp on a hilltop again, trusting the dragon's presence for protection, when he remembered that Santana had flown off the previous night. He camped hidden in a ravine instead. When Santana showed up he rested atop the hill on one side and spoke down to Gerald.

"You have come far today."

"I have a good horse."

"And a good will to ride. What will you tell me of your mate?"

Gerald spat out his drink. "I don't have a 'mate!'"

"Intended mate."

"Intended wife. Betrothed."

"Very well."

"What will you tell me of your wife?" Gerald asked mischievously.

"Mate."

"Very well."

"You grow bolder."

Gerald shrugged. He was in a fey mood but unsure what to say.

"My mate is Selene. She was named for the Moon; she is like liquid moonlight. Men would find the name appropriate, thinking her cold and barren, but she is warm in dragon ways."

"But not barren?"

"Oh, yes. Barren as the Moon. Her mother, of course, foresaw this, and hence named her Selene."

"You say, 'of course.' Is this common among dragons?"

"Of course." The tongue of fire appeared briefly. Gerald was beginning to recognize this as a form of dragon laughter.

"I'm sorry. That she's barren."

"It is of no matter to us, though it may matter to dragons as barrenness is becoming more common. But dragons mate for love. Making more dragons is necessary for there to be dragons in the world, but it is only a side effect for us. We guard our eggs fiercely, but once a dragon hatches it is on its own. It means no more or less to its parents than to other dragons."

Gerald wasn't sure how he felt about the idea of being a mere side effect of his parents' feelings for one another. "Do you mate for life?"

"Yes. Many humans know that. Most, however, do not realize that a dragon normally has but one mate. If that mate were killed after only a week, rare is the dragon who would mate again."

"I had an aunt who married four times because her husbands kept dying."

"She would be considered very strange if she were a dragon. Now, tell me of your lady of the green eyes you dream of waking up to."

Gerald only blushed a little. "I met her, Sally, when I was eight. A dragon, perhaps Argyll, took her father the next day. Her mother adopted me. She and her husband's brother raised me. Sally and I were always friends. We probably would have handfasted, anyway, because each of us secretly loved the other. But when another dragon took Mother, we had to handfast to save Sally from having to marry her crazy cousin, and so we could keep the land."

Santana was looking at Gerald intently. "You named Argyll. Do not think that because I call you dragon lord you can use dragon names with impunity!"

"Of course not! But he's dead."

"And when did this happen?"

"Several years ago, I guess. Captain Murdoch and the king killed him after he killed Wallace. That was Sally's father."

The dragon's eyes lost their focus and were unnaturally still for a few seconds, then resumed their usual, molten lava pattern. "My mother's brother's mate had only one clutch of three eggs. She was slightly mad. When they hatched, she named them all Argyll after herself. They were crazier than their mother. No human knew of this.

"The Argyll who killed your mother, father, and next father is not the Argyll your captain and king killed. He and his sister, also Argyll, yet live. And here he is."

The land lit up with dragon flame as a second dragon alighted on the hill across from Santana's. "Well met, Santana! You have my upstart already cornered, I see. My thanks."

"Greetings, Argyll. No, this is one with whom I have struck a bargain, not yet anyone's prey."

Argyll's head, in hue slightly greener and duller than Santana's eyes, turned this way and that. The great blue eyes sought out every shadow around. "But there is no one else here. I would see, hear, and smell them!"

Gerald started to speak, but Santana beat him to it. "This is the upstart, but he and I have made a bargain, and none may touch him until he has played his part. A week hence, you may try your luck. But be warned, he is tricky, and his skills belie his age."

Argyll snorted, which ought to have singed Gerald but somehow did not. "Fine. Play your games, cousin. I will deal with him later." As quickly as he had arrived, Argyll was gone.

"You did well not to attempt battle, Gerald."

"You seemed to think it best I stay out of even the discussion."

"Yes, you are protected for now, but had you attacked, that protection would have been gone. The Argylls are not dragons to be trifled with. Their motto is 'Eat first and ask no questions later.'"

"If I were as ugly as him, I would need a clever motto as well!"

"He is considered a good dragon to gaze upon . . . by dragons."

"Does he have a mate?"

Santana hesitated a heartbeat, two, before answering. "He is mated to his sister."

"What? That's disgusting."

"Not in the dragon world, Gerald. Though it is very rare."

"Then why did you hesitate to answer me?"

"I know how humans look on this. And while not disgusted, I am ill at ease. I have discussed this with many dragons. I think it is a part of the Argyll madness. At least there have been no offspring."

Gerald shook his head. "I like this dragon less and less."

"You will like him still less if you have to deal with him."

"Oh, I'll deal with him. But when I'm ready and he's not."

"You are either bold or foolish. Perhaps both. Time will be the tell of that."

"Santana, I am hungry and tired. Will I be safe here tonight?"

"I cannot say. But if you mean from Argyll, yes. Our specific bargain protects you from all dragons unless you do something faithless or foolish (or both). I trust you will do neither?"

"If you mean regarding Ar . . ., that dragon, you may be sure of it. Beyond that I know not what a dragon considers foolish, but I am seldom reckoned foolish by men, and I am faithful."

After Santana departed, Gerald ate some stale bread and drank some water. Then he snuggled into his bedroll as the first frost appeared on nearby grass. He grimaced to think that if he hadn't met Santana yet, he might be dead.

How ironic that a dragon he had once sworn to kill had saved his life. On top of that, Santana had confirmed that Argyll had killed all his parents but Samantha.

Then it occurred to him that if he could attack Argyll while Santana was present, the larger dragon might fight for him to be sure of finding the egg!

As he dozed off, his last thought was that he'd forgotten to find out the color of Selene's eyes. He dreamed of gorgeous, blue eyes. Waking in the middle of the night, he realized the blue eyes in his dream were Argyll's. He gagged, rolled over, and went back to sleep—but not until he'd promised those eyes their death.

Before dawn, Gerald awoke from a long night of too little sleep and too many dreams involving Argyll. As he lay thinking how best to attack Argyll, it hit him that he would then owe a life debt to Santana. Owing a dragon that way, even Santana, might be a fate worse than death. He gave up, ignored the rising sun, and went back to sleep.

Five minutes later, Santana's scolding awoke him. Even his horse looked at him reproachfully. Too sleepy to talk much, Gerald apologized to Santana and Fionnlagh, packed and mounted, and started across the barren, rocky landscape as the dragon disappeared in the sky ahead.

CHAPTER SEVENTEEN

AWAKE IN A NEW WORLD

The morning was unseasonably warm, which is not to say warm, but not as cold as Gerald had expected. Here and there grass or heather peeked greenly, if foolishly, from the rocks. The sages had been saying the weather patterns were changing. Gerald only knew that he'd never been able to trust the weather. There could be warm days in winter and cool days in summer. Today was a warm day for winter, but if spring had arrived he was a dragon. Glancing at the sprigs of heather, he reined in Fionnlagh.

Dismounting, he saw faint, small tracks. Soon he was sure he was after a stoat. Sneaking a look over a hill, he found it, bright in its white winter fur, dining on a small rabbit. As soon as its teeth were buried in the meat behind the rabbit's head, Gerald's sling was out, and the stoat—like the rabbit—was food. It wasn't his favorite but it was meat, with nice fur as a bonus.

He cleaned and rolled the fur while he waited for the meat to cook. After this early lunch he rode on. As the moors opened up he let Fionnlagh gallop a while. They slowed as they came back into steeper hills. The temperature dropped, a light fog rolled in, and Gerald made camp in a stone hut abandoned long ago. A rotting bench was the only thing left inside. What

was left of the door wouldn't hold for long, but at least he'd
have notice of anything or anyone coming in.

Supper was a scrawny ptarmigan and bread. Gerald had
never missed vegetables before but would have paid well for
peas, beans, or carrots. Wherever Samantha was, she must
be laughing at him. How many times had he tried to hide his
peas under his plate or feed his carrots to the goat? Santana
didn't show that night. Gerald slept well save for waking to
the distant howling of wolves. It stayed distant, so he and
Fionnlagh caught up on their rest.

The next day and a half passed uneventfully. He noticed
Santana flying overhead more often; was the dragon getting
anxious? Gerald laughed until realizing he was also anxious
somewhere under his excitement. He'd pushed his horse all
morning, but as he came around a small mountain, he stopped.
Before him was a set of mountains he recognized from his
dream. He was near.

It took all afternoon. Gerald completely forgot to eat until
Fionnlagh insisted on stopping when he found some black
grass. After wolfing down some bread, Gerald climbed a
small cliff to scout the area. He was astonished to see nothing
resembling the cliff face where the cave should be hidden. He
climbed down the other side and scouted for a good hour.
Finding nothing he turned back, frustrated. As he approached
the cliff he'd climbed down, he laughed as he realized it
contained the cave. There was the pile of rubble from his
vision.

He screamed to the skies. "Santana!" Less than a minute
later, the dragon arrived.

He had not seen Santana land like this. The dragon barely
slowed, and smote the ground like a group of boulders from
British catapults. Gerald had never seen those, but his father
had described them—Angus had seen them in use against
a group of plague-ridden savages. The force with which the
dragon struck sent small rocks and dust everywhere; the beat
of his great wings kept it moving.

"Gerald! Get to your horse and find shelter. Do not go near the egg. Go now!"

Before Gerald could reply, Santana was back in the air, one wingtip nearly hitting the young warrior. Blinded by the dust, Gerald had to wait a few seconds before he could move. His eyes itching and burning, he scrambled up the cliff, across and down, fairly leapt onto Fionnlagh, and rode hard down the biggest trail. Nervous, angry, wanting to meet whatever threat arose, Gerald still obeyed Santana. A minute's ride from where he started, Gerald found a small cave mouth he could just get his horse into.

He took Fionnlagh as far back as he could see and tied his reins to a stalagmite. He then walked warily to the cave mouth and waited. He heard nothing at first, but eventually noted faint, roaring noises. A while after those stopped, he chanced calling Santana's name. A moment later, the ground shook, and Santana lay, apparently exhausted, outside the cave.

"Santana! Are you hurt? What happened?"

"Gerald, I will live. I am wounded, tired, and angry. Let me rest, go find water, and then I will return and explain. You can stay in the cave or come out as you wish."

"But. . . ."

"Hold! I will return soon." Much more slowly than before, Santana stood, then flew off. Gerald took his horse into the waning sun; the cave was chilly. He really wanted to explore it; there was a strange scent, somehow very old and intriguing, coming from the bowels of the rocks. But there was no time and Gerald had nothing for a torch that would last more than two minutes. He would try to return one day and explore.

As dusk arrived Gerald gathered some wood and started a fire back in the cave. With only sticks as thick as his thumb, Gerald spent a lot of time gathering wood and feeding the fire. He filled his water skins from a nearby spring. An hour later as the half-moon peeked from between two hills, Santana returned, landing somewhat more gently than before.

"Gerald, let us move quickly. It is safe for now, but for how long I am not sure." He stopped and stared past Gerald into the cave, green eyes twirling rapidly. "Have you explored the cave?"

"No. I have no torch. These branches would not last long."

"Bring me the largest, longest branch you have."

Gerald grabbed a three-foot branch a little thicker than his thumb—the biggest he had.

"Stand it upright in the ground or between rocks, and step away."

Knowing Santana was tired and hurting, Gerald did so without questioning, but he was nearly dancing with curiosity and excitement.

As Gerald stepped back, Santana breathed an odd flame the color of his eyes onto the branch. The top of it caught and blazed more brightly than it should have, with a definite greenish color.

"Take the torch. It will last the night."

"I never heard of such a thing."

"Dragons seldom need it, but we sometimes provide this for dragon lords when they need it. Take the torch and your horse and go back in the cave. Hopefully you can both make it. You should find something interesting. If so, bring out whatever you can."

"What is it?"

"I am not quite sure, but it is dragonish and ancient. It is long dead."

Curious and excited, Gerald did as Santana said. Twice he had to choose a direction when the tunnel split. Once he had to turn back, as neither he nor Fionnlagh would fit. Gerald was impressed that the horse had no qualms about going with him; he'd heard horses did not like caves. Just as he thought he'd come to a point the horse could not continue, the cave opened up into a room nearly the size of Cair Parn's Hall of

Warriors.

Gerald stopped. He could hardly breathe. In the middle of the cave, on a bed of logs, rested the egg. Stunned at the sight, he stared for at least a dozen heartbeats before moving to it. It was more beautiful than he remembered from his dream. The colors were odd, but perhaps that was the green torch light. He leaned over to look closer. The torch touched his face; he nearly dropped it before he realized that the heat was bearable and he wasn't burned. Wonderingly, he passed his hand through the flame. It was very warm, but he felt no pain. He touched it to the edge of his coat, which promptly caught fire.

Gerald yelled and dropped the torch. He beat at the coat and put out the flame before it could spread very far. He slumped onto a rock. Dragon magic! How many times had his parents (all of them, including Cle) warned him never to trust it? He wouldn't forget again! Standing the torch in some rocks, both because he didn't trust it not to go out on its side and for better light, he considered the egg. It was much too big to carry, or even to lift onto his horse. "Aha! The wood. I bet that's how they got it here!"

Inspection suggested this was true. Two of the logs on one side of the bed were scraped at one end as if they had been dragged. They also showed evidence of having been tied at each end and in the middle. It took him half an hour, but Gerald rigged up a sling between the logs. He fastened it to his horse. Using all his furs and bedroll as cushions, he managed to roll the egg onto the sling. It was lighter than he had expected.

Carrying the torch once again, Gerald led the horse slowly back through the tunnel, taking longer to return despite having lost time to his wrong choice on the way in. When at last he reached the cave mouth, Santana's green eyes were dancing impatiently. "It took you longer than I expected. The hill is not that big."

Gerald bowed. "My apologies, great one. I took a wrong turn, caught my clothes on fire, and built a sling to bring back the spoils of war."

"Spoils of war? Few dragons have hoards; only those who collect it to teach men a lesson or anger them do so. And I smell more than mere metal or jewels. Did you find nothing else?"

"Move aside so that we may get this out, and you can see for yourself." He somehow managed to look stern despite his excitement. Santana moved back and Gerald led his horse out. As the sling emerged into the light, Santana's eyes went berserk. They spun, they pulsed, they rotated, they did things Gerald couldn't describe. Feeling more than slightly nauseous, he looked away. "Here, Santana, is my part of the bargain."

"Excellent! I wondered, but refused to speculate. Oh, yes, this is an egg of the Lord of the Western Isles! It dates back to Merlin's time!"

"You know of Merlin?"

Santana looked at him reproachfully. "Dragons must know human history to understand humans. We learn all we can, are far seeing, and have long memories. Beyond that, Merlin was half faerie. Merlin spoke with many of us, though none of you seem to know that unless we tell you."

"We have only legends. Perhaps you can tell me more someday."

"Perhaps. When you have something to trade or wish to be in my debt." A slight flame escaped the dragon's mouth.

Gerald laughed. "It can wait. What cannot wait longer is an explanation of this evening."

"That is true." Santana was now peering at the egg from every side, making Fionnlagh a bit nervous. Gerald rolled the egg off the sling, which he began dismantling as he listened to the dragon's tale.

"I had seen dragons in the distance the past two days. I was sure they were the Argylls. Normally we only listen for our own names, but we can hear far more if we try. The Argylls were apparently listening for you to call my name.

"They could not know the nature of our bargain. I think he just hates you because I protected you. They planned to pounce as soon as the bargain was finished. I heard them call to one another when you called my name. They flew up high to wait and see what we did. So I warned you and went to fight them.

"They are younger and stronger, but their madness hinders them. I am bigger, wilier, and more subtle. I tricked them time and again so that I seldom fought both at once. He escaped, sorely wounded, but she fell to the earth after I crushed the bones in her wing with my teeth. She is dead or dying.

"I will live but need to recover. After I hide the egg, I will eat a small herd of cows or sheep. Then I will sleep and heal for a month."

"A month?"

"A month. Dragons live on a completely different timescale. We can go weeks without sleep, weeks without food, weeks without waking. Or we can alternate sleep and waking every five minutes. You are not in my debt for knowing these things, as Cuthbert will teach you all this, anyway. But you must learn not to ask questions carelessly, or I will put you in my debt. Better I than another dragon!"

"And why do you think me careless? Do you think I have not considered all this?"

"No, I do not."

Gerald sighed. "You are right. Thank you, Santana. I am in your debt after all, for your patience, mercy, and teaching me this."

Santana gazed at him a while.

"Did you ever think you would say that to a dragon? Especially without anger?"

"Not until recently, at any rate. Now, what of my debt?"

"I think it can wait. Perhaps leaving it, like a shackle on your leg, will help you learn. . . ."

"Stop! I do not need to be more indebted to you!"

Flames slipped mirthfully from Santana's mouth. "You do learn fast. I release you from your debt; this egg and your honor pay for much. Your sword is in the top of the lightning blasted tree behind me. Farewell, dragon lord!"

"Farewell, yourself, great dragon!" Gerald yelled as Santana took to the skies. He definitely looked tired, Gerald thought.

He shook his head in wonder. *Friendship and pity for a dragon? Who was he, and where was the old Gerald?* Then he thought of Argyll, or rather the Argylls, and found *that* Gerald immediately.

CHAPTER EIGHTEEN

INSULT ON TOP OF INJURY

Gerald went at once to the tree. Trees were few and far between here, so it was somewhat depressing—if unsurprising—that this one had been killed by lightning. Whatever sort of tree it had been, it was now merely a very tall stump—a pale white shaft save the black streaks which ran down to its roots and into the rocky soil.

The top was completely black, a broken spear pointing into the night sky. The tree being six or seven yards tall, Gerald wasn't quite sure how he was supposed to get the sword. The tree was devoid of bark and too slick to climb. He hacked at it with his knife, but the wood seemed hard as rock. Finally he tried tossing a grappling hook over the top. It took three tries to get his smallest grapple to stick, but the third time it stayed. No amount of jerking pulled it loose, so he decided to chance it. The rough leather soles on his supple boots gave enough traction, and he was soon up.

The top of the tree, almost a cubit across, was hollow. The sword, still in its scabbard, was inside the hollow. Gerald was relieved and surprised, having feared the sword would be bare and embedded in the tree. There was no belt.

Lacking another choice, Gerald tossed the weapon to the ground, wincing as it struck. Once down, he could find no damage to the sword or scabbard. Draehamar was highly polished, covered in runes, and had a finely honed edge. The handle was an odd material, rather like ivory, smooth yet not slick. It fit his hand well and didn't slip, as he had thought it might. Perhaps the king's armorer or Cuthbert could tell him what it was made of.

On the other hand, he could not get the grapple to loosen for anything. He climbed back up, carrying a second rope after tying the end in a slip knot. Slipping the new rope around one of the hooks, he climbed back down, went to the other side of the tree, and yanked. On the third try, the grapple came loose and fell, trailing its rope.

Gerald packed the ropes and hook, shoved Draehamar into his bedroll, and rode like the wind toward home.

After an hour he could tell Fionnlagh was tiring, so they slowed. Despite Santana's warning, he didn't want to tire his horse without imminent danger. Sometime after midnight he noticed a small cave. It only went a few yards back and showed no signs of major inhabitants. They slept 'til shortly after dawn.

Breakfasting and watering at a pool in a small stream, his horse suddenly screamed and jumped. Gerald's sword was instantly out. As the stallion danced and pawed at something, Gerald moved in. He saw a snake moving away and sliced it in two. The dark zigzag pattern on its back and orange eyes told him it was a female adder.

"You ninny," he chided the horse. "Adders don't bother you if you leave them alone. I suppose it's safest to not have her running loose, but you'd best hope her husband and children don't come looking for revenge."

He contemplated eating the snake but wasn't sure if the meat was poisonous. In the end he threw it as far from the stream as he could for scavengers to eat, or not, as they chose.

It had taken him almost seven days to get to the cave. With his head start last night, he could probably make it back in six, but Gerald wasn't sure he needed to push that hard. Seven days out and seven back was his original plan. He decided to stick with that.

The next two days were rather boring in terms of both scenery and food. Gerald stayed in the stone hut that night, while the weather turned colder with a north wind. Grateful for the shelter, Gerald hung a fur across the lone window and huddled in a corner with his fire, as far from the door as possible. His horse seemed content, but Gerald dreamed of fire and smoke and slept fitfully. Once he awoke to wolves nearby, but the howls moved on and he settled back to his broken sleep.

Morning dawned with a great deal of red in its artwork. Gerald pondered staying by the hut an hour or two in case storms were coming, but after considering his dwindling food supply and the lack of game nearby, he decided to move on.

At mid-afternoon, after yet another meal of stale bread and having seen nothing more interesting than a hedgehog, Gerald noted a reddish glow on the nearby hillsides. Sunset was still over an hour away, and the sun's position could not account for the glow. Gerald rode into the valley, sword in hand. When he saw the dragon, he leapt from Fionnlagh's back, prepared to fight.

The dragon appeared to be sleeping at first. Gerald stared with confusion at its right wing, which was not furled against the body as usual when at rest. He realized it was possibly broken in several places. In fact the dragon, a rather annoying yellow, was generally in terrible shape—scraped, slashed, and losing quite a bit of dark red, nearly black blood.

The eyes opened. They were red, and though still alive, rather dull and barely moving. The dragon reminded him of Argyll. It dawned on him. "You're the sister. Santana did this."

"Santana did this," she agreed. She sighed, and the reddish flame nearly singed Gerald, despite stopping at least two cubits short of touching him. "Sorry. You are Gerald?"

"I am," he replied grimly.

"Good. I called and you came. I always wondered whether that worked with humans. If it works with us, it should. . . ."

"I don't think it does."

She smiled, an expression oddly like one he recalled Sally wearing at eight years old. "It must! I called but a moment ago and here you are, faster than I would have thought possible. If I were to live, I would go into your debt to find how you managed that. We still have to fly to find those who call."

Gerald shifted on his feet uneasily. "Why did you call me? One may intentionally not call a dragon to its doom, so I would not think you could thusly call us, either." He had no doubt that his arrival was unrelated to her calling, but if she wished to believe that, Gerald would not disillusion her. Better a contented dragon than an angry one.

And even if she couldn't call him that way, nothing could stop her from roasting him if she wished. Definitely best to play along.

"I am dying. I wish you to speed that process by slaying me. Then take the sword and kill my brother. It is his fault I am here dying, and he is not even here with me. I hate him! I wish I had never taken him to mate. Kill me, then take your sword and kill the last living Argyll. I offer you a dragon sword at no peril, so you are already in my debt. Kill my brother and you are free, as well as a dragon lord, having already consummated a bargain with Santana."

Gerald stood frozen, thinking furiously. What she said made sense. Her offer had indebted him, but actually getting a dragon sword would indebt him far more . . . except that she would be dead . . . unless he horribly failed at his job. He saw no way out. She had offered the best bargain he could think of given the circumstances. She must be mad through and through.

"Are you sure?" He had to ask.

"Fool! Of course I am sure. Should my death mean nothing? No! Only tell my story to both man and dragon, that all would know I brought about my brother's downfall and helped make you a dragon lord. Being nearly dead, I see clearer than ever, Gerald, and I see you a mightier dragon lord than you dare hope. And I see you killing my brother, only he looks so odd. . . ."

Gerald tried but could get her to say no more on the subject. She merely grew angry with him for delaying.

"Do it! Do it now! Why do you wait? Why do you torture me?"

"Very well," he sighed. He was nervous, not just about killing this pitiful, if bizarre dragon, but about approaching her. Still, since that one blast of fire had not come close enough to harm him, he assumed she was being truthful. He advanced, sword up.

"Foolish human! Not that sword. Get Murder Most Foul for the deed!"

"Why? It is no more to me than this one, as I have never used it for anything, much less to slay a dragon!"

"I heard rumors Cuthbert was teaching you. Either he is now a dotard or you are an inept pupil. Or perhaps both."

Gerald attempted to interrupt, but Argyll kept speaking. "It is true that dragon swords serve only those who have drawn dragon blood with them. But can you truly not know that once you have drawn blood with a sword that already served against dragons, that all the power accumulated under its previous owners belongs to you? It will be as if you had used that sword to vanquish every dragon it has fought! And that is why you must use Murder Most Foul; you will need all the dragon bane you can get to destroy my brother. He is the mightiest of the Argylls. The sword you hold, though it killed me even in full combat, would be little better than any other sword against my brother."

As she spoke, the young warrior swapped his sword for Draehamar. He noticed it seemed to glow even in the shadows between the hills. As he drew it, it seemed to sing, the metal ringing for many heartbeats after it was free. He waved it to get the feel of it and it rang just from cleaving the air. The runes appeared yellow and red, as if it were already drawing power from Argyll.

"What must I do? Is there anything else?"

She coughed and great drops of blood and bits of flame flew across the space between them. She rolled over on her side. He saw a deep wound on her chest. "Stab me right in the middle of this wound and you will pierce my heart. Move away fast, or you might die in my death throes. And ware the flames! Now promise me you will kill my brother!"

"I will do my best."

"Do it or don't. There is no best. Will you kill him?"

Gerald closed his eyes. He didn't want to lie but decided he was just going to speak words this mad dragon could understand. "Yes. I will kill your brother."

He realized life had returned to her eyes as they talked; the pupils had been flowing and spinning wildly. Now the movements slowed and they dulled again. She seemed to relax. She moved her head well away from Gerald. He took a breath, ran forward, and plunged the sword deep within her breast.

Her screams echoed off the hills. Dark blood spurted, and it burned where it touched his skin. Gerald ran back toward his horse as Argyll's great head and tail thrashed wildly for a few heartbeats. She slowed quickly, then lay still. Her once fiery eyes were a dull maroon. A final breath escaped her lips and nostrils, with no hint of flame.

Slightly stunned, Gerald wiped the sword on a small patch of grass; the grass withered and smoked as the blood came off the sword. Gerald realized his skin was blistered where blood had touched it. He shuddered and tore off a piece of his shirt to wipe the drops from his skin.

The sword now glowed, and not just with the moonlight sneaking through the space between the hills in the darkening sky. It glowed a dark red, as if Argyll's blood ran just beneath the surface. He looked in wonder for a moment. "Thank you, Argyll, and fare well wherever you are," he whispered. Sheathing Draehamar, he turned to look for his horse, who was nowhere in sight. He found him a hundred yards beyond the valley, shivering slightly.

Gerald had planned to leave immediately, but another thought occurred to him. They went back into the valley. He let Fionnlagh loose to graze and walked over to contemplate Argyll's corpse. Once again, the sheer size of a dragon was nearly overwhelming.

Gerald had returned because he wondered if he could make a crude scale mail. He grabbed a scale, and it cut right through his leather gloves; had he not worn them, it would have sliced his finger to the bone. He tried using his knife to pry one off, but the knife broke first. His sword worked no better but at least did not break. Finally he drew Draehamar, but it was too unwieldy. He sighed and turned to leave.

Just as he reached his horse's side, he heard wings. A dragon landed gracefully in front of him, a greenish dragon with lovely, liquid blue eyes. The last, living Argyll had returned.

Small flames flew from the dragon's mouth as he spoke. "You called me, I think."

"I did not!" Gerald hardly even noticed that he held Draehamar before him as if he could ward off the dragon with its mere presence.

"Oh, yes. I distinctly heard you whisper my name. In thanks."

"It was your sister's name I uttered!"

"Ah, but the name belongs to all three of us. If you call one, we all hear. Alas that my siblings cannot answer as well. But what is this? You have killed her!" Argyll's voice crescendoed nastily. "I planned to eat you, foolish child, but now I shall do that slowly, enjoying your every scream as I do!"

Gerald's response would later cause many to claim that he was as mad as an Argyll, but he was sure of himself, and so he spoke.

"Ha! Argyll, you will do no such thing. You are in my debt!"

Argyll froze. "What madness is this? You have murdered my sister, and you wave a tiny, metal stick at me. How am I in your debt?"

But Gerald noted that his eyes had ceased spinning. They stared at him like cold, blue rocks.

"You wanted your sister dead. She was useful, but you had long planned to kill her when you had a chance. I have saved you the trouble, so you owe me and cannot harm me! This 'tiny piece of metal' is Draehamar, the twelfth most revered sword in all of Scotland and Ireland!" With a terrible yell, Gerald spun the sword over his head once and charged.

Great blue flames shot toward Gerald, flowed around him, and went well beyond. He heard Fionnlagh scream once. There was heat everywhere, but it was bearable. He wasn't sure whether his clothes would catch fire or not, but he ran unwaveringly at Argyll. "Die, vile wyrm, die!"

As quickly as it had started, the fire stopped. While he was yet three steps from the monster, it leapt into the air and took flight. He hacked at the tail as it flew by. Draehamar struck at an angle and glanced off it. A few scales broke loose. Argyll roared—probably in fury—and disappeared over the nearest hill. Breathing hard with excitement and frustration, Gerald spun around.

Every bit of plant matter in the valley was gone, or at best blackened and smoldering. But far worse, Fionnlagh was a smoking mound of thoroughly burnt flesh and bones. There was little trace of Gerald's gear. His other sword was a pool of liquid metal glowing in the night. Rocks were blackened and radiating heat; some were split. Only the dead dragon seemed untouched, save that her spilled blood was gone. Realizing that the ground around him was extremely hot, Gerald ran as fast as he could from the valley. He just made it to cooler ground before he doubled over and lost his last meal.

When he stood up, the full weight of the situation struck home. He was five days ride from the castle with no horse, no pack, no food, and no bedroll.

And it was starting to snow.

CHAPTER NINETEEN

FEVER DREAMS

Gerald shook his head and reminded himself that he was a warrior, if only in training. Thinking hard, he recalled seeing no caves for at least two hours ride behind him—much farther on foot. He could not recall any shelter close ahead.

He'd heard of men killing a large animal and getting inside for warmth, but he was not about to climb inside Argyll's corpse. While he would probably fit through the great tear in her chest, the burns on his hands and arm reminded him of the damage her blood could do. He started shivering in the frigid air.

It was then he noticed the small clump of grass near Argyll's head. Where everything else was scorched or destroyed, this still burned with a reddish flame. He hurried to it. It was warm, but it did not burn his hand. Whether this was a final gift or an accident, he had no idea. "Thank you, regardless," he said, as he bowed low to the corpse. Remembering what had just happened, he added, "Argyll," and gripped Draehamar tightly. Nothing happened.

Using his broken knife, he dug up the clump of grass. Carrying it by its roots, he began exploring off to the side of the route he'd taken. He found a sheltered overhang—not quite a cave, but better than nothing. He set his torch down to explore nearby. There was precious little to burn, but after an hour he had enough for a decent cooking fire.

He then went in search of food. Thankfully he had his sling! He managed to kill a rabbit and a ptarmigan, although why the ptarmigan was out in this weather, he couldn't guess. He told himself that most birds were stupid. Looking about, he grimaced and thought, *Just like me.*

After cleaning and gutting both animals, Gerald put the rabbit hide aside. He started his cooking fire easily enough, but as he feared, it seemed to burn normally. He tended it carefully, with the meat just far enough above it to not burn the spits. As the meat cooked he cleaned, cut, and sewed the rabbit fur into a hat. The stoat's fur from the day before he made into crude mittens with no thumbs. He wished there had been enough for boots. His old ones would have to do.

When the cooking fire started going out, the meat was of necessity done. He ate half and put the rest in his small game bag for later. He was stiff from sitting in the cold, even with the fire. He stood and ran a bit to warm up. He collected rocks and made a wall around the dragon fire. It wasn't much, but it might keep him alive. Curling up by the fire, he tried to think.

Mostly he thought of Fionnlagh, his faithful horse, or more correctly, the king's faithful horse. A horse dead by no fault of its own, but by Gerald's foolishness. *I would trade my dragon sword for that horse at this moment. Or would I? The heather is always greener on the other side of the wall. He sighed. Were the choice between me and a sword, which would Sally choose?* His mind wandered back to the day he met her, when they slept together. How young and innocent they had been! He could feel her head on his shoulder, their arms around each other. He settled deeper into his dreams, never feeling the cold.

He woke once, just enough to drag the rest of his supper from the meat bag and start eating, but after a bite or two he fell asleep again without noticing the snow settling on his food . . . and him.

After a lifetime of dreams of good days and bad, of Sally's joyous welcome and her accusations of trading a horse for a toy sword, of killing Argylls over and over, of being whipped by the king's guard for losing the horse, of being made prince for killing an Argyll and recovering Draehamar, his dreams were all of heat and fire. He felt sharp prickles and wind. He was shivering. He decided he was hallucinating and dying of cold.

Forcing his eyes open, he became certain that was the case. He was far above the frozen moors, lying against a hot, damp bed like the banks of a stream he had heard of in England, yet icy winds buffeted him. When he finally looked, he saw slender white stones digging into him above and below. . . .

They were teeth.

Dragon teeth.

He was in a dragon's mouth.

He was wide awake now. He tried to reach for his sword, but even as he realized he couldn't reach it, he also realized his folly. Threatening the dragon would likely get him dropped or eaten. If he simply stabbed it, the dragon would roast him or drop him. All of these would be quick deaths, but pointless. He closed his eyes, prayed, and waited. To his later amazement, he slept.

He awoke in a bed, sweating under thick layers of fur. A large fire blazed in a fireplace nearly as tall as Gerald. There was a pitcher of water by the bed. He drank it all and slept again.

"Ah, the water is gone. Wake up, wake up!"

Gerald groaned and sat up, blinking furiously against the

light. The morning sun shone through a window right into his eyes. Torquil moved a stand with a banner to shield Gerald's eyes from the blazing dawn.

Nearer to the bed was a sinuous, dark-skinned woman clothed in red and purple, with gold jewelry on her arms and neck. "Can you feel your toes?" Her accent was strange and melodic, but she spoke in a tone much like the captain's command voice.

"Yes. I feel the covers against them."

She pulled the covers off his feet, causing him to jump. He'd just realized he was naked, and he wanted those covers!

"Be still, young warrior. It's your feet I need to see." She stared straight into his eyes. "I've seen the rest of you anyway."

He blushed furiously.

She pulled on a toe he couldn't see with the covers in the way. "Do you feel that?"

"Yes."

"Which toe?"

"The big one on my left foot."

This was repeated with several toes. "Can you wiggle them?"

He obliged by wiggling them all.

"Good." She replaced the covers. "Give me your hands. Close your eyes. Now, which finger am I touching?"

Feeling the faintest of touches, he told her.

She repeated this several times. "Now wiggle them." He did.

She turned to Torquil. "He's fine. He has some ice burns on his sides and back. Amazingly, his feet and hands are fine, along with his ears and nose. I'm surprised. And the dragon blood did little damage to his hands and arm. This one is watched over by Someone." She turned back to Gerald. "You need to rest another day. Eat and drink all they bring you, but do not ask for more." Imperiously, she turned and walked to the door.

"Thank you!"

She stopped and turned back. "For what?"

"Um, for saving me?"

"I didn't save you. I just treated a few ice burns and kept your hands and feet the right temperature."

"Well, thank you for that."

Her expression softened. "You're welcome." She turned and left before he could speak again.

"Who was that?"

Torquil gazed at Gerald with a slight smile. "A healer, K'pene. She came to us with traders from across the ocean. Her home was ravaged by dragons. The few survivors fled and settled in a village of caves on the coast. K'pene dreamed of a land of safety, a stone castle, and a king of white men with skin painted blue. She fed many traders for their tales of distant lands and people until some told her of Scotland and brought her here.

"She healed some of the traders and their sailors over the course of a month with fruits, foods, and herbs. She set a broken bone better than their ship's surgeon. This earned her passage. On the way she taught the ship's cook things he had never heard of. When they brought her to port, they gave her enough gold to barter her way across Scotland several times. She asked many questions, got too many answers, and sought us in a dream. Three weeks later, she arrived here."

Gerald pulled on his covers. "Most healers talk as if they are oracles, but this one speaks both as an oracle and as if she were a queen."

Torquil. "She is a princess. She became queen after the dragons killed her parents. But after her dream of Scotland, she handed that title to her cousin."

"I have heard that a true king is a healer; is it then true of a queen as well?"

"It is often true of both."

"What of King Donald?"

"I doubt he has ever had cause to find out."

A page hurried in bearing a tray. He set it on the table beside Gerald, stared for a moment at the young warrior, blushed, and left.

"What was that about, seer?"

Torquil flashed a rare mischievous grin. "It is not every day he serves a dragon lord spit out of the mouth of a dragon."

Gerald groaned and fell back toward the pillow, smacking his head on the wooden headboard. "I hoped that was a fever dream." Rubbing his head, Gerald started to settle down under the covers, but Torquil grabbed his arm.

"Sit up and eat, Gerald. Healer's orders."

"I suppose I must."

"Yes, you must!" Cuthbert walked in, looking as inscrutable as usual. "I am grateful to know you are well, as are all. Today you rest. Tomorrow you will speak with the captain and king. After that, if K'pene agrees, you may see your friends. I suspect that will be the case." He looked inquiringly at Torquil, who nodded.

After his dinner of bread and vegetable soup (Gerald had never been so happy to see peas and carrots in his life), they gave him a potion to drink. It was rather foul, but honey and lemon helped. Soon, he slept.

Sometime during the night he awoke. The captain sat nearby, gazing into the fire. He glanced at Gerald from time to time, but Gerald's face was in the shadows. He couldn't tell what the captain might be thinking. While he tried to decide what to say, he fell back asleep. In his dreams, Jillian, the captain's daughter, alternately flirted with Argyll and Gerald. He woke at dawn to an empty room.

After an embarrassing check of his ice burns, K'pene said he was well. When she finally left, Gerald leapt out of bed. Though dizzy, he dressed quickly in clothes the page had left. As he finished washing his face, the captain entered the room. Gerald stood straight, not sure what would happen. His captain nearly ran to him, hugged him, and clapped him on the back.

"It's good to see you up and well, Gerald."

"Am I?" He seemed doubtful.

"Aren't you?" The captain looked at him sternly.

"I suppose I am. A little weak and dizzy. And..."

"And?"

"Miserable."

"Why?"

"Fionnlagh, the horse. He's dead."

Murdoch slumped back against the wall. "Really? You accomplish your quest, apparently befriend a powerful dragon, reclaim a much sought-after dragon sword, come home in a dragon's mouth—not my preferred means of travel—and you're miserable over a horse?"

Gerald stared a moment, then smiled weakly. "Maybe not too miserable."

"You may yet be, but I personally think a horse is a fair trade for a dragon sword."

Gerald gaped, remembering his own thoughts back in the snow.

"I suspect Donald will feel the same, but we won't know until he tells us. Are you ready to face him?"

"I don't suppose I can breakfast first?"

"Oh, no." Murdoch looked severe. "Definitely not. But there's a reason for everything. Come on."

The two-minute walk to the king's chamber told Gerald he was not quite well. He felt pins and needles in his feet and legs, as well as his shoulders and back. By the time they reached their destination, he wanted only to lie down. Murdoch presented him to the guard, who immediately had someone open the door. They entered.

A table sat in the middle of the room with several chairs. The king stood talking with Cuthbert. Torquil spoke nearby with K'pene. Conversation stopped as they entered. The king spread his arms wide.

"Welcome home, young warrior and dragon lord! Let us eat."

To Gerald's surprise and horror, his captain seated him while pages seated the others. He turned bright red and stared at the plate in front of him.

Food was brought. While the others had bacon, eggs, and toast, Gerald had only dry toast and two eggs.

"Tomorrow," said K'pene, "you may resume eating normally."

Sighing as he noted the butter and jam the others were putting on their toast, Gerald broke off a bite of bread and ate.

Sylvi walked in carrying a sheathed sword. Proudly descended from Viking warriors and Frögärd i Ösb—the first known woman runemaster—she was the king's artisan in charge of heraldry and runes. She drew and held up Draehamar. "Lord Gerald, this sword should have runes to bear record of what you did. How many dragons did you vanquish?"

"It matters not. I would add no runes."

"But you must!"

"Why? Will the sword lose power if I do not?"

"Nay, but a dragon sword always bears testimony to its lineage."

"Then mark it that Argyll gave her life to make me the owner of the sword and remove an execrable blot of a dragon from the world."

"I know of no rune for that. It would take several in any language."

"Then do your best, but speak to me no more of dragons for now."

Murdoch spoke up. "Apparently he killed one Argyll and another fled before his righteous fury."

"Thank you, Murdoch," Sylvi said.

She stared at Gerald a moment, nodded to King Donald, and left the room cradling the sheathed sword .

"Your quest was well done, Gerald." The king gazed at him intensely. "We will eat, and after you have eaten your fill, you will tell us of your adventures." He looked around the table as he added, "Questions can wait until the story is told."

He would rue saying this many times as Gerald related his story. King Donald forgot himself once and started to interrupt, but the captain and Cuthbert joyfully hushed him, to Gerald's discomfort.

CHAPTER TWENTY

UNBALANCING DEBTS

"And that is the last of it, I think. I dreamed a great deal there by the small fire in the ice and snow. I remember little of these dreams, except that they included many of my friends, and at times I thought I saw heaven. I thought I was going there, but it was never quite time.

"Then I awoke in what seemed to be a dragon's mouth. I could see no way out, so I rested. I was thinking to act when we landed, but I fell asleep and did not awaken until I was in bed under the ministrations of the healer." He nodded to K'pene, who nodded back. "When I woke I decided the dragon's mouth was a fever dream until Torquil mentioned it."

The men chuckled but K'pene looked angry.

Gerald thought he understood. He looked at her. "How shall I address you? Princess?"

Surprised, she simply said, "You may call me Healer or K'pene."

Gerald kept looking.

She blushed a bit. "I renounced my titles when I decided to leave my people."

"Very well, K'pene. I know that you have lost far more than

I, but I have lost two sets of parents to dragons. I am sorry for your loss. I know some of your pain."

K'pene looked at Gerald and softened a bit. "Thank you, Gerald."

"And yet, now dragons have saved me more than once." He sighed. "My feelings are a bit conflicted."

The dishes had been cleared away as he told his story. Each of them had gone through a goblet of wine, and Gerald drank water as he talked. He was tiring but knew the questions must come, and come they did. Gerald answered most of these as best he could. But there were some he would not answer.

"What was your vision about the egg that so upset the dragon?" Kind Donald asked.

Gerald looked at the excited faces and sighed. "Something few have seen. He made it clear I could tell no one. I have no idea why."

K'Pene looked astonished and somewhat angry. "Not even your king?"

"Especially me," King Donald answered. "If Gerald told anybody one of the dragons' great secrets, he would be faithless in the eyes of all dragons. Were he to outlive the dragons, he would still be in their debt. And I will not know such a secret unless it is given willingly.

"Gerald, I notice you also did not say whose egg it was, or exactly why it was so valuable. I assume these are also great secrets?"

"I am not sure, but I think so. Whose egg it was ties in with the vision. Why it is so valuable I cannot say."

Gerald noticed that Cuthbert was smiling slightly. He probably suspected, or even knew, much more than he was letting on.

The steward entered and announced. "Lunch is served." Noting the king's look of surprise, he added, "It is already past noon."

"No more questions while we eat. Then we can all rest for an hour before we finish."

Again, Gerald had plain fare while the others feasted. At least this time there was soup with his bread. The bread was fresh, a huge improvement over the past week.

Gerald rested in the room he'd awakened in the day before, with a guard outside his door to make sure he got that rest. He woke feeling better than he had since he'd found the egg, although his mouth was tired and his throat was dry from so much talk. The guard escorted him to the king's chamber.

This time there was no table. The king sat and the others stood. As Gerald bowed, the king spoke.

"I am afraid we must make haste, young dragon lord."

Gerald stiffened and started to protest, but was immediately silenced by the expressions of the king and everyone else. "Things have arisen I must attend to, but there are things here I need to know.

"Twice today you spoke the name of Argyll." Gerald flinched, as did K'pene. Gerald felt badly that it made him feel better that she did so. "Why do you feel safe doing so?"

"The dragon already hates me; I do not think he can desire my death more. But he is in my debt, so he cannot hurt me. But why do you speak his name?"

"Murdoch and I slew his brother. He hates us as much as he does you, but will not dare move against us, between our swords and skill. At least for now." Something in his manner and tone told Gerald there was more, but he knew better than to ask.

"Now why," asked the captain after a nod from the king, "did Santana send that dragon to get you?"

"What?" Gerald blushed slightly at his confusion and outburst. "I had no idea he did!"

The king nodded at Cuthbert, who spoke.

"Torquil dreamed that you were in trouble. He saw you

frozen in a large block of ice, with red candles burning all around. A dead dragon watched over you as if it were alive. He sensed urgency. I sent a Voice to Santana. We were awaiting Santana's reply when this other dragon appeared. We were preparing in case it was an attack, when a Voice appeared and said the dragon was Santana's reply and to welcome it. I thought two of the guards were going to fight anyway, but Murdoch steadied them."

Gerald glanced at the captain, who explained:

"They were from a village near England hard hit by dragons. One lost his child, another his wife. I have sent them home to guard their village. They would not last against a dragon, but there are bandits and savages preying on weakened villages, so they will be useful there. These are strange times; we cannot chance men here who might not listen to orders, and I will not punish men simply for being weak, especially for reasons such as theirs."

Cuthbert took the tale back up. "The dragon landed on top of the keep, but immediately took off again. He circled, then landed outside the walls. He dropped you reasonably gently, then raised his head and screamed at us. 'Murderers! The castle is full of dead dragons!' He said a great deal more, none of it nice, but once he finished, the king addressed him."

The king stood and paced as he talked. "No dragon bone in this castle is from a dragon murdered in cold blood. Every beast whose bones, skin, or scales lie here attacked a dragon lord or innocent people, or died at the hands of another dragon. It took some time before your dragon would listen, but eventually he calmed. We thanked him and asked him how we could repay him. He laughed."

"He laughed?" Gerald sat in wonder.

"He laughed," agreed Cuthbert. 'Santana alone answers for this,' he cried as he rose and flew off west. When we brought you inside, Ivor looked at you and sent for K'pene. She is from a hot region, and he wanted to teach her of ice burns and ice fever. It turns out that she has visited a great mountain near her home and learned of these things before." He bowed to K'pene, who smiled and bowed back. "And that is all we know."

"Who was the dragon?" Gerald asked. Everyone tensed.

"He did not offer his name and we did not ask," replied the king.

Gerald looked at Cuthbert. Cuthbert looked back. Gerald raised an eyebrow. Cuthbert sighed. "Yes, of course I know who it was. Are you sure you want to know?"

A sense of dread overwhelmed Gerald, but he nodded.

"It was Drachmaeius."

Gerald felt as cold as he had in the wilds before he slept.

"And you had to let him go."

"We had no reason to do aught but thank him," the captain replied sternly.

"He took my mother!" Gerald said, barely managing not to snarl.

Cuthbert interrupted. "He said you tasted familiar." Everyone smiled but Gerald and K'pene.

"And now Santana is in debt to this murderous beast?"

"No. It appears Drachmaeius was in debt to Santana, and this nearly paid that debt off. It must have been quite a debt. Only thrice do we know of a dragon carrying a man except for ill purposes. Always it was a dragon lord, and the other two times the dragon owed a great debt to the dragon lord, a life debt, and paid it off by carrying him."

"Did either of them ride on the dragon's back?" Gerald could see the answer on their faces.

"No. The only dragon lord who ever suggested that was allowed onto the dragon's back, but he was then dropped into a volcano."

"We don't really count that one," noted the king wryly.

"Nor do we mention it to dragons," Cuthbert commanded.

Gerald nodded. That seemed like obvious wisdom. He

looked at Cuthbert. "And how is Santana?"

"He said he is doing well enough, but we sent Ivor to tend to him."

"What? Ivor?"

"Oh yes! Ivor and I have worked together to learn much of a dragon's health. Ivor is one of four men and women alive in Scotland who can help dragons heal."

Even though Gerald was glad Santana would recover, something in him still rankled at the concept of healing dragons. He noticed K'pene gripping her chair tightly. He wasn't alone in these feelings.

"And now, Gerald," the king said with a smile, "it is time to truly test your patience and strength. K'pene has released you and we must be done. I have other business. You are free to go to your friends, and may they have mercy on you."

Gerald groaned. He didn't want to think or talk about dragons for a week, but that was all anyone else would want to hear about. He arose, bowed low, and walked toward his doom.

"Gerald!" The king's voice brought him up short. He turned. "Your Majesty?"

"A horse is not too much to trade for a dragon sword such as Draehamar. But try to keep the next one, will you?" He smiled as he spoke, but Gerald left as quickly as gracefully possible.

CHAPTER TWENTY-ONE

DRAGON MADNESS

I t took far longer to tell the story in the barracks, between incredulous interruptions, demands for explanations and repetitions, retellings for people coming in after he started, and discussions and arguments about dragons and how to deal with them. It would have taken even longer, but Gerald was the first back from this year's quests, so his inquisitors were older and knew basic dragon lore.

"Gerald, that was insane, charging Arg. . . ."

"Stop!" Dree's hand covered Drinn's mouth. Once Drinn nodded, Dree removed his hand.

"But Gerald said we're safe in the castle!"

"For now, yes," responded Dree with a knowing look toward Gerald. "But they hear, and they know, and they remember. They have been known to simply bide their time and come for someone later. And this one's as mad as they come, from all I've heard."

"What have you heard?" asked the next McCulloch. "Besides what Gerald said."

"I asked Cuthbert a bit when I heard that there were mad dragons. He told me some stories. There was one dragon who waited over a hundred years for revenge. A king bandied this dragon's name about but never left his home, which was a dragon hide with scales and skeleton intact. . . ."

"He lived in a dragon carcass?" asked Iain, the only Welshman in the group. "Who was crazy in this story? The dragon or the king?"

Dree laughed. "Perhaps both. But the dragon got so angry he started burning fields and homes nearby. The king's men laid a trap. The dragon got away but lost a claw in the process. He went to live atop a nearby mountain from where he could watch the castle. He challenged anyone going in or out. If they were related to the king, they died.

"The king died and his son became king. The dragon offered to cease the siege if the son came out to be eaten. He refused. The son died and his nephew became king. He died and his son became king. It had now been over one hundred years since the king first called the dragon's name. The dragon tired of waiting. He flew to a great height above the king's home. He ceased breathing. He passed out and fell to his death, crushing the dragon home and all within it."

Iain about fell off his bed with agitation. "But a skeleton is protection, never mind a whole dragon hide with it!"

Gerald spoke. "Only against magic."

Dree nodded. "The dragon fell like a rock, a gigantic rock. There was no magic involved. He might have used magic to try to live and they would have been safe. He killed himself for revenge on a great grandnephew. Mad."

Drinn shuddered and covered his mouth. They all laughed.

"But back to Drinn's point," said Peter. "What possessed you to charge the dragon?"

Gerald sighed. He knew this would be the hardest bit to explain. He went with the method Torquil and Cuthbert had suggested. "You know I had a true dream that led to this quest."

They nodded.

"And I had the true vision with Arg . . ., the dragon. No, I'm not afraid to say the name; he already hates me. But I don't want to chance indebting myself or impacting Santana's debt."

"Wait," interrupted Iain. "The other dragon and San . . ., your savior, were the ones with a debt."

Gerald shrugged and winced; he still had a tender spot in one shoulder from a dragon's tooth. "I'm not taking any chances. And I won't name Santana unnecessarily out of respect for him, and I don't want any of you to get too comfortable with his name.

"Anyway, I had a true vision, the one that showed me why he wanted the egg, and no, I can't tell you what that is or all of dragonkind might be at war with us. Anyway, the king decreed I should keep that to myself. In fact, please don't bandy any of that about. I had a true vision, because he started treating me differently and was really upset that I knew. Right?"

They nodded. They weren't all sure, but nobody had any basis for disagreeing, especially if their king and his council hadn't.

"Good. Dream true, see true, know true. I just knew it. It was like knowing what you know from a dream or vision, only without having the dream or vision. Does that make sense?"

Some shook their heads. A few nodded. Iain just stared into the distance. Peter looked rebellious, but he generally did, although every one of them would trust him with their lives.

"Anyway, I just knew that he'd been looking for a way to get rid of his sister and that I had done him a favor. Once a dragon's in your debt, it can't intentionally hurt you. Either nothing will happen, or it will backfire and hurt the dragon."

Dree spoke up. "But he killed Fionnlagh."

Peter nodded, looking stricken. Next to his own beloved Padraigh, he had thought Fionnlagh the best horse any of the young warriors had ridden.

"Accidents happen. If he'd tried to hurt Fionnlagh, it wouldn't have worked, but because he was focusing on me, Fionnlagh became a casualty of war."

"Too bad it didn't backfire on him," Iain growled.

"I'm not sure it didn't."

"Why do you say that?"

Gerald shrugged. "I'm not sure, but he fled without trying again, without even a threat. He never came back, even when I said his name. I think the roar of rage I heard might have been partly pain. I wish I knew."

"Why?" Dree leaned in close.

"Knowledge is power. One of you told me that Cuthbert says that dragon lore isn't just facts about dragons, but facts about each dragon, and history, and what happened to them, and how they reacted, and what they said, and everything.

"If I knew how Argy had . . ."

The others laughed.

"Brilliant!" Drinn said, looking ruefully at the drink he'd just spat on his tunic from laughing. "Is it safe?"

"It's not his name, so it should be. We should check with Cuthbert before you use it, though. Anyway, if I knew what had happened, and why he reacted as he did, it might help in the future."

"With him, anyway," Peter noted glumly.

"Right. Since he's mad. But even knowing for sure how it rebounded and what it did to him—that might apply to all dragons."

Dree grinned. "Maybe the mad dragon just recognized a fellow madman running at him with a sword and no dragon scale mail and fled in fear."

Gerald bared his teeth. "Perhaps you had better flee!"

Dree laughed. "I bet Cuthbert will tell us whether it could have been a backfire. I'll ask him tomorrow."

"What's tomorrow?" Gerald asked.

"He goes out to speak with a dragon face to face, and I help escort him. They don't like to come here, as your trusty dragon steed found out."

"Please! Don't joke about that!"

"What? Why not?" Peter stared at Gerald, who sighed.

"Because he already hates my family and Santana. Because he's one of the nastier dragons out there."

Drinn tried not to smile. "Sounds like you've gone soft for that dragon you traded with. I thought you hated dragons!"

"I do. I did. I mostly do, but I think maybe there are a few that are all right. Sant . . ., he could have left me for dead when I was freezing. He could have had another dragon make sure I was dead. Instead he saved my life."

"And called you dragon lord. I'm sure that had nothing to do with it." Iain smirked.

Gerald smiled. "You're right about the second part. I'm still uncomfortable with that whole concept. I can barely spell the word; I don't think I can lay claim to a title. Cuthbert, the captain, my cousin Cle, some of the warriors here— these are dragon lords. King Donald only helped kill one dragon. Between that and not wanting to upset his people unnecessarily, he refuses the title."

Gerald left it at that, but secretly suspected there was more to it. From what he'd garnered from Murdoch, little things others had said, and the fact that Donald's kingdom was left alone by dragons except at the fringes, Gerald was fairly certain that the dragons considered King Donald a dragon lord, and not a trivial one. He'd have to ask the king about dragons he'd spoken with.

To everyone's surprise, Dree was back before noon the next day. At lunch they quizzed him.

"The dragon didn't show, nor did his Voices. Cuthbert is concerned. Whatever he planned to speak with the dragon about was important, though he wouldn't say what, of course.

He did say that the dragon had requested the meeting, and that in all his life, the only times a dragon failed to show, it couldn't."

"Couldn't?" asked Drinn.

"Couldn't. Dead, wounded, fighting for its life, bound by a debt."

"And he never said the dragon's name?" Gerald pressed.

"Never." Dree seemed slightly irked. "Almost as if he didn't trust us."

"No," Gerald said thoughtfully, "that wasn't it. At least I don't think so. Cuthbert can say almost any dragon's name with impunity and knows he can trust us. I think they hold him in higher regard than any other human alive. But since they are so picky about their names. . . ."

"Weird about their names," Iain interjected.

Gerald laughed. "Cuthbert is careful to honor them. He and the dragons respect one another and each other's ways."

"I suppose," said Dree. "Anyway, I asked some questions on the way out. Good thing, too, because he was brooding all the way back. 'No talking, I need to think.' He fair growled at us."

"So, Dree . . ."

"Careful, Gerald, I might be a dragon in disguise!"

Everyone laughed.

". . . So, elder young warrior who wishes he were a dragon in disguise, what did you learn from our lore master?"

"First, that nicknames, if they aren't too close, are fine. Argy, for instance, is about the limit. He said that Arg followed by Ull as one word would be too close. And you can't just drop a syllable such as Drach since it just means Dragon.

"He also said your guess about backfiring was a good one. He wouldn't be surprised if that were true, but he wouldn't want to guess what the result was. He said that might be getting burned by his own flame, or scales falling off, or going deaf or mute, or almost anything. He told some stories, which he assured me he'll tell everyone in class. I think the best was about a slightly mad dragon who loved to look at his reflection in a lake. He got angry at a dragon lord he was indebted to and tried to get at him by burning his wife and children. It didn't work, but forever after when he looked at his reflection, he saw the dragon lord's face. He couldn't abide water after that and ended up killing himself."

"How did he do that?" Peter wondered.

"Took some doing," Dree allowed. "He tried to fall to his death, but at the last minute his wings spread and he saved himself, though he sprained them badly. All anyone nearby heard for a week was him cursing himself for weakness.

"After that he tried flying into the side of a cliff at full speed, but again he changed his mind at the last minute and slowed down. Had a headache the rest of his short life. Cuthbert reckons he cracked his skull.

"Finally he flew off over the sea. Cuthbert heard later that he tried to pick a fight with the Lord of the Western Isles, but the great wyrm just laughed and ignored him. Eventually he went to Iceland, flew to a great height, and dove into a volcano. Witnesses say he tried to spread his wings again, but he was going so fast they broke and flapped uselessly around him. He fell, screaming with rage and pain, into the volcano. It erupted rather weakly for several days.

"Years later the Icelanders discovered the hide and bones of a dragon embedded in lava on the side of the volcano. Yes, I know: dragons are immune to heat other than dragon fire. Cuthbert believes he either died from the impact, or went so deep into the molten rock that he couldn't breathe and died that way.

"Whatever happened, the volcano was going cold, so the Icelanders tunneled under the dragon and built a refuge there in case of dragon attacks."

"I notice you haven't mentioned his name," Gerald remarked. "Was Cuthbert quiet on that?"

Dree gave Gerald an odd look. "Actually, no. He told us, indirectly. It seems he had the same name as your three mad dragons. In fact, while there have been mad dragons with other names, the only six named Argy he's ever heard of were mad. He said if he believed in curses, he'd think that name cursed, at least for dragons."

"He doesn't believe in curses?" Iain demanded, amazed. Peter and several others clearly felt the same way.

Dree hesitated. "Not in the way you mean, no."

Peter jumped in. "I bet at some point a dragon did something so despicable his name forever became cursed. If we could get all the dragons to name all their dragonlets Argy, we'd be safe!" Most of the others laughed, but Iain clearly agreed with Peter.

The meal over, they each went to their afternoon classes or duties. Peter and Iain walked together, trading stories about people and animals they'd heard of who brought curses on themselves. Gerald had an hour free and went in search of Cuthbert, but that worthy didn't seem to be anywhere.

That meant he was with the king in chambers, and even a victorious dragon lord back from a successful quest knew better than to interrupt unbidden. His questions would have to wait.

TWO MORE RETURN

James returned a week later wrapped in linen, his head reverently packed with straw in a basket. The five men James had led stood in the courtyard and waited. Within moments the king and all the warriors were assembled. Many of the young warriors looked ill or shocked. The five fell to their knees before the king and said nothing.

"Arise, warriors," said Donald solemnly. "Food and drink are being brought." He looked at Alan, the patrol leader. "What happened? And where are your weapons?" His face showed neither anger nor pity yet. He reserved judgment until he heard their story.

"My king," began Alan, "we rode nine days, following the map James had made. The tenth day we made camp and began scouting the area. I urged that we go in pairs, but James, eager to find the thieves, insisted we go separately to search more rapidly. Liam remained to guard the camp; no one approached it.

"The rest of us met back at noon to report. James never came. This time two stayed in camp while three of us went the direction James had gone. We found him cut up and full of arrows, his head on a pole, eyes gouged out. The look on his face was horrible. I think he died in despair and pain.

"We turned to check the woods around us and found them full of ruffians with arrows drawn and spears ready. They let us live but bound our hands and took our weapons. They marched us to camp. There we found Liam and Nelson in the same way. They told us to leave their lands and never return, and to 'take the young brat what killed two of us with ye.'"

His voice shook. "I dinna what we could do better, but James is dead and we return in shame. I was surprised they let us keep the horses."

The king stared at the men a moment. "I'm surprised they let you keep your heads."

Liam raised his eyes from the ground for the first time. Seldom had the king seen such hatred in a good man. "Their leader calls his self a king. I think he sent us to give you notice that he could have killed us all, to make sure you get the message. Sire, it's not my place, but I must ask. What will ye do about this?"

King Donald looked at his council. "You will know soon. Get food and drink, then see the healers about those wounds." He stopped. "How did you get such wounds without battle? Those are not from crawling through brush."

Alan replied, "They cut us as we walked if they didn't like our answers, or if we didn't seem proper respectful, or because they felt like it." He pointed at a bound wound on the upper arm of the warrior on his right. "When they asked Donald where he was from, he told them. One of them cut him saying, 'One o' yer steenking lasses cut me when I was last in your village. But I had some fun with her before she died. This was hers. Do ye like it?' He showed us a copper armband."

Donald almost spat. "It was Brenda's. My sister's."

The king froze. "You are sure of this? Are these the men you and James sought?"

"Aye, my king."

The king looked at Alan, who nodded. "We saw many things we recognized beyond all doubt. I recognized my mother's brooch; I have never seen another like it. I saw swords I know well. Martin recognized one of the leaders—a man with thick black hair and a beard covering scars on his head and face. He saw him in the battle for the village before getting clubbed out of the fight. He had described him many times. Och, it was them."

The king stood tall. "Then no council is needed. We ride three mornings hence. We will leave them all dead, loot their village, and burn it to the ground."

Cuthbert spoke so quickly he almost interrupted. "Do you mean to leave no warrior alive, or no villager?"

"What do you say, Lore Master?"

"I have heard of raiders who start villages with only men, taking wives or slaves from the villages they raid. Let us first determine whether their families are willing or no before deciding the fate of the village. Armed men should, of course, be fair game."

King Donald nodded. "You are right." He looked again at Alan and the others. "You may hold yourselves at fault, but I do not. Alas, James was young and impatient and ignored your counsel, Alan. Since he was quest leader, there was naught you could do. If any bear blame, it is I for allowing the quest."

Alan and Liam looked as if they wanted to argue, but the king's gaze silenced them.

"Do not blame yourselves. Murdoch and I were nearly caught so once."

"But we were caught, not just nearly!" Liam said in despair.

The king smiled ironically. "Murdoch?"

"We were caught, actually. But the next thing we knew, a dragon appeared, set their leaders on fire, and scattered the rest. It was a dragon we had worked hard to indebt to us, as we had need of her services later. But now we owed her. She nearly burnt us to a crisp laughing before she flew away. So we were caught. We simply had an unexpected savior—something you, sadly, did not."

"Now," repeated the king, "go eat, drink, and see the healers. Be ready to ride Thursday. We will give James a warrior's burial on Wednesday." He nodded at the chief steward. "Have a cist prepared in the cemetery." He strode inside.

The crowd dispersed. Gerald, Dree, and several of the others took the body and laid it on a trestle in the chapel. The young warriors, the men from James's village, and the captain took turns standing guard over it. The healers had done things to preserve it and reduce the stench, but the duty was still foul and each welcomed the fresh air when he was relieved.

Justin arrived to a subdued hero's welcome Wednesday at dawn, leading two horses behind his, one with a comely lass aboard. Though dressed in rags, her fierce, proud smile dared anyone to come near. Her fine red hair, fully a yard long, floated behind her in the morning breeze. The third horse plodded in under two bearskins. After the courtyard welcome, some of the ladies took the girl, whose name was Cara, off to bathe, find new clothes, and see K'Pene. The other young warriors and several of the warriors gathered round Justin for details as he ate breakfast.

"Pretty boring, actually."

Gerald and Dree looked at each other and rolled their eyes.

Justin continued. "I rode for a week, then searched for a week before finding the hermit, after finding several other hermits who had no slaves. Two would happily have taken them, I think, if they could have." He gulped some wine. "There was a young woman there. I watched for a day, and it was clear she was a slave.

"I hid my horse, changed into old rags, and stumbled into his yard carrying a skin of wine. Wanting no visitors, he was angry 'til I offered him wine, after which he welcomed me. We sat and drank. His name was Maurice, and he bragged about his slave girl.

"I asked about children and he got angry again. I found out later that Cara had hurt him every time he went near her. She's a brave lass." His eyes shone as he talked. "Of course, he didn't say anything of the sort. Just that she wasn't that kind of slave."

They all laughed except Drinn, who spoke softly. "Most of his sort would have killed her."

"He would have if she'd tried to flee. But he had other plans. He just hadn't found a way to make them work yet.

"Anyway, I offered to buy her and he just laughed. I asked where she came from, and he told me. She was, indeed, the one I'd heard of, my mother's cousin's daughter. I took my leave, went back to my horse, changed, rode back, called him out, and ordered him to release Cara. He reached for a knife and I speared him before he had it out. The bears. . . . Did I mention the bears? No?

"He had two as pets. They'd been quite friendly, but when I slew their master they went berserk. I managed to get one right away, but its mate got hold of my spear. As I reached behind me for my sword, Cara ran out with Maurice's sword and brought it down on the bear's head. The bear fell, dazed and hurt. I started to finish it but saw Cara glaring at me, so I backed off and she killed it. What a lass!"

They all laughed. "Next," Gerald managed to get out, "you'll be engaged!"

Justin didn't reply but turned red.

"What?" shouted Gerald, earning glares from tables across the room. "You're not!!"

Justin grinned shyly. "We are. We need a proper handfasting, but we're betrothed."

Dree choked on his wine. "Gerald's just jealous that he's not the only young warrior in love and betrothed."

Everyone congratulated Justin, who was happier than they'd ever seen him. They toasted him and Cara.

Gerald leaned back and laughed. "Kiergenwald won't know

what to do. Two of its young warriors handfasted."

Justin lost his smile. "And one dead."

"Right. But we're used to that, more or less." Gerald thought of his birth parents; Wallace and Samantha; Smeert, Karyn, and Freda; and all the others he'd lost or seen die in his short life. James dying this way hurt, but not like it once would have. He mainly found himself angry at those responsible.

Justin nodded and raised his goblet. "To the dead! Long and happily may they live, in memory and in the afterlife."

Everyone drank to that. With breakfast over, the groups broke up to go to work or training. Justin went to check on Cara. He met K'Pene by the women's quarters. K'pene bowed, which flustered Justin, having heard from Gerald that she was a princess and once a queen.

"Cara is doing well, but resting. You can see her later. You have done a great thing, young warrior, freeing this woman." She grabbed his shoulders and kissed his cheeks, making him blush again. "And congratulations." She smiled, showing no trace of the sternness Gerald had described.

"Thank you. And it is an honor to meet you, princess."

"You seem to be getting rather used to it."

"What do you mean?"

"I mean Cara, of course."

Justin just looked confused. "She's my mother's cousin's daughter."

"And a princess. Cara's mother remarried but three weeks ago. She did not know this, having been a slave for two months. Her mother is now Queen of the Lothians. Did you not know this, either?"

Justin stared at her, fascinated as much by her appearance as her words. "Nae. I have been gone several weeks seeking and returning Cara. I have heard no such news. Mother must be thrilled; she long felt that her cousin deserved better. Her first husband tried hard, but everyone thought him cursed. He failed at all he did. Even his death was paltry. He sought to kill a small dragon that had been eating the family's sheep. He found it sleeping, told his companions to wait while he cut its throat, crept up to it, and it rolled over on him and killed him without bothering to wake up. The others took it as a portent and fled.

"By all counts he was homely as well. But Cara takes after her mother in every way."

"Save two."

"And what would those be?"

K'Pene's smile lit up her face. "She will marry a fortunate, or let us say blessed, warrior, and a fine-looking one at that." She walked away, leaving Justin blushing furiously.

The captain found him like this and sent him to clean up. "This won't do," Murdoch said to a nearby goose. "That lad will ride off a cliff in this state." He walked off pondering how to wake Justin up without coming down on him too hard. The young warrior had certainly done well on his quest, and deserved respect. "Ah, youth."

CHAPTER TWENTY-THREE

JUSTICE FOR JAMES

They buried James that evening. Gerald was amazed at how quickly they'd managed to dig the hole for the cist and line it with rocks. It was just wide enough at the top for the body, but wider below. They laid James inside wearing battledress, an empty scabbard on his back. His weapons would go to his family. His head was in its proper place but unrecognizable.

Gerald, inured to death more than most of his friends, simply glared at the body. He had no idea, of course, that he was doing so. He was thinking of the raiders who'd caused this—murdering, raping, and looting a village, carrying women and children off, then murdering his friend. Of course, James had gone seeking these men, and knew this could happen. Still, Gerald was glad he would get to go along to help mete out justice.

Justin cried, just a little; Iain and Peter looked close to doing so. Peter was especially livid when he realized that James had died on the anniversary of St. Patrick's death.

"We'll drive those snakes out!" he snarled.

As the priest finished speaking, the grave was sealed. A lone bagpipe wailed its dirge as each of James's comrades, and indeed everyone in the castle stood alone with their thoughts, whether of grief, anger, or something unrelated to James. Unlike Gerald, the fallen young warrior had never gotten to know many people outside his fellow trainees and the warriors they'd dealt with. A likable enough young man, he had not quite outgrown his shyness. To the cooks, for instance, his death was sad, but no sadder than that of any stranger they'd fed.

Afterward, Gerald noticed Cara speaking quietly to Justin. Loneliness hit him like a mad sow, and he wished Sally was by his side. Then he remembered that Sally and James were cousins. He wondered who would carry the message to their families.

That afternoon and evening were spent in final preparations for the ride. After long discussions with the survivors and his council, King Donald had decided to go with some speed to a point an easy day's ride from the village. They would then proceed east with more caution, circling behind the village. They would camp two miles away and time their attack to hit the village from several directions at once. Captain Murdoch had suggested splitting up before making camp, but the king had refused, wanting to ensure they were a superior force every step of the way.

The trip was cold but uneventful. The night before the attack, Gerald drew midnight watch to the north, paired as usual with an experienced warrior. This time his mentor was Ryan, a Scot with an Irish name. Normally quiet in groups, Ryan taught Gerald a good deal during their watch on topics ranging from navigating by the stars, to identifying a warrior's home by the shape of his knife, to better use of shadow and stance to blend in with his surroundings. In turn, he was impressed with Gerald's ability to move through the woods noiselessly, and admitted after a long discussion that he envied Gerald this ability.

Gerald felt he had hardly gotten to sleep when he was roused with a hand over his mouth. Dree gave him the all clear sign, then whispered it was time to eat and break camp.

Chewing a bitter chicory root to wake up (and as Ivor liked to remind them all, to avoid worms), Gerald packed and made sure Dealanach was ready for battle. His new horse seemed as fast as lightning, living up to her name, but Gerald wasn't as comfortable with her as he'd been with Fionnlagh. He hoped he didn't get her killed, too. Still fighting sleep, he wondered whether horses were superstitious, and whether she was nervous carrying him. He laughed quietly to himself, then sobered and muttered aloud, "Wake up, lad, or you'll both die today!"

Gerald, Justin, Dree, and Drinn were told off to Captain Murdoch's troop of about fifty men. Gerald hadn't realized how many men would be riding with them. The king had called in some of the border patrol. From all he'd heard, Gerald was certain that his troop alone could take the village, but King Donald wanted a rout. "In battle there is always the risk of death, and if need be, we accept that risk. But I will not lose so much as a finger to these vermin for lack of men!" The whole castle had cheered loudly at these words.

Murdoch's troop left first, having the farthest to go. After an hour of carefully walking their horses far around the village, the lead scout hooted twice like a snowy owl, a bird seldom heard in this area. They had arrived. Murdoch spread them out across the hills. They hid in copses, in wild hedges, or behind ridges. They mounted their horses, stroked them, whispered in their ears to keep them steady, and waited. Gerald could feel that Dealanach was as excited, and perhaps as nervous, as he was.

The captain told ten of his men to wait in the trees, and to kill any men who escaped the village battle. If they were disappointed, it was impossible to tell in the night time shadows.

From far away, Gerald heard a bird call he didn't recognize.

Then he heard the snowy owl hoot three times. After a brief pause he heard it again. He urged Dealanach slowly and quietly out of the wood and started down the hill toward the village. What fools these men were to build in a hollow rather than atop a hill! Perhaps they valued concealment above defensibility. Gerald shrugged and smiled grimly. So much the better.

He heard a shout from the village.

"Raiders on horses! Wake and fight!"

He saw the captain's sword flash suddenly in the weak moonlight, and then he was thundering down the hill with his brothers in arms, straight into the village. He didn't remember drawing his claymore.

As Dealanach pounded by the first home at the edge of the village, moonlight glinted off a blade. Without thinking, Gerald swung his sword to his right. His arm was jolted badly and he nearly dropped his claymore—how many times had he been told to never use it one-handed—but his assailant howled in pain as his sword flew from his hand. Then Gerald was past him, still asking himself why he was using a claymore on horseback. He hoped no one else had seen.

He pulled into a shadowy area, made sure it was clear, and sheathed his claymore. He whipped out his axe and galloped back onto the road he had been riding, using his axe to split the head of a man hiding in the shadows with a halberd. He had made his first battle kill! He felt proud, thrilled, and sick all at once. Before he could think further about this, he sensed something and looked up in time to see a man leaping off a roof at him, bringing around a claymore in both hands. Gerald threw his axe and ducked. The man hit, knocking him off Dealanach. They bounced off a wall and into the dirt, Gerald's assailant still on top.

Gerald managed to throw the man off and leaped to his feet, dirk in hand. His attacker was already dead, Gerald's axe buried in his chest. Gerald reached out, stopped, gritted his teeth, grabbed the axe, and jerked it from the man, splattering blood on his leggings and boots. He heard footsteps, whirled, and saw a man staggering toward him dragging a sword. Suddenly weary and ill, Gerald didn't want to have to kill this man, but he had his orders. And he could see the hatred in the man's eyes.

"Thought ye'd stopped me when ye knocked the sword out of my hand, did ye?" the man wheezed. Gerald realized there was blood on the man's lips. "Lost your horse, did ye? More even now, are we?" He tried to raise the sword, but fell with an arrow through his neck. The captain rode up, bow in hand, another arrow fitted to the string.

"Where's your horse?"

"He knocked me off." Gerald pointed to the man he'd killed.

"She'll be nearby. The battle's done, unless some of the scum are hiding. Find your horse and meet in the square."

Gerald climbed the tallest tree he could find and looked around. He quickly found Dealanach, being led by Dree toward the square. He scrambled down. As he hit the ground, Gerald heard steps. He whirled around, axe up, to find a woman holding an infant and staring in fear.

Gerald lowered his axe. "Please go to the square. If you are not our enemy, you have naught to fear."

The woman nodded and moved that direction. Gerald followed, constantly alert. The woman kept looking back to see where he was. Gerald could not read her expression. She looked dirty and exhausted.

Once in the square, Gerald moved to Dealanach and made sure she was well. He mounted her and thanked Dree, who merely nodded. As others arrived, Gerald noted one of the king's men had no horse, another led a limping horse, and a third lay on the ground being tended by Ivor. Not as clean as the king wanted, but not too bad. Nowhere did he see the sort of grief or anger that would indicate the king's men had suffered real loss. Gerald managed a smile and prayer of thanks.

A small group of prisoners was brought in at spear point.

The king appeared in the middle of the torchlight, staring impassively at the prisoners.

Gerald recognized one by his description—the man with oddly thick, unkempt, black hair and a beard over a scarred face. While the others looked sullen or afraid, this one looked angry. He sneered a lot.

A horse galloped up. Its rider reported to the king, then rode back off the way he came. The king spoke.

"Seventeen men fled the town. Seventeen men died at the wood's edge. We are still counting the dead here and searching the village. Who is in charge here?"

Unkempt spoke up. "It would seem you are, for the moment."

"For the moment," agreed the king, "and so long as I reign. Which of you styles himself king?"

Unkempt's eyes flashed. "I saw Strachan die, so it appears I am."

The king dismounted and walked up to Unkempt. His dirk slashed Unkempt's throat before the barbarian realized Donald held a weapon. As the man collapsed, struggling to breathe, hands at his throat, Donald kept eye contact. "It would appear you are not." Wiping his dirk on the dying man's shirt, he nodded at Murdoch.

Murdoch spoke in a loud voice. "For treason, for murder, for kidnapping and rape, you men have forfeited your lives. Do any of you have anything to say?"

One man spat. Another called the king's mother a whore. Spears ran them all through.

Some of the women gasped. A few cried out. Some cheered.

It took two days to sort things out. At noon on the second day, the women and children returned to the square to hear the king's judgment. Most of them had been brought to the village as the spoil of raids, but a few had come willingly; these were now the captives. The king and his men hated killing women and said so. One of the former captives, Morna, came forward and spoke with the king. After a moment he nodded. He addressed the crowd.

"I said we would take no prisoners. Concerning the men, we have not. The women we freed have said they will accept the raider women as their slaves if they choose that over death. Otherwise, they will deal with them. I deem this just."

Two of the prisoners looked at each other and began a long, high laughter. Finally one of them spoke.

"We'll no slave for these . . ."

Before she could say more, Morna had run her through with a sword. The other woman stopped laughing and fell to her knees, begging mercy. Morna ignored her and returned to where she'd been standing, holding the sword ready.

The king spoke. "Any other dissenters?"

None of the prisoners spoke. None even moved. After a moment the king finished.

"Very well. You shall live at the mercy of those you helped enslave. Serve them well and they will you treat you better than you treated them. Perhaps one day some of you may even earn your freedom.

"Play the traitor and suffer a traitor's death."

Over the two days after the battle, the village had been thoroughly looted—every home and other building searched, wells and trees checked, disturbed earth dug up. Three carts were piled high with the results, and every man carried some as well. It would all go back to the three villages known to have been plundered by the dead raiders.

With the prisoners walking in front, the army rode one hundred yards from the village and stopped. A dozen men rode through the village, setting it afire. All watched it burn, waiting until the last building had collapsed into a mound of smoldering ashes, little tongues of flame still shooting up at random.

"Thus," noted the captain, "we deal with plagues and their

breeding grounds."

The army turned its back on the smoking ruins. Prisoners were roped together and made to walk. Some of the freed women rode on the few horses the villagers had owned, while the others rode behind smaller warriors or young warriors. A woman named Myra rode with Gerald. She reminded him of Samantha, and he told her as much. They exchanged stories over the course of the week's ride. By the time they reached her village, Corbie, he felt toward her almost as he had toward Samantha.

When she dismounted Dealanach the last time, she hugged Gerald and thanked him. "For a week, you were the son I lost to those murderers. I will pray every day for your safety, and for your future with your Sally." She hugged and kissed him and ran toward several children yelling and running to her.

All the next day they rested and feasted with the village which, after six months, had recovered somewhat from the raid. That evening the village paid the king tribute. They gave silver and copper jewelry and filled a now empty cart with food. Myra put a copper armband that had belonged to her dead husband on Gerald's upper arm. Then she gave him a pearl on a simple necklace.

"Here, my son," she whispered. "It's little enough. No, do not argue. The necklace is for your lady Sally. My husband got them from gypsy traders who claimed they came from Atlantis, but we recognized the armband as my cousin's work." Laughing, she hugged him again, kissed him, and blessed him.

He stammered his thanks and mounted Dealanach, hoping he wasn't as red as he felt.

He was, and the men around him laughed to let him know.

A horn sounded; it was time to move to the next village. Dealanach was happier with his lighter load, but Gerald missed Myra. He shrugged and sat up straighter. Everyone missed someone. He simply had more parents to miss than most. He glanced back at the crowd waving goodbye. Myra was sitting atop a donkey, waving. The way her face was shining, she might have been crying,

He hoped not.

He hoped so.

He did not look back again.

CHAPTER TWENTY-FOUR

ANCIENT BLESSINGS & CURSES

The army arrived back at Cair Parn a little after midnight Wednesday. Captain Murdoch had sent a scout ahead to make sure the gates would open without fanfare. The king and his men simply wanted to sleep; everything else could wait until the morning. Or so the troops were told. Donald and Murdoch really expected to be up half the night catching up on whatever had happened in their absence. Thankfully, they were wrong. Having no advance notice of their arrival, the king's counselors were all asleep, so the king and his captain went to bed as well.

Gerald and his fellow young warriors dragged themselves into their quarters and managed to get into bed without too much noise. *Not that it matters,* Gerald thought to himself. *No one else is here.*

When Gerald woke up, everything felt wrong. For starters, he was in a bed. Beyond that, the sun had clearly been up for a while. Why had no one awakened him? The barracks was empty. He jumped out of bed, finished dressing quickly, and strode outside. Seeing the sun at its highest point brought him fully awake. He hurried to the mess, where he found his comrades eating or just sitting down to eat. Feeling starved, he snatched meat, cheese, and greens from the serving table and sat down by Justin.

"Eoin's back," Justin managed between two, huge mouthfuls.

"Where?" Gerald asked, eagerly looking around in vain.

Dree snorted. "Good question. He's here, but we aren't sure where."

"Right here!" Hands slapped Justin and Gerald on the back, causing them both to choke.

Leaping up, they bear-hugged Eoin, squishing the meat and cheese he had tucked into his vest.

"Argh!" Eoin pushed his two friends away, threw down his soiled meat and cheese, and went for more. When he returned, he sat across from Gerald and said, "You got to go to battle! I want to hear everything!"

Dree laughed, but before he could speak, Eoin rolled his eyes.

"I know. Elder's rights. But I need to eat first. And we all have the day off, anyway."

As everyone filled up, Eoin finally spoke again. "I only got back yesterday. I had a nice long chat with Cuthbert in the king's absence, but this morning I reported to him and the captain." He shuddered. "They took my quest apart piece by piece. I thought I had completely screwed up. Then they said, 'Well done.' I got to eat breakfast with them!" He seemed mildly stunned.

"We know," Justin said. "We did the same thing."

"Oh." Eoin wasn't sure whether he was relieved or disappointed.

"Anyway, I saw Cuthbert afterward. He said they want to make sure we learn all we can from the quests and not get swollen heads. No danger of that now, that's for certain."

Others laughed as they recalled their own receptions.

"Cuthbert told me about yours," Eoin beamed at Gerald and Justin. "He was really proud of you both. But, Gerald, a . . ."

"No!" Gerald cut in. "Don't start that."

Drinn jumped in. "You might as well face it, Lord Gerald. We'd all give our eye teeth to be dragon lords, and you're there already."

Dree grinned. "He's right. Give it up. You are what you are."

Gerald sighed and looked at his goat milk. "What I am is the idiot who rode into the raider's town waving a claymore in one hand."

"What?"

"You didn't!"

"Ho ho!"

"Yes, I did. Nearly lost it on the first stroke. If I'd had any dreams of being the battle hero, that would have taken care of them. Thankfully I got it sheathed and my axe out before I met anyone else."

Eoin wanted all the details. Gerald, Justin, Dree, and Peter had killed adversaries. Iain had unhorsed two, whom others had finished. Drinn had been pinned by two men with halberds, both of whom died at another's hand, leaving Drinn alone of their group unbloodied in the battle. As penance he would have to groom each of their horses once in the coming week.

He had some minor revenge telling Eoin of Myra's kiss and gifts for Gerald, which in turn earned Drinn a dunking in the pond later that day.

Gerald explained. "She reminded me of Samantha! She was like a mother to me, and she'd lost her husband and oldest son to the raiders."

After an awkward silence, Justin grinned. "I'm engaged!"

Eoin's dagger struck the table by Justin's right hand. Eoin jumped to his feet, hands on his hips. Everyone else froze.

"It had better not be my sister!" Eoin growled.

The table howled with laughter. Eoin reached across the table and cuffed Justin lightly on the head.

"Congratulations! Who is it?"

"Cara, the lass I saved from the hermit."

Eoin just stared.

"And it turns out she's a princess."

"She's not!"

"Only by marriage. Her mother's, that is. She wasn't a princess when she was kidnapped, but a week before we left on quest, she became one without even knowing it."

Eoin started to ask for details of Justin's and Gerald's quests, but at least three of the older lads interrupted. Eoin was going first, like it or not. He started to argue, then grinned and relaxed. Elbows on the table, he propped his chin in his hands and began.

"It took over a fortnight to get to the southern coast and find the druid. I thought I had found him near the Firth of Forth, but it was another druid, who claimed only to have a knife Merlin had blessed, and indeed it was."

"How could you tell?" Peter asked.

Eoin hesitated. "It sort of glowed a beautiful, pale blue light. But nobody else could see that, only me. And I knew it meant Merlin or someone like Merlin had blessed it in some fashion."

"We all know there's nobody like Merlin!" Iain said.

"There is that! Anyway, he told me of a druid down near the sea, who lived in a cave at the easternmost end of Hadrian's wall..."

"I've heard of him," Gerald cried. "Wallace, Sally's father, met him on his quest. Wallace was wounded in an attack by a group of outlaws and had to flee for his life. He was sick from infection and a bad turn of the weather. The druid took him in, cared for him, and used a knife he said was Merlin's to clean out the infection. Wallace said the infection had been bad and, indeed, when he returned to the castle it was still an ugly scar. But within a year it had faded to where you could no longer see it."

Eoin nodded. "Aye, that's the sort of story I'd heard of this druid. And I may have seen something of Wallace's. The druid had a shield like ours. He said a warrior he'd healed had given it to him when as he fancied the design."

Gerald shrugged. "I never heard that, so I don't know."

"Anyway, I eventually found my druid, whose name was Elisedd. He met me a day's journey from his cave, said he'd been awaiting my arrival. We rode to his cave and he showed great hospitality, treated me like a king." His face fell. "And then I returned here, and not even a warrior yet."

"Well, it's a good thing ye aren't styling yourself a king," laughed Peter.

"And why is that, my Irish friend?"

Peter leaned across the table with a wolfish grin. "Because King Donald would slit your throat!" They all roared with laughter.

Eoin continued. "I had brought him a gift, a fine sword. In turn he gave me an ancient brooch he had no use for. 'It's just a brooch, gold and emerald, no value to me,' he said. No value! The king's treasurer offered me two oxen and ten acres of land on the Tieth, the Forth, or Loch Lomond for it, whichever I chose. King Donald said not to take it because he suspected it was worth even more than his treasurer knew. Cuthbert says he wants to show it to a dragon; he thinks it may have history we can't guess at."

"How will he know which dragon would know?" wondered Gerald aloud.

Dree replied. "Dragons all seem to know everything any dragon knows. Not quite, but an awful lot. We don't know how they do it. It's eerie."

Gerald's eyebrows shot up. "I bet it's the Voices, the birds!"

"I bet you're right!" Then to Eoin, "Anyway, go on!"

"He showed me all sorts of things the next few days, some really interesting, some boring, some . . . strange. But a few knives really stood out: one with a pale, almost sickly, yellow light; one with a faint, green light; and two with a brilliant blue light that put the first druid's knife to shame.

"Those, of course, were Merlin's—a short sword and a finger bone. The green one was a pearl. When I held it I saw a young Merlin with his mother, Adhan—a slender woman who might have been a faerie. She wore the pearl on a long chain down between her breasts. The yellow light was from a scroll, and I saw an equally beautiful, but deadly, dark woman reading from it, and terrible things happening. It could only be Morgen le Fay.

His friends around the table, as well as stragglers at other tables, were quiet. Every eye was on Eoin, but his eyes were focused afar.

"When I looked on Adhan, I knew such peace and joy as I cannot recount. When I looked on Morgen, I was starved for everything—food, mead, women, blood, lands, everything. When the druid took the scroll back, I wanted nothing more than to behead him and offer the head to Morgen as a gift, until Elisedd touched me with the finger bone. Then she vanished, my lust vanished, and I felt a fool.

"Elisedd asked what I had seen. I told him all, ashamed as I was. He only nodded, saying he had seen similarly but not as strongly. But then he caught me off guard. 'What,' he asked, 'of this?' and he held out a jeweled dagger. It threw off light of varying colors, but when I took it, it was dead in my hands. Long I pondered it. 'Others have sensed much about this knife,' Elisedd hinted. But I saw nothing beyond a decent work of art, though it was nearly useless as a weapon. Eventually I said as much, noting that the only light I saw was reflected from his fire and candles. 'Are you sure?' he demanded in a harsh voice. 'Yes!' I cried, not knowing what game he played. And then he laughed, long and low.

"He bowed. It had been a test. Others had come and guessed at what was what, but each had assured him the knife was a valuable relic—of Arthur, of Merlin, of Morgen, of William

Wallace, and so on. But as Elisedd himself had seen the knife made by a craftsman from Glasgow, he knew them all to be liars."

Eoin pulled a dazzling knife from his belt. "He gave it to me in thanks for confirming what he knew and what he believed, and for my promise to back him in having his shrine built."

Drinn asked to see the knife, looked at it a long time, and whistled. "I don't know what your lovely brooch is worth, but this is excellent work and holds fine jewels. It's worth a small fortune. How did he get it?"

"I've no idea," admitted Eoin as the knife was passed among his friends and comrades. "That cave was full of things I could scarce believe he owned. Anyway, I expect I'll have to give it to a priest as penance for backing a druid. The king says not to be hasty, but things are tense between the old and the new holy men again."

Iain spoke up. "Eoin, I hate to mention this, but you do know James died."

Eoin smiled sadly. "Yes."

"I only wondered because you two were so close, but you don't seem upset."

Eoin's gaze wandered back off into the distance. "The night before I planned to return home, I dreamed of James's death. It was horrible. Then I saw him on a funeral pyre, greatly honored, like something the Vikings might do. I knew he had been murdered. I awoke crying in pain and rage.

"Elisedd brought me Adhan's pearl fastened to a necklace with fine wire and bade me wear it. I instantly felt peace and fell asleep. Apparently I slept three days! During that time I walked and talked with James. We laughed, we cried, we told tales, we talked of this life and the afterlife. When I awoke, I was at peace, even after returning the pearl."

Everyone sat in silent awe for a moment. Then Gerald laughed.

"So now we've a Christian druid seer in the first-year

warrior class, descended in power and blessing, if not blood, from Merlin." He looked at Justin. "And royalty. And, of course, a dragon lord." He bowed, then looked at Dree, Drinn, Peter, and Iain in turn. "Whatever happened to your year?"

That earned him a dousing from all their goblets—water, wine, and mead.

They broke up so those who needed it (all of them, really, but they mainly meant Gerald) could bathe and the rest could begin unpacking and cleaning their clothes and gear. The rest of the day was lazy except for a muster of the whole castle, during which the king and captain summarized their journey. They praised all who went, those who stayed and kept the castle ready, and Eoin—for the successful completion of his quest.

The next day the schedule returned to normal. Gerald and his friends finished breakfast as the sun peeked over the nearby hills, then moved on to taking care of animals, sharpening weapons, and discussing the battle.

But they were all thinking about the next Monday. Between Gerald's adventures and the rumors about the king or Cuthbert meeting a dragon to discuss the brooch (and of course more), Cuthbert had decided to give the younger warriors a brief introduction to dragons. He said a day would be sufficient.

For once he was wrong.

CHAPTER TWENTY-FIVE

GLASGOW CALLING

Sundays were as close to a day of rest as they ever got at the castle, with those who attended church having two hours free from chores for the service, and all having every other Sunday afternoon off. This fine afternoon Justin and Gerald were far afield, having raced across the countryside until their horses needed to rest.

"Look!" Justin pointed ahead and to the left as their horses grazed on thick, southern highland heather. "That peak is Ben More. We should climb it. I hear the view is great from there."

"And how do you know it's Ben More?"

"Ma described it many a time. When she was a lass our age, they lived somewhere near here. When her pa was away on business or patrol, she'd climb it every day to look for him. She said she could see him comin' a long ways off."

"Then let's . . ." Gerald kicked his horse lightly to get her started, ". . . go!"

Laughing with delight, Justin and Flora chased Gerald and Dealanach the two miles to the base of Ben More. Gerald won, as much by trickery as anything. They rode at a careful pace halfway up the mountain, then dismounted and let their horses graze. They hiked the rest of the way up, occasionally slipping on the loose scree.

At the top, the view was all Justin had promised and more. They knew there were higher peaks to the north, but at these distances, everything else looked smaller. To the west the view was beautiful, with the isle of Iona just visible on the misty horizon. Looking south they saw a rider not a half hour away.

They went as quickly down to their horses as they could, slipping more than once. Regaining their mounts, they rode almost recklessly southwest to intercept the newcomer.

At the bottom of Ben More, they thundered down to the roadway to find a lad their age, looking proud and fierce atop a magnificent horse.

"Ho, stranger!" called out Justin. "Who are you and where do you go?"

The stranger scarcely moved; his horse was well controlled. "And why should I answer vagabonds from the hills?"

Both the young warriors sat up straight. Gerald spoke. "We are in service to King Donald. This is his domain, and we have right to challenge anyone we meet on the road." Both boys looked perfectly at ease, though inwardly they were tense and ready to fight if necessary.

"A thousand pardons! I am Afagdu of Glasgow, sent to learn better the arts of war, to learn more of dragons, of healing, and whatever else I might at Cair Parn. May I ride with you?"

Gerald and Justin looked at each other and shrugged.

"Yes," replied Gerald, "if you are in no great hurry. We will arrive back after dark, as we have ridden the horses hard this afternoon."

The newcomer nodded and they started moving.

"I am Gerald. This is Justin. We have been in training over a year now. Though the month long dragon class is not soon, Lord Cuthbert will teach us some basics tomorrow. What do you know of the things you come to learn?"

"I have some small skill with throwing knives. I am told I

hold great promise with a sword, but feel utterly useless. I can hit a man in the head with an arrow at fifty paces. I can ride. I know little of healing, and suspect much of what I know of dragons is wrong; it all comes from the old folk, and they say all kinds of crazy things."

"Withhold judgment on what the old folk say of dragons. Some of them are useless, but some know a great deal."

Justin laughed. "Gerald should know."

Gerald shot him a look.

Afagdu waited, but no explanation was offered. "What you said is true for many subjects."

The others nodded in turn.

After a few minutes of silence, Justin asked, "How do you come to Cair Parn? Surely you could learn these things in Glasgow."

"Of course! But Balfour, lord of Glasgow, sends some of us to all the surrounding areas to learn, and many of them send some of theirs to be trained in Glasgow. That way everyone knows at least some of what everyone else knows."

"Like the dragons!"

"Like the dragons."

"So, Voice of Balfour. . . ."

"Do not call me that!"

"Why not?" Gerald and Justin asked in astonishment.

Afagdu shuddered. "One of my uncles decided to call himself that and began issuing decrees as if he were Balfour. Everyone knew he was crazy, but Balfour decided he was mocking him and his office. One night my uncle went to bed, and no one ever saw him again."

The boys rode on in silence for a bit.

Afagdu, as the others would find, was seldom quiet for long. "I hear you have a really young dragon lord at Cair Parn. He's what, ten?"

Justin looked shocked. "Ten?"

Gerald replied quietly. "Don't believe all you hear."

Afagdu laughed. "I knew it! I told my friends that was crazy. Maybe at eighteen or something, but hardly ten."

Justin wanted to say something, but caught the look in Gerald's eye.

Gerald smiled gently. "I'm pretty sure he's at least eleven."

"What?"

"Perhaps he's thinking of our healer," Justin suggested. "I think she's only ten."

Afagdu looked back and forth between the two. He couldn't fathom if they were joking or not. He decided to wait and see.

The trio arrived back at the gates after dark hungry, despite having stopped to eat. A scullery maid gave them some cheese and wine. They ate before taking Afagdu to Captain Murdoch.

The captain, it seemed, was a distant relative of Afagdu. They spoke of kin on the way to the Hall of Warriors, where King Donald awaited them. After receiving Afagdu's oath of fealty, Donald promised to train, protect, and provide for Afagdu while at Cair Parn, not to exceed two years' time. There was no service expected or provided for afterward as there was for the king's own subjects. Afagdu knelt and the king blessed him. Murdoch released him to the others, who escorted him to their barracks and introduced him to their comrades.

They were rather late getting to sleep, swapping stories of their lives growing up in various countries and regions of Scotland. Only a couple of hours after getting to sleep, they were awakened. Daylight was still far off.

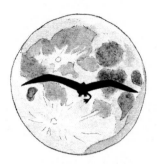

CHAPTER TWENTY-SIX

AN UNEXPECTED VISITOR

C uthbert wanted them atop the keep a half hour before dawn. Afagdu, used to a relative life of ease in the city, grumbled at having to be ready earlier than he was used to waking. The rest were just as sleepy, but proudly staggered through breakfast and muster without complaint. Afagdu quickly ceased griping.

Cuthbert greeted them wrapped in a robe that shimmered even in the darkness, looking for all the world as if stars shone from it. Gerald knew immediately that it was covered with dragon scales. A robe, not even mail! Cuthbert was either the most honored or the most protected man in all of Scotland. Perhaps both.

"Do any of you know why I have called you here at this time?"

No one seemed to know. Everyone glanced at Gerald, but he merely looked at Cuthbert, awaiting the answer.

"Good. No one told you. All right, then. Look around. Really look! And tell me what you see." The young warriors looked down at their feet, at the walls atop the keep, at each other, at Cuthbert. But Gerald looked into the distance and up. As his eyes slid past the moon near the western horizon, he froze. The face was wrong. And the wrongness was moving, shifting, slowly growing larger. He grinned.

"I think I know."

"By all means, tell us."

"Look to the moon, brothers! Look to the moon!"

The other lads turned immediately to the moon, but Cuthbert gave Gerald an encouraging smile before doing so. Soon they all had it.

"A dragon! A dragon is coming!" yelled Afagdu.

"Don't wake the castle!" Cuthbert reprimanded him. "Yes, dragons are wont to attack just before dawn, often coming out of the moon."

Gerald stood his ground, but the other young warriors ducked as the dragon sailed past, enormous claws mere feet from their heads.

Cuthbert laughed. "Very good! No one yelled."

Justin stood indignantly. "How could I? That was terrifying!"

Most of the others chimed agreement.

"They will not say why they fly out of the moon. It would seem to give notice to their enemies or prey, but there you have it. I have asked this one to simulate an attack to show you what could happen and how quickly they arrive. He looked small and distant when Gerald first spied him, did he not?"

They all agreed, then jumped as a voice boomed from behind.

"Hopefully I am not disappointingly small."

Spinning around, everyone somehow managed to remain standing. Gerald smiled as he noted the tongue of flame that indicated dragon laughter. Apparently they were amusing. Once, this would have infuriated Gerald, but already he found he could reserve judgment on the dragon. This surprised him. More than that, it made him uncomfortable. He almost felt like a traitor to his family, both dead and living.

"Greetings Lord Cuthbert, Lord Gerald, young warriors."

Afagdu gasped as the dragon addressed Gerald. The dragon hung silently before them for a moment as Cuthbert, then Gerald, then the others (haltingly at first) greeted and welcomed him. Gerald marveled at his size; the dragon was easily twice as long as any he had seen. His wings beat slowly but deliberately, the wind rocking the humans in time with each beat. His long tail was constantly in motion, curling and meandering across the sky, throwing vague reflections of starlight as it went. The "stars" all had a strange, colorless tint; Gerald guessed this dragon would look a shimmery gray in sunlight.

"I am Nain. I am the third oldest dragon alive today. Cuthbert honors me by requesting my presence. What can I tell you of my kind?"

Afagdu spoke first, making Gerald and Cuthbert nervous; he was an unknown. They needn't have worried. "Most noble and generous Nain, who names himself before us and graces us with his presence, may we know how you know Cuthbert?"

Again a flame hissed from Nain. Most of the lads ducked. Gerald noted that Afagdu did not.

"All the dragons know Cuthbert, and Cuthbert knows the dragons. But Cuthbert and I know each other as well, perhaps, as is possible. Cuthbert?"

"Nain and I each had occasion to spare the other's life at some point. Later, each of us saved the other. We have chosen to forget the rules of debt and simply treat each other as friends and equals. Dragon and dragon lord may always choose to do so."

Nain turned his gaze fully on Gerald, who started to look away. "No, Lord Gerald, you have nothing to fear from me."

Gerald realized the eyes were almost a pure bright white, like miniature moons. "Tonight none of you have anything to fear from me. If you live your lives as do Cuthbert, Murdoch, Donald, and Gerald, then you also never need fear me. Nor I you."

That was a strange concept for most of them, having grown up in a world where dragons were the most feared adversaries on the planet, beyond any invader, beast, or even the plague.

"Gerald, well done. Seldom has any achieved the title, much less such respect, so young."

Gerald was glad it was dark; nobody could see him blush, at least no human. He suspected Nain saw quite well in the dark.

Aed, a fiery boy from the moors whom Gerald barely knew, spoke up. "Lord Cuthbert, how do we know we can trust this dragon?"

The flame that followed was not born of mirth. The heat was fierce, and Aed and Justin cringed.

Nain did not wait for Cuthbert. "Have a care, child. Dragons have no need of lying to humans, and certainly I have no reason to lie to you. Not all of us see every human as evil. I, Nain, am willing to live at peace with all who are willing to live at peace with me. When the Norsemen began to invade the areas I fed upon, we clashed. But soon one of them came to treat, and now they leave my lands alone and I leave theirs alone. If my animals roam onto their lands, they are theirs, and if theirs roam onto mine, they are mine. But there are others who come by sea with whom I am at war until their kind is gone—pirates who made a treaty with my sister's sister. The treachers killed her the first chance they got. I do not judge you by their actions, and if you are wise, you will not judge dragons by the actions of Timberlake and the like."

Cuthbert spoke up. "I will tell those of you who do not know of Timberlake that tale later."

"And of course there are the Argylls. I suggested their eggs be dropped into a volcano, but..." Hesitating, Nain looked each lad in the eyes in turn. He did not look at Cuthbert. "We did not, and they have spread much havoc."

Gerald would have given a lot to know what Nain had intended to say, and why he had not said it.

Enthralled (or perhaps nervous) with Nain's presence, none

of the young warriors had noticed the lightening sky. But dawn now burst gloriously behind Nain with reds, oranges, and yellows in abundance. Nain roared in song, a sound like nothing the young warriors had heard—a cross between an avalanche and a glorious cacophony of flutes, trumpets, and bagpipes. Looking down, a couple of them noticed that everyone in sight was staring up, but not with alarm. Perhaps they had all seen and heard this before.

As Nain ceased his roaring, Justin spoke up.

"What was that?" Nain's laughing flame came scarily close to Justin's hair. It was all the young warrior could do to make sure it wasn't burning or simply gone.

"Most dragons greet the day in song. That many of you also do so is one of the things that drew me to Scotland."

"Not that gloriously, great Nain," Afagdu said as he bowed. Nain shifted his whole body so that he reoriented toward Afagdu. "Are you a flatterer?"

Afagdu silently returned his gaze.

Nain continued. "I do not believe you are. No, you are not. I know you, yet I do not know you. Who are you?"

"I am Afagdu of Glasgow. My father is a jewel merchant. My uncle . . ."

"I see! Yes, Afagdu of Glasgow, I see. Your father owes me his life. I owe your uncle my life. Your uncle owes your father his life. The debts do not cancel, so the circle of debt exists, like a worm eating its own tail, yet growing as fast as it eats."

"They will not speak of it, but I knew something must have happened."

"If they do not speak of it, neither do I."

In the quiet after the beautiful, calamitous noise of Nain's singing, the boys had begun to relax. The slow, steady beat of giant wings, the slow, sinuous writhing of Nain's tail, and the white eyes constantly in motion all had a calming effect. Nain's claw moved to within a foot of Gerald. He barely flinched. The claw was huge, easily thrice his size.

"May I, Lord Gerald?"

He wasn't sure what the dragon was asking, but he agreed after noting Cuthbert's nod. The claw closed around him, and he found himself hovering a dozen yards above the castle. By the time his heart sped up, Nain was placing him gently back on the keep.

"I wanted to show you that the proximity of dragon relics could not stop me from having my way with you. I could not penetrate the castle and would not want to rest upon it, but the mere presence of relics is not absolute protection. What this means will hopefully become evident as Cuthbert teaches you."

The dragon looked at Cuthbert, who asked his students, "Any other questions?"

"Yes," said Aed. "Great Nain," he bowed as he spoke, "why do dragons fly out of the moon?"

Nain hung in silence for a few heartbeats before answering. "I will only answer that to a very great dragon lord, and not in anyone else's presence. If you become a dragon lord, perhaps you may get your answer." Nain and Aed stared at each other intensely for a few seconds before Aed looked down.

"Thank you, Nain."

"Why do you thank me, Aed?"

"How do you know my name?"

"I only used your word for fiery. It matches your hair and your temper, but you are well on the path of training yourself to use that temper wisely. Now, why do you thank me?"

"Because you answered with respect, and held out hope I might one day attain the title of dragon lord."

Dragon mirth barely lit the sky against the rising sun. "Just remember that there are multiple ways to attain that title. Cuthbert?"

"Thank you, Nain, for coming. Do you have any requests

of us?"

Nain looked each lad in the eye again. "Only that you keep an open mind and deal faithfully with dragonkind." He looked at Cuthbert. "The eldest brother wishes to see you soon, before the next full moon."

The young warriors looked at the moon—full, huge, and orange on the western horizon. Cuthbert had up to a month.

Cuthbert smiled and bowed. "So be it. Please give him my regards."

"You will see him before I do. Give them yourself."

"Very well. Where shall we meet?"

"On the coast at Skye, by Cair Nonesuch." Nain bowed his head a full ten yards on that impossible neck.

Cuthbert bowed. "Thank you, Nain."

With that, the wings beat stronger, the wind nearly knocking them down. As Nain turned to fly away, his constantly moving tail swished perilously close to their heads. Even Cuthbert ducked. Gerald, without thinking, raised his hand to slap the tail away. It almost knocked him over and his hand went numb from the shock.

"Just like his father's mother's sister's son, Cle," Nain laughed fire as he flew northeast.

"What did he mean by that?" Gerald demanded, massaging his stinging hand.

Cuthbert looked after the rapidly receding Nain. "Your cousin Cle did something similar, but it was far cheekier as he wasn't a dragon lord yet. Nain chose him for his demonstration that he could snatch any of us up. As he reached out and asked Cle's permission, your cousin slapped at his claw with his hand and said, "I think not!""

"And?"

Cuthbert grinned hugely. "Nain said, 'Oh, my apologies,' and withdrew his claw. As Cle smirked, Nain brought the tip of his tail around, ran it between Cle's legs, and picked him up off the ground before he knew what happened. 'If you insist,' Nain responded, 'we can do this the hard way.' Cle held on for dear life. I must have laughed for five minutes. I only stopped because I was choking. Nain didn't put Cle down until I stopped laughing."

"What did Cle do?"

"Pulled out his dirk and said, 'My turn. Can you move a bit closer?'"

The others gasped. "That was the most danger we were in that day, not from anger, but because Nain was laughing so hard he almost roasted us! You were tame by comparison, but I suspect that is only because you have already been treating with dragons."

Afagdu snorted. "Not bad for an eleven-year-old."

For once, Cuthbert looked confused.

Before he could ask about it, a thought hit Justin. "You're meeting at Skye! Do you think you will see the Lord of the Western Isles?"

Cuthbert smiled. "I'd better. That's Nain's eldest brother."

The class stared, awestruck, and not just because of how regal and powerful Cuthbert looked in his dragon scale robe with the rising sun shining through his long hair. Even Gerald was mildly surprised.

Aed finally found his tongue. "But he's the eldest, isn't he?"

"As far as we know, yes. Certainly he's the eldest in Europe, and the most revered, knowledgeable, and powerful."

"What does he want with you?"

"Not to eat me, certainly, if that's your concern."

Aed shook his head negatively.

"I don't have any idea. Hopefully I'll find out in Skye." Cuthbert smirked, catching everyone off guard. (As Justin later said, "He looked like my six-year-old brother when he's just gotten away with mocking me.")

Cuthbert looked around. "Afagdu, you have a concern?"

"No, sir. A question. What is Cair Nonesuch?"

"Ahhh. . . . You would ask that." Cuthbert stared off into the west a while, almost as if he were looking for an answer himself. "You have heard of Dunvegan Castle, home to Clan MacDonald for some time?"

Everyone nodded but no one spoke.

"Many of you know some of the story, but it's easier if I tell all. Dunvegan, a stronghold if ever there was one, was suddenly and mysteriously deserted almost two generations ago. The MacDonalds who lived there had simply disappeared, including their leader, known as the Lord of the Isles. It was then that the eldest took the title of Lord of the Western Isles. He also decreed Dunvegan Castle should remain uninhabited until the rightful heir should appear. He renamed it Cair Nonesuch until that time. Even though Skye was not actually part of the Western Isles but a neighbor, nobody wanted to argue with the eldest dragon.

"It wasn't quite deserted. People were hired to care for the castle. The Lord of the Western Isles made sure provisions and payment were provided for those keeping the castle prepared for the return of Clan MacDonald. At the same time, he would not discuss what had happened, or why things were as they were.

"The MacDonalds were not, as you might guess, exactly thrilled. But while the Lord of the Western Isles is protecting the castle from invaders and usurpers, and providing well for it, they're willing to wait, though I am not sure for how long.

"Anything else?"

"Yes," Gerald said thoughtfully. "Why did he tell us so much? Such as the limits of relic protection?"

"You would have learned that anyway, but this way you know. It is an offer of goodwill, of trust. Technically it indebts you, but because he allowed questions, the result is that no one incurred a debt. This happens most naturally in a neutral zone with many relics.

"And now, let us withdraw to this castle's dragon treasure room below the keep to see what relics we have and hear some stories."

It was all the others could do not to race each other down the stairs.

CHAPTER TWENTY-SEVEN

HISTORY LESSONS

They stopped after many flights of stairs, including several below ground, when they could go no farther. Before them stood a massive stone door with two guards. Cuthbert produced a large iron key, which one of the guards used to unlock the door. The guards then pulled on a massive rope across a pulley system to open the ponderous door. When Cuthbert and the young men were inside, the guards used a second rope to close the door. Cuthbert then locked the door from inside and returned the key to somewhere in his robe.

"This room is locked at all times. It is the heart of the castle's defenses and offenses, the safest place in all of Donald's kingdom." Cuthbert used his torch to light the oil in a trough on the wall by the door. The flame spread quickly along each wall until reaching the other side of the door. Cuthbert pointed at the walls.

Everyone gasped. They knew the walls were stone, but they could scarcely see any for all the dragon bones, hide, scales, teeth, and nails. A central beam across much of the ceiling was a seven-yard long horn. Horned dragons had not been sighted in over a century and had always been rare. Few of the young men knew of anyone who spoke of seeing a horn, much less one this large.

"This is the safe room. Here are not only dragon relics and weapons guarded against dire need, but also food for a year for two dozen people. Water comes in here," he indicated a hole in a wall to his right, "flows through this trough across the floor, and out there." He indicated a hole at floor level on his left. "The water comes from an underground spring discovered while building the castle. I know of no way an enemy could touch it.

"If all the dragons in Europe came against us, the castle might not stand, but we believe this room would."

"But there's no way to know that, is there?" asked Afagdu.

"Not without inviting all the dragons to assault us, no." Cuthbert smiled wryly. "But we have been able to perform some tests. Do not ask, for I am not at liberty to say. But the results were most satisfactory."

The class looked around. Gerald went to a rack of swords.

"May I?" he asked.

Cuthbert nodded. Gerald pulled out a claymore. It wasn't the longest or the most ornate, but it drew him.

"Why that sword?" Aed asked.

Gerald stared intently at the sword. "It called me. See how it shines?" He moved away from the others to a more open space and swung it carefully over his head. It hummed powerfully as it clove the air, shimmering and leaving reddish trails behind it like miniature dragon fire.

Cuthbert studied Gerald a moment. "That is the second most powerful dragon sword in all of Great Britain. We believe the first to be permanently lost. You say it called you?"

Gerald was barely listening, staring raptly at the sword. "Yes. Yes, it called me. I heard my name. And I can almost see battles. . . ." He slowly lowered the point to the ground, staring off into the distance as if atop the keep rather than deep under the ground. "I see much death. I see dragons fighting dragons, men fighting men. I see men and dragons fighting. I see a dragon flying weakly, a sword in her breast, falling at last into a volcano. I see this sword . . ." He paused. ". . . I see this sword being used finally against a man rather than a dragon."

Shaking his head, he seemed to realize where he was. "Why? Why, Cuthbert?"

"I cannot say, Lord Gerald."

Gerald started at the title, suddenly noticing how everyone was staring at him.

"But know this: the sword was brought here from Dunvegan shortly after the castle was cleansed of MacDonalds. You have seen more than most who have held that sword. We believe the sword that flew into the volcano with the dragon was the most powerful dragon sword in history. You must speak of this to Torquil and the king first chance you get."

Gerald nodded. At Cuthbert's gesture, he returned the sword to the rack.

"Cuthbert, who was she? The dragon who fell into the volcano?"

"She was the eldest then, and mother of the current eldest and Nain."

He waited, but Gerald asked nothing else.

"All right, then. King Donald and Captain Murdoch have both mentioned they've heard that many of you ask why Cair Parn is situated here along the Orchy rather than atop one of the peaks within a day's ride?"

All the students nodded.

"I'd have wondered had you not asked!

"When Cair Parn was built, almost four hundred years ago, the nearby mountains, Ben Cruachan, Ben Heasgarnich, and Bidean nam Bian all had dragons living upon them. These dragons were not opposed to men but had no intention of giving up their homes on the mounts. The MacGregor clan had already come to a truce with the dragons, but they were afraid that if they built a fortress, the dragons might be upset. So they went about indebting the dragons.

"They informed Arvis, atop Bidean nam Bian, of a plot by a clan to the north to kill him. Gorgon, who had but one head though five horns atop it, nearly lost her wings in a typhoon. When she limped home to Ben Cruachan, the MacGregors slaughtered a herd of cows and several herds of goats and sheep, hauling them up the slope to feed her. When Vajay, atop Ben Heasgarnich, wiped out another herd of cattle, the greatest MacGregor dragon lord, Ulf the Hammer, led a party of men into hiding while Vajay was off west. When she returned, they sprang their trap, and Ulf had Drachlaird, the sword Gerald held, against an unprotected spot on her throat. But he spared her.

"Having secured debts, Clan MacGregor called the dragons down to Glen Orchy a week later. There they forged the Treaty of Orchy, agreeing that so long as the treaty was honored, the dragons and the MacGregors would owe each other nothing beyond the treaty, which called for peace between the parties, and for each party to inform the others if they heard of plots or attacks coming against them. It also stated that each dragon was entitled to its mountain, and that Cair Parn would be built along the Orchy. It would be safe against dragons: the three dragons would breathe their fire upon it, adding to its strength against other dragons but rendering it vulnerable to these three."

Aed interrupted. "How does that work? It makes no sense to me, and I see not why the MacGregors would do it in any event."

Cuthbert nodded in respect. "Excellent points! Because the treaty canceled debts yet is in itself a debt, it allowed the dragons to participate in ways they could not otherwise. And dragon fire on dragon relics always has that effect, if the owners agree. They knew they could trust these dragons, and now had protection against others.

"When the MacGregors brought their great store of dragon

bones and such from hiding, which was about half what is in the castle walls today and a quarter of what you see in this room, the dragons were amazed and angry. 'Why have you killed so many dragons?' they demanded. But Donald MacGregor was able to account for every relic. The MacGregors had killed only three of the dragons, all in self-defense. The rest they had found in caves, in the forest, on the coast, or had taken from raiders. As you know, dragons can sense truth, so they calmed down.

"The dragons breathed fire in turn and together on the relics. These were then incorporated into the building of Cair Parn. The MacGregors in turn helped the dragons each recover an egg from one of its nemeses as protection from those dragons. That treaty held as long as the dragons lived."

"Excuse me," Justin said. "Why Cair Parn? Why not Castle MacGregor, or Orchy Castle, or Donald?"

"Cair is the word dragons use for an enhanced natural fortress. They consider this castle natural for reasons unclear to men." He smiled. "Parn is simply their name for this valley. It means, more or less, 'Place of Life and Refuge.'"

Cuthbert now moved to the table farthest from the door. He indicated three goblets made to resemble dragon horns and covered with dragon scales—one red, one orange, one a pale green. "These are the Horns of Treaty, made by men, the scales given freely by the dragons—a great gift. Such scales from a living dragon live as long as the dragon lives. A great enough dragon lord, especially a seer, can speak to the dragon through the scales and hear from them the same way.

"What happened to the dragons?" Aed demanded.

Cuthbert smiled sadly. "Dragons from the Far East tried to move in. There was a great battle. All were killed but Vajay, who flew east a week later to either treat or exact vengeance for the attack. We never heard of her again, and no one knows what happened. But a month after she left, someone thought to check the goblets and her scales were dead.

"Before she left, she entrusted her last clutch of eggs to the McGregors. She set logs on fire around them, and they guarded the eggs against other dragons until they hatched. The dragonlets came out of their eggs to sword point to deepen their debt to the people, that they might not ever attack the clan. They flew away, and no MacGregor saw them again."

They spent the rest of the morning learning the history of various swords and relics, and a great deal more history of the castle and the clan MacGregor. At noon, Cuthbert grabbed a stone hammer and struck once upon a gong mounted to the door. As soon as he unlocked it, the guards opened the door and they left the heart of the castle behind. Gerald wished he could have a month in the room with the lore master.

Cuthbert left them at lunch time and did not return for two hours. Giving no explanation, he led the class back atop the keep.

"What sorts of questions have you still?"

Gerald spoke. "I've been wondering about using dragons' names. When is it safe? I've some idea, but from things you and the dragons have said, I'm guessing I know less than I thought I did. . . ."

"This is certainly true for all of us, and a crucial lesson to learn about anyone, but especially about dragons. The rules are tricky and amorphous. Too much use of a name can put one in debt. Using your own name can sometimes balance the debt, but can never indebt a dragon to you. Also, too much use of your name can lead to contempt. In that case, instead of balancing the debt, the debt becomes much worse, often catastrophically."

Shantaigh, a quiet lad from the east, spoke up. Gerald had heard him so seldom, he didn't recognize his voice.

"Why do we know so little about them? Our village elders, all dragon lords, said that nobody knows where they come from, or why at times they seem so many and at others so few."

"We know far more than your elders realize, but until

recently that knowledge was limited to a few. In discussions between the greatest dragon lords and the dragons, it was decided that both groups should know the history of the other as much as possible. We . . . the hope is that this will foster understanding and peace between us."

He paused to gather his thoughts. "We do not know where dragons began, or when. We assume it was at creation, when men were made, but we know not. All the stories say that men come from the east, below Europe, near where two great rivers meet. There are only rumors of where the dragons began. One set of rumors says that they began near men along those great rivers. Another says that dragons came from somewhere here in Britain. No rumor, even from other lands, suggests that dragons came from anywhere else. This seems telling.

"But while Britain has always had more than its share of dragons, we have no evidence that the dragons began here. We know only that they have long been here, often in large numbers. Certainly, nowhere else man lives seems to have the sheer number of either dragons or relics that we do.

"As to the waxing and waning of dragonkind, dragons are not immortal, but they might as well be from man's perspective. From the fragments of records that have survived mankind's constant wars, we know that dragons existed as far back as the great floods, and likely before. We have the dragons' word that some of them have lived several thousand years. The Lord of the Western Isles has told the best seers that he is almost four thousand years old, and that his mother was among the first dragons on earth.

"He has said this both while looking them in the eye and while they looked away. None have sensed anything but truth. Whether he is correct, we cannot of course know, but he certainly believes it. He is almost certainly correct as far as his own age goes."

There was a moment of silence as Cuthbert let that sink in. Nothing of man's was known to be that old. That was a hundred generations or more. Even given a long life of 100 years, that was almost forty lifetimes.

Gerald shook his head in wonder.

Cuthbert continued. "Dragons do not seem to have sickness as we know it, though their wounds often seem to spread as if rotting. Dragons die mainly from three causes: natural disasters, other dragons, or battles with men. I have not heard of any dying of old age, although some have gotten old and tired and simply chose to cease living."

Peter interrupted. "The church teaches that suicide is a sin."

Cuthbert raised an eyebrow. "Dragons are not humans and are not subject to all of the same laws. It is said that past a certain point, it is left to them to pick their time.

"According to the oldest dragons, men and dragons originally existed in peace, even friendship. Some great calamity happened, known interestingly enough to both dragons and Christians as 'the fall.'"

"What do the druids call the fall?" asked Iain.

"The druids do not believe such an event happened.

"The dragons blame men for this fall, and men blame a woman, though as I hear it, the man was equally to blame! At any rate, men and dragons slowly grew to distrust one another, eventually becoming mortal enemies. And just as men turned against each other, dragons turned against each other. Many dragons died, and most of those who survived fled far from each other.

"Times of peace between men and dragons have come and gone. For the most part there has been at best an uneasy, scattered truce between the two, except with humans the dragons respect or to whom they owe debts.

"At some point in the not too distant past, dragons disappeared from the Isles, and indeed from most of Europe. For almost two hundred years, long enough to relegate dragons to mythical status, no dragon was seen across most of Europe. But almost overnight, Britain was invaded, then all of Europe. This led to speculation that they came from the west."

Justin interrupted. "Speaking of the west, what of Wales? Why has it no dragons?"

"Ah. Either no one knows, or that is the best kept secret in the history of the world. I believe it to be unknown, but judging by Aed's and Afagdu's expressions, they are not so sure?"

"Lord Cuthbert, I am not," Afagdu said, while as Aed shook his head in agreement. "I trust no dragon."

Cuthbert nodded knowingly. "Neither did Gerald." He looked inquisitively at Gerald, who sighed and thought briefly before responding.

"I still don't know how I feel about dragons. But having dealt with several, with one having saved my life, and even a mad one having helped me, I no longer either hate them all or mistrust them all. I would trust the one who saved my life with anything. I think I trust Nain as much. As to the others, I know not, save for those with a certain name. Only one of those remains, and I plan to see him dead.

"Speaking of which, we are in Argyll, Lord Cuthbert. Were the dragons with that name from here?"

"No man knows how dragons choose names. I know that the three of whom one is your bane (and you his) come from near the lake on the Thurso River in the north. I know of no connection between them, or their mother, and the region here."

Since there were no more immediate questions, Cuthbert spent the rest of the afternoon telling them of various battles, of famous dragons and dragon lords, and of ways that problems were settled cleverly, without loss of life. After supper, the young warriors tended their horses and spent the evening in lively discussion. Most of them now had more questions than before the lessons started.

Gerald fell asleep pondering Wales. Much of the night he dreamed of walking across that country. He saw no humans, but the skeletons of dragons gathered about him—walking, running, even flying—until a great army of them had amassed. As he pondered what to do with all the skeletons, they collapsed, turned to dust, and blew away. He awoke feeling very lonely and sad. It was at least an hour before dawn. He gazed at the moon through the window until he fell back asleep. Twice he thought he saw dragons fly across it, but they might have simply been birds.

If he dreamed after that, he never remembered it.

CHAPTER TWENTY-EIGHT

FAIR TRADES

Late in the week a merchant caravan began its trek through the valley (which Gerald and his class now thought of as Parn). A rider came a day ahead to announce them, but of course, a border guard had arrived with the news well before that.

The following morning, during the brief time between breakfast and axe drill, Donald of Lochlorien hailed Gerald and his friends and waved them to come up on the wall. Behind the castle was a trader's caravan spread along the Orchy River, with dozens of colors glowing, shimmering, and waving in the early sunlight and breeze. Gerald and Justin had never seen one so large, but others said it was merely a decent size. Large or not, all were eager to go down.

When they reported to drill, Folkvar had them line up with Dree's class and march to the gate—one of the few times they all marched anywhere. From there they were free until noon. They scattered quickly across the caravan, joining adults already haggling with the vendors. Men and women, jauntily dressed to attract the opposite sex, called out from each wagon. Most vendors carried several types of goods, but some specialized. Gerald and Justin halted in front of a display of intricate jewelry. Afagdu nodded his approval but hauled Aed toward a display of unusual weaponry.

"Welcome, young warriors!"

Gerald and Justin looked up from the jewelry and stared. The merchant was a young woman in her twenties of almost unearthly beauty, dressed in bright colors, with long, reddish-blonde hair that wandered well down her back, ringlets constantly in motion like so many dragon tails. Her eyes were hazel, fading between green and blue as she shifted her gaze.

"I am Kenna of Bennu. Do you like my jewelry?"

Both young men nodded mutely. Gerald turned red as he realized he'd been staring at a pendant on Kenna's chest, afraid she would misinterpret his gaze. But she laughed, reached to her left, and pulled one very like it from the wall. She offered it to Gerald as Justin examined rings.

It was a miniature dragon in flight, wrought of fine silver threads, with slivers and curlicues of something that wasn't quite ivory woven throughout where a skeleton would be. It had eyes of jet black, reflecting the sunlight far too much for such dark material. As he held it near his face, fire washed over his hands. He nearly dropped the pendant but caught himself as he realized it was a vision. In seconds all was normal, except that the dragon still seemed to be breathing fire.

"Justin, what do you think of this?"

Justin glanced at it and whistled appreciatively. "It's beautiful, all right." He went back to looking at a ring. Clearly he had seen nothing unusual.

Gerald looked at Kenna. "This isn't ivory. It's dragon bone. And the eyes . . ." He stared at them a moment until he was sure they were really shimmering. ". . . Dragon scales?"

Kenna stared. "Who are you to recognize such a thing so young?"

Justin spoke, as if from far away. "This is Gerald, the youngest dragon lord."

Kenna spun and gently took a ring from Justin. "I'm sorry.

I should have warned you. Don't stare at this one too long."

Justin shook his head dully. "What just happened?"

Kenna sighed. "That isn't exactly a jewel. It's what we call the heart of a dragon's eye. I've only seen one other. They're beautiful, but I'm starting to think they are too dangerous despite their beauty. Some people respond to one as they would any amazing jewel, but some people get sucked in and take a long time to come out." She looked at Justin until he looked back into her eyes. "What did you see?"

"I . . . I'm not sure. It was constantly in motion, like the sea, only it was a sea of love. I wanted to drown in it." He shook his head. "That sounds crazy. It felt crazy. I don't think I want that ring."

Kenna dropped it into a pouch at her belt and sighed. "It ought to be worth a fortune, but either nobody wants it or it reduces them to gibbering idiots. No offense."

Justin shook his head again. "None taken; I was well on my way to gibbering. Thanks for putting it up. Doesn't it affect you?"

She shrugged. "To me it's simply beautiful. Like a living ruby, thinking out loud."

Gerald and Justin looked at each other.

"Right," said Gerald. "Anyway. Is everything you do made from . . ?"

Kenna placed a finger on his lips and called out to a man walking up. "Good day, steward! What can I do for you this trip?" She winked at Gerald, who resumed looking over the merchandise.

Justin found a matching ring and bracelet of intricately interwoven silver wire sprinkled with tiny emeralds of exquisite quality. Gerald found several things Sally would like, but nothing quite matched the dragon Kenna wore.

After a few minutes of selection and arguing, the steward sauntered off with a fine set of buttons of silver, ebony, and ivory, sure he'd gotten the better end of the deal. Gerald arched his eyebrows at Kenna.

Kenna smiled. "Yes, everything here is made from dragons and silver. The dragon bone and scales are from the same dragon, washed in dragon fire by his mate before she left his side the last time. My father, who rides with the fall caravan, is doing something with the hide. He won't say what."

"Your work is exquisite," Gerald said. Justin nodded vigorously. "But I have yet to see anything as lovely as the dragon you wear."

Kenna laughed. "I'm afraid this one's not for sale. I made everything else here, but this one was a gift from my father. He taught me the trade after I came up with the idea of incorporating dragon relics into the jewelry. Someday I hope to equal his work. But here," Kenna reached beneath a shelf and brought out a small cloth, "is the best I have for sale."

Gerald held out his hand and gasped as Kenna dropped something into it. Where her other works and the dragon on her breast were flat, this one had depth, like a sculpture. It looked very much like a real dragon falling on prey, wings arched high, claws extended, mouth open as if flaming something. There was incredible detail in it for something less than two inches long. He looked at it from every angle. It was perfect.

"Kenna, who made this?"

"I did. Is something wrong?"

"Yes. No! You were wrong. This is above even that which you wear. I have seen a dragon in battle that looked just like this. Where have you seen such?" he asked intensely.

Kenna moved uncomfortably. "Only in my dreams." She hesitated, then blurted out, "But I am not a witch!"

"What?" Gerald laughed. "I never thought that. But you must be a seer if you have seen this without seeing a live dragon. A seer with vision to match her beauty."

Now it was Kenna's turn to blush.

Justin grinned. "He's engaged. Don't fall for his flattery."

Gerald cuffed Justin. "Don't talk crazy! I'm serious."

Kenna broke back in. "What do you know of seers, Gerald?"

"I have a gift, and I have spoken much with Cuthbert and Torquil. When I first held your pendant, I saw dragon fire."

Kenna relaxed and her face softened. "There have been dragon lords in every generation of my family, as far back as we can know. But seeing deeply began with my father and flowed to me."

"So who treated with the dragon for the bones, hide, and scales?"

"I did."

"Are you then a . . ."

"No! I spoke with only the one. That was more than enough for me."

Gerald laughed. "I know the feeling!"

"I was terrified. But she was gracious, and I have enough to last a lifetime and then some."

Gerald thought that an understatement but said nothing more on the subject. "What did she want in return? Unless she was mad?" He looked concerned.

"No, I had what she wanted, and I gave it—my promise that all my works would show the beauty, the grace, and the power of dragons, and that it would never be in a form to cause men to hate them, only to admire them. She lost her mate to a man maddened by dragons killing his family for no reason. She seeks peace with men."

Gerald nodded a bit uncomfortably; while he was comfortable with certain dragons, he still wasn't sure about them as a group. "How much for this?"

"One tenth ounce of gold."

Gerald didn't hesitate. He brought out a small nugget from

his pouch and she shaved off small flakes onto her scale until it measured the right amount.

"Is this for your betrothed, Gerald?"

He nodded.

She wrapped the dragon in red silk and sealed it with a white ribbon. She turned to Justin. "The ring and the bracelet are a quarter ounce of silver."

Justin reddened. "I have no silver, but I have something I want to sell."

Kenna looked skeptical. "Let's see it."

Justin pulled out the jewel-encrusted knife. As he held it up in the sunlight, Kenna gasped, but a cry from two wagons down got everyone's attention.

"I'm buying that, Justin! First rights!" Afagdu ran up, pushing Justin's hand with the knife down and out of sight. "I forgot you had that, friend! Has she made an offer yet?"

Gerald stared at Afagdu, sure he hadn't seen the knife before. "No, I . . ."

"Good, good. How much for your presents for the princess?"

"Princess?" Kenna demanded.

"Princess," Gerald affirmed, grinning. He'd explain after things calmed down.

Justin told Afagdu the price, and Afagdu pulled out the exact amount from a belt pouch, surprising Kenna. She looked closely at him for a moment.

"I know you! I have seen you in Glasgow, at Sinclair's shop!"

Afagdu stared. "You know my uncle?"

"If Sinclair is your uncle, yes. My father and I have dealt with him often."

"Of course! That's where I have seen you! I work with the buyers; he's not yet had me working with sellers. But I have seen you and your father."

"So let's see this knife again. Don't worry; I won't start a bidding war." Kenna smiled a dazzling smile.

Gerald knew right then he would not want to have to argue with her.

The three young warriors and Kenna made a close circle. Afagdu held the knife up for all to see.

"I thought so, even from twenty yards away. This is the bastard art of Gillean, the greatest weapon maker in Scotland until his death twenty years ago. He sometimes made what he called art on commission. It was big and gaudy, but it usually brought him good money. This piece was paid for in advance, but the buyer never returned. When Gillean died, the piece was found to be missing, with no clue as to where it had gone."

"How came you by it?" Afagdu demanded.

Justin provided an abbreviated version of his quest. "By all accounts, this druid was above reproach. I assume he was given this either as a gift or in payment for something."

Afagdu shuddered. "It's hideous. Maybe they were mad at him."

Kenna nodded vigorously.

Gerald laughed. "It's a terrible knife, even though the blade is exceptional quality."

Justin held out his hand. "Ugly or not, may I have it back?"

Afagdu handed it over. "Kenna, what would you pay for this knife?"

"It's worth more than I could pay. It's worth at least eight ounces of gold, even to someone who doesn't know of Gillean."

"On the open market, yes. Justin, Uncle Sinclair could get you twice that by shopping it to collectors. He'll want a commission, of course, probably ten percent, maybe as much as twenty. But I promise, you'll come out richer than you would otherwise."

Kenna shook her head. "I don't think so."

"What?" Afagdu asked angrily.

"A pound of gold? No. I think your uncle can get even more

than that for Gilean's Lost Knife."

Justin laughed and handed the dagger to Afagdu.

"What?" the latter asked. "Just like that?"

"Just like that," said Justin. "I trust you. And I have witnesses." He waved his hand across the display. "Including dozens of dragons."

Afagdu handed Justin an ounce of gold. "This is a downpayment. Will it do for now?"

Justin looked stunned, having never held an ounce of gold in his life. "Yeah. I reckon it will."

The rest of the morning was spent in similar fashion among the other merchants, although none of them had goods as exciting as Kenna's or Justin's to trade. Gerald found a brass buckle with an onyx dragon for Cle's sword belt, and a few trinkets for friends back home. The only other purchase of note was a dozen yards of silk by Aed, who wanted it for his sister's wedding gown.

"Few merchants come to small villages on the moors, so we have a day's trek to a market where there is seldom anything this nice. My sister is betrothed to a wealthy farmer on the coast. I want her to have a nice gown."

He'd haggled a long time for it. The others suspected he'd used all his savings but said nothing. They'd have done the same. The lunch bell tolled. As they turned to leave, Gerald waved farewell to Kenna.

A mist covered the landscape. Gerald froze. He could see nothing around him, but a soft, blue light shone dimly through the mist before him. He walked toward it. He came to a tree, a great oak where he knew no trees grew. In fact, he ought to have been standing in water. The light came from overhead. He looked up.

A boy and a girl—perhaps six years old—sat holding hands in the tree, laughing and talking. The boy glowed with a bluish light, the girl an emerald green. The girl could have been a younger Kenna. They looked at him, laughed, pointed, and vanished.

The tree vanished with the children. Now a stag stood immobile before him, bathed in blue light. A green light appeared and Kenna stood with her arm lightly and tenderly across the stag's back. They both looked alertly north. He realized it wasn't quite Kenna. They faded.

The mist cleared; the day was bright again. Gerald stood not in the river, but where he'd stopped. His friends had gone a few steps farther and now looked back at him impatiently. He waved them on, and ran back to the caravan.

Kenna was counting the morning's take. "Do you need something else?"

Gerald shook his head. "Who are you?"

She tilted her head. "I told you. Kenna of Bennu."

Gerald looked around to make sure no one could hear, then looked back into Kenna's eyes. "You are of the faerie."

"I'm sorry. What did you say?" Clearly wary, Kenna's face had become a stone mask.

"Are you descended from Merlin?"

Kenna looked at Gerald a long time before she spoke. "Gerald the youngest dragon lord, please ask me no more questions. But if I were you, I would never doubt my sight." She turned back to her counting.

Exhilarated and nervous, Gerald turned and ran for lunch.

He was late; the boar meat was gone. They offered him venison. Remembering the stag in his vision, he took only cheese and bread. One of the cooks mentioned Gerald's refusal to eat meat to Ivor and K'pene. He spent the afternoon reassuring everyone he saw that he felt fine.

Late in the evening, Gerald cornered Justin. "Was Kenna the trader you fell for a couple of years ago?"

Justin looked blank for a moment, then laughed. "No. She could easily be related, but I don't think it was her."

Just as he fell asleep, Gerald realized that faerie powers might have confused Justin—if indeed Kenna had been the same one. He decided it didn't matter, rolled over, and went to sleep. He tossed and turned all night and awoke sweaty, exhausted, and nervous. He couldn't remember dreaming.

CHAPTER TWENTY-NINE

VISIONS

The next two weeks passed routinely. Gerald and his classmates honed their skills with axe and dirk, tested their bow and arrow skills on horseback, and worked with different sized targes to see which they liked best. Evenings were spent comparing notes, speculating about dragons, or talking about home. The midsummer harvest and planting break was nearly upon them.

A week before they were to head home, a page startled Gerald at breakfast with a summons from the king. Gerald was even more surprised when the page led him not to the king's chambers but to the keep's dining room. Inside he found King Donald sitting in a window much as Gerald liked to do—one leg across the sill, one dangling to the floor. The king glanced at Gerald, smiled, then resumed staring thoughtfully out the window.

Cuthbert sat at the adjacent table along with Captain Murdoch, Torquil, and K'Pene. They all nodded and smiled at Gerald as Cuthbert waved him to an empty seat between Murdoch and K'Pene.

The king turned to face them. "Gerald, I have a favor to ask of you."

Off balance, Gerald still answered quickly. "How may I

serve you, my king?"

Donald smiled tiredly. "It will take some explaining. I assume you are looking forward to going home for the midsummer harvest and planting?"

"Of course, sire."

"And you know that Cuthbert leaves the day after tomorrow for Skye, to meet with the Lord of the Western Isles?"

"Yes, sire."

The king glanced at Cuthbert and continued. "The Lord of the Western Isles dwells on North Uist, across the Little Minch from Skye. He has called Cuthbert to Dunvegan on Skye. Cuthbert will cross to meet the dragon in the ruins of Lochmaldie. Normally, this would be no cause for concern."

Gerald sat up straighter as Donald continued.

"Cuthbert, it seems, has been dreaming of disaster and not bothering to tell us. I only found out after both Torquil and K'Pene also dreamed of danger and came to me."

Ivor walked in from behind the wall-hanging leading to the roof. "I have had no such dreams. But then, I never do." He sat on the window sill near Donald.

Cuthbert sighed. "While I was troubled by the dreams, I hoped to have an explanation before I went to the king. Never has the Lord of the Western Isles proved faithless. But I dreamed of other dragons, of fighting, of treachery."

K'Pene smiled enigmatically at Gerald. "Torquil and I dreamed of Cuthbert going with a standard escort, but we both also dreamed of him taking you. Each time we dreamed this, disaster was averted, or at least lessened."

Everyone looked at Gerald.

"There's more," the king said. "Murdoch?"

"Gerald, what do you know of Kenna?"

Gerald looked confused. "Kenna? The trader?"

"Yes. You have dealt with her."

"Yes, sir. I bought a pendant for Sally."

"And was that all?"

"Yes, that was all I bought."

"Gerald!" The king's tone froze him. "What other dealings have you with this woman?"

"Oh. I had . . . a vision."

"Go on."

Gerald sighed and started over. "I had a vision. I believe she is of the faerie folk, descended from Merlin."

Torquil looked excited, the others slightly skeptical.

The captain asked, a bit more gently than the king, "And did you ask her? How did she answer?"

"I asked. She did not answer directly, but seemed to give assent."

The king spoke again. "Cuthbert insisted we could trust her. He would not say why. Normally that would have been enough, but I knew there was something eerie about her."

Cuthbert spoke quietly. "I have never found the faerie to be anything but faithful."

"You knew she was faerie?"

"I did."

"Then why did you not say so?"

"It was not my secret to tell. They are a wary folk, having been much maligned and persecuted by man."

"Do you know this Kenna?"

Cuthbert smiled. "Now that Gerald has let the cat out of the bag—and I believe that to be a good thing so long as it stays within this room—I can say that I do."

"I hate secrets," Donald grumbled. He nodded at Murdoch to continue.

"The caravan left ten days ago. Yesterday, Kenna reappeared alone at the castle gate on the most impressive mare I have seen. Kenna asked if Cuthbert was going to the coast to meet with dragons. She had seen a vision … or rather, several: In one she saw Cuthbert dead or wounded while dragons raged in battle. In another, she saw you, Gerald, and Cuthbert watching from a castle while the dragons battled. In yet another, she saw herself with the two of you, and you were all speaking to dragons; there were far fewer battles.

"She asked to accompany the two of you to Skye."

"But, but I am not going to Skye," Gerald stammered.

"And therein lies the great favor I have to ask, my Lord Gerald," the king noted. "Would you delay your trip home and accompany Cuthbert to Skye? I will not command this. I only ask."

The room was as quiet as anywhere Gerald had ever been. Far away, somewhere on the Orchy, he heard gulls cry.

"You need not answer now," the king added. "But we must know by this time tomorrow morning."

Gerald nodded, unable to find his voice.

K'Pene spoke. "If you wish to speak with Kenna, she is staying in the women's quarters near me."

The king rose, waving the rest to stay seated. "Gerald, today is yours to do with as you wish. I'm sorry to burden you with this. I know you wish to see your family, your betrothed, and your friends, and to help with the harvest and planting. But you have some idea of Cuthbert's value to this kingdom, and indeed to all of Scotland. No other human in Great Britain, or as far as we know in Europe, is so respected by the dragons, or knows as much about them."

"I know, Your Majesty. I cannot fathom Scotland without him."

Cuthbert's eyebrows twitched, but he said nothing.

"I must be about other business now. If you have questions for me, inform Captain Murdoch and he will bring you to me." The king strode from the chamber, lost again in thought.

The captain took over. "The time until you answer is yours, Gerald. You may speak with any of us about anything that will help you make your decision, but the king must know by tomorrow after breakfast. And please, do not speak of this unnecessarily."

"Yes, sir. And no, sir."

"Do you need anything from me now?"

"No, Captain."

"Very well. I, too, have work to do." He left.

Torquil smiled wryly. "The rest of us, of course, have naught to do but laze around and watch the scullery maids and pages."

Gerald laughed, realizing he had not even come close to smiling since his summons a half hour earlier. "Unless they have had dreams or visions, I have no business even with them at the moment." He looked more somber. "Please, tell me more of these dreams."

But there was no more to tell. If Cuthbert went alone, things looked dire—certainly for him, definitely for some dragons, probably for Scotland. If Gerald went as well, things looked better. They looked best if Kenna accompanied them both. What would happen if only Kenna and Cuthbert went, no one knew.

"Not that we seem to know much at all," Torquil admitted.

Gerald stared out the window for several minutes. He envisioned dragons fighting, falling into the sea, great clouds of steam rising. He thought of them falling to land, crushing homes, fields, cattle, people. He saw endless lands on fire. But in the end it was just his imagination. These were not visions.

"What does it mean?"

"We don't know," Cuthbert spoke plainly. "Except that it means no good for any of us if I go alone. I cannot imagine anyone challenging the Lord of the Western Isles; he is not only the eldest, but the largest, cleverest, and wisest. But something is brewing, and if he should fall, our peace would likely fall as well."

"But I thought we had treaties with many dragons and debts to hold most of the rest at bay."

The other three exchanged grim, knowing looks.

Cuthbert stroked his beard. "To some extent we do. But much of the peace we currently have was brokered by the Lord of the Western Isles. In bringing about that peace, many debts were wiped out. And the laws of debts between dragons are somewhat different than those between dragons and men. Many debts dragons owed men were canceled through this peace as well.

"I doubt the Lord of the Western Isles is indebted, but where he was once nearly untouchable, if enough dragons rose against him now, he might lose. And we might then have war with dragons such as we have not had in centuries."

"If that were to happen," K'Pene said, "people would again distrust all dragons. All the peace we have won would turn to hatred and war, and most dragons would again distrust all of us—man, woman and child. Many would die; much land would be burned and lost. I came here hoping to one day take a dragon lord back to my home, to train my people to slay or indebt dragons, to help bring about peace there. Now I wonder if I will not flee back there to seek a hiding place safer than here." She smiled wistfully. "I do not wish to go home that way."

Gerald nodded. He really felt he had no choice, but he wanted to think. "Thank you, all. If I have more questions, I will find you." He bowed his head to each, for he respected and loved them, and left.

Staring somewhere inside himself, Gerald wandered aimlessly through Cair Parn. He noticed only enough to avoid collisions or falling down stairs. Eventually he went through the front gate, arbitrarily taking the leftmost path down to the Orchy. Or perhaps it wasn't arbitrary. He found himself near where he had bartered with Kenna and was not surprised to find her there.

She sat on a log, arms holding her legs to her chest. Chin on her knees, long hair gently in motion despite the lack of a breeze, she gazed peacefully into the pool before her. Her hair looked slightly redder today, but perhaps that was mere contrast to her layered green dress—some type of gauze over something silky. Gerald froze when he realized the green was the same shade as the light he'd seen about her in his vision.

"Welcome, Dragon Lord. Yes, that is your title. More than that, it is truly your identity. You did not want it solely to kill dragons because of your pain and anger; it is part and parcel of who and what you are." Still she had not looked up.

"May I join you on the log?"

Slowly she sat up, dropping her long slender arms by her sides and her lithe legs to the ground. She turned and smiled, patting the log. "Come. Sit."

Gerald's world was unmade. He felt as if the Faerie Queen had just offered him her hand in marriage. He trembled.

Her radiant smile dimmed somewhat, as if she realized her effect on him. "Have no fear. I will not bite, nor would I enchant, even if I could, in the way you are thinking. Come and sit by me. Please?"

Gingerly, Gerald joined her. He tried to relax but felt like a warrior preparing for battle. He laughed inwardly—he felt more like a stag ready to flee the unknown.

"That is better, Dragon Lord! Laughter, even quiet laughter, is a far better defense than most people know. Now, why did you seek me out?"

"I didn't seek you out. I just went for a walk."

She looked at him carefully. "So I see. And yet a part of you sought me, expecting me to be here."

He shrugged. "If you say so. If I did, I didn't know it." He wasn't quite sure how to deal with the faerie world. It threw him off guard more than visions, dreams, or dragons ever had.

"Why do you fear me, Gerald?"

His answer surprised them both. "I see beauty. I see power and grace. I see heaven and hell. I see a servant and a mighty queen. I have never seen anyone or anything like you, and I know not who or what you are, or who or what you may become." He halted there, ever so slightly red-faced.

She stared at the pool a long, quiet time. "I see all of that and more, and neither do I know who or what I may become. But I know who I am, and what I choose to accept and reject." She looked up at Gerald. "One thing you missed in your vision two weeks ago, Dragon Lord, and it was key. Yet I am glad you saw nothing of it then.

Kenna cut Gerald off before he could react.

"No, do not ask! You will know when it is time. But know this now: I utterly reject evil and have no desire to take anything that is not mine, including men's hearts. I wish to see peace among men and dragons. I wish to see Cuthbert safe. I wish to see King Donald live to a ripe old age on his throne, with a line of worthy successors."

She turned to him and smiled, this time intentionally veiling it to avoid blinding him. "And to see you grow into the dragon lord you already are."

It was Gerald's turn to smile. "That makes no sense."

"Oh, it does. But don't worry about it. What else do you wish to know?"

"Everything."

"Everything about what?"

"You know. Everything."

She laughed. "As do I!"

"Then tell me of your vision."

She did, but it was no more than he already knew. "And before you ask, if I try to see myself with Cuthbert without you, I see only empty night. As if it cannot be. Certainly there is no point in it."

Gerald nodded. He'd suspected something like that. In fact, he'd felt quite sure since hearing the various dreams and visions that he really had no choice. He realized his mind was made up, but he didn't have to discuss that just yet.

"Why is it so hard to be around you?"

She looked up, surprised. "Is it?"

He reddened again. "I'm sorry. But yes, it is. I feel like . . . I feel like . . ." He couldn't really explain it, and it would sound silly if he said it out loud.

Her face softened. "I am not quite human. You have seen just a little of the faerie in me, but I am still a created being like you. Do not worship me. And do not fear. You will not fall madly in love with me, though it may have first felt like that. Gerald, I told you that you see clearly. It is difficult for men to look on faerie. Your eyes are not used to it. Perhaps human eyes cannot get used to it, or at least only the strongest may do so, but you are strong and will become stronger.

"Remember to laugh! If you feel strangely toward me, or toward anything of faerie, just laugh. The odd feelings will soon pass if you do."

She looked at him thoughtfully. Suddenly, she laughed. It was the laugh of a silly, teenage girl, not a woman in her twenties. It was the laugh of a child. It was the laugh of a crazed, old woman. In it he heard Sally laughing, and Samantha, Freda, Myra, K'Pene, and many others. And suddenly he was laughing too, laughing so hard he nearly fell into the pool before the log. It lasted only a minute, but once it passed, he was sitting next to Kenna the trader, not Kenna the faerie queen.

He wiped tears from his eyes, gasping for breath. "Thanks. I needed that."

She grinned mischievously. "I think I did too. Now go, and think on the things you need to think on. Ask the questions you need to ask. Don't bother Cuthbert; you can talk to him on the trip."

Gerald jumped down off the log. He bowed, thanked her,

and walked off toward the wood. More than anything, he wanted an hour with Sally and Cle—both for their counsel and his love for them. And perhaps an extra hour with Sally. He laughed again at that, just a bit. He really missed her.

But the one thing it seemed he would not be getting any time soon was time with Sally and Cle.

He talked it through with them in his head. They laughed at the idea he would even consider not going. Then Cle looked at him seriously. "You will find favor and safety in the strangest of places, cousin."

Gerald found himself in a strange place about then, sitting six feet off the ground in a tree. He didn't recall climbing a tree, and looking around saw no reason to do so. The last part must have been a vision. It didn't seem as clear as his visions normally did, but it had to be one. He shrugged, climbed down, and headed back toward the castle. There was no point in delaying telling the king of his decision; it would make everyone's planning easier, including his own.

Gerald slept peacefully that night, happily untroubled by dreams.

CHAPTER THIRTY

ILLUMINATION
IN THE FOG

Cuthbert had prepared for a month and Kenna was always ready to travel, but Gerald spent a rather frantic day preparing. By supper he was ready. They left before dawn the following morning.

It seemed to Gerald that adventures should start on glorious days, but the morning had arrived shrouded in fog. If anything, the fog had thickened by the time they left. Gerald stuck close to Cuthbert and Kenna, their escort ranging loosely ahead and behind, Folkvar close by.

They rode in silence at first, some affected by the dismal damp ride, others pondering the coming days. Between the muffled sound of the horses' hooves on the damp trail and the constant drip of condensation from the trees and rocks about them, Gerald had to fight to stay awake. It felt like the fog was creeping into his brain. His thoughts were gray, misty, and hard to see through, dripping into oblivion.

Cuthbert broke the silence as they climbed yet another invisible hill in the drab world. Gerald was thankful for the interruption until Cuthbert's words worked their way through the mists of his mind.

"Young warrior, at some point we must duel. Did not the fate of my life, and perhaps Scotland, hinge upon your presence at

Dunvegan, I would already have challenged you."

"What?"

"You heard me! You let that dragon call me a dotard and never answered her! Unless you were calling yourself a fool!"

Gerald laughed. He heard Kenna and Folkvar snort nearby.

"Certainly I am a fool! Only a fool loses his horse, especially far from home, and only a fool incurs a larger debt thereby to a dragon!"

"Ah! Then all is well, and you need not feel my wrath."

"My Lord Cuthbert, you cannot imagine the depths of my relief."

"Good. I am glad you are contrite."

"No, Lord. I meant that your mind could not conceive of anything so minute!"

Everyone laughed. Then Kenna spoke. "Gerald, what did you wish to ask Cuthbert?"

"Who said I wished to ask that old dragon anything?"

"I did."

He could hear the smirk in her voice. He thought a minute. "Very well, you are right. In fact, I will question him until my voice gives out, or until his gives out answering . . ."

Cuthbert growled, "Young pup, do your worst!"

". . . And if his voice gives out, I shall keep asking questions until it returns!"

Cuthbert groaned. "I may have created a monster, but you, Kenna, are playing mother to one all too well, nursing his demands this way!"

Kenna feigned innocence. "I? I am merely a teacher, encouraging the young warrior to learn all he can from the wisest and best known of lore masters."

"I am ambushed from all directions. Ask away, young dragon lord."

Gerald almost choked hearing the affection in the banter.

It felt like they were family—Cuthbert his venerable great grandfather and Kenna his sister, older by a few years.

Or was she? It suddenly struck Gerald that in stories of faerie, age was deceiving. But he would not ask that, at least not here and now with others about.

"My lord, it is no flattery to call you the greatest dragon lore master, and all know you are one of the greatest dragon lords alive."

"Only one of?" Cuthbert protested.

"I have seen no definitive list."

"Very well, go on."

Gerald was surprised at how relaxed the lore master was away from the castle. But that question, too, could wait.

"Since you are respected by all, including the dragons, why do you wear dragon scale mail for this trip?"

"I wondered when you would ask!" Cuthbert paused, reverting from easy banter to his teaching mode of speech—slow and thoughtful, even when he knew the answer well. "For one thing, it is my right, as a lore master and as the dragon lord who earned the scales of these dragons. Yes, dragons. Surely you noticed the multitude of colors?"

"Of course. At first I thought they were like Kenna's eyes, reflecting light differently based on surroundings, but I soon saw that they truly varied in hue. And I wondered ever more, for I spent an hour looking at that mail in the treasure room yesterday eve."

"What? How did you get back in there?"

"The king asked what I needed for the journey which I did not yet have. I said that so far as I knew, I lacked only a deeper understanding of dragons. I knew I could not get all I needed in a lifetime, much less an evening, but it was the truth. And King Donald, bless his soul, escorted me to the safe room and left me there from supper 'til nearly midnight.

"At first I thought there were only a few colors, but the longer

I looked, the more colors I saw. There were definitely at least two dozen, and probably more. Yet from what I have heard and seen, I cannot believe you killed twenty-four dragons, much less fifty. Whence came those scales?"

Everyone could hear the delight in Cuthbert's voice as he answered. "Gerald, no one besides Donald and Murdoch has ever asked me this!"

Kenna laughed. "I did not need to ask."

"No, of course not. I do not believe I could have any secrets from you, my lady, even if I wished to."

"Nae, Lord. I would respect your secrets. And I do."

"So I do have some?"

"Three, I think."

"Now that I think more on it, I have at least three, and perhaps five. But perhaps not. Never mind.

"Gerald, I am, indeed, too old to be your father, by more years than you reckon. In my time I have slain fifteen dragons, but I have treated with far more. From some whom I defeated in battle but did not kill, I took a scale, preferably one they lost in the battle, as that in no way incurs or impacts a debt.

"Some were given me as a token of appreciation, and a few to pay or pay down debts."

"But why?"

"Can you not guess?"

"Does it protect you more from those dragons?"

"That, my young friend, is an excellent question. But for reasons unknown, protection in general is always greater when the relics come from multiple dragons. This is true no matter the relic. It is so with bones, hide, claws, teeth, horns, the hearts of their eyes, or anything else.

"If all the dragons in Europe were to use their flames at once, the very rocks at my feet might burn or explode, but I would be unharmed."

"So a dragon cannot harm you while you wear that!"

"Not quite, young warrior. Remember what happened to Samantha? The scales only work against magic. Flying is not magic, and neither is dropping something—whether that is me to my death or a boulder to crush me.

"I am sorry to bring that up."

Gerald was quiet for a few seconds. "It's all right. I cannot hide from the past, and not a day goes by that I don't think about it."

"And what do you think about it?"

"Once I wanted to kill every dragon on earth. Today, I want to kill one dragon, or possibly two. There may be others I will yet want to kill, or have to kill. But today I want to understand them, talk with them, watch them, learn all about them. Only then will I know what I truly think of them or want to do about each of them. It is not as simple as it was in my youth."

"Wisdom is seldom simple, and even less often simply gained."

Gerald could not see Kenna, but her voice held a gentle smile. "I have seen boys grow to men, never losing their shortsightedness, their hatred, their hurts, their rejection, or their prejudice. I have watched them die old and bitter, cursing even those who loved them."

It just popped out. "How old are you?"

She laughed out loud, low and musically, befitting her looks of twenty-five years. "Ask not questions you do not wish to know the answers to! For I assure you, you do not wish to know. But know this, I am as I appear. Among the faerie, I have lived only a small portion of life, enough to have been an adult for a little while, but still young, adventurous, and full of the joy of youth. When we first met you thought me, what, twenty-five?"

"Um, more or less."

"In my people's years, that is about right." Her voice became wistful. "Just don't be surprised that I always look this way to you, Gerald. I know it is rough on humans."

"Perhaps so, but there's actually something refreshing about knowing that beauty and good are forever."

"Thank you, Gerald, for that, but we are not immortal. Rather, like the dragons, we are very long lived, appearing immortal only to humans."

"Immortal enough. Forever enough for me."

Cuthbert laughed. "Yes, that is true. Give up, Kenna; the young man knows who he is and who you are."

"And who am I?"

Gerald thought only a few seconds. "If Cuthbert is right that you are nurturing my inquisitiveness, then I suppose you are like a mother to me, despite our both being only recently out of childhood. So you are my faerie godmother."

Even the scouts in the van laughed, albeit nervously. Most of them were not as comfortable around the world of faerie as Gerald seemed to be. In fact, some of the guards had discussed only the evening before whether Gerald might not be of the faerie, or under their enchantment.

Gerald continued. "Kenna, when you came as a trader, you pretended to be human. Why do you now speak freely as faerie?"

"It was hard to let go of my disguise because many humans fear us, but we can have no secrets from one another on this trip. Cuthbert and King Donald trust every man here with us; therefore, I will trust them as well."

Gerald was silent for several minutes before remembering to ask more questions. "Lord Cuthbert, what sword do you wear on this journey?"

"Some things are better left unsaid in the open, Gerald."

"Very well. Of what use is the heart of a dragon's eye?"

Kenna spoke somberly. "Some things are better left unsaid in the open."

Gerald sighed.

"Fine. What is this meeting with the Lord of the Western Isles about?"

Cuthbert waited at least a minute before answering. "We might guess, but at this point I do not wish to do so out loud. Yet given the visions and dreams around the trip, and around us, there is much more afoot than whatever the Lord of the Western Isles has planned."

"I saw visions in the safe room last night, and I dreamed once in the barracks. Though I do not recall all I dreamed, I recognized some of the dragons. What is odd is that in my dream I knew several of them, yet there are only three dragons I have met who live." He thought briefly and added, "If you can count being carried in a mouth as meeting one."

"Three? Are you forgetting Nain?"

"Yes. Four."

Cuthbert nodded seriously. "And what were these dragons doing in your dream?"

"They were arguing. They were fighting. They were . . . posturing? Such as men might do when they try to provoke others into attacking first, or attempting to convince others that they must go along with them to avoid battle. But I don't recall what they were arguing about, or even whether I knew that in my dreams."

"And your visions?"

"Were silent, as silent as if I had no ears. I remember reaching up to make sure I had ears. At one point, with my hands over my ears, I could hear my blood pounding. I realized I could hear my breathing. I spoke aloud and it seemed wrong to do so, but the visions were as silent as the grave."

"Such were not mine," said Kenna, "save one. And in that one, dragons died."

Someone in the rear guard murmured, "Better them than us."

"Perhaps," Cuthbert replied. "Perhaps. And yet perhaps not. We do not go to this meeting to prevent my dying, but apparently to prevent war among, and almost certainly with, the dragons."

A deep voice spoke from overhead. "Happy am I to hear you say that, Cuthbert!" Dragon wings beat the air. The wind in their wake swirled the mist, which was finally fading. Before any could reply, the dragon was too far off to hail. Sunlight poured through rifts in the fog. Perhaps it would be a glorious day after all.

"Who was that, Cuthbert? Do you know?"

"Young warrior, I cannot say. But now you have met five dragons who yet live."

Kenna spoke close on Cuthbert's words. "Nor can I say who that was. But she is a friend, or at least an ally. Whoever she was, we were well met."

"She?" Gerald asked.

"Oh, yes. Of course! Could you not tell?"

Cuthbert replied for Gerald. "Remember, Kenna, that our young warrior has not spent much time among dragons. And few dragon lords can tell from a voice in the mists what sex a dragon might be."

"If you say so. I am primarily familiar with you and with Murdoch, and you two have no trouble."

"But we are, if I may say so, exceptional."

"You certainly are, my Lord Cuthbert. And Murdoch is a jewel among men."

"Aye."

The fog melted away. A moment later they topped another in the endless series of low mounts they seemed to always be going up or down.

"Why did we come this way?" Gerald asked. "Would not the plains have been easier?"

Folkvar replied. "Why came we this way? Because this trail

was easiest in the fog. I know that seems odd, but it's true. Highwaymen and ruffians love to wait up high and ambush the lower trails on such days, and we have no time to fight or deal with injuries. Were I not detailed with getting you all safely to Skye, I would be leading men down those trails to hunt the hunters. Also, while the trail would be flatter it would be much farther, with fewer landmarks."

"We won't be scaling the highest peaks, will we?"

"Binnein Mor is the tallest. We will pass east of Ben Nevis shortly before we stop for the night. But that is hours away. Today is the longest ride of the journey."

"I am sorry you are saddled with such wearisome folk," Cuthbert replied.

"Nay, my lord! We are thrice honored by the company we escort. And if I hear any more grumbling from the rear, I will feed someone to dragons at Skye!"

"If it will free me from your high and mighty words, I will leap into the dragon's mouth!"

Gerald twisted around to see who challenged Folkvar, but Folkvar merely laughed. "Fret not, young warrior; that is my half cousin, Norbert. Yes, I know you had a cousin with that name! I am his senior in life by five minutes, and his senior in the army by a day and a half. I can best him with a bow or spear, but I know of few who can best him at sword or knife work."

"Name one, cousin!"

"Murdoch, and Donald."

"That's two, not one!"

"No, it's three. I meant both Donalds." The men around Norbert laughed.

"Look, Gerald." He turned at the sound of Kenna's voice. She wasn't pointing, but staring in the distance, as was Cuthbert. It took a moment but finally Gerald made out (just barely) three dragons in the distance, probably miles apart, all flying toward

Skye.

"Three dragons?"

"More," said Cuthbert, but offered no number.

"I see six," Kenna replied. "No, eight."

Gerald stared but was rapidly losing the three in the distance. "I wish I had your eyes, Kenna."

"But then how should I see?"

Gerald wasn't sure why he laughed as hard as he did, but he was still snickering occasionally as they descended into the last of the fading fog. The morning was only half over, but he was ready for lunch. The day was flying by and crawling at the same time. He was ready for Skye. He was ready for dragons.

As he recalled his visions, he decided the dragons could wait.

CHAPTER THIRTY-ONE

MERLIN, ELIJAH, & DUNVEGAN

A n hour before sunset the third day, they approached a stone tower.

Gerald pointed. "What is that tower? It looks ancient."

Kenna glanced around, but the others simply nodded at her. "This is Dun Troddan, one of two broughs, or stone towers, here. It is over a thousand years old. Folkvar's people called them borgs. As their names imply, they were originally forts. They fell into disuse for hundreds of years, but some came back into use, such as this and Dun Telve, the brough two-and-a-half furlongs farther on. They needed work: while the main part of the brough is dry stonework, the floors and roofs were wood and thatch. The old wood rotted. Newer wood was cut, dried, and sealed to make it last. The roofs are now slate, brought from one of the islands in Argyll.

"Legend has it that this brough was set to watch inward while Dun Telve watched outward, but I don't believe that; an outward facing tower should have been nearer yon larger river. Whatever their origin, when the dragons returned, the towers were set as both watchtowers and refuges. The stone itself is just that, but there are relics in the storage spaces between the inner and outer walls and beneath the slate."

Folkvar spoke up. "Few hereabouts will speak of these. Even some of the king's men avoid them if they can. But they are merely old forts and, at times, guard towers. I have heard that Danes and Picts worked together to build these. As Kenna said, they were rebuilt as watchtowers. Since the Lord of the Western Isles has taken up residence nearby, they now mainly serve as storehouses, lodgings for those like ourselves traveling through, and markers to let travelers know they are near Fionn's Bridge."

"Fionn's Bridge?" Gerald asked as they passed Dun Telve.

"Aye. Fionn's Bridge. It's where we cross the Kylerhea. Otherwise we'd have to take the ferry, which would take many trips for our horses and gear, or go a little up the Kylerhea and swim the horses across. Either way would take longer."

Gerald heard grumbling from the rear.

Folkvar laughed. "There's nothing to fear from the bridge or from talking about it. We will spend the night in Kylerhea."

"What? The river?" Gerald asked.

"Of course in the river, my Lord Gerald."

Gerald managed not to react to the title or the sarcasm.

"The town across the river is also called Kylerhea. It is the gateway to Skye from the mainland, the strait just up river being the narrowest nearby crossing from the mainland. And, of course, there is the bridge, but the ferry was here well before the bridge. Ah, here we are."

The company was quiet as they crossed the bridge, concentrating on the path in front of them. The bridge was of a black rock unlike anything Gerald had seen—pockmarked, uneven, and somewhat shiny, reflecting the sunset dimly in myriad directions. The horses took their time on the uneven footing. There appeared to be many sharp edges; Gerald knew he would hate to fall on this roadway.

"And here we are," Folkvar announced a few minutes later. He turned aside and led them to the edge of town as the last daylight began to fade. "Tonight we will stay here at the King's Inn, run by warriors who retired from service only because of injuries. They keep one wing set aside for the king's envoys, warriors, and other such groups. Dree and Drinn rode ahead to secure quarters for us."

"Will they still be here?" Gerald asked hopefully.

"No," Cuthbert replied. "They were to give word of our arrival and return to patrol. King Donald and others have all sent men to scour the coasts for raider camps. And here we are!"

"Is this an inn or a fortress?" Gerald demanded. The outer walls slanted and entrance ways showed the rock was very thick before the doors. Crenellated walls ran the perimeter of the roof.

Norbert responded. "It's somewhat of both. Vikings and pirates have plied these waters. Raiders still come to Skye. A wise man keeps his sword handy here, just as in Argyll."

"You've been here before?"

"My father was one of the owners 'til a pirate stove his head in."

"Oh. I'm sorry."

"As were we all. But Ma cut the pirate's head off. Da would have been proud."

Stable hands came out to help as they dismounted. A big man with a limp approached with a lantern.

Folkvar spoke. "This is Gilchrist Cameron, clan leader in Kylerhea and master innkeeper here. He will show you to your rooms." He hugged Gilchrist like an old friend and handed the reins of his horse to a stablehand. "Breakfast at first light, Cuthbert?"

"Yes, Folkvar. We will camp in the open tomorrow. We should make camp while there is plenty of light. Stow your gear and let us eat. Gilchrist keeps a fine table."

The next morning, Gerald ate two of the biggest eggs he had ever seen. "What are these?"

Kenna replied. "Have you seen the cormorants?"

"The what?"

"Cormorants. The big black birds out on the water."

"Ah, of course."

"Big birds lay big eggs. They usually lay several at a time. The faerie only take one from each nest so that each family of birds has offspring. The local people do the same."

"That's very thoughtful. Do they do the same with humans?"

"Of course! Unless there are twins. It's cruel to separate twins."

Folkvar interrupted. "Do not joke about this; there are those about who will always believe the worst of the faerie, and I for one wish better relations between us, not worse."

"As do we all," Cuthbert added.

"Of course," Gerald and Kenna agreed.

A half hour later the sun rose redly through wispy clouds and they set off across Skye. Gerald moved close to Kenna and asked her softly, "Why Fionn's Bridge? And why do the men seem nervous?"

Kenna glanced discreetly around before answering softly. "Legends say Fionn forced giants to build the bridge and they resented it, promising to return and wreak havoc on those who use it. I believe dragons built it, but that story should wait for another day."

That day and the next passed in similar fashion. There was banter. There was silence. Gerald ran out of questions near the end of the third day. Late afternoon the fifth day near Dun Beag Broch, Gerald remembered to ask something he had pondered a long time.

"Cuthbert, it seems that for much of history, dragons are seen as mythical creatures. How is this possible?"

Kenna and Cuthbert exchanged an odd look. Eventually Cuthbert began.

"As I have told you, in the beginning dragons and men got along quite well. But anger, hurt, and suspicions ran deep after the fall. Men blamed the dragons—called serpents at the time—for leading them astray. The dragons blamed men for believing foolishness. Mistrust grew like an evil weed.

"The dragons soon tired of the taunts and harangues by men. Eventually one dragon ate a woman who had harassed her for months. Afterward, aghast at what she had done, she went before the council of elder dragons. News had already reached them of the humans' anger at the woman's death. They decided to move away from the lands where humans dwelt. And so they left.

"The dragons were comparatively few. They spread out across the face of the earth and dwelt mostly alone or with only a mate. At times they met together; each time seemed more tense. Yet they still avoided humans. Within perhaps two hundred years, they had become myths. It is common, I am afraid, that within a few generations, people quit believing the tales of their ancestors. Fact becomes legend, legend becomes myth, myth becomes merely an old story. After a thousand years or so, men walked into a valley where a dragon named Elijah lived."

"Elijah? You're kidding!"

"I am not. Many of the old names of prophets and other justly famous men, such as Merlin, were first borne by dragons."

"Merlin? A dragon's name?"

Kenna broke in briefly. "Yes, and later the mage was right proud to bear that name. The dragon Merlin was a prince among dragons."

Gerald wore an odd look. "Did you know him? Merlin, the dragon?"

She laughed. "Of course not. I told you, I am young!"

Her laughter slid down Gerald's spine with a dangerous thrill. Sometimes he was afraid being around Kenna would draw him somehow into the land of faerie and he would never come out. Part of him loved the idea. This scared the rest of him. Gerald returned his gaze to Cuthbert.

"Elijah had never wanted the dragons to separate from humans. He was glad to see the men. He invited them to come feast with him. They accepted, but deep inside they were terrified that Elijah planned to eat them, or worse yet, bend them to some evil will. They had listened to the rumors and speculations of the fearful and hateful that if there had ever been dragons, they were evil. So though they ate as his honored guests, when Elijah relaxed after the meal they slew him with their newly perfected weapons, their swords.

"From that day forward, there has been a great deal of enmity between us."

Gerald shuddered. To kill your host at a meal was base treachery. Even the savages they faced knew this much.

"Why? Why did they do this?"

"Because it had been a thousand years since anyone had seen a dragon. The stories changed in that time to the point that all dragons were deemed evil, wanting sometimes to seduce men to some dark purpose, and at other times to simply eat them. And men, as ever, wanted someone to blame for their problems and foolishness.

"During the days of war that followed, many men were killed but few dragons. Yet because mankind was multiplying like ants and dragons seldom laid eggs, men were coming out ahead. The dragons fled all areas containing people. As generations again passed without dragon sightings, the dragons again became mere myths in men's minds.

"People eventually stumbled upon them wherever they were. When this happened, whoever struck first usually survived. But always, someone knew of the encounter and took word back to others of their kind. And so the enmity became a deep-rooted hatred. Mankind would sink back into smug superiority until dragons faded into myth. Then something incontrovertible would happen and reality would reassert itself.

"For nearly two hundred years before the year of the Truce of Carlisle, no dragons had been seen, at least in Europe. Few believed in them beyond the most superstitious, despite a plethora of skeletons and hides.

"Then, seemingly out of nowhere, hordes of dragons appeared from the west. They battled each other all round Wales. Eventually the survivors flew farther east, plaguing Ireland, Scotland, and England. They were drawn to battles, where men were too busy to notice them coming and too weary to fight well. Had not Danbury, Wallace, and Moray the good sense to ally, or had the English Crown refused to treat, we might all be dead save a few—reduced to near savagery—hiding in caves.

"Both the druids and the Augustinians had preserved the knowledge of dragons. They brought their knowledge to the lore masters, and where possible to men high in the armies and to royalty. The English Crown refused to listen to the druids, still declaring them under the Ban, which meant their heads if they identified themselves. England did, however, listen to the Augustinians.

"The reinstated Balliol here in Scotland, and most of the kings under him, were happy to listen to anyone who might aid them in defeating the dragons. Balliol charged Robert the Bruce with bringing peace between the druids and the church, something unheard of since Merlin's time. The Bruce never said how he did it, but accomplish peace he did, at least here in Scotland. It has held until now, although there is again tension between the two.

"So for the past two hundred years we have fought and treated with dragons. The uneasy peace uniting the kingdoms here in our land, and uniting Great Britain with most of

Europe, always starts to unravel when the dragons are quieter. But wherever men gather to fight in large numbers, dragons arrive and we soon band together against a common enemy. Or what we perceive as our enemy."

Cuthbert sighed and drank long from his water skin.

"Fifty-three years ago, the Lord of the Isles—John MacDonald II—plotted rebellion. He planned to carve out the Isles as their own nation and make a treaty with the English Crown, which still hated the idea of Scotland being equal rather than subservient. Word reached King Donald, our king's grandfather, who sent word to the high king of Scotland, MacIver, in Stirling. MacIver prepared an army to march to Dunvegan, but the day before they were to leave, a flock of Voices showed up craving audience with the high king."

Cuthbert smiled. "His majesty's advisers were sure it was an evil enchantment and demanded that boiling oil be thrown on the birds. Thankfully an old druid prevailed, offering to speak with the birds himself. When he returned, explaining that they brought news from a dragon, the king was beside himself. Eventually, although two visiting bishops renounced him, he listened to the birds.

"This is what he heard: 'Your Gracious Majesty, High King of Scotland, I am now Lord of the Western Isles, the eldest dragon alive in Europe, if not the world. I wish only peace with men. The castle at Dunvegan is empty of MacDonalds; I now call it Cair Nonesuch. I have taken steps to make sure it is kept in good repair against the day the rightful successor to the castle appears.

"'If it please the king, I will dwell in the ruins of Lochmaldie, and sometimes in a cave near Stornoway, and I shall guard the Isles against all invaders and treason. If it does not please the king, I shall still dwell there, but we will likely have war. If the king will grant me the island of Taransay and all the animals thereon, with herdsmen unafraid of dragons to tend them, I will continue to keep up Dunvegan, and no dragon shall trouble the Western Isles.

"'I, the Lord of the Western Isles, have spoken.'

"The high king of Scotland called the kings of Scotland together. It took only a day for all to agree to accept the offer, truly a modern miracle."

Kenna interrupted. "Or perhaps they were all thinking of MacDonald and Dunvegan."

"Perhaps. In any event, there have been Voices of the Lord of the Western Isles at Stirling Castle since that day, should the king wish to speak with the dragon in the Isles."

After a moment Gerald asked quietly, "And to this day, nobody knows what happened to MacDonald and his court?"

"The night watch had seen nothing. When the staff awoke that morning, they soon found the castle had only two people present who were not castle staff. Both were visitors—Farquhar the Bruce, and the high king's great niece, Hilary, who was there to reject suitors."

Kenna laughed. "That seems a strange reason to be somewhere."

Cuthbert shook his head. "Several suitors were present to lay claim to her affection. She wanted nothing to do with them. But until she had heard them out and rejected them, she was not free to discuss her true desire in life—to become a dragon lore master."

"Good for her!"

"Yes, good for her, save that most of her family was against the idea. They all wanted her to marry well. All, it seems, but the high king, who was content to back her.

"At any rate, when it was realized that so many people . . . if I recall correctly, the number was in excess of one hundred . . . had disappeared, the staff began to panic. With the help of Farquhar, mainly using his imposing appearance and great sword to bar people from leaving until they heard Hilary out, she calmed most of them. She sent word to Stirling, but of course they already knew. In fact the king's emissaries arrived at Dunvegan before word from Dunvegan reached the king."

"But how could that many people simply disappear?"

"Gerald, it is one of the great mysteries of this age. I assure you it was discussed to death at the time. I was there for the discussions, as were some of Kenna's relatives."

"Some of my longer-lived relatives," she said, with an impish grin.

"Nothing of note has happened at Dunvegan since, except that the Lord of the Western Isles somehow convinced most of the staff to stay on permanently. They say he pays handsomely, which I assume helped. While most of them have retired or passed on, their children and children's children have stayed on in their places.

"We don't know how the Lord of the Western Isles forged a truce or imposed his will on the other dragons, but the Western Isles have been free of dragon troubles, and indeed of most other dragons, until now. But we have seen dozens of dragons heading that way, and a Voice has told me of yet more coming."

"I didn't think there were dozens of dragons left in all of Great Britain," Gerald said thoughtfully.

"The number is unsure, but I do know that some of these dragons come from other lands."

Gerald started to ask another question when a Voice landed behind him on his horse and addressed Cuthbert.

"The Lord of the Western Isles knows that you planned to arrive in the morning, but he asks that you make haste and come tonight, whatever hour that may be."

Before anyone could ask questions or remark on his arriving alone, the Voice was gone.

"Only one," said Gerald. "I thought they always flew in groups."

"The groups may split up and travel separately. But I do not like this. Let us make haste!"

Most of the day they had kept the horses to a fast walk or gentle trot, but now Cuthbert had them gallop as long as he thought they could, then cantered the remaining few miles across Skye. They came at last to the castle at Dunvegan.

Though it was after dark, the castle was well lit.

A dragon crouched between them and the castle gate.

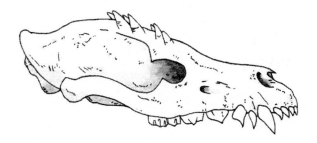

CHAPTER THIRTY-TWO

A STRANGE NAME

As the escort scrambled to move between their charges and the dragon, Cuthbert yelled, "Hold!" and they halted. Cuthbert then spun around as he heard steel being drawn. "Gerald!"

But Gerald already had his claymore aloft in salute. He waited on Cuthbert, but the lore master simply stared at him as if he had forgotten the dragon, so Gerald spoke. "Hail, Santana!"

The dragon nodded. "Hail, Gerald. Tread softly here, young warrior."

Gerald nodded in turn.

Cuthbert recovered. "Hail, Santana, Protector of the Good, Defender of the Weak, Deliverer of Lore Masters . . ."

A flame of laughter escaped Santana's lips.

Cuthbert ignored the flame. "What brings you here?"

"The same thing that brings us all—or rather most of us—here, a summons from the Lord of the Western Isles. But there are unwanted guests coming soon as well. You must all," and he looked at each in turn, though some of their escort refused to look in his eyes, "be constantly alert. Trust in nothing and no one unless you know them."

Cuthbert nodded. Santana stared at Kenna for a moment. "Lady Kenna, I am both concerned and ecstatic that you are here. Welcome. And you must beware more than the others."

She nodded, a grim smile playing across her lips.

"And now, my Lord Cuthbert, you must come with me across the Little Minch. I will carry you."

"Wait!" cried Gerald. "I thought we were all three to go! We must!"

Santana turned his head sideways to look at Gerald fully with one eye. "When you dreamed of this day, and when you foresaw it, where were you?"

Gerald thought for a moment. He pointed with his sword at the castle ahead. "Some of the time I was in the castle, and some of the time we were on the island."

"Exactly. For now you and the lady Kenna must remain here on Skye. You should probably share the room at the top of the keep, from which you can best see across the Minch. I suspect you will be sent for tomorrow. Cuthbert?"

"Gerald, sheath your sword!" Cuthbert smiled, then prodded his weary horse toward the dragon. About twenty paces away, he dismounted, turned the horse, and slapped its rump. It trotted gratefully back toward the others as Cuthbert walked up to Santana. In an instant, a great claw was about the lore master and the pair was in the air, flying toward South Uist.

As they watched the dragon disappear into the night, Gerald turned to Kenna, but before he could open his mouth, she spoke in her command voice.

"We must get into the castle immediately!"

All obeyed without thinking. Guards and servants awaited them inside the gate, which shut as soon as they entered. Their horses were unlade and sent to stables, the escort was taken to the mess for a late supper, and Kenna and Gerald were shown at Kenna's request to the upper floor of the keep. The maid and page exchanged knowing looks as they left.

"Well, Gerald, it appears that I have impugned our honor in doing as Santana suggested!"

Gerald cocked his head. "My lady, I will happily remove their heads for sullying your reputation, but not before they bring us food and drink."

"My lord, I greatly appreciate your offer, but perhaps if they spend some time with us, they will recognize the error of their ways and save you the trouble of cleaning your sword."

"My lady is ever wise and gracious." Stowing his weapons, Gerald slumped onto a window ledge facing northwest. He saw fire in the distance, some miles across the water. "What is that?"

Kenna joined him at the window. "It appears that something—I've no idea what on those barren hills—has been set ablaze with dragon fire. Perhaps that is for Cuthbert's sake. Dragons have keen eyes and see nearly as well in the dark as during the day."

"As do the faerie folk?"

She smiled. "The dragons' sight is as far above ours as ours is above yours."

Gerald shuddered. "It's a wonder they didn't simply kill us all."

"They tried for a while, but you had too much of a head start on breeding. There were ten thousand or more humans for every dragon by that time, and it only took the right human out of a thousand to kill a dragon." She looked sadly at Gerald. "Too many people and dragons were lost. It is time to stop the madness."

"Is that why we are here?"

"I hope so."

"You do not know?"

"Do you?"

"Of course not, Kenna!"

"Nor do I. I know what I saw, what you and the others saw. I know what Santana said and what others have said. That is all."

They were staring out the window, wondering if Cuthbert was safe, when the servants returned with their meal—goat, quail, greens, bread, and apples. It was better fare than Gerald had seen in weeks.

Kenna laughed. "Take this back!" She handed the surprised maid a cluster of saxifrage flowers from the tray. "We are neither married nor lovers, but are in this room together only to keep watch upon South Uist. You two need this where we do not."

The maid blushed, glanced at the page, and fled the room. Grinning foolishly, the page followed her.

Kenna turned back to Gerald. "On Skye, saxifrage is in vogue as a blessing for young lovers, whether engaged or newlywed. Those two are not yet engaged, but it is written all over their faces that they soon will be."

"Of course it was, my lady." Gerald had seen nothing but wasn't about to admit it. Not that she wouldn't know...

"May I sit beside you on the window, my lord?"

"Please do," Gerald said as he turned, patting the ledge beside him. "And fear not, I shall not enchant you, at least not in that way."

Both laughed as she joined him. They sat like children, feet dangling outside, unafraid of the long drop to the rocks below. Sunrise found them asleep against one another. How they had not fallen is anyone's guess.

Gerald awoke first. As he gently awakened Kenna, he laughed. "It's a good thing the servants did not find us sleeping together, if only in the window!"

When he heard giggling behind him, he very nearly did fall as he spun around. A laughing Kenna caught him. The page and maid were laying out breakfast on the table. Kenna nodded, and they left.

Kenna feigned horror. "Now you have truly besmirched my honor, sleeping with me!"

"On a windowsill."

"Still."

"That's what got me engaged, you know, sleeping with a girl."

"I know."

"You don't!"

"Gerald, your story is legend among my people."

"What? Now I know you are teasing me."

They walked to the table, sat, and talked as they ate, watching all the while through the window.

She smiled. "No, I am not teasing. One of my folk heard of Argyll eating your parents. Then he had a vision of you asking for help. He went to watch over you. He arrived the day you took to the woods. He followed you all those months you wandered. Have you never wondered that a child should survive so long in the woods?"

Gerald laughed. "Not when I was a child. Later I did a bit, but since I had survived, I didn't worry about it. But if someone were protecting me? That would explain it."

Kenna rolled her eyes. "If? I'll give you 'if.' Three bears, six wild pigs, an eagle, at least a dozen poisonous creatures, and a mad skunk. Never mind several rogues."

Gerald whistled. "I had no idea. Please thank him for me, whoever he is."

Her face softened. "It was my father. And I will."

"So your father is not a jeweler?"

She laughed again. "No. Only I in all my family have been in such a trade. The human I call father is more of a godfather. And he is fully human, by the way. When he 'adopted' me, as it were, he was only twenty-four. Now he is near sixty. These days that is old for a human, though once you were longer lived." She gazed sadly into the distance.

"Most of my people do not form friendships with humans. It is painful to see you age and die, and many humans come to resent our seeming immortality.. . . ."

Dropping her spoon, she gripped Gerald's arm and pulled him to the window. Even Gerald could see a great many dragons hovering like flies about something.

"What are they doing?" he demanded.

She stared for a few heartbeats. "There are two large dragons; the others are flying around them. Some of the outer dragons seem agitated."

"How can you tell that?"

"By how they fly, just as you can tell when a man is agitated by how he moves. Remember, I have been around dragons a long time."

After a moment Gerald asked, "Are there more of them or are they moving closer?"

"Both, but only a few more have joined the flight. Wait. . . . One of the large dragons in the middle has broken away and is coming toward us. None of the others are following."

They ran down the stairs and through the castle, coming out the front gate just as the dragon landed fifty paces from the gate.

"I have come to carry you to the ruins of Lochmaldie. Are you ready to go?"

Hands on his hips, Gerald stared at the dragon, though this was hard to do since its white scales reflected the sun almost blindingly. "Who are you?"

"You may call me Younger." His voice, the deepest Gerald had heard, boomed off the castle walls.

Gerald slitted his eyes, trying to make out the dragon's expression. Kenna smiled and bowed to Younger. Gerald bowed as well before continuing.

"Younger is a strange name for a dragon."

"My brother gives no other name and neither do I. I am the second oldest dragon alive. My brother summoned your friend Cuthbert, inadvertently summoning you two as well." Flames of laughter licked the ground in front of the dragon. "And as I know who you two are, may we not fly?"

"But . . ." Gerald started to protest.

"Gerald," Kenna suggested gently, "if he wanted us dead, we'd be dead."

Gerald had to agree, and there was really no alternative. He and Kenna walked forward into those terrible claws more than twice their height. In less than five minutes, they were deposited gently on the shore beside an utterly devastated city.

"What happened here?" Gerald asked.

"Dragons fought, and men," Younger replied. "The city is littered with the bones and hides of dozens of dragons and the remains of countless men. My brother ordered them left as a memorial to the dead, as a reminder why we must not fight each other. He declared this a haven where all may meet without fear of magic being used against them."

"But does that not leave dragons susceptible to the tricks of men?"

Younger shook his great head. Gerald got dizzy watching. Despite having smaller claws, Younger was even larger than Nain.

"While it is certainly possible, it is unlikely, unless the man were mad. To even plot against a dragon under such circumstances, and more so to attack, indebts one to the dragon. Likewise, a dragon cannot safely try to use claws or other, non-magical means against a human here.

"So go quickly into the ruins. You are somewhat safe out here, but safer within."

The walked into the ruins. Kenna's eyebrows shot up.

"Seldom have I felt such power in a graveyard."

Younger's beautiful white eyes darkened. "Seven of the

twelve eldest dragons, including all five of the females, died here in the fight alongside numerous others. It was not a good day for dragonkind."

"What were they fighting over?" Gerald asked.

Kenna opened her mouth to answer, but Younger spoke first.

"I will not say. But you may guess before you leave."

Kenna closed her mouth. She would not speak a dragon's secret where the dragon would not speak it. Gerald didn't seem to notice.

"Thank you, Younger," Kenna said as she bowed.

Gerald did the same.

The dragon bowed his head and replied. "You are most welcome. Thank you. Cuthbert should join you soon. Perhaps he can tell you what will come next." With that enigmatic remark, Younger took wing.

Within a moment he was gone. Gerald and Kenna stood staring at rubble. Not far away was the skull of a dragon. It was large enough they could have stood side by side in it, peering out the eye sockets. Half of its teeth were broken.

Gerald wondered what it took to break a dragon's teeth. He looked at Kenna. "I don't think I'd want to live here."

She couldn't argue with that.

CHAPTER THIRTY-THREE

THE DECREES

Their original plan was to explore the city while they waited, but there was no city to explore. There were only piles of rubble intermixed with dragon and human remains.

They found a stunted tree and sat in its meager shade. Occasionally they sipped water as they talked and watched dragons flying in the distance. Sometimes the dragons landed for a bit, but some of them quickly took to the air again. Some appeared to remain agitated about whatever was being discussed.

"He seemed almost human. Younger, I mean. At least, he was the easiest dragon to talk with so far."

"Gerald, most dragons would be offended, but Younger would be delighted to hear that. You should tell him."

"Why?"

"He is the dragons' lore master, their master of human lore." She smiled at the astonishment on his face. "And why not? You have those who study dragons; why should dragons not have those who study humans?"

"Those . . . you mean they have more than one?"

"Of course! Oh, the Voices make sure the information gets

passed on, but each human culture is different. Once, at a lore master convocation, Younger grumbled that if every dragon did nothing but study humans, they would still need twice as many dragons as existed just to cover Europe."

"That's crazy."

"On the contrary, I think he underestimated."

Gerald stared at her. "You're not just being difficult?"

"No!" she laughed. "Many of the faerie live among humans as humans. But while we are much closer to humans than dragons, we do not completely understand you."

"I guess that makes sense."

"Good."

"I've lived my whole life among girls and I still don't understand you, either the short- or long-lived type."

That earned him a cup of water dumped on his head. As he wiped it from his eyes, he laughed. "You act awfully human at times."

"I told you, we are close to human. And we live with you. We know how you act and react. But that was genuine fun. In many ways we are the same." She stood and stretched. "I need to walk, but we should stay together. Will you come?"

As he leapt to his feet Cuthbert walked from behind a mound that might once have been a house, hailing them.

"Cuthbert!" They both ran to him. Gerald bowed, but Kenna hugged the lore master and kissed his brow.

"Walk with me, children."

Kenna laughed at this.

"Walk with me and listen." He pointed toward the dragons. "And watch."

"Where have you been?" Gerald asked.

"With the dragons, of course. As soon we shall all three be with them. The Lord of the Western Isles has called all the dragons from Europe, Asia, and Africa together. No, they are not all here yet, Gerald. Some may not come, but if those here agree to something, they will force the rest to comply or chase them away into wastelands far from humans or dragons.

"So far about two hundred have arrived. The Lord of the Western Isles hoped to get nearly all of them together before introducing you, but events are happening too quickly. Any moment now, those two hundred dragons will descend on Lochmaldie. Many Voices will be about the Isles here to greet incoming dragons and explain things to them before they land. Thus all will be aware of the situation by the time they arrive."

Gerald started to speak.

"A moment, Gerald! The Lord of the Western Isles has been speaking with many dragons and many people. He believes that evil times are upon us unless a truce such as he has forged with Scotland is forged with all, or at least most, men and dragons. Of the four others remaining of the eldest dragons, he has dispatched two to speak with humans and kept two with him here to help convince the dragons and to help keep order.

"We must all be on our toes! Make no adversary if you can help it, but do not give ground unnecessarily. If you are unsure, look to me, and I will help if I can."

Gerald had so many questions he couldn't get one out for a moment. Then it was too late. They had walked into a large, open, grassy area, presumably Lochmaldie's commons, when the dragons began to arrive. Some lit atop mounds around the perimeter while others landed near the center.

Kenna whispered, "These in the middle have either decided which side they support or they are going to demand answers about something."

Gerald nodded and followed Cuthbert to the highest point they could see in the grass.

About a dozen dragons had landed when Cuthbert nodded to the south. A huge group of dragons was coming. There was a constant formation in the center—the largest dragon was surrounded by ten or so mostly large dragons in the center of a vast, shifting cloud of dragons.

Gerald saw a lone, greenish dragon diving on the group from far away and high up. "I'd guess that was Argyll, but he's much too big."

The cloud of dragons opened up in front and underneath as the formation dropped near the ground, the largest dragon landing quite near Gerald and his friends. Hundreds of dragon wings stirred up winds that buffeted them from every direction. As the largest dragon's escort surrounded him, the rest began to land around the commons. With a cry of rage, the green dragon flew overhead, its tail lashing violently.

"Now I'd swear that was Argyll, save for the size," said Gerald.

"Trust your eyes, young warrior," Cuthbert advised. Kenna caught Gerald's gaze and nodded.

"But how..."

Cuthbert shook his head in disgust. "Dragons normally grow throughout their lives, but never quickly. The only way a dragon can grow that fast is by eating other dragons. Seldom is that done save with mortal enemies. But Argyll . . ."

Argyll roared again as his name was spoken,

". . . is mad by the standards of both dragons and men, and is undoubtedly responsible for at least one, and probably two, recently missing dragons. It's uglier than I thought."

Kenna directed Gerald's eyes to the largest dragon. "That's the Lord of the Western Isles. The largest dragons near him are the next group of eldest dragons. When the last of the current eldest have all died or exiled themselves from among the eldest, the next dozen become the eldest. Nothing but age matters, save that if a dragon has been declared mad by the current group of eldest, he or she may never be eldest.

"The Argylls were all declared mad within a week of their births. That has never happened with any other dragons."

The Lord of the Western Isles roared Argyll's name to

summon him back, but Argyll was rapidly dwindling into the distance. Flame flashed from Argyll's mouth, and the humans' ears were buffeted by an angry din of Voices and dragons.

Cuthbert put his mouth next to Gerald's ear and yelled, "Argyll just killed a Voice who asked him to return here. Attacking a Voice is considered the same as attacking its dragon. With this attack, Argyll has made himself the enemy of every other dragon, save rogues and lunatics like himself. There are, thankfully, precious few of those."

After a moment the din died. Gerald quietly asked Cuthbert, "Where is Younger?"

Cuthbert smiled. "He is one of the two sent to speak with humans, of course."

"So the eldest who left trust the eldest to speak for them?"

A handful of small flames played about the three as the dragons around them all laughed. A medium-sized orange dragon spoke.

"They trust their eldest no more than you trust your king."

Gerald stared at the dragon. "Excuse me?"

The dragon looked the humans over. "Lord Gerald? Yes, I was sure! Greetings, Lord Cuthbert, Lady Kenna."

Those two bowed and returned the greeting.

Cuthbert smiled. "Gerald, this is Goyim from Samaria. Beware her wit. It is razor sharp."

Goyim bowed her head briefly in thanks. At this point Gerald noticed that most of the nearby dragons were looking at him.

"Why are they staring at me?" he hissed to Kenna and Cuthbert. Kenna moved her head close to him, and whispered quietly through her cupped hands. Gerald could barely hear the answer.

"They know of you, but you are an unknown. They cannot understand why the youngest dragon lord is here in such august company."

"Meaning you and Cuthbert?" Gerald smiled.

"Yes," she said quietly. "And the dragons."

"Oh. I won't forget them again."

"Gerald," Kenna sighed as more flames erupted around them, "please be more discrete."

He smiled weakly. "At least they're laughing."

"Small favors."

Gerald suddenly noticed that a silvery dragon a hundred yards beyond the eldest was looking at him. He saw pale yellow eyes with green irises. "Santana!" he yelled. Santana bowed his head but kept talking with another dragon.

"Wait! He's in the circle around the Lord of the Western Isles. Is Santana in the next group of eldest?"

"Yes," said Cuthbert with a smile. "Now be still. I want to listen."

It was then Gerald realized that all the dragons were deep in conversation. As he turned full circle, taking it all in, he came very close to laughing. The dragons who were sitting tended to wrap their long tails around their legs, while the standing dragons tended to lash them back and forth. They reminded him of cats and dogs. He decided to keep this observation to himself for the time being.

Kenna laughed and moved her head next to his. "I have often thought the same thing."

Gerald pulled back to stare. "How do you know what I am thinking, lady who swore she was not a witch?"

"A girl can tell what her younger brother is thinking when his face betrays him."

A moment later Gerald realized that the dragons were not using any language he had ever heard. The words rolled from their great mouths like waterfalls, avalanches, raging fires, thunderclaps, and howling winds. He remembered the name his mother had spoken. Apparently it had been in a dragon tongue rather than any human language. He was awestruck that she could have spoken it recognizably. He doubted he could repeat anything he was hearing.

A clump of bushes served as a privy as the day wore on. The dragons talked through the day. Cuthbert, Kenna, and Gerald snacked on waybread and water at first, but mid-afternoon Cuthbert spoke with the nearest dragon—the only deep purple dragon Gerald had seen—who promptly flew away. Fifteen minutes later she returned with a goat—skinned and ready to cook—and a skin of wine. She also dropped a bundle of wood. Gerald prepared the wood while Cuthbert cut and spitted the goat. Kenna dug through her bag for dried herbs and spices. She combined these and oil into a paste and coated the meat with it. When all was ready, a nearby dragon lit their fire. An hour later they ate supper. The dragons talked on.

Men and faerie spread their bedrolls and took turns sleeping as the dragons talked through the night. No dragon spoke to them during the night.

Dragons continued to arrive. By dawn the group's size had doubled.

Cuthbert sat up, yawning and rubbing his eyes. He looked around and smiled a tight smile. "That looks to be about it."

The discussions went on this way for three days. As conversations would dwindle, dragons would move to new groups and join conversations there. Gerald realized that over time each dragon spoke with most of, if not all, the others. Late the third afternoon, he asked Cuthbert, "Don't they ever sleep?"

"Of course they sleep. But unless they are exhausted, they only sleep if they choose to. Under normal circumstances, a dragon might go two weeks with no sleep, food, or drink. He might then sleep for several days. Given the choice, most males will eat every two to three days; most females every three to five. Look, there is one sleeping now."

Gerald followed Cuthbert's gaze to the reddest dragon he had seen. It was lying down, head on its side, left eye against a sharp boulder.

"Doesn't that hurt, Cuthbert?"

"Apparently not."

"Is it snoring?"

Cuthbert listened a few seconds. "Just barely, yes. Good ear, Gerald!"

Gerald looked around. "Where is Kenna?"

"Bathing. Unlike most Scots, she prefers to bathe every day if she can."

Gerald shuddered.

"The faerie prefer to be clean, Gerald, as do I."

"Me too, but every few days seems sufficient."

Cuthbert laughed.

"Where is she bathing? Is it safe?"

"She's just over the hill behind me. It's perfectly safe."

"Ever since I was nearly bitten by a large snake while bathing in a stream, I've been a bit wary."

"Wary is good. Wary tends to survive."

"You spoke openly of faerie just now."

"We are among dragons, not humans. Dragons see clearly. A dragon can tell upon seeing you from afar whether you are human, faerie, or a mix; and if a mix, how much—at least to the fifth generation."

"Do the faerie and dragons get along?"

A large, dull-gray dragon rumbled, "If I may answer, Lord Cuthbert?"

"Of course, Selwyn." Cuthbert bowed, as did the dragon.

"Lord Gerald, it was man who fell, not the faerie or dragons, and yet we went down with you. We have no quarrel with the faerie, nor they with us. At times a mad dragon will cause problems, but the faerie know that is only one dragon. They do not blame the rest of us, as men often do.

"The faerie folk are by nature dragon lords. We consider them equals in every way."

Gerald, still reeling emotionally at being addressed as Lord Gerald by dragons, stammered an apology.

"No need. Unlike some, I deal with each human separately, just as I would a dragon. I do not hold you accountable for what Cuthbert, or Donald, or William Wallace, or anyone else has done. I ask only that I am treated the same way."

"And are you?"

"Do you care?"

"Yes, I do!" Gerald was surprised at just how much he cared. What had happened to him the last few months?

"I am treated the same way far less often than I would like, but more than I used to be. A great deal of that is due to Cuthbert and Kenna, and to those like your parents who worked to understand us and to help others do so."

As Gerald turned all this over in his mind, something else struck him. "Magic!"

"I beg your pardon?" Selwyn said. Cuthbert raised his eyebrows.

"Magic! In the old tales, the faerie always did magic. Merlin was different, of course, being part druid, but still..."

"And what is your question, my young warrior?" Cuthbert asked.

"I haven't seen any hint of magic around Kenna!"

"Really? Nothing? Never felt enchanted with her or anything?"

"I mean anything active."

"I see," said Cuthbert, who really did, even though Gerald did not. "Selwyn?"

Selwyn bowed. "Lord Gerald, you should know that I am the chief faerie lore master for Africa. I could tell you tales of faerie magic."

Gerald rolled his eyes. "I should have known. Oh, not about Africa, but that there are such positions and that you would have one."

"Why should you have known?" Selwyn puzzled.

"Cuthbert?"

The lore master tried to explain. As he did, Kenna strode up looking and smelling like a field blooming with flowers on a spring day. He was overwhelmed with beauty, joy, peace, and love.

"How's this?" she asked.

"How's what?" Gerald replied, staring in sheer joy.

Suddenly the sunlight dimmed, the scent wafted away, and Kenna stood before him with a mocking smile. "The magic."

"Oh." He shook his head. "Very nice, but I was wondering about other things."

"Aha! Yes, lots of other things. But some other time when it's not so crowded." She laughed, a fey laugh that made Gerald want to run, screaming his own laughter, through the crowd. But as the crowd was dragons, he found it easy enough to simply stand and wait. He forgot to ask Selwyn what he had meant to say about faerie magic.

An hour after dusk, the common suddenly grew quiet.

A powerful, deep voice spoke in Gerald's native tongue, slowly and rhythmically like a giant heartbeat. "Are we all in agreement, then, to send the Voices, and such emissaries as we can find among men and faerie, to all the kingdoms of Europe, Africa, and Asia, to declare that dragons will henceforth live in peace with humans, unless first attacked by humans?"

A roar of approval came back.

"And any dragon who refuses shall be exiled?"

The approval was, if anything, slightly louder.

"And any dragon who kills or destroys a human, save in self-defense, is outlawed, and may be killed on sight, just as if he or she had killed a dragon or faerie?"

The din was deafening. After it subsided, Gerald spoke.

"That's incredible! I had no idea anything would happen this quickly."

"You helped it along, Gerald," Cuthbert replied somberly.

Kenna nodded.

"How?" Gerald asked, completely confused.

"Mainly," said Cuthbert, "by staying here patiently, showing them how confident, how insightful, how nonjudgmental, how graceful you are. And by your courtesy and honor to them."

"Me? Are you serious?"

"That is what they saw. Granted, I did a lot of talking you up before you arrived, but so did Santana, which helped immensely. The fact that Argyll hates you, and that you have not tried to kill Drachmaeius over Samantha, helps as well. And of course Kenna has been radiating her sense of soothing peace."

"So that's what I've been feeling." He looked at Kenna strangely.

"I'm sorry, Gerald. It was meant for the dragons, but it's not something easy to control in great quantity. You caught the overflow, as it were."

"So long as it's not a false sense of security or anything, I have no problems with it."

"I would have stopped immediately had anything happened."

Wind nearly knocked the three of them over. Gerald realized the dragons were starting to fly away. "They're leaving now?" he asked.

Cuthbert laughed. "You forget that they see in the dark as well as the day. And they are well rested, having done nothing taxing the past three days."

"Some of them brought us food and such."

"That is as if you or I walked from the mess hall to the kitchen to bring back a loaf of bread. A trifle."

Soon only the Lord of the Western Isles and his escort remained. The circle opened, and the eldest of the eldest approached. He lay down. "Forgive me. I have not slept in a month or eaten in a week. I am what you would call bone weary.

"No, Cuthbert, I need nothing. Three dragons have gone to Taransay for cows to fill my belly, and I will sleep right here until noon tomorrow. Then we will talk, if that suits each of you."

Cuthbert nodded and spoke for all. "You are most welcome to rest, old friend. We will rest also."

As the escorts lay down to sleep or stood watch over their eldest, the humans and faerie lay down in their bedrolls as well. Just as he was about to fall asleep, Gerald noticed a shape cross the moon. The third time it happened, he poked Kenna and Cuthbert and pointed.

"Argyll," they both mouthed.

"Argyll," agreed the dragon nearest their makeshift bedroom.

Against all reason, Gerald fell asleep almost immediately.

CHAPTER THIRTY-FOUR

A BRIEF RESPITE

Gerald awoke at sunrise. Cuthbert stirred soon after, but Kenna was already away somewhere. Probably bathing again, Gerald thought with amusement.

The eldest and a third of his escort were asleep. Another third were in the air nearby on patrol. The remainder were off in parts unknown. Gerald wanted to talk, but he didn't want dragons nearby. Before he could say anything, Cuthbert spoke.

"Breakfast will be here soon, have no fear. I need to speak with Santana." He scanned the sky, waved his arms in an odd pattern over his head, then looked at Gerald and pointed east. "Kenna will be down by the shore." He slapped Gerald affectionately on the back as Santana landed nearby.

Gerald and Santana bowed to each other. Cuthbert moved closer to Santana and began speaking in a low voice.

A little irritated, Gerald headed for the nearby cove. As expected, he found Kenna there. She was sitting on a rock, staring dreamily out over the bay. The tide was coming in, booming and splashing on huge, jagged rocks off shore. Without turning, Kenna called loudly over the crashing waves.

"Those are the Hounds' Teeth, after which the village was named—Loch nam Madadh, Loch of the Hounds. This was originally a rendezvous for pirates, you know. They would hide off the coast somewhere and chase ships this direction. If the victims didn't heave to, they met their end on the teeth. The pirates would collect what washed up. If they hove to, the pirates plundered their ships. More often than not they then killed the crew anyway."

She patted the rock and Gerald climbed up beside her. After a few moments of brooding over the sea, he finally spoke. "Why are we here?"

"I came to enjoy the sunrise and the ocean." She smiled.

"You know what I mean."

"I do, but I have no answer beyond what I gave before. We came to avert disaster."

"But we haven't done anything!"

"What would you have done? Did you think to sway them with great oratory? Cuthbert can talk rings around you. Did you plan to fight? Again, Cuthbert, old as he is, can probably kill dragons in his sleep if need be.

"I confess it was easier than I expected. I asked a dragon about it. Just our presence here said a great deal. The youngest and oldest living dragon lords and a faerie princess—yes, really!" She somehow managed to curtsy sitting down. "We came at a dragon's call. We showed respect, we did not attempt to interfere, we were here if they wanted us. Gerald, they are not used to humans, or even faerie—we tend to keep to ourselves—treating them with such honor.

"As for myself, I concentrated on peace and goodwill, and they felt it. It wasn't meant for you, but you felt it. None but the eldest dragons know that my people can do this. Cuthbert told me that he asked what we could do to help, and the Lord of the Western Isles requested I bless the proceedings with peace."

Gerald let all that soak in.

"And Gerald, he requested that you be here."

"What? But I already planned to be here."

"He did not know that. He asked Cuthbert as soon as he

arrived how to convince you to come. Cuthbert told him that you already planned to be here and explained why. He will want to speak with you later, I am sure."

Gerald thought of something. "Was Drachmaeius here? I've only seen a bit of the inside of his mouth."

"He was, yes. He agreed early on."

Gerald gritted his teeth but said no more about Drachmaeius. He would never forgive him for killing Samantha and the others merely for speaking his name.

He stared quietly out to sea. "I don't hate all dragons anymore. I can even admire them. I'm not completely sure how I feel about them as a race, or about how quickly I seem to be making friends or comrades with so many. I guess it's like trading with an unknown clan. You can work with them, eat with them, stay with them; you don't have to be enemies or friends with all of them. I can live with that for now." He shrugged.

"I trust you and Cuthbert, so I can accept what you say about why we're here. But it still feels pointless." Gerald sighed. "I'm going to see if breakfast is ready. You want to come?"

She nodded and jumped lightly down.

He noticed she barely made indentations in the damp sand. "How much do you weigh?"

She laughed her musical laugh. "Pick me up and see!"

He shrugged and reached out. She leaped into his arms. He braced and then nearly fell forward because there was so little impact.

"You hardly weigh anything! I've held goats that weighed more!"

"Goats! No wonder Sally found you enchanting."

He acted as if he would drop her, then lowered her back to the ground. He looked at her seriously for a moment. She stared back.

"Lady, I am glad I have Sally to focus on. I used to think the legends of faerie must be greatly exaggerated. The more I am around you, the more I feel the legends have diminished in potency with age. Do mortals fall in love with faeries often?"

She looked at him pointedly, then relaxed. "There are things we do not discuss with humans, as naught but trouble ever came of such. But I will say that we have to be ever on our guard with mortals lest they become enchanted. Some more than others." She looked at her feet. "I forget sometimes and am simply myself with you. You are one of the few humans I am truly comfortable with. I am sorry if that makes it more difficult for you."

He reached out and tenderly lifted her chin, noting the deep wells of love and concern in her eyes. "Lady, there are many types of love." He dropped his hand. "While at times I have had to tear my mind from you to think of Sally, it has gotten easier each time. I love and value you as a friend, and as an elder sister." He fought a grin. "An extremely elder sister."

He wasn't sure what she did, but he found himself sitting on the sand just as a wave washed over his backside and legs. He joined her in laughter.

"I am glad you can be yourself around me. Think no more about it."

As he fought the backwash to stand, she reached out to help. He threw her over his shoulder into the sea. She spluttered in the water, stood, ran lightly over the top of his head, and fled over the sand dunes to breakfast, laughing the whole way.

Gerald rubbed sand from his hair where she had stepped on him and followed her inland.

As promised, the Lord of the Western Isles awoke at noon. Gerald watched in fascination as he ate each of the tethered cows in two bites. His mouth was immense; Gerald realized the dragon could have eaten each cow in one bite had he so desired. It was messy but efficient.

"I thirst. Wait here; I will soon return." He walked over the dunes toward the beach.

"Cuthbert, where is he going?"

"To drink, Gerald, as he said."

"But there is no fresh water here."

"Dragons can eat and drink much that we cannot. Think on the cows. He left nothing but the blood spilled when he bit half the cow from the whole. Hide, teeth, bones, all gone. Saltwater is fine for dragon thirst."

Gerald thought about the time he had tried drinking saltwater and shuddered.

Cuthbert smiled. "You are squeamish for a man who has killed dragons and men."

"One dragon and two men. The dragon was dying, and the men were trying to kill me or my friends. But I was squeamish then too."

"That will pass. It is a good sign. A man with no qualms about killing is a danger to himself and all about him."

"Did you and Santana find the time profitable?"

"Very. I was sorry to have to exclude you, but I really had no choice."

"I understand."

"Thank you. You will know what matters to you in time."

"Is our work here done?"

"I think nearly. We will see what the Lord of the Western Isles wishes to discuss."

The dragon returned shortly after that. "I tire of this mausoleum. It has served its purpose. Let us retire to the top of Bienn Mhor where I make one of my homes. I will carry Cuthbert."

Santana, who had been laying patiently nearby, immediately got to his feet and stepped over, offering his outstretched front claws to Kenna and Gerald.

Gerald marveled at how quickly Santana traveled. But even though the eldest seemed to work no harder, he outpaced

Santana by virtue of his greater wingspan. Gerald noticed that three others followed. He yelled at Santana. "Does the Lord of the Western Isles always have an escort?"

Santana's voice was loud even over the wind. "Only when he wishes it. The occasion required it, but he still does not trust Argyll. Any dragon who would eat other dragons simply to grow is extremely dangerous. He considered outlawing Argyll, but felt the peace he managed between the others was all he could count on for now. We will wait on him as long as he desires."

"And then?"

"And then we will go each to our home."

"Is your mate here?"

"Is yours?"

"No."

"Humans are fickle. I wondered if you had traded for Kenna."

"What?" the lady in question yelled.

Gerald saw Santana looking at him with one eye. "I tried to, but couldn't afford the dowry."

"What? Gerald! When I. . . ."

Flames escaped Santana's lips and trailed back the way they had come. "And what was the dowry?"

"A dozen of your scales." Gerald grinned across at a fuming Kenna.

"I should drop you for that impertinence, Kenna," Santana said solemnly.

"I would sprout wings, fly to your mate, and tell her you were leaving her for a pirate ship with a cute dragon's head on the bow."

Santana looked at Gerald. "She probably would." Santana landed and let the pair down gently onto the bare rock atop Bienn Mhor.

Before Kenna could say anything, Gerald looked at Santana. "And your mate?"

Santana hesitated a few seconds. "You met her. She brought you your first meal."

"She is purple?"

"Yes. You remember!"

"You said she was white. I remember because her name sounded so fitting."

Again Santana hesitated. He looked at the eldest, who merely looked back. Gerald realized that everyone was staring at Santana.

"Gerald, any response I give will put you in my debt."

"I leave that up to you, Santana."

"I will not burden you unduly. This is a great dragon secret. To speak of it with others without permission would bring you death. White dragons are rare; even rarer are those like Selene. Normally they look white, but they can take on any colors they choose. We have no word for this in your language.

"Her choice of colors at the convocation signified her support for your presence."

Gerald stood in silence a moment, awed by what he had just heard. He decided not to pursue it further now. "She is truly beautiful, even to my eyes."

Santana froze, staring into Gerald's eyes. The dragon's eyes, always in motion, hardly bothered Gerald anymore.

Finally Santana spoke. "I see you speak truly. Seldom have we heard such words from human lips, unless they were lies or spoken in fear, or when men wanted to kill dragons for their scales.

"Lord Gerald, have a care."

Santana looked at the Lord of the Western Isles. "And you have a care. This one tilts the scales of debts in ways I cannot calculate. He is sane, but what he inadvertently does could drive me as mad as Argyll."

"Do not say that, even in jest," the eldest replied. "Yet I can see why you speak so." He turned to Gerald and Kenna. "Welcome to my home. Do you desire anything before we talk?"

Both they and Cuthbert were hungry, so they sat and ate and drank from their breakfast leftovers. Gerald found himself staring at the eldest dragon's eyes. They were black but might once have been red, green, blue . . . every color there was.

"Gerald, are my eyes so very like those of my unhatched offspring?"

"Yes. Yes, they are." Gerald doubted he would ever get used to what dragons could see with their minds' eyes.

"I cannot read your mind. But dragons can see much that human seers may not. When I saw your reaction to my eyes, I also saw you staring into my offspring's eyes in your dream."

The Lord of the Western Isles said no more until they finished eating. "Gerald, I would hear your story from your own mouth, even though I know a great deal."

"And what story is that, my Lord Eldest?"

"The story of your life! You need not provide every detail, or you will die of old age here, always fifteen years behind." He laughed tiny flames. "But I would hear of the things that have shaped you, of your hopes and dreams, your visions, your love and hate, whatever you would tell me. While I can see a great deal, I cannot see all, especially these things."

Gerald wasn't sure that most of this would excite anyone, much less a dragon, but he did as requested, starting with his life as a child. He thought it might take half an hour, but as the dragon asked questions, he thought of more details and kept talking. Eventually he realized that he was losing his voice and that it was dark.

Kenna laughed gently, suggesting they continue the following morning. She found a mixture of dried fruits and herbs in her pack which she boiled in water for him to drink. She suggested he talk as little as possible that night. After exacting his promise to do so, she proceeded to spin tales of Gerald as a star-crossed lover of a mermaid, a dryad, a dwarf woman, a sphinx, and finally a rock. Eventually, she explained, there was no one and nothing else left, so he settled for a human.

When she stopped, Gerald spoke ruefully. "Never again will I challenge you that way, Kenna."

Santana sighed, nearly blowing Gerald over. "That is a shame. The two of you could spin more legends than all of human history has done so far." They all laughed, but when Gerald started coughing, Kenna insisted it was really time to quiet down for the evening.

The eldest lay across an area of bare rock that was clearly his bed, the sparse heather ceasing entirely near the outline of his great bulk. Three of the remaining escorts lay around them at three points a hundred yards away. The fourth flew up high to keep watch through the night.

Kenna, Cuthbert, and Gerald built beds of heather and lay near each other close by the eldest. Gerald had wanted to move farther away until the Lord of the Western Isles assured him that he did not roll or thrash about in his sleep. Or sleepwalk.

Cuthbert fell to snoring almost immediately but Gerald and Kenna watched the sky, occasionally seeing shooting stars. Kenna spoke softly, telling Gerald interesting bits of her life. He fell asleep to the lyrical sound of her voice and dreamed of wedding Sally amidst dragons and faeries. In the dream they lived in a cave, where they raised their children who turned out half faerie and half dragon.

CHAPTER THIRTY-FIVE

ARGYLL POUNCES

Dawn arrived with a vengeance for Gerald, who opened his eyes with the sun peering directly into them. He closed them tightly and rolled over. After a minute he gingerly opened them a second time to see that once again, Kenna was already up and gone. At least Cuthbert and the Lord of the Western Isles still slept. He hated being the last to wake.

After breakfast their host spoke with the other dragons for a few minutes and decided to send two back to their homes, keeping only Santana and Wandap, a scarred, dark gray, one-eyed female dragon from southern Africa. The dragons spent another half hour with their Voices, who came and went constantly, before turning their attention back to Gerald.

Just as he started to speak, Wandap screamed and took to the sky. Before Gerald could react, the other dragons were in the air as well, gaining altitude as quickly as possible.

"Argyll!" shouted Kenna, pointing at the sun. Gerald could not see anything for the sun's brightness, but Cuthbert stared as if it didn't matter.

"And others," he muttered. "Wait here!" he commanded and ran off across the hilltop.

Kenna grabbed Gerald as he tried to chase Cuthbert. She was amazingly strong and Cuthbert amazingly quick.

"Let me go! What is he doing?" Aghast, he watched as Cuthbert disappeared over the edge. "He was running too fast! He'll fall!" Gerald strained but could not budge from Kenna's grip.

"He said to stay! Trust him!"

Gerald stared furiously at the cliff's edge, knowing there was no way a man could survive that fall. A white dragon shot from behind the cliff, clawing skyward rapidly. "Younger! Cuthbert went to get him. But where is Cuthbert? In Younger's claws?"

Kenna stared at the sun. "He's safe. Well, as safe as any of us."

Gerald looked up; the eldest and his escort were closing rapidly on the intruders out over the ocean. A few seconds later, a wall of flame erupted between the dragons. They all flew into it.

They almost immediately emerged, scattering in various directions. Santana and a lovely green dragon flew around each other—vying for position, clawing, snapping, breathing fire. Younger flew straight at Argyll, but that dragon was already diving on the eldest. Those two met with a mighty crash and locked in a vicious embrace. They started falling, clawing and biting as they descended. Just before hitting the sea they broke off and strove for altitude, circling each other warily. Younger was now engaged with a brown dragon. Wandap was fighting a brilliant blue behemoth, the largest of the newcomers after Argyll.

Gerald couldn't tell how the battle was going at first, although he could guess in part by the amount of blood on the dragons' scales. Younger looked the worst; Gerald thought. He hoped it was because the dragon was so white.

Kenna's grip tightened painfully on Gerald's wrist. "Look!" She sounded scared. Her free hand pointed at the sun.

Squinting, Gerald realized at least one more dragon was coming. "Whose side are they on?" he demanded.

"I don't know, but I fear the worst."

"What can we do?"

"Nothing for now. Wait. Take my hands!"

He took her hands. She held them gently at first and closed her eyes, but soon her nails dug painfully into the backs of his hands. He held on, but realized he was sweating and scared. He felt dizzy. She was using her magic, somehow drawing power from him as well.

"Give in to the feelings, please! I know it is hard but I need your help!"

He gave in. It was hard at first, but he spiraled faster and faster down into a vortex of fear and despair. From somewhere he heard whimpering and screams of anguish. Everything went black.

Seconds later he came to. Kenna held him, pouring strength and joy into him. "It worked! Oh, thank you! Two of the dragons fled in fear, and one was so distracted, Santana was able to kill it. But there are still so many."

Gerald looked; there were still six against four. Unbelievably, Younger broke free and flew straight toward their mountain. "What's he doing now? He can't leave!"

Kenna just held his arm again and waited. When Younger was nearly on top of them, he flared his wings and slowed. Kenna pushed Gerald away. As he stumbled to stay upright, Younger snatched each of them up in a great claw and started aloft, back toward the battle.

"It goes ill! You two must fight as well!"

Gerald screamed back. "But how can we?"

"Use your sword!"

As they approached the dragons, Younger dove at a dragon not engaged at the moment. As he passed over the other dragon, Younger dropped Gerald. Though terrified, Gerald drew his claymore. As he fell beside the dragon's great neck he swung with all his might. Out of the corner of his eye, he saw Younger closing rapidly on Argyll, who left off chasing the eldest to meet the threat.

His arms were nearly torn from their sockets as his claymore sliced into the dragon's neck, biting deeply, cutting halfway through before being jerked from Gerald's hands. Gerald continued falling. The dragon flew on maybe another second or two, then crumpled and fell with Gerald.

Fascinated and thrilled to have helped, regrets flooded his mind at dying young as Gerald watched the waves rush up toward him. A brilliant flash from above and behind reflected off the sea, momentarily blinding him, as screams of rage and pain overcame the wind whistling in his ears. Something snatched him up. He waited for death until he heard Younger's voice reassuring him.

A moment later he was back on Bienn Mhor, stumbling to his knees. When he could see again, he looked around frantically. Bruised and battered, the eldest and Santana were landing—alone—before him. Argyll and his party were nowhere in sight. Cuthbert lay naked before him, bleeding from many wounds.

Santana took to the air again, obviously laboring. "I will get help. Tend his wounds as best you can. Stop the bleeding!"

Gerald looked around, stunned at the condition of both Cuthbert and the eldest. "Whose?" he demanded in frustration.

"Both!" came the fading cry from Santana, gaining speed as he flew toward Dunvegan.

"I will live. Tend to Cuthbert, Lord Gerald." The eldest's voice was labored but still commanding. Gerald ripped fabric from his shirt and began to staunch the blood flow from the worst wounds, desperately wishing for cleaner rags.

CHAPTER THIRTY-SIX

A BITTERSWEET VICTORY

"**W**hat happened? Why did he leap off a cliff? Where are the others?"

The Lord of the Western Isles did not answer.

Gerald glanced at Cuthbert and started to rise to check on the dragon, though how to do that he wasn't sure.

"Keep working on Cuthbert, Lord Gerald."

"Eldest, there is nothing more I can do!"

"Then keep pressure on the worst wounds."

Gerald looked and picked two of the worst to press his hands against. Looking again, he moved one hand to another spot and laid his body across Cuthbert's chest to stop the bleeding there. He could feel a heartbeat and labored breath. There was still hope.

"I cannot tell you why he leaped off the cliff."

"Why was he naked? Where was the dragon scale mail he wore on the way here?"

"He always said the mail itched after a few days. He had changed into his robes for comfort but probably abandoned them for the battle. They catch the wind, and if flames come near they burn."

"Where is everyone else?"

"I do not know where the others are."

A Voice arrived, then another. They spoke rapidly. Gerald could catch little more than names.

"Wandap lies among the teeth in the ocean; her head is underwater and she moves only with the waves. Three of those who attacked us are also dead. The Voices report no other dragons in sight, and their eyes are near as good as ours."

"What of Kenna? And Younger? He took me into the fray, and he caught me as I fell and brought me out!"

"Of Kenna, there is no word, but I think she is alive. I hear something that reminds me of Kenna in my mind, but it is hard to say. . . ." His speech trailed off. Gerald hoped he was just tired.

"And Younger?"

"He is alive."

"And?"

"Later. Here is Santana with the first of those to help."

Santana landed gently. K'Pene emerged from one great claw, and a giant of a man Gerald did not know leapt from the other. Both carried packs and bags. Santana was gone almost before he had let them go.

The giant ran straight to the dragon. He asked a few questions and ordered the eldest to roll onto his side.

As K'Pene fell to her knees beside Cuthbert, Gerald moved aside, pulling rags away as he did. She hissed, uncorked a water skin, and began bathing the wounds. She had Gerald put clean cloths on each as she moved to the next. She told him to apply pressure to the arm and shoulder wounds he had held before, and began applying various salves and herbs to the chest wound. The skin looked as if sharp rocks had torn it. Gerald was amazed he had survived.

"What made this?"

K'Pene, concentrating, said nothing.

"Voices! It must have been Voices. There were several

around..."

"Hush. Later," was K'Pene's reply.

Gerald glanced at the eldest. The giant had applied something to his neck wounds and was now applying bandages. Gerald had to laugh.

"Why laugh you, Lord Gerald?" the dragon rumbled.

"Because you will have a pretty necklace. Perhaps he can tie a large bow on it."

Flames erupted from the dragon's mouth.

"I hope that was laughter."

More flames.

"Gerald, please, not now!" K'Pene worked desperately.

Gerald hushed. He watched as the giant worked all around the dragon, clambering onto him and over him as necessary, his bare feet somehow unfazed by the dragon's scales. Finally he made the dragon roll over to work on his other side.

K'Pene sighed. "Gerald, I am done with the worst wounds. His chest, head, and neck worried me the most, even though the latter were not deep. There was much poison in them."

"Poison?" Gerald gulped.

"Poison. Not of the sort you are thinking, but a dragon's teeth and claws carry things that can kill you, much like the infection you can get from an untreated sword wound."

"But these wounds were much too small to be from a dragon!"

K'Pene pushed her hair back from her forehead with the back of her hand. "Cuts and scrapes full of dragon blood. Drool. Who knows?"

The giant was now inspecting the dragon's wings. He looked almost pleased as he spoke. "He is very blessed. I suppose he was in Younger's claw and mostly protected."

K'Pene sat back for a moment, looking pleased herself. "He will live, and I think he will heal well."

"He's amazingly strong and healthy for someone his age."

"I admit, I am surprised at how well he is. Already he breathes more easily. I expected that to take days." She looked puzzled.

Gerald looked around. "I don't see his sword anywhere. I suppose he lost it as I lost mine."

The giant came over. "I be Sterling MacLeod."

"Gerald of . . ."

The dragon interrupted. "That is Lord Gerald, a great dragon lord. Though young, he has slain two dragons, one in battle today, thus helping save us all. He has earned the respect of dragonkind, save for the mad and rogues."

Gerald reddened deeply.

"And this is K'Pene, a great healer and seer from another land. K'Pene, the MacLeod is a healer of dragons, the greatest in Scotland and likely Great Britain. He is a seer as well."

A Voice nearby cried, "Santana returns!" just as Santana landed, bearing Torquil and a warrior almost the size of Sterling. The warrior's name turned out to be something Norse that Gerald couldn't quite pronounce.

"No matter," the stranger laughed. "My friends and foes alike call me Hamar!" He loosed a great hammer and swung it in a circle over his head.

Gerald was reminded of the legendary Thor.

Hamar climbed a great rock and stood lookout. "The boat is coming from Dunvegan."

"What boat?" Gerald asked.

"One with food, drink, and more medicine." Hamar looked at the eldest and grinned. "And perhaps more necklaces."

The eldest growled. "Hamar, I will eat your offspring yet to save the world a great deal of trouble and embarrassment."

Hamar laughed. (Gerald had never seen a warrior who laughed so much.) "This is why I have no offspring, Lord; I am trying to starve you!"

K'Pene rolled her eyes.

"K'Pene, I'm fine!" Gerald said as she started to check him.

"I'll tell you if you're fine. Does this hurt?" She raised his right arm straight out and up, and he winced.

"Yes, it does. All along the top of my shoulder and arm. But it's just..."

She began rubbing something on it. "Probably just a sprain, but we need you in top shape in case the dragons come back. Hamar is strong, but I suspect he can only manage a half dozen Argylls by himself."

Hamar grinned as he scanned the sky and horizon.

"Santana saw what you did with your sword. As he described it, I was afraid you might have torn something or pulled your shoulder apart. Are you related to Cuthbert?"

"Not that I know of." He started as flames slipped from the eldest's mouth. "What are you laughing at?"

"Later, Lord Gerald."

K'Pene went to work on the other arm. After checking the rest of him, she relaxed and said tiredly, "All right. You're almost fine. You'll be there in a day or two."

A Voice flew past Santana, chattering away. He leapt immediately up and flew off, bellowing in joy.

The Lord of the Western Isles got to his feet, annoying MacLeod. He stared east toward the ocean. "A Voice found Kenna. She is half dead, but she managed to swim or float to Wandap and climb onto her back. Even in death, Wandap saves someone." He bowed his head, but there was renewed light in his eyes.

Gerald looked at the dragon, then at K'Pene, then back at the dragon, his eyes raised. The eldest nodded.

"K'Pene, what do you know of faerie?"

"I have lore, Lord Gerald. Why?"

"Kenna is of the faerie."

K'Pene hissed. "They are not too different from us in body, beyond lighter and stronger."

Gerald rubbed his forehead and eyes a moment as he thought. "Lord of the Western Isles! What was that light?"

"Ah, yes. The light. Kenna called on every bit of power within her or available to her. She even took strength from us. It was as if a small sun appeared in her hand, blinding and hot. She threw it at Argyll and two of his band who had just flown near him. It exploded in their midst. Argyll survived but was sorely hurt. I wonder that he could fly. It killed one of the others outright and burned the wings off the third, who fell to her death on the Teeth. Argyll and the rest fled.

"Gerald, Kenna will likely live, but she will be changed. Use of power that way always changes one. For a while she will be very weak. A seer saw the battle in a vision and sent for healers for humans and dragons. Torquil is here as well, having seen that he was needed by Kenna, though we do not yet know why.

"No one foresaw Kenna's nearly dying. We have sent for a healer from her family."

As the Voices began talking all at once, Santana arrived, more Voices flying about him. He laid Kenna nearby. Before Gerald could get to her, Sterling had run over, picked her up, and carried her to Cuthbert's side for Torquil and K'Pene to care for. But it seemed that there was little they could do, save wrap Kenna up, pour broth down her throat, and tend minor wounds.

Torquil rubbed his eyes. "The saltwater has served her well for those. And her kind are strong and heal easily." He looked around. "There seems little point in my being here, but at least I may learn something from studying Sterling's treatment of the eldest." He walked over to the dragon and began discussing the wounds with the dragon healer.

Santana spoke. "The boat will put in at Lochmaldie. We will carry Cuthbert and Kenna there, where craftsmen will build shelters." He bowed to the eldest. "With your permission?"

The Lord of the Western Isles sighed. "It is against my decree that none may dwell there, but it is necessary. Yes. Do whatever it takes to protect these two. I owe them as much, or more, than you, Santana. In fact, is there a dragon alive who does not?"

"Are you expecting Argyll back, then?" Gerald hoped.

"I will take no chances. Clearly I did not expect him here so soon. I will not make that mistake again. But you, at least, are safe, Lord Gerald."

"How is that, Lord Dragon?"

"You do not know? Gerald, he has long sought to scare and trick you so that he might be free to kill you. He owes you blood price for taking your parents when you were so young, which puts him greatly in your debt, even more than your killing his sister."

"All this time I feared him. . . ."

"I thought you hated him."

"That too."

"Perhaps you should not fear him but respect the danger he poses. He is mad but wily."

"Water. . . ." Kenna struggled to sit.

K'pene tried to stop her, but Gerald helped Kenna up, moving so that she could lean back against his chest. K'Pene gave her small sips, making her wait between each one. The healer looked at Gerald oddly.

He smiled. "Kenna is like a sister to me as Cuthbert is like a grandfather. I would do the same for him."

Cuthbert moved a hand weakly.

"And hope to before long." Gerald relaxed. It looked as if his friends—no, his family—would live after all. He looked toward the sun. "Go hide, Argyll. Hide as deep in the belly of the earth as you can, and grow strong and well. I want to hew your head from your neck myself, not find your carcass rotting because you were too mad or too stupid to heal."

Kenna relaxed. She leaned back and looked up at Gerald. "Then we won?"

"This time, yes. Most of us. We lost Wandap."

"I saw. And yet she saved me after all." She looked into Gerald's eyes and a mischievous grin crept onto her face. "My one true love."

K'Pene's eyebrows crawled well up her forehead.

Gerald looked at K'Pene. "She is hallucinating. Do you have something to make her sleep? Perhaps for a year?"

Kenna laughed. "I yield! You have won this round. Let me sleep without her draughts, and we shall see who wins tomorrow."

They looked at Cuthbert, and each reached out and put a hand on his arm. He twitched, but the corners of his mouth turned up. They sat like that until the boat arrived and it was time to move to Lochmaldie.

END OF BOOK ONE

The story continues in

NEMESES
UNEXPECTED
Volume II of the Dragon Lord Chronicles

PRONUNCIATION GUIDE

TERM	PRONUNCIATION
cist	kist (kissed)
targe	tarj

NAME	PRONUNCIATION
Aed	Eyd (between aid and I'd)
Afagdu	Uh-făg-due'
Ailsa	Ayl'-sah
Argyll	Arr-gile'
Cle	(halfway between klee and kleh)
Dealanach	Jyal'-awn-akh
Draehamar	Dray'-ă-măr
Druze	Drooz
Eoin	Oh-en (similar to Owen)
Fionnlagh	Fin'-lay
Orchy	Orkh'-ey

GLOSSARY

TERM	DEFINITION
blood price	Compensation paid to the family of a person who was accidentally killed. No blood price was required for fair combat or just killings. It could be offered in the case of murder but was seldom accepted when justice was possible.
cist	A stone-lined grave. The top was narrower than the rest.
claymore	A Scottish variant of a two-handed broadsword, or great sword, with a cross hilt.
crenellated	Having rectangular gaps, such as the typical battlements atop castles.
scree	A collection of broken rock fragments typically found at the base of a mountain, cliff face, or hillside shoulders; typically a hazard to travel.
targe	A round shield approximately 18-22 inches in diameter, made of wood and covered with cowhide and metal decorations. Some had spikes in the center; these could often be removed and fastened to the backs of the shields.

AFTERWORD—
AND FORWARD

For years I have written short stories. I've published articles and coauthored a technical book, but there was one thing I was convinced I couldn't write until...

I awoke one morning in early 2012 with vivid memories of the beginning and ending of a dream about a young man and dragons. I could focus on any instant in those few, incredibly vivid scenes and see, taste, and feel everything.

The dream's middle—spanning many years of the main character's life—was gone. I didn't have a clue about what happened there, but I knew that this could be one of the best short stories I'd ever written. Quite possibly the best.

It took a few tries before I could actually get anything written, but I finally found myself typing away on a laptop late one evening. A couple of hours and 1,200 words later I had written . . . an opening scene. There was more to the first part of the dream than I had time to describe. "This will be a long short story," I mused.

The next evening I wrote another 1,400 words and still hadn't finished the beginning. My inward conversation picked up again. "Uh oh, this might be a novella."

By the fourth evening, I realized I had a novel, and by the sixth, I realized it might be two or three. The current plan is four books (a tetralogy). The one thing I knew I couldn't write was a novel, but within a month, I had finished the first draft of one of several.

75,000 words. (Now close to 90,000.) I was amazed. I'd done it! Three-and-a-half years later, after much research and numerous rewrites and editing cycles, we have a book.

I love it when a dream comes together.

What are your dreams? As they said in *Galaxy Quest*, "Never give up! Never surrender!" That thing you don't know if you can do, or are convinced you can't? Go for it. I know the feeling. But in the end I did it. The world needs people who aren't afraid to chase their dreams. It's what you were made for. Go for it. Try to find like-minded people who will support you; they are out there. I pray more blessings on you than you believed possible.

ACKNOWLEDGEMENTS

Thanks to Jason Chin and others for the revelations that redirected me toward indie publishing.

Thanks to all those involved with the Ragged Edge/Re:Write conference for convincing me I already had the tools to handle marketing. Special thanks to Page Vandiver for not just providing me with a great web site and social media that really reflect who I am and what I want to do, but for truckloads of encouragement and for teaching me so much about marketing.

The book is much better thanks to the early readers who gave me invaluable feedback and encouragement: Kenneth Riviere, Josiah O'Neal, Lisa Mikitarian, Lyndsay Bila, Abi and Derek Penner, Maria Buodono, Rachel Schober, Charlotte Macmillan, Chelsea Boyd, and Grant Howard.

My wife, Sharon O'Neal, is an amazing editor and my biggest cheerleader. She doesn't read much fantasy but every night when I would finish writing a chapter or two she would read through them and ask where the rest was. This told me that I was on to something. Thanks, babe. I seriously doubt it would have happened without you, and I know it's a far better book because of you!

Thanks to Alli Gray for the great artwork prefacing each chapter, and lots of other great art.

Thanks to Allison Metcalfe for the design, cover, and production. You turned a manuscript into a beautiful book!

Thanks to Sally Hanan for all the advice on writing, editing, and other aspects of producing a book, for final editing, and for encouragement, insight, revelation, and general awesomeness.

A special thanks to my dad and mom for giving me a real love for reading and thirst for understanding, and for indulging my imagination and experimentation in so many areas.

Thanks to Bill and Traci Vanderbush, and Joel and Cheryl Davis for believing in me and encouraging and helping me to pursue my dreams and passions.

Thanks to all of the above for your beautiful friendship and for being a part of my family.

Thanks to all the fantasy and science fiction authors I have read over the years; the librarians and booksellers who directed me to new material; Marvel, DC, and the rest of the comics world; a variety of movie makers; and everyone else who fueled my imagination.

Finally, thanks to all of you who read my writing. I'd love to hear from you!

ABOUT THE AUTHOR

Miles O'Neal has written most of his life—short stories, songs, poems, software, documentation, government computer system contract proposals, you name it. His first failed attempt at writing a book was in conjunction with Claude Thompson the summer after the sixth or seventh grade. This is his first published novel.

Miles is a husband, lover, father, grandpa, friend, storyteller, author, musician, and former youth pastor who believes passionately in young people. He lives just outside Round Rock, Texas, with his wife, Sharon, whoever else is living with them at the time, and all manner of people and creatures that wander in and out of his imagination.

"One of my goals is to live to be at least 120 years old. If I write two or three books every year for the rest of my life, I'll still have ideas sitting on the shelf at the end of my days."

ABOUT THE ILLUSTRATOR

Alli Gray graduated from Texas State University with a BFA in studio art with an "all level teacher's certification" in 2009. She really loved teaching art, but realized she wasn't ready to manage classes of her own. Alli currently works as an accountant at a local dealership by day and as a freelance artist and crafter by night.

Her art uses a wide variety of media, including unconventional combinations such as coffee and salt with india ink. Alli has had a number of successful art shows in the Austin area.

Follow Alli: https://www.facebook.com/alli.gray.96

ABOUT THE DESIGNER

Allison Metcalfe is a graphic designer, typesetter, and photographer. She has a deep love for the beauty in people and good design. Her goal in producing any work is to capture the client's voice and design with innovation, style, and longevity. Bestselling author Ted Dekker is one of her recent clients of note.

Allison's skills include publishing, book cover design, typesetting, logo design, and working with Adobe CS: Illustrator, Photoshop, and InDesign.

Follow Allison: https://www.facebook.com/
allisonmetcalfephotography

ABOUT THE EDITOR

Sally is a copywriter, editor, and author of four books. She has been writing and editing for over ten years, and is passionate about excellence in everything she does. Bestselling author Shawn Bolz is one of her recent clients of note.

Sally and Allison often work together to produce books authors can be proud of, and Sally's skills include Word and a smattering of Adobe CS's Photoshop and InDesign. You can see more of their projects at www.inksnatcher.com.

Follow Sally: https://www.facebook.com/inksnatcher

COMMUNITY, NEWS, AND MORE

Blogs, news, short stories, books, merchandise, and more about the author, his upcoming works, backstories, etc.:

http://www.milesoneal.com/

Facebook:

https://www.facebook.com/milesonealauthor

Twitter:

https://twitter.com/miles_oneal